FANTASISTS ON FANTASY

For enjoyment, enrichment, and enlightment — or as a primer for would-be writers — this splendid collection of twenty-two writings on the subject of fantasy surveys almost a hundred years of provocative, important ideas by eighteen prominent practitioners of the genre.

Who better than H.P. Lovecraft could define "the literature of cosmic fear" and interpret the chaos and daemons of unplumbed space? And what could be more fascinating than discovering how J.R.R. Tolkien came to begin *The Hobbit* or brought the tree-like Ents to life? Or where else could we learn Ursula Le Guin's feelings and thoughts about her subconscious and the Earthsea Trilogy, "a dream I have not stopped dreaming"?

Academic investigations, definitions, the importance of folk lore and fairy tales, the witty observations of Thurber, the philosophy of Sir Herbert Read, and so much more, all make this an essential anthology for both serious students and delighted fans of the magic worlds made real in FANTASISTS ON FANTASY.

D1546023

Other Avon Books Edited by
Robert H. Boyer and Kenneth J. Zahorski

THE FANTASTIC IMAGINATION:
An Anthology of High Fantasy

THE FANTASTIC IMAGINATION II:
An Anthology of High Fantasy

THE PHOENIX TREE:
An Anthology of Myth Fantasy

VISIONS OF WONDER:
An Anthology of Christian Fantasy

FANTASISTS ON FANTASY
A Collection of Critical Reflections.
Edited by
ROBERT H. BOYER
and
KENNETH J. ZAHORSKI

A DISCUS BOOK/PUBLISHED BY AVON BOOKS

FANTASISTS ON FANTASY: A COLLECTION OF
CRITICAL REFLECTIONS is an original publication of
Avon Books. This work has never before appeared in
book form.

The Acknowledgments of this book serve as an extension
of this Copyright page.

AVON BOOKS
A division of
The Hearst Corporation
1790 Broadway
New York, New York 10019

First Discus Printing, February, 1984

DISCUS TRADEMARK REG. U.S. PAT. OFF. AND IN
OTHER COUNTRIES, MARCA REGISTRADA, HECHO EN
U.S.A.

Printed in the U.S.A.

OP   10 9 8 7 6 5 4 3 2 1

PREFACE

We are grateful to the following people whose help in producing this book has been essential: Terry Maguire, our student assistant, for his substantive contribution in reading and evaluating a large number of essays and acting as a tiebreaker for the co-editors; Karen Donahue, interloan librarian of the St. Norbert College Library; Peggy Schlapman, typist-proofreader; Robert L. Horn, Dean of St. Norbert College, for his unfailing encouragement; and Barbara Boyer and Marijean Zahorski.

ACKNOWLEDGMENTS

George MacDonald, "The Fantastic Imagination." Reprinted from *A Dish of Orts* (London: Edwin Dalton, 1908).

G. K. Chesterton, "Fairy Tales," in *All Things Considered* (New York: Sheed and Ward, 1956). Reprinted by permission of A. P. Watt Ltd. and the Estate of G. K. Chesterton.

H. P. Lovecraft, "Introduction" from "Supernatural Horror in Literature" in *Dagon and Other Macabre Tales* (Sauk City, Wisconsin: Arkham House, 1965). Reprinted by permission of Arkham House Publishers, Inc., Sauk City.

Herbert W. Read, "Fantasy (Fancy)," in *English Prose Style* (Boston: Beacon Press, 1928). Reprinted by permission of William Morris Agency, Inc, on behalf of author; and by Random House, Inc.

James Thurber, "The Wizard of Chitenango," *The New Republic,* Dec. 12, 1934, 141–142 and "Tempest in a Looking Glass," *Forum*, April 1937, 236–238. Reprinted by permission of Helen Thurber.

CONTENTS

FANTASISTS ON FANTASY

INTRODUCTION

"Believe an expert," said Saint Bernard. "Believe one who has had experience." Like all wise sayings, Saint Bernard's is as meaningful to us as it was to his contemporaries nearly 1,000 years ago. The thesis inherent in his commonsensical advice, as a matter of fact, represents the philosophical foundation of our anthology. We could not think of a better place to turn for material on fantasy literature than to the "experts," to those with the requisite "experience"—in short, to writers of fantasy literature. Thus, *Fantasists on Fantasy* is a collection of twenty-one writings on the subject of fantasy literature by eighteen prominent practitioners of the genre.

This is a unique collection. While other anthologies containing critical essays on fantasy do exist, none has the particular focus and format of this volume. For example, there are a few single-author collections of essays on fantasy such as *Language of the Night* (1979), a fine gathering of Ursula K. Le Guin's essays edited by Susan Wood, and also anthologies composed of critical essays on fantasy written by critics and scholars, such as Roger C. Schlobin's *The Aesthetics of Fantasy Literature and Art* (1982), but up to this time no one has put under one cover a representative sampling of

1

reflections about fantasy made by recognized authors in the field. Another kind of distinctiveness results from our attempt to include neglected or relatively inaccessible writings. Chesterton's "Fairy Tales," for instance, is taken from *All Things Considered,* a collection of his essays relatively unknown in this country; James Thurber's two articles, "The Wizard of Chitenango" and "Tempest in a Looking Glass" are even more difficult to obtain since both were published nearly a half century ago in *The New Republic* and *Forum;* Michael Moorcock's "Wit and Humour in Fantasy," published in a low-circulation British fan magazine, *Foundation,* is relatively unknown to American readers; August Derleth's and Herbert Read's writings are excerpts from texts which, although fine, are not easily obtained (of the two, Derleth's is especially difficult to find); and even the essays that we have taken from *The Horn Book Magazine* (those by Alexander, Hunter, and Langton) are probably not familiar to fantasy readers in general because *Horn Book* is not as well known outside the field of children's literature as it ought to be.

In addition to being unique, *Fantasists on Fantasy* offers enjoyment and enlightenment to a broad spectrum of readers. To begin with, it will be of value to anyone who is interested in either fantasy literature or in any of the writers we have chosen for inclusion. The volume, however, should also appeal to more specific audiences. Both the teacher and student of fantasy literature, for example, should find *Fantasists* useful as a source of background and enrichment readings. As a matter of fact, it was our experience as teachers of a course in Science Fiction and Fantasy Literature for the past twelve years that was primarily responsible for the decision to undertake this project. We found that we were frequently searching for articles and essays containing material on the definition, theory, and aesthetics of fantasy literature. In particular, we wanted our students to discover what the fantasists themselves had to say about these things. What we needed, in short, was a collection of reflective writings on fantasy: a vol-

ume containing readings to be assigned in conjunction
with the required novels and short stories. Then, too,
this anthology serves as a primer for would-be writers,
especially of fantasy. While not all of the selections deal
specifically with the technique of writing fantasy fiction, those that do, such as Le Guin's "From Elfland to
Poughkeepsie" and Derleth's "The Fantastic Story," are
must-reading for aspiring fantasists. Librarians, we feel,
will also welcome this versatile volume, since it serves
a multitude of functions. While some may wish to shelve
it next to works such as Edward Blishen's *The Thorny
Paradise: Writers on Writing for Children* (1975), others
may decide to place it beside other collections of essays
on science fiction and fantasy. It will also serve as a
handy reference tool for fantasy readers who want to
find out more about the lives and writings of particular
fantasists. Our headnotes are specifically designed to
satisfy that need.

We have already mentioned two criteria used in selecting writings for this volume: (1) the author of the
work must be a recognized writer of fantasy; and (2)
the subject of the writing must be fantasy literature,
that is, literature in which nonrational phenomena play
a significant part. While these were our primary criteria, they were not the only ones. In addition, we tried
to find writings that nicely blended the autobiographical and the theoretical and that were witty and sty-
listically charming. Above all, we wanted the author's
personality to shine through clearly. We were fortunate
in our search. Although a few of our selections, such as
Herbert Read's "Fantasy (Fancy)," smell faintly of the
lamp, most are light and refreshingly informal. We are
confident that you will know our subject authors much
better after you have had an opportunity to hear them
speak about fantasy in their inimitable styles.

Still another criterion was to provide diversity within
the boundaries set by our primary criteria. Note, for
instance, the many different forms of writing included.
In addition to either formal or informal essays taken
from various periodicals, *Fantasists on Fantasy* in-

cludes reviews (Beagle), published talks (Tolkien, Alexander, Hunter), prefaces (MacDonald), editorial essays (Martí-Ibáñez), excerpts from texts (Lovecraft, Read, Derleth), interview-essays (Kurtz), and even letters (Tolkien). This multiformity we consider to be one of our volume's unique strengths, since it is possible to learn more about each author by examining his or her chosen medium. It is only proper, for example, to allow Martí-Ibáñez to speak through a medium he found particularly suited to his writing temperament—the editorial essay. In addition to diversity of form, there is also variety in length. This, too, we feel works to the reader's advantage in that there is something here for nearly every reading occasion. Some of the short works, such as the Martí-Ibáñez essay, the Lewis essay, and the Tolkien letter, for example, are perfect as before-bed snacks, while longer and more theoretical essays such as those by Alexander, Langton, Le Guin, and Hunter are more suitable for leisurely and substantive literary dining. The different styles will also serve to satisfy different tastes.

Yet another type of diversity appears in the form of a wide variety of fantasy authors whose work covers nearly a century of literary endeavor in the field of fantasy literature. The earliest piece is MacDonald's "The Fantastic Imagination," which first appeared in 1893 as the Preface to the American edition of *The Light Princess and Other Tales,* and the most recent is Katherine Kurtz's interview-essay, first published in the May 1980 issue of *Fantasy Newsletter* but updated for this volume in July 1982. Writers from both sides of the Atlantic are represented here, but it is interesting to note that while the authors representing the first half of the century are primarily British, the representation from about 1965 on is predominantly American. There is also a shift in terms of gender: before 1965, primarily male representation; after 1965, primarily female. Thus our table of contents—partly by design, partly by happy coincidence—accurately reflects current trends in the fantasy field. Since 1965 the fantasy balance of trade has shifted from England to America, and the male-dominated genre of the first half of the century is now dominated by a number of excellent women fantasists. A final point about diversity. It should be noted that the entire spectrum of fantasy literature is represented in this volume. Although the majority of our selections are by writers of myth and fairy tale fantasy (what we call high fantasy*), we have also included selections by writers of Gothic fantasy (Lovecraft, Derleth), Sword and Sorcery fantasy (Norton, Moorcock), and "historical fantasy" (Kurtz's own designation for her Deryni books). In short, there is something here for all readers of fantasy.

We should like to conclude by addressing in particular the teachers and the students of fantasy literature. The general readers are invited as well, but they may choose, as Chaucer recommended, to "turn over the leaf" if they are not interested, and begin with the essays. As already mentioned, our major objective was to collect noteworthy essays on fantasy by people who were also among its more important practitioners and thus to provide the inside view of the art. We were familiar with a sufficient number of the fantasist-essayists at the outset to reasonably hope that the collection would at the same time provide an overview of the field, and thus some sort of systematic approach to it. Our findings have surpassed our hopes. A surprising degree of concurrence exists among our authors on what they consider important and about which they have written. And these recurring concerns—ten or eleven prime ones—are those that we have encountered as teachers and researchers of fantasy literature, covering a broad spectrum ranging from the theoretical and philosophical to the practical and technical.

More to the theoretical end of this spectrum lie four major topics: fantasy and the imagination; definition and classification; effects; meaning or moral.

---

* The secondary world, with its discernible though nonrational causality, is what characterizes high fantasy. Low fantasy, on the contrary, features nonrational happenings that are without causality or explanation because they occur in the rational world where such things are not supposed to occur.

The more purely theoretical essays originate, not surprisingly, from three of the academicians of the group. MacDonald, Tolkien, and Read all discuss fantasy as a faculty of the mind in relation to the imagination, and all three use Coleridge's definitions of imagination, fancy, and fantasy. In defining and classifying fantasy, the three academicians are joined by five other writers: Derleth, Chesterton, Langton, Cooper, and Kurtz. MacDonald, Tolkien, Chesterton, and Langton all insist upon the careful adherence of fantasy to its own internal laws, an adherence that belies the anything-can-happen fallacy. Derleth and Read define fantasy in stylistic and rhetorical terms. Cooper contrasts it to mainstream literature, while Kurtz distinguishes among three types: historical, heroic, and fairy-tale fantasy. And Langton offers a fine classification system based, in Tolkien's terms, on the relationship of the primary to the secondary world.

Another way of defining fantasy is by describing what it does, as do a number of our authors. Tolkien and Cooper write about the beneficial escape enjoyed by the reader, with Cooper adding some interesting notes about escaping into ourselves to Tolkien's classical statement. MacDonald compares the effect of fantasy to that of a sonata. Lovecraft similarly sees fantasy as affecting the emotions or the sensitive imagination. A group of writers—Alexander, Hunter, Cooper, and Martí-Ibáñez among them—reflect on the workings of fantasy upon children and adolescents, but we will return to this area shortly.

The last of the four theoretical topics takes the form of the question, should fantasy have a moral? MacDonald, who especially in his earlier stories became occasionally too moralizing, believes that a good fantasy ought to "wake" a meaning rather than preach a meaning. Langton agrees, but recognizes how difficult it is to succeed in this wakening. C.S. Lewis, who has been called a christian apologist, reveals that he would have been incapable of writing his Narnian books—or any novel—with a moral as a starting point. Chesterton on the other hand, makes the boldest assertion by insisting that some form of moralizing is necessary since a code of ethics is of the essence in the fairy tale. Kurtz explores the very specific question of the nature of religion in both its private and public forms.

The middle portion of the theoretical-to-practical fantasy spectrum contains five topics: comedy; style; realism; the unconscious; children.

It must be admitted that the first topic, comedy, receives attention from only three writers—Derleth, Tolkien and Moorcock—and of these three, only Moorcock deals with it as a central issue (Tolkien's statement does not appear in our excerpt). This relative silence is the more surprising since so many of our writers employ a good deal of humor, and two are in fact primarily known as wits or humorists—Chesterton and Thurber. The relative silence is perhaps most eloquent in speaking of the general attitude of a churchlike seriousness about fantasy. It is as a reaction against just this attitude that Moorcock writes his thought-provoking article, in which he sees a traditional and almost necessary relationship between comedy and fantasy. Derleth, though he only mentions comedy in passing, agrees.

Derleth's major focus is on the importance of style and on what constitutes a good descriptive style for fantasy. Le Guin's "From Elfland to Poughkeepsie" complements the Derleth essay by exploring the high style of speech or dialogue essential to good fantasy. While Le Guin definitely promotes the pure Elfland style, Kurtz favors a style somewhere in between that and the common or Poughkeepsie speech. MacDonald apparently agrees with both in ruling out the use of cockney.

Two of the more fascinating areas of fantasy literature in this mid-spectrum are the functioning of the unconscious mind (reader's and writer's) and the importance of realistic detail. While these two may appear to be either unrelated or opposed, they actually are complementary. When Beagle, Hunter, and Langton talk of realism, they are not talking of following inner laws; they mean that fantasy should correspond to the real world. Yet Langton's expression, "realism sharpens fantasy," reveals the complementarity. The presence of or awakening of the unconscious—largely through archetypes—is more startling and more convincing in the company of more familiar realistic circumstances. Several of the authors write of the unconscious mind in very Jungian terms, including Tolkien ("To W. H. Auden"), Le Guin ("Dreams Must Explain Themselves"), Cooper, Kurtz, and Hunter.

A number of our authors—mainly those whose writings appeal to young readers—address the perennial objections to fantasy-escapism and violence. Susan Cooper presents the defense against the former, and Thurber against the latter, attacks. Then several others make convincing cases for the positive effects of fantasy on children. Martí-Ibáñez suggests that fantasy is especially therapeutic for the young, Hunter that it enables children to adapt to the real, and Alexander that it helps young readers develop a capacity for belief in values.

At the most practical end of our spectrum are treatments of two important areas: influential works and writers; the technicalities of writing fantasy.

Many of our writers refer to the writers who influenced them; others simply speak of their favorite fantasy authors. This anthology thus provides an informal and delightfully eclectic survey of the history of fantasy literature. Informal and eclectic it might be, but such a survey would be, for the careful readers, extensive and varied in terms of time periods and types of fantasy. Readers will be fascinated—and perhaps bewildered for a time—by the fact that Read includes as examples fitting his definition of fantasy both *A Thousand and One Nights* and *Finnegan's Wake*, or that Lovecraft does the same with Dickens and Henry James. Derleth has one of the more extensive collections of names, extending from Dante through Milne. Norton's and Moorcock's lists are seemingly the most diverse, including, as they both do, Robert E. Howard and Edgar Rice Burroughs on the Sword and Sorcery side, along with E. R. Eddison (Norton's) and even Homer (Moorcock's) on the more classical side. Langton favors children's writers like Nesbit and Lofting but also includes Swift. And Kurtz offers a long and impressive catalogue, primarily of contemporary women fantasists.

A number of the essays touch upon the technicalities of writing fantasy in ways that might be helpful to other writers and that are of considerable interest to the general reader. Norton and Kurtz both rely heavily on historical research as a basis for their work. Hunter is also a researcher, but more in the area of folk tales and local legends than of ancient or medieval histories and texts. Along somewhat different lines, Cooper and Le Guin ("Dreams Must Explain Themselves") both speak of discovering their stories as they proceed, though both are clearly well versed in myth and legend. Langton's method, one certainly shared by others, is to ask the question "what if" and then introduce an impossible element and make it seem plausible. Le Guin ("From Elfland to Poughkeepsie") and Derleth offer numerous helpful stylistic hints and cautions. And, for those who wonder how to get their characters into the otherworld, Langton offers eight possible ways to do so.

In addition to agreeing on what is important—what they should write about—our authors had a second mild surprise for us: how much they agree on particulars. So strong is this concurrence that the few disagreements stand out by contrast. These disagreements add a needed ingredient of healthy debate: Moorcock versus Beagle on Tolkien; MacDonald versus Derleth on allegory; Le Guin versus Kurtz on style. Together the broad concurrence and occasional divergence of views are instructive and enhance the value of the anthology in offering an overview of fantasy literature.

GEORGE MACDONALD

(1824–1905)

"That man is richest who, having perfected the functions of his own life to the utmost, has also the widest
helpful influence . . . over the lives of others" *(Unto This
Last,* 1862). Although John Ruskin's words are meant
to reveal an important truth about the human condition
in general, he might just as well have been describing
his friend George MacDonald in particular. MacDonald,
it is true, had little material wealth, but he was exceedingly rich in other things, possessing a sunny dis-
position, a lively intellect, a fertile imagination, a fine
literary talent, and, above all, an almost ethereal spiritual quality that manifested itself in a devotion to high
ideals. Through the wise use of these exceptional attributes, MacDonald "perfected the functions of his own
life to the utmost," thus naturally acquiring what Ruskin refers to as the richest gift of all: the ability to
favorably influence the lives of others.

C. S. Lewis provides one of the most striking examples of MacDonald's pervasive influence. In his preface to *George MacDonald: An Anthology* (1947), Lewis
acknowledges his indebtedness to his chief literary and
spiritual mentor: "I have never concealed the fact that
I regarded him as my master; indeed I fancy I have
never written a book in which I did not quote from him."

Lewis goes on to declare that MacDonald's *Phantastes* (1858) made such a powerful impression upon him that it served to "convert, even to baptise...[his] imagination." J. R. R. Tolkien and W. H. Auden were also deeply influenced by MacDonald, in particular by his two Curdie books, *The Princess and the Goblin* (1872), and *The Princess and Curdie* (1882). Perhaps of greater importance than these individual instances, however, is the benign influence that MacDonald has had upon the millions of children who have read and who continue to read, his works of fantasy. The steady demand for MacDonald's works has resulted in two fine collections that have recently made his short stories more accessible: *The Gifts of the Child Christ: Fairy Tales and Stories for the Childlike* (1973, 2 vols.) and *The Complete Fairy Tales of George MacDonald* (1977). Most recently Glenn Edward Sadler has resurrected *The Portent* (1979), a story involving second sight, originally published in 1864, and he has also edited *The Fairy Stories of George MacDonald* in four volumes (1980). George MacDonald's influence shows little sign of waning.

George MacDonald, Scottish clergyman, novelist, poet, mythmaker, and father of modern fantasy, was born on December 10, 1824 in Huntly, Aberdeenshire, the son of a farmer. He attended Aberdeen University from 1840 to 1845, where he took prizes in chemistry and natural philosophy. After preparing for the ministry at Independent College, Highbury, he assumed his duties as Congregationalist pastor at Arundel, England, in 1850. However, because of theological disagreements with the church deacons he was forced to resign after only three years, thereafter making a meager living through free-lance writing, teaching, and lecturing. One of the highlights of his postministerial career was a highly successful lecture tour of the United States in the years 1872–73. MacDonald was such an effective and inspirational speaker that he was offered a lucrative pastorate in New York City ($20,000 per annum), but he turned it down, preferring to return to England, where he felt more at home.

Despite serious health and financial problems, and the loss of four of his eleven children, MacDonald seems to have led an extraordinarily full, eventful, and rewarding life. He not only became a popular and famous author, but also established friendships with some of the leading literary figures of his time, including Ruskin, Carlyle, Browning, Tennyson, Carroll, Morris, Emerson, Holmes, and Longfellow. He seemed happiest, however, when reading one of his stories to his large and adoring family. He died on September 18, 1905, at the age of eighty, at Ashtead, Surrey. His remains were cremated and sent to Bordighera, Italy, where they were buried next to the grave of his beloved wife, Louisa.

MacDonald was a prolific, imaginative, and highly talented writer who is probably best known in the United States for his works of fantasy, which include all-ages fantasies such as *At the Back of the North Wind* (1871) and the previously mentioned Curdie Books and fairy tales, as well as his adult fantasies, *Phantastes* and *Lilith* (1895). But he also published dozens of other books, including popular novels of Scottish peasant life, of which *David Elginbrod* (1863), *Alex Forbes* (1865) and *Robert Falconer* (1868) are perhaps his best. Details of his long and fascinating life may be found in a full-length biography written by his son, Dr. Greville MacDonald, (*George MacDonald and His Wife*, 1924), and in his own autobiographical novel, *Wilfrid Cumbermede* (1872). In addition, C. S. Lewis and Glenn Edward Sadler have written excellent short appreciations.

First printed in 1893 as the preface to the American edition of *The Light Princess and Other Fairy Tales,* and later reprinted in *A Dish of Orts* (1893), "The Fantastic Imagination" is a seminal work on the laws that govern the world of the fairy tale. It was not until 1938, with J. R. R. Tolkien's Andrew Lang Lecture "On Fairy-Stories" (published in longer form in 1947), that the new critical territory entered by MacDonald was further explored. It seems safe to assume that some of Tolkien's thinking on fundamental concepts regarding fantasy and the fairy story—for example, that of the secondary world and the laws governing it—was influenced by MacDonald. There are many memorable statements in "Imagination," but perhaps the most often quoted is MacDonald's cautionary reminder: "For my part, I do not write for children, but for the childlike, whether of five, or fifty, or seventy-five." MacDonald, steadfast champion of the concept that fantasy literature should not be relegated to the nursery, would have been pleased by the fact that his fantasy works are now being enjoyed by readers of all ages.

The Fantastic Imagination

George MacDonald

That we have in English no word corresponding to the German *Mährchen,* drives us to use the word *Fairytale,* regardless of the fact that the tale may have nothing to do with any sort of fairy. The old use of the word *Fairy,* by Spenser at least, might, however, well be adduced, were justification or excuse necessary where *need must.*

Were I asked, what is a fairytale? I should reply, *Read Undine: that is a fairytale; then read this and that as well, and you will see what is a fairytale.* Were I further begged to describe the *fairytale,* or define what it is, I would make answer, that I should as soon think of describing the abstract human face, or stating what must go to constitute a human being. A fairytale is just a fairytale, as a face is just a face; and of all fairytales I know, I think *Undine* the most beautiful.

Many a man, however, who would not attempt to define *a man,* might venture to say something as to what a man ought to be: even so much I will not in this

place venture with regard to the fairytale, for my long
past work in that kind might but poorly instance or
illustrate my now more matured judgment. I will but
say some things helpful to the reading, in right-minded
fashion, of such fairytales as I would wish to write, or
care to read.

Some thinkers would feel sorely hampered if at lib-
erty to use no forms but such as existed in nature, or
to invent nothing save in accordance with the laws of
the world of the senses; but it must not therefore be
imagined that they desire escape from the region of
law. Nothing lawless can show the least reason why it
should exist, or could at best have more than an appearance of life.

The natural world has its laws, and no man must
interfere with them in the way of presentment any more
than in the way of use; but they themselves may suggest laws of other kinds, and man may, if he pleases,
invent a little world of his own, with its own laws; for
there is that in him which delights in calling up new
forms—which is the nearest, perhaps, he can come to
creation. When such forms are new embodiments of old
truths, we call them products of the Imagination; when
they are mere inventions, however lovely, I should call
them the work of the Fancy: in either case, Law has
been diligently at work.

His world once invented, the highest law that comes
next into play is, that there shall be harmony between
the laws by which the new world has begun to exist;
and in the process of his creation, the inventor must
hold by those laws. The moment he forgets one of them,
he makes the story, by its own postulates, incredible.
To be able to live a moment in an imagined world, we
must see the laws of its existence obeyed. Those broken,
we fall out of it. The imagination in us, whose exercise
is essential to the most temporary submission to the
imagination of another, immediately, with the disap-
pearance of Law, ceases to act. Suppose the gracious
creatures of some childlike region of Fairyland talking
either cockney or Gascon! Would not the tale, however

lovelily begun, sink at once to the level of the Burlesque—of all forms of literature the least worthy? A man's inventions may be stupid or clever, but if he do not hold by the laws of them, or if he make one law jar with another, he contradicts himself as an inventor, he is no artist. He does not rightly consort his instruments, or he tunes them in different keys. The mind of man is the product of live Law; it thinks by law, it dwells in the midst of law, it gathers from law its growth; with law, therefore, can it alone work to any result. Inharmonious, unconsorting ideas will come to a man, but if he try to use one of such, his work will grow dull, and he will drop it from mere lack of interest. Law is the soil in which alone beauty will grow; beauty is the only stuff in which Truth can be clothed; and you may, if you will, call Imagination the tailor that cuts her garments to fit her, and Fancy his journeyman that puts the pieces of them together, or perhaps at most embroiders their button-holes. Obeying law, the maker works like his creator; not obeying law, he is such a fool as heaps a pile of stones and calls it a church.

In the moral world it is different: there a man may clothe in new forms, and for this employ his imagination freely, but he must invent nothing. He may not, for any purpose, turn its laws upside down. He must not meddle with the relations of live souls. The laws of the spirit of man must hold, alike in this world and in any world he may invent. It were no offence to suppose a world in which everything repelled instead of attracted the things around it; it would be wicked to write a tale representing a man it called good as always doing bad things, or a man it called bad as always doing good things: the notion itself is absolutely lawless. In physical things a man may invent; in moral things he must obey—and take their laws with him into his invented world as well.

"You write as if a fairytale were a thing of importance: must it have a meaning?"

It cannot help having some meaning; if it have proportion and harmony it has vitality, and vitality is truth.

16

The beauty may be plainer in it than the truth, but without the truth the beauty could not be, and the fairytale would give no delight. Everyone, however, who feels the story, will read its meaning after his own nature and development: one man will read one meaning in it, another will read another.

"If so, how am I to assure myself that I am not reading my own meaning into it, but yours out of it?"

Why should you be so assured? It may be better that you should read your meaning into it. That may be a higher operation of your intellect than the mere reading of mine out of it: your meaning may be superior to mine.

"Suppose my child ask me what the fairytale means, what am I to say?"

If you do not know what it means, what is easier than to say so? If you do see a meaning in it, there it is for you to give him. A genuine work of art must mean many things; the truer its art, the more things it will mean. If my drawing, on the other hand, is so far from being a work of art that it needs THIS IS A HORSE written under it, what can it matter that neither you nor your child should know what it means? It is there not so much to convey a meaning as to wake a meaning. If it do not even wake an interest, throw it aside. A meaning may be there, but it is not for you. If, again, you do not know a horse when you see it, the name written under it will not serve you much. At all events, the business of the painter is not to teach zoology.

But indeed your children are not likely to trouble you about the meaning. They find what they are capable of finding, and more would be too much. For my part, I do not write for children, but for the childlike, whether of five, or fifty, or seventy-five.

A fairytale is not an allegory. There may be allegory in it, but it is not an allegory. He must be an artist indeed who can, in any mode, produce a strict allegory that is not a weariness to the spirit. An allegory must be Mastery or Moorditch.

A fairytale, like a butterfly or a bee, helps itself on all sides, sips at every wholesome flower, and spoils not one. The true fairytale is, to my mind, very like the sonata. We all know that a sonata means something; and where there is the faculty of talking with suitable vagueness, and choosing metaphor sufficiently loose, mind may approach mind, in the interpretation of a sonata, with the result of a more or less contenting consciousness of sympathy. But if two or three men sat down to write each what the sonata meant to him, what approximation to definite idea would be the result? Little enough—and that little more than needful. We should find it had roused related, if not identical, feelings, but probably not one common thought. Has the sonata therefore failed? Had it undertaken to convey, or ought it to be expected to impart anything defined, anything notionally recognizable?

"But words are not music; words at least are meant and fitted to carry a precise meaning!"

It is very seldom indeed that they carry the exact meaning of any user of them! And if they can be so used as to convey definite meaning, it does not follow that they ought never to carry anything else. Words are live things that may be variously employed to various ends. They can convey a scientific fact, or throw a shadow of her child's dream on the heart of a mother. They are things to put together like the pieces of a dissected map, or to arrange like the notes on a stave. Is the music in them to go for nothing? It can hardly help the definiteness of a meaning: is it therefore to be disregarded? They have length, and breadth, and outline: have they nothing to do with depth? Have they only to describe, never to impress? Has nothing any claim to their use but the definite? The cause of a child's tears may be altogether undefinable: has the mother therefore no antidote for his vague misery? That may be strong in colour which has no evident outline. A fairytale, a sonata, a gathering storm, a limitless night, seizes you and sweeps you away: do you begin at once to wrestle with it and ask whence its power over you, whither it is carrying you? The law of each is in the mind of its composer; that law makes one man feel this way, another man feel that way. To one the sonata is a world of odour and beauty, to another of soothing only and sweetness. To one, the cloudy rendezvous is a wild dance, with a terror at its heart; to another, a majestic march of heavenly hosts, with Truth in their centre pointing their course, but as yet restraining her voice. The greatest forces lie in the region of the uncomprehended.

I will go farther— The best thing you can do for your fellow, next to rousing his conscience, is—not to give him things to think about, but to wake things up that are in him; or say, to make him think things for himself. The best Nature does for us is to work in us such moods in which thoughts of high import arise. Does any aspect of Nature wake but one thought? Does she ever suggest only one definite thing? Does she make any two men in the same place at the same moment think the same thing? Is she therefore a failure, because she is not definite? Is it nothing that she rouses the something deeper than the understanding—the power that underlies thoughts? Does she not set feeling, and so thinking at work? Would it be better that she did this after one fashion and not after many fashions? Nature is mood-engendering, thought-provoking: such ought the sonata, such ought the fairytale to be.

"But a man may then imagine in your work what he pleases, what you never meant!"

Not what he pleases, but what he can. If he be not a true man, he will draw evil out of the best; we need not mind how he treats any work of art! If he be a true man, he will imagine true things; what matter whether I meant them or not? They are there none the less that I cannot claim putting them there! One difference between God's work and man's is, that, while God's work cannot mean more than he meant, man's must mean more than he meant. For in everything that God has made, there is layer upon layer of ascending significance; also he expresses the same thought in higher and higher kinds of that thought: it is God's things, his embodied thoughts, which alone a man has to use, mod-

ified and adapted to his own purposes, for the expression
of his thoughts; therefore he cannot help his words and
figures falling into such combinations in the mind of
another as he had himself not foreseen, so many are the
thoughts allied to every other thought, so many are
the relations involved in every figure, so many the facts
hinted in every symbol. A man may well himself discover truth in what he wrote; for he was dealing all the
time with things that came from thoughts beyond his
own.

"But surely you would explain your idea to one who
asked you?"

I say again, if I cannot draw a horse, I will not write
THIS IS A HORSE under what I foolishly meant for one.
Any key to a work of imagination would be nearly, if
not quite, as absurd. The tale is there, not to hide, but
to show: if it show nothing at your window, do not open
your door to it; leave it out in the cold. To ask me to
explain, is to say, "Roses! Boil them, or we won't have
them!" My tales may not be roses, but I will not boil
them.

So long as I think my dog can bark, I will not sit up
to bark for him.

If a writer's aim be logical conviction, he must spare
no logical pains, not merely to be understood, but to
escape being misunderstood; where his object is to move
by suggestion, to cause to imagine, then let him assail
the soul of his reader as the wind assails an æolian
harp. If there be music in my reader, I would gladly
wake it. Let fairytale of mine go for a firefly that now
flashes, now is dark, but may flash again. Caught in a
hand which does not love its kind, it will turn to an
insignificant, ugly thing, that can neither flash nor fly.

The best way with music, I imagine, is not to bring
the forces of our intellect to bear upon it, but to be still
and let it work on that part of us for whose sake it
exists. We spoil countless precious things by intellectual greed. He who will be a man, and will not be a
child, must—he cannot help himself—become a little
man, that is, a dwarf. He will, however, need no con-

solation, for he is sure to think himself a very large creature indeed.

If any strain of my "broken music" make a child's eyes flash, or his mother's grow for a moment dim, my labour will not have been in vain.

GILBERT KEITH CHESTERTON

(1874–1936)

Few twentieth-century writers have titillated the public imagination as potently as G. K. Chesterton. His very name conjures up a host of vivid images: Chesterton the man about town, heavily sauntering down Fleet Street, sword stick in hand, floppy-brimmed brigand's hat atop his massive head, and great cloak draping a body well over six feet and weighing more than 300 pounds; Chesterton the "vagabond lecturer," so absentminded he once sent a telegram to his wife in London which read: "Am in Market Harborough. Where ought I to be?"; Chesterton the debater, sufficiently clever and articulate to regularly get the best of formidable opponents such as George Bernard Shaw and Clarence Darrow, but frequently so amused by his own jokes that he laughed himself into fits of uncontrollable hiccups; Chesterton the radio broadcaster, mischievously assuring his audience in one of his final talks that "they [might] go with a whimper, But [he would] go out with a bang"; and Chesterton the conversationalist, regularly engaging, with his close friends and fellow writers, Hilaire Belloc and Maurice Baring, in orgies of talk, food, and drink. In brief, Chesterton's life was an exercise in hyperbole. He was the caricaturist's dream come true.

G. K. Chesterton, journalist, essayist, cartoonist, poet, novelist, fantasist, and "Prince of Paradox," was born on March 29, 1874, at Campden Hill, a suburb of London. In 1887 he was sent to Saint Paul's School, but the revered institution, at which such luminaries as Pepys and Milton had been educated, did not inspire Chesterton, who later confessed that he spent most of his time writing bad poetry rather than studying. In fact, some of the poems Chesterton contributed to *The Debater,* a school magazine he had helped establish, were very good. Chesterton, however, believed that he ought to pursue a career in the graphic arts. Thus in 1892, after a brief stay in a smaller art school, he enrolled in the Slade School of Art, University College, London. It was a costly decision. Lonely and under a great deal of pressure, Chesterton lapsed into what he later called his "period of madness," a time of lethargy, self-doubt, and profound inner torment. At least two good things came out of his stay at Slade, however: he left convinced that he loved literature more than art; and he met Sir Ernest Hodder Williams, who invited Chesterton to write reviews for the *Bookman.*

Chesterton's acceptance of Williams's offer marked the beginning of his brilliant career as a journalist. A remarkably rapid and prolific writer, Chesterton contributed hundreds of essays to several different journals from about 1895 on, but he is probably best remembered for his work with *The London Illustrated News;* Chesterton submitted weekly essays to the *News* from 1905 to 1930, missing only two numbers for the entire twenty-five-year period.

One of the reasons for Chesterton's reliability was the stabilizing influence of Frances Boggs, whom he had married in 1901. Indeed, the first eight years after his marriage were among Chesterton's most happy and and productive: he not only wrote several books and hundreds of fine articles, but also conceived the idea for his famous Father Brown detective stories. The next ten years were nearly as productive, but not nearly so happy, since they were plagued by a series of personal misfortunes. The first occurred in 1909, when Frances insisted that they leave their London home in Battersea for a home in Beaconsfield, Buckinghamshire, about thirty miles from London. Although this was a move that ultimately helped both Chesterton and his writing career, it was extremely painful for him to leave the bustling city. Then, in November 1914, Chesterton began suffering from a life-threatening illness which left him in a state of semiconsciousness for several months; his recovery was miraculous. And, finally, not long after Armistice Day, his brother Cecil, with whom Chesterton had a very close relationship, died in a hospital in France.

Once through this painful decade, the indomitable Chesterton resumed his active lifestyle: writing, lecturing, debating, traveling, and editing *G. K.'s Weekly*, a vehicle for spreading the gospel of "Distributism" (i.e., the widest possible ownership of property). Following his conversion to Roman Catholicism in 1922, at the age of forty-eight, Chesterton turned even more of his attention to religious writings (he had already defined his idea of Christianity in *Orthodoxy*, 1908), publishing works such as *St. Francis of Assisi* (1923), *The Everlasting Man* (1925), and *St. Thomas Aquinas* (1933). Although he was not in the best of health the last few years of his life, his spirits were never dampened. He died at Top Meadow, his Beaconsfield home, on June 14, 1936.

Dudley Barker, in his *G. K. Chesterton: A Biography* (New York: Stein and Day, 1973), points out that "Chesterton's output was so vast that even John Sullivan, in his two excellent volumes of bibliography...does not claim to have included all." (p. 289) All that we can do here is provide a miniature sampler. *New and Collected Poems* (1929), *The Napoleon of Notting Hill Gate* (1904), *The Man Who Was Thursday* (1908), and *Manalive* (1912) offer a taste of Chesterton's poems and novels; *The Coloured Lands* (1938) is a fine showcase for Chesterton's illustrations and short fantasy pieces, and *The Father Brown Omnibus* (1947) contains the corpus of

Chesterton's short detective fiction; some of Chesterton's finest literary criticism appears in *Robert Browning* (1903), *Dickens* (1906), and *The Victorian Age in Literature* (1913); two representative volumes from among his many collections of essays are *Generally Speaking* (1929) and *Come to Think of It* (1930). Further information on the life of Chesterton can be found in his *Autobiography* (1936) and Maisie Ward's *Gilbert Keith Chesterton* (1943).

In his prefatory essay to *All Things Considered* (1908), the collection from which "Fairy Tales" has been taken, Chesterton puckishly explains that the "chief vice" of these particular essays is that "so many of them are very serious." While it is true that some of his subjects are serious, his treatments are generously spiked with imaginative wit, ingenious paradox, and high-spirited good humor. "Fairy Tales" is a case in point. Although it is clear that Chesterton strongly defends the morality of fairy tales, he defends his thesis in a lively, witty, lucid, and entertaining manner. Like his good friend Bernard Shaw, Chesterton believed in, and knew how to effectively use, the sugarcoated pill approach. It is always a pleasure to take Chesterton's medicine.

·❈ Fairy Tales ❈·

G. K. Chesterton

Some solemn and superficial people (for nearly all very superficial people are solemn) have declared that the fairy-tales are immoral; they base this upon some accidental circumstances or regrettable incidents in the war between giants and boys, some cases in which the latter indulged in unsympathetic deceptions or even in practical jokes. The objection, however, is not only false, but very much the reverse of the facts. The fairy-tales are at root not only moral in the sense of being innocent, but moral in the sense of being didactic, moral in the sense of being moralising. It is all very well to talk of the freedom of fairyland, but there was precious little freedom in fairyland by the best official accounts. Mr. W. B. Yeats and other sensitive modern souls, feeling that modern life is about as black a slavery as ever oppressed mankind (they are right enough there), have specially described elfland as a place of utter ease and abandonment—a place where the soul can turn every way at will like the wind. Science denounces the idea of a capricious God; but Mr. Yeats's school suggests that in that world every one is a capricious god. Mr. Yeats himself has said a hundred times in that sad and splendid literary style which makes him the first of all poets now writing in English (I will not say of all English poets, for Irishmen are familiar with the practice of physical assault), he has, I say, called up a hundred times the picture of the terrible freedom of the fairies, who typify the ultimate anarchy of art—

> "Where nobody grows old or weary or wise,
> Where nobody grows old or godly or grave."

But, after all (it is a shocking thing to say), I doubt whether Mr. Yeats really knows the real philosophy of the fairies. He is not simple enough; he is not stupid enough. Though I say it who should not, in good sound human stupidity I would knock Mr. Yeats out any day. The fairies like me better than Mr. Yeats; they can take me in more. And I have my doubts whether this feeling of the free, wild spirits on the crest of hill or wave is really the central and simple spirit of folk-lore. I think the poets have made a mistake: because the world of the fairy-tales is a brighter and more varied world than ours, they have fancied it less moral; really

it is brighter and more varied because it is more moral.
Suppose a man could be born in a modern prison. It is
impossible, of course, because nothing human can happen in a modern prison, though it could sometimes in
an ancient dungeon. A modern prison is always inhu-
man, even when it is not inhumane. But suppose a man
were born in a modern prison, and grew accustomed to
the deadly silence and the disgusting indifference; and
suppose he were then suddenly turned loose upon the
life and laughter of Fleet Street. He would, of course,
think that the literary men in Fleet Street were a free
and happy race; yet how sadly, how ironically, is this
the reverse of the case! And so again these toiling serfs
in Fleet Street, when they catch a glimpse of the fairies,
think the fairies are utterly free. But fairies are like
journalists in this and many other respects. Fairies and
journalists have an apparent gaiety and a delusive
beauty. Fairies and journalists seem to be lovely and
lawless; they seem to be both of them too exquisite to
descend to the ugliness of everyday duty. But it is an
illusion created by the sudden sweetness of their presence. Journalists live under law; and so in fact does
fairyland.

If you really read the fairy-tales, you will observe
that one idea runs from one end of them to the other—
the idea that peace and happiness can only exist on
some condition. This idea, which is the core of ethics,
is the core of the nursery-tales. The whole happiness
of fairyland hangs upon a thread, upon one thread. Cin-
derella may have a dress woven on supernatural looms
and blazing with unearthly brilliance; but she must be
back when the clock strikes twelve. The king may invite
fairies to the christening, but he must invite all the
fairies or frightful results will follow. Bluebeard's wife
may open all doors but one. A promise is broken to a
cat, and the whole world goes wrong. A promise is broken to a yellow dwarf, and the whole world goes wrong.
A girl may be the bride of the God of Love himself if
she never tries to see him; she sees him, and he vanishes
away. A girl is given a box on condition she does not

open it; she opens it, and all the evils of this world rush out at her. A man and woman are put in a garden on condition that they do not eat one fruit: they eat it, and lose their joy in all the fruits of the earth.

This great idea, then, is the backbone of all folklore—the idea that all happiness hangs on one thin veto; all positive joy depends on one negative. Now, it is obvious that there are many philosophical and religious ideas akin to or symbolised by this; but it is not with them I wish to deal here. It is surely obvious that all ethics ought to be taught to this fairy-tale tune; that, if one does the thing forbidden, one imperils all the things provided. A man who breaks his promise to his wife ought to be reminded that, even if she is a cat, the case of the fairy-cat shows that such conduct may be incautious. A burglar just about to open some one else's safe should be playfully reminded that he is in the perilous posture of the beautiful Pandora: he is about to lift the forbidden lid and loosen evils unknown. The boy eating some one's apples in some one's apple tree should be a reminder that he has come to a mystical moment of his life, when one apple may rob him of all others. This is the profound morality of fairy-tales; which so far from being lawless, go to the root of all law. Instead of finding (like common books of ethics) a rationalistic basis for each Commandment, they find the great mystical basis for all Commandments. We are in this fairyland on sufferance; it is not for us to quarrel with the conditions under which we enjoy this wild vision of the world. The vetoes are indeed extraordinary but then so are the concessions. The idea of property, the idea of some one else's apples, is a rum idea; but then the idea of there being any apples is a rum idea. It is strange and weird that I cannot with safety drink ten bottles of champagne; but then the champagne itself is strange and weird, if you come to that. If I have drunk of the fairies' drink it is but just I should drink by the fairies' rules. We may not see the direct logical connection between three beautiful silver spoons and a large ugly policeman; but then who in fairy-tales ever could see the direct logical connection between three bears and a giant, or between a rose and a roaring beast? Not only can these fairy-tales be enjoyed because they are moral, but morality can be enjoyed because it puts us in fairyland, in a world at once of wonder and of war.

HOWARD PHILLIPS LOVECRAFT

(1890–1937)

> Here rests his head upon the lap of earth,
>   A youth to Fortune and to Fame unknown;
> Fair Science frowned not on his humble birth,
>   And Melancholy marked him for her own.
>   Thomas Gray, "Elegy:
>   Written in a Country Churchyard"

Had H. P. Lovecraft been asked to choose an epitaph to mark his grave, he might very well have chosen the lines quoted above. Indeed, to say that Melancholy marked Lovecraft for her own is to understate the case, and it is most certainly true that Fortune and Fame were to him unknown. Four people attended his funeral services, and at the time of his early death it appeared that his works were destined for oblivion. But "fame is the sun of the dead," Balzac reminds us, and true to the maxim, Lovecraft now basks in the bright rays of posthumous fame and popularity. His life has been meticulously chronicled in biographical works such as August Derleth's *HPL: A Memoir* (1945) and L. Sprague De Camp's *Lovecraft: A Biography* (1975); his regularly reprinted works have achieved international popularity; his fans have formed societies devoted to him and his Cthulhu Mythos; and his literary reputation has steadily improved through the generous critical attention scholars have given his works. As S. T. Joshi notes in the introduction of his voluminous *H. P. Lovecraft: An Annotated Bibliography* (1981), "that [Lovecraft] will continue to ascend in stature is evident; that he deserves to do so is equally clear."

H. P. Lovecraft, American author of Gothic fantasy and science fiction, was born on August 20, 1890 in Providence, Rhode Island, a city for which he developed an unusually strong affection. Frail and shy, but remarkably precocious, Lovecraft mastered the alphabet at the age of two and read with ease at four. He took an early interest in the sciences, and in 1906, when he was only sixteen, he began contributing monthly articles on astronomy to the *Providence Evening Tribune*. Because of poor health and a reclusive nature, he rarely ventured far from the city of his birth, living first with his sheltering mother, Sarah Phillips Lovecraft, and then his aunts. He did move to Brooklyn in 1924 shortly after his ill-fated marriage to Sonia Greene, also a writer, but two years later he returned to Providence, alone, having tired of both the metropolis and married life. The separation was made final through a divorce agreement signed by Lovecraft on March 25, 1929.

Lovecraft, influenced by writers such as Edgar Allan Poe, Jules Verne, Algernon Blackwood, Arthur Machen, M. R. James, and Lord Dunsany, had published a few stories in little magazines from 1916 on, but his career as a professional writer did not begin until 1923 with the appearance of "Dagon" in the October issue of *Weird Tales*, the pulp magazine that carried most of Lovecraft's stories. For the remaining fourteen years of his life Lovecraft published a steady stream of eldritch tales, most written at night, including such classics as "The Rats in the Walls" (1924), "The Outsider" (1926), "Pickman's Model" (1927), "The Colour Out of Space" (1927), "The Call of Cthulhu" (1928), "The Dunwich Horror" (1929), "The Whisperer in Darkness" (1931), "At the Mountains of Madness" (1936), "Haunter of the Dark" (1936), and "The Case of Charles Dexter Ward" (1941).

It is sad to note that even with his successful writing career, Lovecraft's life was essentially an unhappy one. Part of the problem was that he was almost always in dire financial straits, despite the fact that he had over fifty stories published during his lifetime and worked as a revisionist and ghost writer as well. But poverty wasn't his only problem. He seemed constantly to suffer from poor health and from the deep-rooted fear that he, like his parents, would succumb to mental illness; he was dissatisfied with his own work, deprecatingly describing it as being too commercial; he was more at home in the past (he adored the eighteenth century) than in the present; and he was terribly shy and withdrawn, preferring to communicate by letter (he wrote close to a hundred thousand, many of which have been collected in a massive five-volume Arkham House edition) rather than by face-to-face conversation. Ironically, although Lovecraft probably never found true happiness and contentment in his own life, he brought enjoyment to the lives of many others through his writings and voluminous correspondence. He died at the age of forty-six of cancer and Bright's disease, on March 15, 1937, in his beloved Providence.

When Lovecraft died, he did leave behind a solid core of enthusiastic and loyal admirers, but in general his popularity had waned to such a degree that there was very real danger of his fiction gradually fading into obscurity. However, August Derleth, one of Lovecraft's devoted followers, was determined not to let this happen. Shortly after his mentor's death, Derleth and his close friend, Donald Wandrei, attempted to find a publisher for a collection of Lovecraft's stories, without success. Not so easily defeated, however, Derleth and Wandrei published the collection themselves, calling their newly formed company Arkham House, in honor of the fictitious New England village Lovecraft had used so often as a setting in his tales. Since that first collection, *The Outsider and Others* (1939), Arkham House has published in hardback almost everything Lovecraft wrote, including his classic essay, "Supernatural Horror in Literature." Although Lovecraft's talent would probably have been recognized sooner or later, we owe a great deal to Derleth for keeping Lovecraft's works in print.

The rapid rise to classic status of "Supernatural Horror in Literature" is in and of itself remarkable, but even more remarkable is the fact that it has survived at all, considering its inauspicious beginnings. Published in 1927 in the first issue of W. Paul Cook's amateur magazine, *The Recluse,* neither the essay nor the newly born magazine drew much attention. Lovecraft did not lose interest in his essay, however; during the next ten years he continued to revise and polish it, finally putting it into its present form. The excerpt included here constitutes only the introduction of Lovecraft's lengthy essay; however, despite its brevity, this is perhaps the most important segment of the work because it contains Lovecraft's definition of what he termed "the literature of cosmic fear." In this theoretical preamble, Lovecraft emphasizes that an atmosphere capable of creating a profound sense of dread in the reader is vital to the Gothic mode. It is, of course, Lovecraft's own exceptional ability to evoke such a sense of dread that has assured him of a lasting reputation as one of America's most efficacious authors of weird fiction.

·✻· Introduction to ·✻·
Supernatural Horror in Literature
H. P. Lovecraft

The oldest and strongest emotion of mankind is fear, and the oldest and strongest kind of fear is fear of the unknown. These facts few psychologists will dispute, and their admitted truth must establish for all time the genuineness and dignity of the weirdly horrible tales as a literary form. Against it are discharged all the shafts of a materialistic sophistication which clings to frequently felt emotions and external events, and of a naively inspired idealism which deprecates the aesthetic motive and calls for a didactic literature to "uplift" the reader toward a suitable degree of smirking optimism. But in spite of all this opposition the weird tale has survived, developed, and attained remarkable heights of perfection; founded as it is on a profound and elementary principle whose appeal, if not always universal, must necessarily be poignant and permanent to minds of the requisite sensitiveness.

The appeal of the spectrally macabre is generally narrow because it demands from the reader a certain degree of imagination and a capacity for detachment from everyday life. Relatively few are free enough from the spell of the daily routine to respond to rappings from outside, and tales of ordinary feelings and events, or of common sentimental distortions of such feelings and events, will always take first place in the taste of the majority; rightly, perhaps, since of course these ordinary matters make up the greater part of human experience. But the sensitive are always with us, and sometimes a curious streak of fancy invades an obscure corner of the very hardest head; so that no amount of rationalisation, reform, or Freudian analysis can quite annul the thrill of the chimney-corner whisper or the lonely wood. There is here involved psychological pattern or tradition as real and as deeply grounded in mental experience as any other pattern or tradition of mankind; coeval with the religious feeling and closely related to many aspects of it, and too much a part of our innermost biological heritage to lose keen potency over a very important, though not numerically great, minority of our species.

Man's first instincts and emotions formed his response to the environment in which he found himself. Definite feelings based on pleasure and pain grew up around the phenomena whose causes and effects he understood, whilst around those which he did not understand—and the universe teemed with them in the early days—were naturally personifications, marvelous interpretations, and sensations of awe and fear as would be hit upon by a race having few and simple ideas and limited experience. The unknown, being likewise the unpredictable, became for our primitive forefathers a terrible and omnipotent source of boons and calamities visited upon mankind for cryptic and wholly extraterrestrial reasons, and thus clearly belonging to spheres of existence whereof we know nothing and wherein we have no part. The phenomenon of dreaming likewise helped to build up the notion of an unreal or spiritual world; and in general, all the conditions of savage dawn-life so strongly conducted toward a feeling of the supernatural, that we need not wonder at the thoroughness with which man's very hereditary essence has become saturated with religion and superstition. That saturation must, as a matter of plain scientific fact, be regarded as virtually permanent so far as the subconscious mind and inner instincts are concerned; for though the area of the unknown has been steadily contracting for thousands of years, an infinite reservoir of mystery still engulfs most of the outer cosmos, whilst a vast residuum of powerful inherited associations clings round all the objects and processes that were once mysterious, however well they may now be explained. And more than this, there is an actual physiological fixation of the old instincts in our nervous tissue, which would make them obscurely operative even were the conscious mind to be purged of all sources of wonder.

Because we remember pain and the menace of death more vividly than pleasure, and because our feelings toward the beneficent aspects of the unknown have from the first been captured and formalised by conventional religious rituals, it has fallen to the lot of the darker and more maleficent side of cosmic mystery to figure chiefly in our popular supernatural folklore. This tendency, too, is naturally enhanced by the fact that uncertainty and danger are always closely allied; thus making any kind of an unknown world a world of peril and evil possibilities. When to this sense of fear and evil the inevitable fascination of wonder and curiosity is superadded, there is born a composite body of keen emotion and imaginative provocation whose vitality must of necessity endure as long as the human race itself. Children will always be afraid of the dark, and men with minds sensitive to hereditary impulse will always tremble at the thought of the hidden and fathomless worlds of strange life which may pulsate in the gulfs beyond the stars, or press hideously upon our own globe in unholy dimensions which only the dead and the moonstruck can glimpse.

With this foundation, no one need wonder at the existence of a literature of cosmic fear. It has always existed, and always will exist; and no better evidence of its tenacious vigour can be cited than the impulse which now and then drives writers of totally opposite leanings to try their hands at it in isolated tales, as if to discharge from their minds certain phantasmal shapes which would otherwise haunt them. Thus Dickens wrote several eerie narratives; Browning, the hideous poem *Childe Roland;* Henry James, *The Turn of the Screw;* Dr. Holmes, the subtle novel *Elsie Venner;* F. Marion Crawford, *The Upper Berth* and a number of other examples; Mrs. Charlotte Perkins Gilman, social worker, *The Yellow Wall Paper;* whilst the humorist, W. W. Jacobs, produced that able melodramatic bit called *The Monkey's Paw.*

This type of fear-literature must not be confounded with a type externally similar but psychologically widely different; the literature of mere physical fear and the mundanely gruesome. Such writing, to be sure, has its place, as has the conventional or even whimsical or humorous ghost story where formalism or the author's knowing wink removes the true sense of the morbidly unnatural; but these things are not the literature of cosmic fear in its purest sense. The true weird tale has something more than secret murder, bloody bones, or a sheeted form clanking chains according to rule. A certain atmosphere of breathless and unexplainable dread of outer, unknown forces must be present; and there must be a hint, expressed with a seriousness and portentousness becoming its subject, of that most terrible conception of the human brain—a malign and particular suspension or defeat of those fixed laws of Nature which are our only safeguard against the assaults of chaos and the daemons of unplumbed space.

Naturally we cannot expect all weird tales to conform absolutely to any theoretical model. Creative minds are uneven, and the best of fabrics have their dull spots. Moreover, much of the choicest weird work is unconscious; appearing in memorable fragments scattered through material whose massed effect may be of a very different cast. Atmosphere is the all-important thing, for the final criterion of authenticity is not the dovetailing of a plot but the creation of a given sensation. We may say, as a general thing, that a weird story whose intent is to teach or produce a social effect, or one in which the horrors are finally explained away by natural means, is not a genuine tale of cosmic fear; but it remains a fact that such narratives often possess, in isolated sections, atmospheric touches which fulfill every condition of true supernatural horror-literature. Therefore we must judge a weird tale not by the author's intent, or by the mere mechanics of the plot; but by the emotional level which it attains at its least mundane point. If the proper sensations are excited, such a "high spot" must be admitted on its own merits as weird literature, no matter how prosaically it is later dragged down. The one test of the really weird is simply this— whether or not there be excited in the reader a profound sense of dread, and of contact with unknown spheres and powers; a subtle attitude of awed listening, as if for the beating of black wings or the scratching of outside shapes and entities on the known universe's utmost rim. And of course, the more completely and unifiedly a story conveys this atmosphere, the better it is as a work of art in the given medium.

SIR HERBERT EDWARD READ

(1893–1968)

If there is any truth to William Cowper's popular adage, "Variety's the very spice of life," Sir Herbert Read's life must have been a virtual cornucopia of piquancy. Indeed, the variety of his writings and intellectual endeavors is nothing short of phenomenal. During a literary career that spanned half a century, Read vigorously explored dozens of diverse subjects including literature, art, education, philosophy, politics, technology, and sociology. Perhaps even more remarkable than his extraordinarily wide range of interests, however, is the depth of understanding he brings to all his studies. Read has earned the reputation of being one of the most interesting, stimulating, and important thinkers of our time.

Herbert Read, poet, novelist, essayist, editor, educator, polemicist, and critic, was born on December 4, 1893, at Muscoates Grange, Kirbymoorside, Yorkshire, England. The eldest son of a farmer, Read spent the first ten years of his life in relative seclusion, receiving his early schooling from governesses, rather than from teachers at the local school. Shortly after his father's death in 1904, however, he began leading a less isolated life, finally leaving home to attend a boarding school in Halifax, where he pursued his studies for the next five years.

In 1912 Read enrolled at the University of Leeds; he intended to study law, but he soon discovered that his love of literature was stronger than his desire to become a barrister. While only halfheartedly pursuing his major studies, Read wholeheartedly followed a program of extracurricular readings. He also began writing poetry, publishing at his own expense a small volume of verse called *Songs of Chaos* (1915). The title was prophetic. Commissioned in January 1915, before taking his degree, Read spent the next four years with the Yorkshire Regiment, the Green Howards, fighting on the battlefields of France and Belgium. He served his country with distinction, winning both the Distinguished Flying Order and the Military Cross.

From 1919 to 1939, a period he described as "the no-man's years between the wars," Herbert Read moved from one job to another, writing enough in his spare time to establish a solid reputation as poet and critic. His first position after the war was assistant principal in the Government Treasury Office in London, a post for which he had little liking. After three tedious years (1919–22), he resigned to become assistant keeper in the Victoria and Albert Museum, a position he found considerably more stimulating and rewarding. As a matter of fact, it was here that his career as art critic began with the publication of *English Stained Glass* (1928) and *Staffordshire Pottery Figures* (1929). Read left the Museum in 1931 to become Watson Gordon Professor of Fine Art at the University of Edinburgh, a position he held until 1933, when he assumed the editorship of *Burlington Magazine*.

During the last three decades of his life Read continued to write at a furious pace, but he also lectured throughout the world and held a number of prestigious university positions, including that of Charles Eliot Norton Professor of Poetry at Harvard (1953–54) and Andrew W. Mellon Lecturer in Fine Arts, Washington, D.C. (1954). Earlier, in the years 1940–42, he was a Leon Fellow at the University of London, during which time he wrote one of his most important works, *Edu-*

cation Through Art (1943). He received many awards
and honors for his manifold accomplishments, including honorary degrees from several universities, but his
greatest moment came in 1953 when a grateful nation
made him a Knight of the Order of the British Empire
in recognition of his superb literary achievements. Sir
Herbert Read died at his Yorkshire home near Malton
on June 12, 1968. The world lost one of its most productive and erudite men of letters.

It is difficult in any essay of this length to provide
a representative sampling of Read's tremendous literary product. Probably the best introduction to Read's
poetry—mostly free verse—is his *Collected Poems*
(1966); for a good cross section of Read's literary criticism one ought to turn to *Reason and Romanticism*
(1926), *English Prose Style* (1928), *The Sense of Glory*
(1929), *Wordsworth* (1930), *Form in Modern Poetry*
(1932), *In Defence of Shelley and Other Essays* (1936),
Collected Essays in Literary Criticism (1938), and *Poetry and Experience* (1967); some of his finest critical
works on art include *The Meaning of Art* (1931), *Art
Now* (1933), *Art and Society* (1936), *Poetry and Anar-
chism* (1938), *A Letter to a Young Painter* (1962), and
Henry Moore: A Study of His Life and Work (1965); and
a few of his most celebrated studies of education are
Education Through Art (1943), *The Education of Free
Men* (1944), *The Third Realm of Education* (1960), and
The Redemption of the Robot (1966). Although Read
wrote only one novel, *The Green Child* (1935), many
critics consider this intriguing fantasy to be the work
by which he will be best remembered. *The Innocent Eye*
(1933) is a fascinating autobiographical study.

"Fantasy (Fancy)," although complete in itself, is
actually Chapter XI of Read's classic study, *English
Prose Style*. In this selection, one of the most scholarly
and theoretical of our collection, Read introduces several provocative concepts while attempting to "distinguish pure fantasy, and to describe its rhetorical
properties." Perhaps of greatest interest to the fantasy
enthusiast is Read's suggestion that the fairy tale con-

stitutes the purest type of fantasy. In his *Of Studies,* Sir Francis Bacon points out that "some books are to be tasted, others to be swallowed, and some few to be chewed and digested." Although not a book, "Fancy" nonetheless deserves to be chewed and digested.

··❧ Fantasy (Fancy) ❧··

Sir Herbert Read

Extraverted feeling gives rise to 'fancy'; introverted feeling gives rise to 'imagination'. These two words, with their near synonyms 'fantasy' and 'invention', are extremely confusing, and I must begin by trying to give them a clear meaning within the present context.

The *New English Dictionary* points out, with reference to the word *fantasy,* and the almost identical word *phantasy,* that 'in modern use *fantasy* and *phantasy,* in spite of their identity in sound and in ultimate etymology, tend to be apprehended as separate words, the predominant sense of the former being "caprice, whim, fanciful invention", while that of the latter is "imagination, visionary notion."'. This distinction is implied in the use of the word *fantasy* in the present context, and indeed it will be necessary in this chapter to define the special connotation of the word with some precision, in order to distinguish a mode of rhetoric which has not yet been given separate recognition.

Fantasy should not be confused with those separate, disparate and unorganized expressions which give form to a *'passing'* whim or caprice and which are more properly called 'conceits'. A fantasy is more than a conceit, implying a sustained invention in the realm of fancy.

Before we can demonstrate its characteristics as a type
of rhetoric we must further distinguish it from imagination.

Fantasy is extraverted feeling:[1] imagination is
introverted feeling. If in pursuit of the extraversion of
feeling, the mind turns to speculation, the result is fantasy. When, however, feeling is introverted, the product
of speculation is imaginative. The distinction follows
the lines of discursive and non-discursive logic. Fantasy
may be visionary, but it is deliberate and rational;
imagination is sensuous and symbolic. Each mode has
its characteristic style, but the style of fantasy is analogous to that of exposition, while the style of imagination is analogous to that of narrative. Fantasy may
be identified with fancy, though it is customary to apply
the word fancy to the mental activity as such, the word
fantasy to the product of that activity. Of fancy as a
mental process I have no desire to improve on the definition given by Coleridge:

> Fancy...has no other counters to play with, but
> fixities and definites. The fancy is, indeed, no other
> than a mode of memory emancipated from the
> order of time and space; while it is blended with,
> and modified by that empirical phenomenon of the
> will, which we express by the word Choice. But
> equally with the ordinary memory the Fancy must
> receive all its materials ready made from the law
> of association.
>
> *Biographia Literaria,* chapter xiii.

It is necessary, however, to comment on this definition
with special reference to prose composition. We must

[1] I should confess at this point that Jung would scarcely sanction this
statement, for he has remarked *(Psychological Types,* p. 547) that 'phan-
tasy-activity, or reverie...is a peculiar form of activity which can manifest
itself in all the four functions'. But by his use of the word 'reverie' as a
synonym for 'phantasy' Jung shows that he has in mind something quite
different from the English meaning of *fancy.* In German the words *Phan-
tasie, phantasieren* are associated primarily with the phenomenon of 'day-
dreaming', which is far from the sense of Coleridge's 'fixities and definites'.

try to distinguish pure fantasy, and to describe its rhetorical properties.

We notice in the first place that fancy is concerned with fixities and definites. In other words, it is an objective faculty. It does not deal with vague entities; it deals with things which are concrete, clearly perceptible, visibly defined.

Secondly, it is 'a mode of memory emancipated from the order of time and space'. This clearly distinguishes fancy from exposition and narrative, for it deliberately avoids the logic and consistency of these types of rhetoric and creates a new and arbitrary order of events. It is, as the next clause in Coleridge's definition points out, an exercise of choice, an expression of the will. Psychologically the will may follow a direction given to it by the conditions of our mental and physical environment; it may be merely a pattern of behaviour. Coleridge perceived something of this, and added as a qualification that 'Fancy must receive all its materials ready made from the law of association'—meaning thereby that nothing comes to the mind except in some connection with the world of which it is but one unit. But this consideration does not affect the present argument; we are dealing with a mode of expression, with the definite and observable facts constituted by a series of words; and such words do sometimes present that arbitrary appearance which we ascribe to the will and to the exercise of conscious choice.

Fantasy, then, the product of Fancy, is distinguished by two qualities which we may briefly summarize as objectivity and apparent arbitrariness. In what form of literature do we find these two qualities notably expressed? I think only in one, essentially, and that is the fairy tale. But there is more than one kind of fairy tale.

The fairy tale is originally a folk creation. Its analogue in verse is the ballad. It is a common characteristic of these forms of expression, which are handed down from generation to generation by word of mouth, that the slow changes they undergo are all in the direction of the elements with which Coleridge has distinguished Fancy: they become emancipated from the order of time and space because the memory does not carry literally from generation to generation, but only essentially. The idea of theme is constant, but there is a gradual accretion of subsidiary details. And the memory that reaches from one generation to another tends to select only those elements of the story which are vivid and actual, and these will naturally be objective elements, rather than the descriptions of emotional or individual reactions. There is a natural tendency, therefore, for the ballad and folk tale to develop a clear objective narrative, but a narrative encumbered with odd inconsequential but startlingly vivid and concrete details.

At St. Mary's of the Wolf-pits in Suffolk, a boy and his sister were found by the inhabitants of that place near the mouth of a pit which is there, who had the form of all their limbs like to those of other men, but they differed in the colour of their skin from all the people of our inhabitable world; for the whole surface of their skin was tinged of a green colour. No one could understand their speech. When they were brought as curiosities to the house of a certain knight, Sir Richard de Caine, at Wikes, they wept bitterly. Bread and other victuals were set before them, but they would touch none of them, though they were tormented by great hunger, as the girl afterwards acknowledged. At length, when some beans just cut, with their stalks, were brought into the house, they made signs, with great avidity, that they should be given to them. When they were brought, they opened the stalks instead of the pods, thinking the beans were in the hollow of them; but not finding them there, they began to weep anew. When those who were present saw this, they opened the pods, and showed them the naked beans. They fed on these with great delight, and for a long time tasted no other food. The boy however was always languid and depressed, and he died within a short time. The girl enjoyed continual good health, and becoming accustomed to various kinds of food, lost completely the green colour, and gradually recovered the sanguine habit of her entire body. She was afterwards regenerated by the laver of holy baptism, and lived for many years in the service of that knight (as I have frequently heard from him and his family), and was rather loose and wanton in her conduct. Being frequently asked about the people of her country, she asserted that the inhabitants, and all they had in that country, were of a green colour; and that they saw no sun, but enjoyed a degree of light like what is after sunset. Being asked how she came into this country with the aforesaid boy, she replied, that as they were following their flocks they came to a certain cavern, on entering which they heard a delightful sound of bells; ravished by whose sweetness, they went for a long time wandering on through the cavern until they came to its mouth. When they came out of it, they were struck senseless by the excessive light of the sun, and the unusual temperature of the air; and they thus lay for a long time. Being terrified by the noise of those who came on them, they wished to fly, but they could not find the entrance of the cavern before they were caught.

The Green Children.[2]

A story such as this is the norm to which all types of Fantasy should conform. The only difference is, that in the conscious literary inventions with which we are nowadays concerned, the will or intention of the writer has to take the part of the age long and impersonal forces of folk tradition. That this can be achieved is beyond doubt, and Southey's immortal story may be given as a proof of it:

[2] From T. Keightley, *The Fairy Mythology*, p. 281.

Once upon a time there were Three Bears, who lived together in a house of their own, in a wood. One of them was a Little, Small, Wee Bear; and one was a Middle-sized Bear, and the other was a Great, Huge Bear. They had each a pot for their porridge, a little pot for the Little, Small, Wee Bear; and a middle-sized pot for the Middle Bear; and a great pot for the Great, Huge Bear. And they had each a chair to sit in; a little chair for the Little, Small, Wee Bear; and a middle-sized chair for the Middle Bear; and a great chair for the Great, Huge Bear. And they had each a bed to sleep in; a little bed for the Little, Small, Wee Bear; and a middle-sized bed for the Middle Bear; and a great bed for the Great, Huge Bear.

One day, after they had made the porridge for their breakfast, and poured it into their porridge-pots, they walked out into the wood while their porridge was cooling, that they might not burn their mouths, by beginning too soon to eat it. And while they were walking a little old Woman came to the house. She could not have been a good, honest old Woman; for first she looked in at that window, and then she peeped in at the keyhole; and seeing nobody in the house, she lifted the latch. The door was not fastened, because the Bears were good Bears, who did nobody any harm, and never suspected that any body would harm them. So the little old Woman opened the door, and went in; and well pleased she was when she saw the porridge on the table. If she had been a good little old Woman, she would have waited till the Bears came home, and then, perhaps, they would have asked her to breakfast; for they were good Bears— a little rough or so, as the manner of Bears is, but for all that very good natured and hospitable. But she was an impudent, bad old Woman, and set about helping herself.

So first she tasted the porridge of the Great, Huge Bear, and that was too hot for her; and she said a bad word about that. And then she tasted the porridge of the Middle Bear, and that was too cold for her; and she said a bad word about that, too. And then she went to the porridge of the Little, Small, Wee Bear, and tasted that; and that was neither too hot, nor too cold, but just right; and she liked it so well, that she ate it all up: but the naughty old Woman said a bad word about the little porridge-pot, because it did not hold enough for her.

Then the little old Woman sate down in the chair of the Great, Huge Bear, and that was too hard for her. And then she sate down in the chair of the Middle Bear, and that was too soft for her. And then she sate down in the chair of the Little, Small, Wee Bear, and that was neither too hard, nor too soft, but just right. So she seated herself in it, and there she sate till the bottom of the chair came out, and down came hers, plump upon the ground. And the naughty old Woman said a wicked word about that too.

Then the little old Woman went up stairs into the bed-chamber in which the three Bears slept. And first she lay down upon the bed of the Great, Huge Bear; but that was too high at the head for her. And she next lay down upon the bed of the Middle Bear; and that was too high at the foot for her. And then she lay down upon the bed of the Little, Small, Wee Bear; and that was neither too high at the head, nor at the foot, but just right. So she covered herself up comfortably, and lay there till she fell fast asleep.

By this time the Three Bears thought their porridge would be cool enough; so they came home to breakfast. Now the little old Woman had left the spoon of the Great, Huge Bear standing in his porridge.

'SOMEBODY HAS BEEN AT MY PORRIDGE!' said the Great, Huge Bear, in his great, rough, gruff voice. And when the Middle Bear looked at his, he saw that the spoon was standing in it too. They were wooden spoons; if they had been silver ones, the naughty old Woman would have put them in her pocket.

'Somebody has been at my porridge!' said the Middle Bear, in his middle voice.

Then the Little, Small, Wee Bear looked at his, and there was the spoon in the porridge-pot, but the porridge was all gone.

'Somebody has been at my porridge, and has eaten it all up!'

said the Little, Small, Wee Bear, in his little, small, wee voice.

Upon this the Three Bears, seeing that someone had entered their house and eaten up the Little, Small, Wee Bear's breakfast, began to look about them. Now the little old Woman had not put the hard cushion straight when she rose from the chair of the Great, Huge Bear.

'SOMEBODY HAS BEEN SITTING IN MY CHAIR!' said the Great, Huge Bear, in his great, rough, gruff voice.

And the little old Woman had squatted down the soft cushion of the Middle Bear.

'Somebody has been sitting in my chair!' said the Middle Bear, in his middle voice.

And you know what the little old Woman had done to the third chair.

'Somebody has been sitting in my chair, and has sate the bottom of it out!'

said the Little, Small, Wee Bear, in his little, small, wee voice.

Then the Three Bears thought it necessary that they should make farther search; so they went up stairs into their bed-chamber. Now the little old Woman had pulled the pillow of the Great, Huge Bear out of its place.

'SOMEBODY HAS BEEN LYING IN MY BED!' said the Great, Huge Bear, in his great, rough, gruff voice.

And the little old Woman had pulled the bolster of the Middle Bear out of its place.

'Somebody has been lying in my bed!' said the Middle Bear, in his middle voice.

And when the Little, Small, Wee Bear came to look at his bed, there was the bolster in its place; and the pillow in its place upon the bolster; and upon the pillow was the little old Woman's ugly, dirty head,—which was not in its place, for she had no business there.

'Somebody has been lying in my bed,—and here she is!' said the Little, Small, Wee Bear, in his little, small, wee voice.

The little old Woman had heard in her sleep the great, rough, gruff voice of the Great, Huge Bear; but she was so fast asleep that it was no more to her than the roaring of wind, or the rumbling of thunder. And she had heard the middle voice of the Middle Bear, but it was only as if she had heard someone speaking in a dream. But when she heard the little, small, wee voice of the Little, Small, Wee Bear, it was so sharp, and so shrill, that it awakened her at once. Up she started; and when she saw the Three Bears on one side of the bed, she tumbled herself out at the other, and ran to the window. Now the window was open, because the Bears, like good, tidy Bears, as they were, always opened their bed-chamber window when they got up in the morning. Out the little old Woman jumped; and whether she broke her neck in the fall; or ran into the wood and was lost there; or found her way out of the wood, and was taken up by the constable and sent to the House of Correction for a vagrant as she was, I cannot tell. But the Three Bears never saw anything more of her.

ROBERT SOUTHEY,
The Doctor.

This story so perfectly conforms to the requirements of a folk tale that it has actually been adopted as such,

and is everywhere and in almost every language reprinted and retold with little consciousness of the fact
that it is a deliberate creation of an English writer of
the early nineteenth century.

The perfection of 'The Three Bears' is a rare one.
Almost all other fairy tales which are not traditional
fail in some way, and their failure can, I think, always
be traced to an ignorance of the canons of fantasy. King-
sley's *Water Babies,* for example, has one of the true
elements of fantasy—arbitrariness, but it lacks objectivity: it has a subjective, or moralizing, intent, and
this not only destroys its rhetorical purity but in so
doing destroys its rhetorical effect, as any child will tell
you. *Alice in Wonderland* comes much nearer to perfection—it is magnificently arbitrary, and is in a large
measure objective. A good deal of satirical thought underlies the fantasy, and though the fantasy is pervasive
enough to allow children (and perhaps adults) to ignore
the satire (as also in a more recent example of fantasy—
George Orwell's *Animal Farm*), the adult is generally
aware of the sophistication. *Alice* has a suppressed
background of culture which a true fairy tale never has.
Alice will always delight our particular civilization: it
will hardly become a part of our traditional folk-lore,
like 'The Three Bears'.

A primitive, or at least an innocent, outlook seems
essential to a good fairy tale, and it is among the civ-
ilizations which to-day retain something of their primitive spirit that we naturally find the best Fairy Tales.
I refer in particular to Alexey Michailovich Remizov,
whose tales 'Her Star-Bear' and 'Hare Ivanitch' are perfect examples of their kind. The following short passage
from the former tale will illustrate their fantastical
nature:

> Alyónushka's little star was a long time flying
> through the air, and, at last, it fell down into the
> heart of a wood, where the trees were thickest,
> where the firs intertwined their shaggy branches
> and made an eerie humming noise.
>
> A thick blue-grey mist woke up and crawled

across the sky, and the winter night was over.

And the sun, dressed in a scarlet cloak and a laced hat, came down from his crystal watch-tower.

Alyónushka's little star was lying, all transparent, with melancholy blue eyes, on the soft pine needles, not far from a hare's form, and Jack Frost began to breathe on things.

And the old sun marched on and on, over the wood, and went home to his crystal watch-tower.

Snow clouds appeared and lay across the sky, and it began to grow dark.

In a trembling voice the grumbling wind struck up his old winter song.

The dumb snow-storm sprang up, and, dumb though she was, she shrieked.

The snow began to dance.

The poor little star was dozing by the hare's form, and the thaw of a little tear rolled down her star cheek and then froze again.

And it seemed to her that once more she was flying round in the dancing chorus with her little golden friends, and they were so merry and laughed out loud, like Alyónushka. And the cloudy night—an old Nannie, like Vlasyevna—was taking care of them.

The blinds were being pulled up.

All day Alyónushka stood by the open window. Strange people were walking past, furniture removers were jogging along, and look! a waggon is crawling past, piled up with mattresses and tables and beds.

'That means that somebody is off to the country!' decided Alyónushka. The sky was blue and clear, and the sky smiled at Alyónushka.

'Mummie! I say, Mummie! When are *we* going to the country?' she kept asking.

'We'll get ready, darling, and pack up everything and go off far away, farther than last summer!' said Mummie: Mummie was making

Alyónushka a dressing-gown, and she was busy.

'Oh! if only we could go quickly,' teased Alyónushka.

She couldn't as much as look at her toys—they were so wooden and dull. The toys, too, had had enough of winter.[3]

To pass to more sophisticated types of fantasy, written as deliberate artifices, it is easy to quote many quasi-fantastical compositions, but very few have the purity of traditional fairy tales. A 'Utopia', or description of a fantastical country and its civilization, might well exhibit all the characteristics of pure fantasy, but rarely does so because the writer has some ulterior satirical or moral aim, which aim directs his composition, fixes it in space and time, gives it a basis of subjective intolerance. Such objections apply to *Utopia* itself, to *News from Nowhere* and *The Dream of John Ball,* to *Erewhon, A Crystal Age* and Orwell's *1984.*[4] They do not apply to some of the fantasies of H. G. Wells, who comes as near as any modern writer to a sense of pure fantasy. He errs, as in *The Time Machine,* by imparting to his fantasies a pseudo-scientific logicality; it is as though having conceived one arbitrary fantasy he were compelled by the habits of his scientific training to work out the consequences of this fantasy. Real fantasy is bolder than this; it dispenses with all logic and habit, and relies on the force of wonder alone.

The Thousand and One Nights, with its magnificent apparatus of genii and afrits, is the greatest work of

---

[3] From *The Book of the Bear,* being Twenty-one Tales newly translated from the Russian by Jane Harrison and Hope Mirrlees. (Nonesuch Press, 1926.)

[4] W. H. Hudson, in his Preface to the second edition of *A Crystal Age,* remarks: 'In going through this book after so many years I am amused at the way it is coloured by the little cults and crazes, and modes of thought of the 'eighties of the last century. They were so important then, and now, if remembered at all, they appear so trivial.'

fantasy that has ever been evolved by tradition, and given literary form. But it, alas, is not English, and has no English equivalent. The Western world does not seem to have conceived the necessity of fairy-tales for grown-ups—though it has been suggested that the modern detective story is an equivalent—and that is perhaps why it condemns them to a life of unremitted toil. In *Vathek* William Beckford produced a counterfeit of an Arabian Nights' Entertainment which almost deserves to be incorporated in the Eastern collection. But a counterfeit is a counterfeit, and though *Vathek* is one of the best fantasies in the language,[5] I prefer not to give it as a model because I would rather envisage the possibility of a fantasy that is racial in its origins and part, not only of the English language, but of English traditions. Meanwhile I can only suggest that the possibility of such a fantasy is foreshadowed in the dramatic nightmare which makes the climax of James Joyce's *Ulysses*. The first 'stage direction' illustrates the strain of fantasy which is sustained throughout the episode:

> The Mabbot street entrance of nighttown, before which stretches an uncobbled tramsiding set with skeleton tracks, red and green will-o'-the-wisps and danger signals. Rows of flimsy houses with gaping doors. Rare lamps with faint rainbow-fans. Round Rabaiotti's halted ice gondola stunted men and women squabble. The grab wafers between which are wedged lumps of coal and copper snow. Sucking, they scatter slowly. Children. The swan-comb of the gondola, highreared, forges on through the murk, white and blue under a lighthouse. Whistles call and answer.

The only fault of this fantasy is its incoherence, which is not the incoherence of arbitrariness (which is always

---

[5] *Vathek* was written in French by its author, so the Rev. Samuel Henley, who translated it, should have a share in these encomiums.

simple[6]) but of sophistication. This fantasy from *Ulysses* needs for its appreciation an intellectual standpoint of a most exclusive kind; it needs a temper of metaphysical disillusion. As a fantasy it is not therefore completely emancipated from the order of time and space; nor is it completely concrete in its expression. *Finnegan's Wake,* with its reliance on arbitrary word associations, is a better example, but one that is far too complex and sophisticated for the common reader.

Fancy has suffered a certain denigration from its association of contrast to imagination, which latter faculty has been enhanced ever since writers of the Romantic Movement took it as their special endowment. But this aspersion of fancy is entirely sentimental in origin; as I have shown, fancy and imagination are rather to be regarded as equal and opposite faculties, directly related to the general opposition of discursive

---

[6] Compare, for example, Samuel Foote's delightful oddity:

THE
GREAT
PANJANDRUM
HIMSELF

So she went into the garden
to cut a cabbage-leaf
to make an apple-pie;
and at the same time
a great she-bear, coming down the street,
pops its head into the shop.
What! no soap?
So he died,
and she very imprudently married the
  Barber:
and there were present
the Picninnies,
and the Joblillies,
and the Garyulies,
and the great Panjandrum himself,
with the little round button at top;
and they all fell to playing the game
of catch-as-catch-can,
till the gunpowder ran out at the heels of
  their boots.

and non-discursive thought. When a less romantic age has realized this distinction, perhaps it will turn to fantasy as to a virgin soil, and give to English literature an entertainment comparable to the *Thousand and One Nights*.

JAMES GROVER THURBER

(1894–1961)

Most writers would be glad to settle for any one
of ten of Thurber's accomplishments. He has written the funniest memoirs, fables, reports, satires,
fantasies, complaints, fairy tales and sketches of
the last twenty years, has gone into the drama
and the cinema, and on top of that has littered
the world with thousands of drawings. Most writers and artists can be compared fairly easily with
contemporaries. Thurber inhabits a world of his
own.

The New York Times, November 3, 1961

So writes E. B. White of his close friend and colleague,
James Thurber. If anyone knew Thurber well it was
White, and it is instructive to note what point he chooses,
to conclude his perceptive assessment: the uniqueness
of Thurber's artistry. Indeed, Thurber's drawings of
huge, wide-eyed hounds; his informal essays satirizing
domineering women, rebellious children, and pedantic
psychiatrists; his amusing sketches of domestic life—
all are as original as a thumbprint. A lifelong champion
of individuality and nonconformity, Thurber convincingly illustrates the integrity of his strong beliefs
through his artistic legacy.

Although Thurber spent most of his adult life in New York City and Cornwall, Connecticut, he frequently pointed out that he was a Midwesterner at heart. Born in Columbus, Ohio, on December 8, 1894, his early years were generously laced—if we are to believe all that is chronicled in his autobiographical classic, *My Life and Hard Times* (1933)—with hilarious experiences generated by the eccentricities of his friends and relatives. After attending elementary and secondary schools in Columbus, Thurber entered Ohio State University in 1913. Jamie had been happy and popular in high school (he was president of his senior class), but unfortunately his freshman year at the large university was not a repeat performance. Disillusioned and lonely, Thurber dropped out of school, without even informing his family. He returned the next year, however, to give it another try. Encouraged and helped by his friend Elliott Nugent, Thurber became a member of Phi Kappa Psi, as well as a writer for the student paper *(The Ohio State Lantern)* and humor magazine *(The Sun-Dial)*.

Thurber left the university in 1918, without graduating. Deeply concerned about the war in Europe, he tried to enlist, but his examiners failed him because of poor eyesight (his brother William had accidentally shot Jamie in the left eye with an arrow years before). However, Thurber finally did make it "over there" by acquiring a code clerk post at the American Embassy in Paris. Two years later he returned to Columbus as a reporter for the Columbus *Dispatch*. In 1923 the *Dispatch* rewarded Thurber for his good work by giving him his own Sunday column, "Credos and Curios," but Thurber's wife, Althea, whom he had married in 1922, convinced him that he ought to resign so that he might try his hand at free-lance writing. Thus, in the spring of 1925 the Thurbers set out for France, a country that they felt might provide the proper milieu for an aspiring novelist. After a brief sojourn in Normandy, during which time Thurber lost interest in his novel, the Thurbers went to Paris where Thurber took a job first with the Paris edition of the Chicago *Tribune,* and later with the Riviera edition in Nice. Soon after, he decided to return to the United States, this time to work as a reporter for the New York *Evening Post*.

Not long after Thurber took up residence in New York he met E. B. White, who offered to arrange an interview with Harold Ross, founder and editor of the *New Yorker*. Thurber, who had been repeatedly, but unsuccessfully, trying to get his humorous sketches published in the magazine, happily accepted White's generous offer. Shortly after, in February 1927, Thurber had a brief meeting with Harold Ross; he left Ross's office as managing editor of the *New Yorker*. After working at the position for about six months, Thurber finally convinced Ross that he wanted to be a writer, not an editor, so Ross reassigned him to the "Talk of the Town" department. Thurber had finally found the milieu for which he had so long been searching. Although Thurber gave up his position as editor of "Talk of the Town" in 1935, he continued to use the *New Yorker* as a major outlet for his writings and cartoons.

During the last twenty-five years of his life, Thurber enjoyed wealth, critical recognition, and fame, but the luster of his artistic accomplishments was dimmed by his emotional and physical problems. Suffering a prolonged nervous breakdown in the early 1940s would have been bad enough, but this was coupled with a serious cataract problem that began weakening the sight in his remaining good eye. Despite several operations, Thurber's eyesight continued to rapidly deteriorate, finally resulting in total blindness. During the last few years of his life he had to dictate all of his writing, and his career as cartoonist came to an end. He died of pneumonia on November 2, 1961, at Doctors Hospital in New York City. All those who value the priceless gift of laughter lost a great friend on that day.

There are several fine collections of Thurber's many writings and drawings, including *The Owl in the Attic* (1931); *The Seal in the Bedroom* (1932); *The Last Flower* (1939); *Fables for Our Time and Famous Poems Illustrated* (1940); *Men, Women, and Dogs* (1943); *The Thur-*

ber Carnival (1945); *The Beast in Me and Other Stories* (1948); and *The Thurber Album* (1952). His important full-length works include *Is Sex Necessary?* (1929), a bestseller coauthored by E. B. White; *The Male Animal* (1940), a comedy drama written in collaboration with his old friend Elliott Nugent; and *The Years With Ross* (1959), a memoir describing his years with the *New Yorker.* "The Secret Life of Walter Mitty," the classic short story most closely associated with Thurber, was first published in the *New Yorker* on March 18, 1939.

It should not be forgotten that Thurber was also a fine writer of high fantasy. Beginning with *Many Moons,* in 1943, Thurber wrote a number of excellent all-ages fantasy tales. Fairy tales such as *The Great Quillow* (1944), *The White Deer* (1945), *The Thirteen Clocks* (1950), and *The Wonderful O* (1957) all bear Thurber's hallmarks: lively wit, zany word play, and a strong belief in the potential and dignity of the little man. Those who have not yet discovered Thurber's fantasies are in for a treat.

As one would expect of a writer of fairy tales, Thurber had a strong love for the genre and equally strong opinions about it. The two articles that follow vividly exhibit both his love and his ideological resoluteness. "Tempest in a Looking Glass" not only provides good insight into the essential nature of the fairy tale, but also treats us to a characteristic Thurberian attack on psychoanalytic literary theory, one of his favorite targets. The other essay, "The Wizard of Chitenango," smoothly blends a colorful biographical sketch of L. Frank Baum, a useful description of the genesis and evolution of the Oz books, and a perceptive commentary on the nature of fantasy. The two pieces should serve as a convenient portal to Thurber's unique world. Please enter.

·✺· The Wizard of Chitenango ·✺·

James Grover Thurber

I have been for several weeks bogged in Oz books. It had seemed to me, at first, a simple matter to go back to the two I read as a boy of ten, "The Wizard of Oz" and "The Land of Oz" (the first two published), and write down what Oz revisited was like to me now that my life, at forty, has begun again. I was amazed and disturbed to discover that there are now twenty-eight different books about Oz (the latest one, 1934, is "Speedy in Oz"). Since the first was published nearly thirty-five years ago about three million copies of Oz books have been sold; sales of the various books, taken together, run to almost a hundred thousand copies a year. The thing is obviously a major phenomenon in the wonderful land of books. I began my research, therefore, not by rereading the two Oz books I loved as a child (and still do, I was happy to find out later) but with an inquiry into the life and nature of the man who wrote the first fourteen of the series, Mr. L. Frank Baum.

Lyman Frank Baum was born in Chitenango, New York, in 1856. When he was about ten he became enamoured of (if also a little horrified and disgusted by) the tales of the Grimm brothers and of Andersen and he determined that when he grew up he would write fairy tales with a difference. There would be, in the first place, "no love and marriage in them" (I quote the present publishers of his books, Reilly and Lee, of Chicago); furthermore, he wanted to get away from the "European background" and write tales about fairies in America (he chose Kansas as the jumping off place for the Oz books, although he was educated in Syracuse, lived most of his life in Chicago, and spent his last years in Hollywood where he died in 1919, aged 63). There was also another significant change that he wanted to make in the old fairy tales. Let me quote from his own foreward to the first Oz book, "The Wizard": "...the time has now come for a series of newer 'wonder tales' in which the stereotyped genie, dwarf and fairy are eliminated, together with all the horrible and blood-curdling incident devised by their authors to point a fearsome moral.... 'The Wizard of Oz' aspires to be a modernized fairy tale in which the wonderment and joy are retained, and the heartaches and nightmares left out." I am glad that, in spite of this high determination, Mr. Baum failed to keep them out. Children love a lot of nightmare and at least a little heartache in their books. And they get them in the Oz books. I know that I went through excruciatingly lovely nightmares and heartaches when the Scarecrow lost his straw, when the Tin Woodman was taken apart, when the Saw-Horse broke his wooden leg (it hurt for me even if it didn't for Mr. Baum).

But let me return for a moment to the story of his writings. In his late twenties he wrote two plays, "The Maid of Arran" and "The Queen of Killarney." Under the name of Schuyler Stanton he also wrote three novels (I could not learn their titles). In all, he wrote about fifty books, most of them for children. He was forty-three in 1899 when he did "The Wizard of Oz," which to him was just another (the twentieth or so) book for children. It sold better than anything he had ever written. The next year he wrote a thing called "Dot and Tot in Merryland." But his readers wanted more about Oz. He began to get letters from them by the thousands and he was not exactly pleased that Oz was the land they loved the best. He ignored the popular demand for four years, meanwhile writing a book called "Baum's American Fairy Tales," subtitled "Stories of Astonishing Adventures of American Boys and Girls with the Fairies of Their Native Land." He must have been hurt by its cold reception. Here he was, nearing fifty, trying to be what he had always fondly wanted to be, an American Andersen, An American Grimm, and all the while American children—and their parents—would have none of it, but screamed for more about Oz. His American fairy tales, I am sorry to tell you, are not good fairy tales. The scene of the first one is the attic of a house "on Prairie Avenue, in Chicago." It never leaves there for any wondrous, faraway realm. Baum apparently never thoroughly understood that fatal flaw in his essential ambition, but he understood it a little. He did another collection of unconnected stories but this time he placed them, not in Illinois but in Mo. "The Magical Monarch of Mo" is not much better than the American tales; but at least one story in it, "The Strange Adventures of the King's Head," is a fine, fantastic fairy tale. The others are just so-so. On went L. Frank Baum, grimly, into the short tales making up "The Enchanted Island of Yew"; but the girls and boys were not interested. Finally, after four years and ten thousand letters from youngsters, he wrote "The Land of Oz." He was back where they wanted him.

I haven't space to go into even half of the Oz books, nor do I want to. The first two, "The Wizard" and "The Land" are far and away the best. Baum wrote "The Wizard," I am told, simply as a tour de force to see if he could animate, and make real, creatures never alive before on sea or land. He succeeded, eminently, with the Scarecrow and the Tin Woodman and he went on to succeed again in the second book with Jack Pumpkinhead, the Saw-Horse and the Woggle Bug. After that I do not think he was ever really successful. Admittedly he didn't want to keep doing Oz books (he wanted to get back to those American Tales). In the next six years he wrote only two and at the end of the second of these he put a tired, awkward note explaining that Oz was somehow forever cut off from communication with this world. What a heartache and a nightmare that announcement was to the children of America! But of course they didn't fall for his clumsy device: they knew he was a great wizard and could get back to Oz if he wanted to and they made him get back. From 1910 until 1919 he resignedly wrote an Oz book every year and was working on one when he died. This one was finished by Grace Plumly Thompson, a young Philadelphia woman who as a child had adored the Oz books. She has written, up to now, thirteen Oz books. But she has taken them up where Mr. Baum left off, not where he began; she has never found her way into the real Oz.

I think the fatal trouble with the later books (for us aging examiners, anyway) is that they became whimsical rather than fantastic. They ramble and they preach (one is dedicated to a society in California called "The Uplifters"), they lack the quick movement, the fresh suspense, the amusing dialogue and the really funny invention of the first ones. They dawdle along like a class prophecy. None of their creatures comes to life for me. I am merely bored by the Growleywogs, the Whimsies, the Cuttenclips, the Patchwork Girl, Button-Bright, the Googly-Goo, and I am actually gagged by one Unc Nunkie. Mr. Baum himself said that he kept putting in things that children wrote and asked him to put in. He brought back the Wizard of Oz because the children pleaded and he rewrote the Scarecrow and the Woodman almost to death because the children wanted them. The children should have been told to hush up and go back to the real Wizard and the real Scarecrow and the real Woodman. They are only in the first two books.

Too much cannot be said for the drawings of Mr. John R. Neill. He began with "The Land of Oz" and his pictures were far superior to those of Mr. W. W. Denslow who illustrated "The Wizard." After doing more than three thousand drawings (he's still at it), he keeps up beautifully.

Tempest in a Looking Glass

James Thurber

Dr. Paul Schilder, research professor of psychiatry at
New York University, has his work cut out for him. I
have cut it out for him myself. I hope he is a young
man, for there is so much for him to do: What I am
about to outline will take him at least ten years, if it
is to be done properly.

First, I should perhaps introduce Dr. Paul Schilder
to you or, rather, refresh your memory about him. He
is the distinguished scientist who, some weeks ago at
the Hotel Waldorf-Astoria, analyzed, for the members
of the American Psychoanalytic Association in solemn
meeting there, the unfortunate nature of the late
Charles Lutwidge Dodgson, better known to the world
under his escapist pen name of Lewis Carroll. Dr.
Schilder had found in his researches, you may remember, that *Alice in Wonderland* is so full of cruelty, fear,
and "sadistic trends of cannibalism" that he questioned
its wholesomeness as literature for children. (Could it
have been *Alice* that debauched the kiddies in Mr. Richard Hughes's *High Wind in Jamaica*? I suggest that
Dr. Schilder set about the analysis of Mr. Hughes right
now. Maybe *he* was debauched, as a child, by the works
of Lewis Carroll.)

Dr. Schilder seems to have been pained and astonished by his belated discovery that everything in Wonderland and Through the Looking Glass is out of joint. He spoke, according to the report of his lecture in the *New York Times,* of the "unwholesome instability of space" and the "tendency of the time element to be thrown out of gear." He found, in a word, a world of "cruelty, destruction, and annihilation." He also found cruelty inherent in Mr. Carroll's "destructive use of the English language," but that's beside my point, that's something to be fought out, man to man, between Dr. Schilder and some writer younger and stronger than I—I nominate Ernest Hemingway or Jim Tully.

As I said to begin with, I have some further researches to suggest to Dr. Paul Schilder (after he gets through with the cruel and sadistic Richard Hughes). They will keep him even busier and shock him, I am afraid, even more severely than his work with Mr. Carroll did. I submit to him, as a starting-off place, the *English Fairy Tales* collected so painstakingly 42 years ago by Mr. Joseph Jacobs. With the exception of *The Three Bears,* which was the invention of the cruel and sadistic poet Southey, these are all folk tales. In getting at the bottom of the savagery, the mercilessness, the ferocity, and the sadistic trends of cannibalism of these tales, Dr. Schilder will be able to expose the evil nature not of one man, not of one race of men but of the whole of mankind, for there is, of course, scarcely a story in this compilation which has not its counterpart, parallel, or source in the folk tales of another country. Usually, each story may be traced to a dozen countries, from Ireland to India, from France to Russia, from Germany to Iceland. Let us examine, rather minutely, for Dr. Schilder's enlightenment, just one of these tales, the one entitled by Mr. Jacobs *The Rose-Tree.* Dr. Schilder will surely want to analyze *The Rose-Tree* and the depraved soul of man which shines so darkly behind it.

SHE LAUGHED, DR. SCHILDER!

"There was once upon a time [the tale begins] a good man who had two children: a girl by his first wife, and a boy by the second. The girl was as white as milk, and her lips were like cherries." The tale goes on to tell how the stepmother hated the little girl and one day sent her to the store to buy a pound of candles which, when she put them on the ground while she climbed over a stile, a dog stole. Three times this happened, with three different pounds of candles. "The stepmother was angry, but she pretended not to mind the loss. She said to the child: 'Come, lay your head on my lap that I may comb your hair.'" Down to the ground fell the yellow silken hair as the stepmother combed it. Said she, finally: "I cannot part your hair on my knee, fetch a billet of wood." When this was done she said, "I cannot part your hair with a comb, fetch me an ax." So (brace yourself, Dr. Schilder, for here comes cruelty which makes the cruelty of Mr. Carroll seem like the extremely lovely nonsense it really is) the stepmother made the little girl put her head upon the billet of wood, and then she cut off her head with the ax. In the tale as Mr. Jacobs tells it there comes now this sentence: "So the mother wiped the ax and laughed." In all of Lewis Carroll, Dr. Schilder, there is no such sentence as that. There, indeed, is grist for your mill; there is red meat for your grinder. But wait. We are coming to a real trend in cannibalism.

"Then she took the heart and liver of the little girl, and she stewed them and brought them into the house for supper. The husband tasted them and shook his head. He said they tasted very strangely. She gave some to the little boy, but he would not eat." The little boy, the story tells, took up what was left of his little sister and put her in a box and buried the box under a rose tree. "And every day he went to the tree and wept and his tears ran down on the box. One day the rose-tree flowered. It was spring, and there among the flowers was a white bird; and it sang, and sang, and sang like an angel out of heaven." The song the bird sang is, in the version Mr. Jacobs uses, this dainty ditty:

> My wicked mother slew me,
> My dear father ate me,
> My little brother whom I love,
> Sits below and I sing above,
> Stick, stock, stone dead.

The white bird, the tale goes, sang her song for the shoemaker, and he gave her two little red shoes; and she sang her song for the watchmaker, and he gave her a gold watch and chain; and she sang her song for three millers, and they put, when she asked for it, a millstone around her neck. Then the white bird flew to the house where the stepmother lived. And from there I give the tale as it is in the book, on to the end. "It rattled the millstone against the eaves of the house, and the stepmother said: 'It thunders.' Then the little boy ran out to see the thunder, and down dropped the red shoes at his feet. It rattled the millstone against the eaves of the house once more, and the stepmother said again: 'It thunders.' Then the father ran out, and down fell the chain about his neck. In ran father and son, laughing and saying: 'See, what fine things the thunder has brought us!' Then the bird rattled the millstone against the eaves of the house a third time; and the stepmother said: 'It thunders again, perhaps the thunder has brought something for me,' and she ran out; but the moment she stepped outside the door down fell the millstone on her head; and so she died."

Dr. Paul Schilder will want, of course, to trace the extent of this cruel and cannibalistic story among the peoples of the world. To aid him in his quest I should like to quote a paragraph from Mr. Jacobs' notes and references at the end of his book:

Source.— From the first edition of Henderson's "Folk-Lore of Northern Countries," p. 314, to which

it was communicated by the Rev. S. Baring-Gould.
Parallels.— This is better known under the title,
"Orange and Lemon," and with the refrain:

"My mother killed me,
  My father picked my bones,
  My little sister buried me,
  Under the marble stones."

I heard this in Australia, and a friend of mine
heard it in her youth in County Meath, Ireland.
Mr. Jones gives part of it in "Folk-Tales of the
Magyars," 418-20, and another version occurs in
Notes and Queries, vi. 496. Mr. I. Gollancz in-
forms me he remembers a version entitled "Pep-
per, Salt, and Mustard," with the refrain just given.
Abroad it is Grimm's "Juniper Tree," where see
further parallels. The German rhyme is sung by
Margaret in the mad scene of Goethe's "Faust."

Once launched onto the awful, far-spreading sea of
folklore, Dr. Schilder will find a thousand examples, in
the fairy tales of all countries, of fear and cruelty, horror and revenge, cannibalism and the laughing wiping
of blood from gory axes. He must surely know, to give
just one more example, the tale from the brothers Grimm
of how a queen "quite yellow with envy" sang to another
looking glass than Lewis Carroll's: "O, mirror, mirror
on the wall, who is the fairest of us all?" and how, when
the mirror answered that the fairest maid alive was
the queen's own stepdaughter, Snow White, the en-
raged lady sent for a huntsman and said to him: "Take
the child away into the forest... You must kill her and
bring me her heart and tongue for a token."

OF ART AND OUR PSYCHOLOGISTS

Dr. Schilder's work, as I have said, is cut out for him.
He has the evil nature of Charles Perrault to dip into,
surely as black and devious and unwholesome as Lewis

Carroll's. He has the Grimms and Hans Christian Andersen. He has Mother Goose, or much of it. He can spend at least a year on the legend of Childe Rowland, which is filled with perfectly swell sexual symbols—from (in some versions) an underground cave more provocative by far than the rabbit hole in Wonderland to the sinister Dark Tower of the more familiar versions. This one piece of research will lead him into the myth of Proserpine and into Browning and Shakespeare and Milton's *Comus* and even into the dark and perilous kingdom of Arthurian legend. I should think that the good doctor could spend a profitable month on the famous and mysterious beast Galtisant, that was called the Questing Beast and that so plagued Sir Palamides—"The Questing Beast that had in shape a head like a serpent's head, and a body like a leopard, buttocks like a lion, and footed like an hart; and in his body there was such a noise as it had been the noise of thirty couple of hounds questing, and such a noise that beast made wheresomever he went."

When he is through with all this, Dr. Schilder should be pretty well persuaded that behind the imaginative works of all the cruel writing men, further or nearer, lies the destructive and unstable, the fearful and unwholesome, the fine and beautiful cruelty of the peoples of the earth, the men and women in the fields and the huts and the market place, the original storytellers of this naughty world. If Dr. Schilder wishes to expose to the members of the American Psychoanalytic Association, at some far date, the charming savagery and the beautiful ruthlessness of these peoples of the world, these millions long dead—and still alive—that is up to him. I should protest mildly that there is much more important work to be done.

I had planned, to be sure, a small analysis and defense of the nature of the artistic imagination for Dr. Schilder's information. Thinking of this one afternoon, I stood at a window of my house in the country, and as I looked out three pheasants came walking across the snow, almost up to my window. They were so near that, if I had had a stout rubber band and a ruler to snap it from, I could have got one of them. Presently they wandered away, and with them, somehow, went my desire to explain the nature of the artistic imagination, in my humble way, to Dr. Paul Schilder. But I should like to leave with him, to ponder, one little definition, the definition of the word *empathy* as given in *Webster's New International Dictionary:* "Imaginative projection of one's own consciousness into another human being; sympathetic understanding of other than human beings." There's a great deal in that—for some people—Dr. Schilder.

And, at the far end of all this tempest in a looking glass, I should like to set down, for Paul Schilder's guidance, a sentence from the writings of the late Dr. Morton Prince, a truly intelligent psychologist. He was speaking of multiple personality when he wrote it but he might have been speaking of the folk tales of the world or of the creatures and creations of Lewis Carroll: "Far from being mere freaks, monstrosities of consciousness, they are in fact shown to be manifestations of the very constitution of life."

JOHN RONALD REUEL TOLKIEN

(1892–1973)

"The shelves are crammed with dictionaries, works on etymology and philology, and editions of texts in many languages, predominant among which are Old and Middle English and Old Norse; but there is also a section devoted to translations of *The Lord of the Rings* into Polish, Dutch, Danish, Swedish, and Japanese; and the map of his invented 'Middle-earth' is pinned to the window-ledge. On the floor is a very old portmanteau full of letters, and on the desk are ink-bottles, nibs and pen-holders, and two typewriters. The room smells of books and tobacco smoke." This description of Tolkien's workshop is part of the excellent portrait drawn by Humphrey Carpenter in the opening chapter of his fine biography, *J. R. R. Tolkien* (London: George Allen & Unwin, Ltd., 1977, p. 4). It was in this room and earlier rooms like it dating back at least to World War I, that Tolkien produced the works that have provided the chief stimulus in attracting both scholarly and popular attention for fantasy literature in recent decades.

Thanks to Carpenter's biography, we have a clear outline of, and can gain a number of impressions about, Tolkien's life. He was born in South Africa on January 4, 1892, but came to England very soon after, in 1895. Although his father died in 1896 and his mother in

1904 when Tolkien was twelve, Tolkien's early years seem to have been reasonably happy. In fact, Sarehole, just outside of Birmingham, where he moved in 1896, later provided the model for the hobbits and the shire. He began his long and rich association with Oxford when he enrolled in Exeter in 1911. After taking his degree in 1915, he went on active duty with the Lancashire Fusiliers. In 1916 he married Edith Brett, went to war in France where he contracted trench fever, and returned home. He never forgot the horrors of the war, in which he lost most of his close friends. He returned briefly to Oxford, then taught for several years at Leeds before he returned once again to Oxford, where he remained for most of the rest of his life.

The impression one gets from the Carpenter biography is that Tolkien's many years as a professor at Oxford were marked on the one hand by considerable pressure due to family and university responsibilities, and on the other hand by stimulating and congenial associations with colleagues. Having four children, for a number of years Tolkien had to supplement his salary by correcting various examinations, while at the same time performing his teaching and governance assignments. Among the many enriching associations Tolkien formed at Oxford, the most rewarding, certainly the most famous, were with C. S. Lewis, Charles Williams, and a few other "Inklings" as they called themselves. Tolkien's letters (Humphrey Carpenter, ed., Boston: Houghton Mifflin Company, 1981) reflect the joy he found in the readings and conversations he shared as an Inkling.

Before Tolkien became known as a writer of fantasy, he had made a reputation with two outstanding works of scholarship, the enduring and productive sort of scholarship that helps to unlock the treasures of literary texts. "Beowulf: The Monsters and The Critics" (1936) is his classic attack on the many doubtful, frequently allegorical, interpretations of the Old English epic. An earlier work, still the best in its field, is the Tolkien and E. J. Gordon edition of *Gawain and the*

Green Knight (1925), for which Tolkien compiled an extensive glossary to enable students to cope with the difficult Middle-English dialect. Tolkien's own tales are of course from the same mythic and linguistic background as these two great poems that he taught and wrote about so effectively.

While students of Old and Middle English will continue to make Tolkien's acquaintance through his scholarly work, the great majority will know of him as the creator of *The Hobbit* (1937) and *The Lord of the Rings* (1954, 1955). A lesser number will continue the acquaintance through Tolkien's poetry and short stories and, finally, the two imposing posthumously published works, *The Silmarillion* (1977) and *Unfinished Tales* (1980).

The essay-letter "To W. H. Auden" included below provides Tolkien's own account of the genesis of most of the writings just noted. In the course of giving his account, Tolkien reveals numerous tangential details of interest, in particular his "Atlantis complex" and the fact that his tree characters, the Ents, emerged from his unconscious (see Le Guin's "Dreams Must Explain Themselves"). One possibly confusing reference is to there being six books to *The Lord of the Rings*. The work is not a trilogy but a single epic with six books; dividing the work into three volumes was, and is, a publisher's decision.

While the letter is a personal, informal essay, "Fantasy," from "On Fairy-Stories," is in Tolkien's complicated scholarly style. The excerpt that appears here includes Tolkien's definition of fantasy from the point of view of the writer and in relation to a number of other key terms: Art, Imagination, Sub-creation, Enchantment, and Reason (Tolkien capitalizes these terms). Here also readers will encounter these oft-quoted expressions: "inner consistency of reality," "arresting strangeness," and "Secondary World."

❖ Fantasy ❖

J. R. R. Tolkien

The human mind is capable of forming mental images of things not actually present. The faculty of conceiving the images is (or was) naturally called Imagination. But in recent times, in technical not normal language, Imagination has often been held to be something higher than the mere image-making, ascribed to the operations of Fancy (a reduced and depreciatory form of the older word Fantasy); an attempt is thus made to restrict, I should say misapply, Imagination to "the power of giving to ideal creations the inner consistency of reality."

Ridiculous though it may be for one so ill-instructed to have an opinion on this critical matter, I venture to think the verbal distinction philologically inappropriate, and the analysis inaccurate. The mental power of image-making is one thing, or aspect; and it should appropriately be called Imagination. The perception of the image, the grasp of its implications, and the control, which are necessary to a successful expression, may vary in vividness and strength: but this is a difference of degree in Imagination, not a difference in kind. The achievement of the expression, which gives (or seems to give) "the inner consistency of reality,"[1] is indeed

---

[1] That is: which commands or induces Secondary Belief.

78

another thing, or aspect, needing another name: Art, the operative link between Imagination and the final result, Sub-creation. For my present purpose I require a word which shall embrace both the Sub-creative Art in itself and a quality of strangeness and wonder in the Expression, derived from the Image: a quality essential to fairy-story. I propose, therefore, to arrogate to myself the powers of Humpty-Dumpty, and to use Fantasy for· this purpose: in a sense, that is, which combines with its older and higher use as an equivalent of Imagination the derived notions of "unreality" (that is, of unlikeness to the Primary World), of freedom from the domination of observed "fact," in short of the fantastic. I am thus not only aware but glad of the etymological and semantic connexions of *fantasy* with *fantastic:* with images of things that are not only "not actually present," but which are indeed not to be found in our primary world at all, or are generally believed not to be found there. But while admitting that, I do not assent to the depreciative tone. That the images are of things not in the primary world (if that indeed is possible) is a virtue, not a vice. Fantasy (in this sense) is, I think, not a lower but a higher form of Art, indeed the most nearly pure form, and so (when achieved) the most potent.

Fantasy, of course, starts out with an advantage: arresting strangeness. But that advantage has been turned against it, and has contributed to its disrepute. Many people dislike being "arrested." They dislike any meddling with the Primary World, or such small glimpses of it as are familiar to them. They, therefore, stupidly and even maliciously confound Fantasy with Dreaming, in which there is no Art;[2] and with mental disorders, in which there is not even control; with delusion and hallucination.

But the error or malice, engendered by disquiet and consequent dislike, is not the only cause of this confusion. Fantasy has also an essential drawback: it is

___

[2] This is not true of all dreams. In some Fantasy seems to take a part. But this is exceptional. Fantasy is a rational, not an irrational, activity.

difficult to achieve. Fantasy may be, as I think, not less
but more sub-creative; but at any rate it is found in
practice that "the inner consistency of reality" is more
difficult to produce, the more unlike are the images and
the rearrangements of primary material to the actual
arrangements of the Primary World. It is easier to produce this kind of "reality" with more "sober" material.
Fantasy thus, too often, remains undeveloped; it is and
has been used frivolously, or only half-seriously, or
merely for decoration: it remains merely "fanciful."
Anyone inheriting the fantastic device of human language can say *the green sun*. Many can then imagine
or picture it. But that is not enough—though it may
already be a more potent thing than many a "thumbnail
sketch" or "transcript of life" that receives literary
praise.

To make a Secondary World inside which the green
sun will be credible, commanding Secondary Belief, will
probably require labour and thought, and will certainly
demand a special skill, a kind of elvish craft. Few attempt such difficult tasks. But when they are attempted
and in any degree accomplished then we have a rare
achievement of Art: indeed narrative art, story-making
in its primary and most potent mode.

In human art Fantasy is a thing best left to words,
to true literature. In painting, for instance, the visible
presentation of the fantastic image is technically too
easy; the hand tends to outrun the mind, even to over-
throw it. Silliness or morbidity are frequent results. It
is a misfortune that Drama, an art fundamentally distinct from Literature, should so commonly be considered together with it, or as a branch of it. Among these
misfortunes we may reckon the depreciation of Fantasy. For in part at least this depreciation is due to the
natural desire of critics to cry up the forms of literature
or "imagination" that they themselves, innately or by
training, prefer. And criticism in a country that has
produced so great a Drama, and possesses the works of
William Shakespeare, tends to be far too dramatic. But
Drama is naturally hostile to Fantasy. Fantasy, even
of the simplest kind, hardly ever succeeds in Drama,

when that is presented as it should be, visibly and audibly acted. Fantastic forms are not to be counterfeited. Men dressed up as talking animals may achieve buffoonery or mimicry, but they do not achieve Fantasy. This is, I think, well illustrated by the failure of the bastard form, pantomime. The nearer it is to "dramatized fairy-story" the worse it is. It is only tolerable when the plot and its fantasy are reduced to a mere vestigiary framework for farce, and no "belief" of any kind in any part of the performance is required or expected of anybody. This is, of course, partly due to the fact that the producers of drama have to, or try to, work with mechanism to represent either Fantasy or Magic. I once saw a so-called "children's pantomime," the straight story of *Puss-in-Boots,* with even the metamorphosis of the ogre into a mouse. Had this been mechanically successful it would either have terrified the spectators or else have been just a turn of high-class conjuring. As it was, though done with some ingenuity of lighting, disbelief had not so much to be suspended as hanged, drawn, and quartered.

In *Macbeth,* when it is read, I find the witches tolerable: they have a narrative function and some hint of dark significance; though they are vulgarized, poor things of their kind. They are almost intolerable in the play. They would be quite intolerable, if I were not fortified by some memory of them as they are in the story as read. I am told that I should feel differently if I had the mind of the period, with its witch-hunts and witch-trials. But that is to say: if I regarded the witches as possible, indeed likely, in the Primary World; in other words, if they ceased to be "Fantasy." That argument concedes the point. To be dissolved, or to be degraded, is the likely fate of Fantasy when a dramatist tries to use it, even such a dramatist as Shakespeare. *Macbeth* is indeed a work by a playwright who ought, at least on this occasion, to have written a story, if he had the skill or patience for that art.

A reason, more important, I think, than the inadequacy of stage-effects, is this: Drama has, of its very nature, already attempted a kind of bogus, or shall I say at least substitute, magic: *the visible and audible presentation of imaginary men in a story.* That is in itself an attempt to counterfeit the magician's wand. To introduce, even with mechanical success, into this quasi-magical secondary world a further fantasy or magic is to demand, as it were, an inner or tertiary world. It is a world too much. To make such a thing may not be impossible. I have never seen it done with success. But at least it cannot be claimed as the proper mode of Drama, in which walking and talking people have been found to be the natural instruments of Art and illusion.

For this precise reason—that the characters, and even the scenes, are in Drama not imagined but actually beheld—Drama is, even though it uses a similar material (words, verse, plot), an art fundamentally different from narrative art. Thus, if you prefer Drama to Literature (as many literary critics plainly do), or form your critical theories primarily from dramatic critics, or even from Drama, you are apt to misunderstand pure story-making, and to constrain it to the limitations of stage-plays. You are, for instance, likely to prefer characters, even the basest and dullest, to things. Very little about trees as trees can be got into a play.

Now "Faërian Drama"—those plays which according to abundant records the elves have often presented to men—can produce Fantasy with a realism and immediacy beyond the compass of any human mechanism. As a result their usual effect (upon a man) is to go beyond Secondary Belief. If you are present at a Faërian drama you yourself are, or think that you are, bodily inside its Secondary World. The experience may be very similar to Dreaming and has (it would seem) sometimes been confounded with it. But in Faërian drama you are in a dream that some other mind is weaving, and the knowledge of that alarming fact may slip from your grasp. To experience *directly* a Secondary World: the potion is too strong, and you give to it Primary Belief, however marvellous the events. You are deluded—whether that is the intention of the elves (always or at any time) is another question. They at any rate are not themselves deluded. This is for them a form of Art, and distinct from Wizardry or Magic, properly so called. They do not live in it, though they can, perhaps, afford to spend more time at it than human artists can. The Primary World, Reality, of elves and men is the same, if differently valued and perceived.

We need a word for this elvish craft, but all the words that have been applied to it have been blurred and confused with other things. Magic is ready to hand, and I have used it above, but I should not have done so: Magic should be reserved for the operations of the Magician. Art is the human process that produces by the way (it is not its only or ultimate object) Secondary Belief. Art of the same sort, if more skilled and effortless, the elves can also use, or so the reports seem to show; but the more potent and specially elvish craft I will, for lack of a less debatable word, call Enchantment. Enchantment produces a Secondary World into which both designer and spectator can enter, to the satisfaction of their senses while they are inside; but in its purity it is artistic in desire and purpose. Magic produces, or pretends to produce, an alteration in the Primary World. It docs not matter by whom it is said to be practised, fay or mortal, it remains distinct from the other two; it is not an art but a technique; its desire is *power* in this world, domination of things and wills.

To the elvish craft, Enchantment, Fantasy aspires, and when it is successful of all forms of human art most nearly approaches. At the heart of many man-made stories of the elves lies, open or concealed, pure or alloyed, the desire for a living, realized sub-creative art, which (however much it may outwardly resemble it) is inwardly wholly different from the greed for self-centred power which is the mark of the mere Magician. Of this desire the elves, in their better (but still perilous) part, are largely made; and it is from them that we may learn what is the central desire and aspiration of human Fantasy—even if the elves are, all the more in so far as they are, only a product of Fantasy itself. That creative desire is only cheated by counterfeits, whether the innocent but clumsy devices of the human dramatist, or the malevolent frauds of the magicians. In this world it is for men unsatisfiable, and so imperishable. Uncorrupted, it does not seek delusion nor bewitchment and domination; it seeks shared enrichment, partners in making and delight, not slaves.

To many, Fantasy, this sub-creative art which plays strange tricks with the world and all that is in it, combining nouns and redistributing adjectives, has seemed suspect, if not illegitimate. To some it has seemed at least a childish folly, a thing only for peoples or for persons in their youth. As for its legitimacy I will say no more than to quote a brief passage from a letter I once wrote to a man who described myth and fairy-story as "lies"; though to do him justice he was kind enough and confused enough to call fairy-story-making "Breathing a lie through Silver."

> *"Dear Sir," I said—"Although now long es-*
> *tranged,*
> *Man is not wholly lost nor wholly changed.*
> *Dis-graced he may be, yet is not de-throned,*
> *and keeps the rags of lordship once he owned:*
> *Man, Sub-creator, the refracted Light*
> *through whom is splintered from a single White*
> *to many hues, and endlessly combined*
> *in living shapes that move from mind to mind.*
> *Though all the crannies of the world we filled*
> *with Elves and Goblins, though we dared to*
> *build*
> *Gods and their houses out of dark and light,*
> *and sowed the seed of dragons—'twas our right*
> *(used or misused). That right has not decayed:*
> *we make still by the law in which we're made."*

Fantasy is a natural human activity. It certainly does not destroy or even insult Reason; and it does not either blunt the appetite for, nor obscure the perception of, scientific verity. On the contrary. The keener and the clearer is the reason, the better fantasy will it make. If men were ever in a state in which they did not want to know or could not perceive truth (facts or evidence), then Fantasy would languish until they were cured. If they ever get into that state (it would not seem at all impossible), Fantasy will perish, and become Morbid Delusion.

For creative Fantasy is founded upon the hard recognition that things are so in the world as it appears under the sun; on a recognition of fact, but not a slavery to it. So upon logic was founded the nonsense that displays itself in the tales and rhymes of Lewis Carroll. If men really could not distinguish between frogs and men, fairy-stories about frog-kings would not have arisen.

Fantasy can, of course, be carried to excess. It can be ill done. It can be put to evil uses. It may even delude the minds out of which it came. But of what human thing in this fallen world is that not true? Men have conceived not only of elves, but they have imagined gods, and worshipped them, even worshipped those most deformed by their authors' own evil. But they have made false gods out of other materials: their notions, their banners, their monies; even their sciences and their social and economic theories have demanded human sacrifice. *Abusus non tollit usum.* Fantasy remains a human right: we make in our measure and in our derivative mode, because we are made: and not only made, but made in the image and likeness of a Maker.

·✶ To W. H. Auden ✶·

J. R. R. Tolkien

[Auden, who had reviewed *The Fellowship of the Ring* in the *New York Times Book Review* and

Encounter, had been sent proofs of the third volume, *The Return of the King.* He wrote to Tolkien in April 1955 to ask various questions arising from the book. Tolkien's reply does not survive (Auden usually threw away letters after reading them). Auden wrote again on 3 June to say that he had been asked to give a talk about *The Lord of the Rings* on the BBC Third Programme in October. He asked Tolkien if there were any points he would like to hear made in the broadcast, and whether he would supply a few 'human touches' in the form of information about how the book came to be written. Tolkien's reply survives because on this occasion—and when he subsequently wrote to Auden—he kept a carbon copy, from which this text is taken.]

7 June 1955   76 Sandfield Road, Headington, Oxford
Dear Auden,

I was very pleased to hear from you, and glad to feel that you were not bored. I am afraid that you may be in for rather a long letter again; but you can do what you like with it. I type it so that it may at any rate be quickly readable. I do not really think that I am frightfully important. I wrote the Trilogy as a personal satisfaction, driven to it by the scarcity of literature of the sort that I wanted to read (and what there was was often heavily alloyed). A great labour; and as the author of the *Ancrene Wisse* says at the end of his work: 'I would rather, God be my witness, set out on foot for Rome than begin the work over again!' But unlike him I would not have said: 'Read some of this book at your leisure every day; and I hope that if you read it often it will prove very profitable to you; otherwise I shall have spent my long hours very ill.' I was not thinking much of the profit or delight of others; though no one can really write or make anything purely privately.

However, when the BBC employs any one so important as yourself to talk publicly about the Trilogy, not without reference to the author, the most modest (or at any rate retiring) of men, whose instinct is to cloak such self-knowledge as he has, and such criticisms of life as he knows it, under mythical and legendary dress, cannot help thinking about it in personal terms—and finding it interesting, and difficult, too, to express both briefly and accurately.

The Lord of the Rings as a story was finished so long ago now that I can take a largely impersonal view of it, and find 'interpretations' quite amusing; even those that I might make myself, which are mostly *post scriptum:* I had very little particular, conscious, intellectual, intention in mind at any point.* Except for a few deliberately disparaging reviews—such as that of Vol. II in the *New Statesman,* in which you and I were both scourged with such terms as 'pubescent' and 'infantilism'—what appreciative readers have got out of the work or seen in it has seemed fair enough, even when I do not agree with it. Always excepting, of course, any 'interpretations' in the mode of simple allegory: that is, the particular and topical. In a larger sense, it is I suppose impossible to write any 'story' that is not allegorical in proportion as it 'comes to life'; since each of us is an allegory, embodying in particular tale and clothed in the garments of time and place, universal

---

*Take the Ents, for instance. I did not consciously invent them at all. The chapter called 'Treebeard', from 'Treebeard's first remark on p. 66, was written off more or less as it stands, with an effect on my self (except for labour pains) almost like reading some one else's work. And I like Ents now because they do not seem to have anything to do with me. I daresay something had been going on in the 'unconscious' for some time, and that accounts for my feeling throughout, especially when stuck, that I was not inventing but reporting (imperfectly) and had at times to wait till 'what really happened' came through. But looking back analytically I should say that Ents are composed of philology, literature, and life. They owe their name to the *eald enta geweorc* of Anglo-Saxon, and their connexion with stone. Their part in the story is due, I think, to my bitter disappointment and disgust from schooldays with the shabby use made in Shakespeare of the coming of 'Great Birnam wood to high Dunsinane hill': I longed to devise a setting in which the trees might really march to war. And into this has crept a mere piece of experience, the difference of the 'male' and 'female' attitude to wild things, the difference between unpossessive love and gardening.

truth and everlasting life. Anyway most people that have enjoyed *The Lord of the Rings* have been affected primarily by it as an exciting story; and that is how it was written. Though one does not, of course, escape from the question 'what is it about?' by that back door. That would be like answering an aesthetic question by talking of a point of technique. I suppose that if one makes a good choice in what is 'good narrative' (or 'good theatre') at a given point, it will also be found to be the case that the event described will be the most 'significant'.

To turn, if I may, to the 'human Touches' and the matter of when I started. That is rather like asking of Man when language started. It was an inevitable, though conditionable, evolvement of the birth-given. It has been always with me: the sensibility to linguistic pattern which affects me emotionally like colour or music; and the passionate love of growing things; and the deep response to legends (for lack of a better word) that have what I would call the North-western temper and temperature. In any case if you want to write a tale of this sort you must consult your roots, and a man of the North-west of the Old World will set his heart and the action of his tale in an imaginary world of that air, and that situation: with the Shoreless Sea of his innumerable ancestors to the West, and the endless lands (out of which enemies mostly come) to the East. Though, in addition, his heart may remember, even if he has been cut off from all oral tradition, the rumour all along the coasts of the Men out of the Sea.

I say this about the 'heart', for I have what some might call an Atlantis complex. Possibly inherited, though my parents died too young for me to know such things about them, and too young to transfer such things by words. Inherited from me (I suppose) by one only of my children, though I did not know that about my son until recently, and he did not know it about me. I mean the terrible recurrent dream (beginning with memory) of the Great Wave, towering up, and coming in ineluctably over the trees and green fields. (I bequeathed

it to Faramir.) I don't think I have had it since I wrote
the 'Downfall of Númenor as the last of the legends of
the First and Second Age.

I am a West-midlander by blood (and took to early
west-midland Middle English as a known tongue as
soon as I set eyes on it), but perhaps a fact of my personal history may partly explain why the 'North-western air' appeals to me both as 'home' and as something
discovered. I was actually born in Bloemfontein, and so
those deeply implanted impressions, underlying memories that are still pictorially available for inspection,
of first childhood are for me those of a hot parched
country. My first Christmas memory is of blazing sun,
drawn curtains and a drooping eucalyptus.

I am afraid this is becoming a dreadful bore, and
going on too long, at any rate longer than 'this con-
temptible person before you' merits. But it is difficult
to stop once roused on such an absorbing topic to oneself
as oneself. As for the conditioning: I am chiefly aware
of the linguistic conditioning. I went to King Edward's
School and spent most of my time learning Latin and
Greek; but I also learned English. Not English Literature! Except Shakespeare (which I disliked cordially),
the chief contacts with poetry were when one was made
to try and translate it into Latin. Not a bad mode of
introduction, if a bit casual. I mean something of the
English language and its history. I learned Anglo-Saxon
at school (also Gothic, but that was an accident quite
unconnected with the curriculum though decisive—I
discovered in it not only modern historical philology,
which appealed to the historical and scientific side, but
for the first time the study of a language out of mere
love: I mean for the acute aesthetic pleasure derived
from a language for its own sake, not only free from
being useful but free even from being the 'vehicle of a
literature').

There are two strands, or three. A fascination that
Welsh names had for me, even if only seen on coal-
trucks, from childhood is another; though people only
gave me books that were incomprehensible to a child

when I asked for information. I did not learn any Welsh till I was an undergraduate, and found in it an abiding linguistic-aesthetic satisfaction. Spanish was another: my guardian was half Spanish, and in my early teens I used to pinch his books and try to learn it: the only Romance language that gives me the particular pleasure of which I am speaking—it is not quite the same as the mere perception of beauty: I feel the beauty of say Italian or for that matter of modern English (which is very remote from my personal taste): it is more like the appetite for a needed food. Most important, perhaps, after Gothic was the discovery in Exeter College library, when I was supposed to be reading for Honour Mods, of a Finnish Grammar. It was like discovering a complete wine-cellar filled with bottles of an amazing wine of a kind and flavour never tasted before. It quite intoxicated me; and I gave up the attempt to invent an 'unrecorded' Germanic language, and my 'own language'—or series of invented languages—became heavily Finnicized in phonetic pattern and structure.

That is of course long past now. Linguistic taste changes like everything else, as time goes on; or oscillates between poles. Latin and the British type of Celtic have it now, with the beautifully co-ordinated and patterned (if simply patterned) Anglo-Saxon near at hand and further off the Old Norse with the neighbouring but alien Finnish. Roman-British might not one say? With a strong but more recent infusion from Scandinavia and the Baltic. Well, I daresay such linguistic tastes, with due allowance for school-overlay, are as good or better a test of ancestry as blood-groups.

All this only as background to the stories, though languages and names are for me inextricable from the stories. They are and were so to speak an attempt to give a background or a world in which my expressions of linguistic taste could have a function. The stories were comparatively late in coming.

I first tried to write a story when I was about seven. It was about a dragon. I remember nothing about it except a philological fact. My mother said nothing about the dragon, but pointed out that one could not say 'a green great dragon', but had to say 'a great green dragon'. I wondered why, and still do. The fact that I remember this is possibly significant, as I do not think I ever tried to write a story again for many years, and was taken up with language.

I mentioned Finnish, because that set the rocket off in a story. I was immensely attracted by something in the air of the Kalevala, even in Kirby's poor translation. I never learned Finnish well enough to do more than plod through a bit of the original, like a schoolboy with Ovid; being mostly taken up with its effect on 'my language'. But the beginning of the legendarium, of which the Trilogy is part (the conclusion), was in an attempt to reorganize some of the Kalevala, especially the tale of Kullervo the hapless, into a form of my own. That began, as I say, in the Honour Mods period; nearly disastrously as I came very near having my exhibition taken off me if not being sent down. Say 1912 to 1913. As the thing went on I actually wrote in verse. Though the first real story of this imaginary world almost fully formed as it now appears was written in prose during sick-leave at the end of 1916: The Fall of Gondolin, which I had the cheek to read to the Exeter College Essay Club in 1918. I wrote a lot else in hospitals before the end of the First Great War.

I went on after return; but when I attempted to get any of this stuff published I was not successful. *The Hobbit* was originally quite unconnected, though it inevitably got drawn in to the circumference of the greater construction; and in the event modified it. It was unhappily really meant, as far as I was conscious, as a 'children's story', and as I had not learned sense then, and my children were not quite old enough to correct me, it has some of the sillinesses of manner caught unthinkingly from the kind of stuff I had had served to me, as Chaucer may catch a minstrel tag. I deeply regret them. So do intelligent children.

All I remember about the start of *The Hobbit* is sitting correcting School Certificate papers in the everlasting weariness of that annual task forced on impecunious academics with children. On a blank leaf I scrawled: 'In a hole in the ground there lived a hobbit.' I did not and do not know why. I did nothing about it, for a long time, and for some years I got no further than the production of Thror's Map. But it became *The Hobbit* in the early 1930s, and was eventually published not because of my own children's enthusiasm (though they liked it well enough**), but because I lent it to the then Rev. Mother of Cherwell Edge when she had flu, and it was seen by a former student who was at that time in the office of Allen and Unwin. It was I believe tried out on Rayner Unwin; but for whom when grown up I think I should never have got the Trilogy published.

Since *The Hobbit* was a success, a sequel was called for; and the remote Elvish Legends were turned down. A publisher's reader said they were too full of the kind of Celtic beauty that maddened Anglo-Saxons in a large dose. Very likely quite right. Anyway I myself saw the value of Hobbits, in putting earth under the feet of 'romance', and in providing subjects for 'ennoblement' and heroes more praiseworthy than the professionals: *nolo heroizari* is of course as good a start for a hero, as *nolo episcopari* for a bishop. Not that I am a 'democrat' in any of its current uses; except that I suppose, to speak in literary terms, we are all equal before the Great Author, *qui deposuit potentes de sede et exaltavit humiles*.

All the same, I was not prepared to write a 'sequel', in the sense of another children's story. I had been thinking about 'Fairy Stories' and their relation to children—some of the results I put into a lecture at St. Andrews and eventually enlarged and published in an Essay (among those listed in the O.U.P. as *Essays Presented to Charles Williams* and now most scurvily allowed to go out of print). As I had expressed the view

---

**Not any better I think than *The Marvellous Land of Snergs*, Wyke-Smith, Ernest Benn 1927. Seeing the date, I should say that this was probably an unconscious source-book! for the Hobbits, not of anything else.

that the connexion in the modern mind between children and 'fairy stories' is false and accidental, and spoils the stories in themselves and for children, I wanted to try and write one that was not addressed to children at all (as such); also I wanted a large canvas.

A lot of labour was naturally involved, since I had to make a linkage with *The Hobbit;* but still more with the background mythology. That had to be re-written as well. *The Lord of the Rings* is only the end part of a work nearly twice as long which I worked at between 1936 and 53 (I wanted to get it all published in chronological order, but that proved impossible.) And the languages had to be attended to! If I had considered my own pleasure more than the stomachs of a possible audience, there would have been a great deal more Elvish in the book. But even the snatches that there are required, if they were to have a meaning, two organized phonologies and grammars and a large number of words.

It would have been a big task without anything else; and I have been a moderately conscientious administrator and teacher, and I changed professorships in 1945 (scrapping all my old lectures). And of course during the War there was often no time for anything rational. I stuck for ages at the end of Book Three. Book Four was written as a serial and sent out to my son serving in Africa in 1944. The last two books were written between 1944 and 48. That of course does not mean that the main idea of the story was a war-product. That was arrived at in one of the earliest chapters still surviving (Book I, 2). It is really given, and present in germ, from the beginning, though I had no conscious notion of what the Necromancer stood for (except ever-recurrent evil) in *The Hobbit,* nor of his connexion with the Ring. But if you wanted to go on from the end of *The Hobbit* I think the ring would be your inevitable choice as the link. If then you wanted a large tale, the Ring would at once acquire a capital letter; and the Dark Lord would immediately appear. As he did, unasked, on the hearth at Bag End as soon as I came to that point. So the essential Quest started at once. But I met a lot of things on the way that astonished me. Tom Bombadil I knew already; but I had never been to Bree. Strider sitting in the corner at the inn was a shock, and I had no more idea who he was than had Frodo. The Mines of Moria had been a mere name; and of Lothlórien no word had reached my mortal ears till I came there. Far away I knew there were the Horse-lords on the confines of an ancient Kingdom of Men, but Fangorn Forest was an unforeseen adventure. I had never heard of the House of Eorl nor of the Stewards of Gondor. Most disquieting of all, Saruman had never been revealed to me, and I was as mystified as Frodo at Gandalf's failure to appear on September 22. I knew nothing of the *Palantíri,* though the moment the Orthanc-stone was cast from the window, I recognized it, and knew the meaning of the 'rhyme of lore' that had been running in my mind: *seven stars and seven stones and one white tree.* These rhymes and names will crop up; but they do not always explain themselves. I have yet to discover anything about the cats of Queen Berúthiel. But I did know more or less all about Gollum and his part, and Sam, and I knew that the way was guarded by a Spider. And if that has anything to do with my being stung by a tarantula when a small child, people are welcome to the notion (supposing the improbable, that any one is interested). I can only say that I remember nothing about it, should not know it if I had not been told; and I do not dislike spiders particularly, and have no urge to kill them. I usually rescue those whom I find in the bath!

Well now I am really getting garrulous. I do hope you will not be frightfully bored. I hope also to see you again some time. In which case we may perhaps talk about you and your work and not mine. Any way your interest in mine is a considerable encouragement.

With very best wishes. Yours sincerely,
J. R. R. Tolkien.

AUGUST WILLIAM DERLETH

(1909–1971)

Writing in the November 1945 issue of *Esquire,* Sinclair Lewis had this to say about a promising young writer by the name of August Derleth:

> When he was very young, he had a notion worthy of a giant, and with gigantic industry he has pursued it: that his Wisconsin village is a microcosm of the whole world.... He has not trotted off to New York literary cocktail parties or to Hollywood studios. He has stayed home and built up a solid work that demands the attention of anybody who believes that American fiction is at last growing up. It is a proof of Mr. Derleth's merit that he makes one want to make the journey and see his particular Avalon: the Wisconsin River shining among its islands, and the castles of Baron Pierneau and Hercules Dousman.
>
> 100 Books by August Derleth, Sauk City: Arkham House, 1972, p. 109

Lewis's comments underline Derleth's attachment to his place of birth. Indeed, few writers have been so devoted to a place as August Derleth to his beloved Sauk City, Wisconsin. This village and its environs was the setting for all the major events of Derleth's life: his birth February 24, 1909; his elementary and secondary school education; his marriage to Sandra Winters in 1953; the birth of his daughter, April Rose, and his son, Walden William; his founding of Arkham House in 1939 (see the Lovecraft headnote); and his death from an apparent heart attack on July 4, 1971.

What he couldn't do from Place of Hawks, his home near Sauk City, he tried to do nearby. Thus he pursued his higher education at the University of Wisconsin-Madison, located just twenty-five miles southeast of his home. He received his B.A. there in 1930, and later, from 1939 to 1943, he served as a Lecturer in American Regional Literature at his alma mater. He also took advantage of Madison's proximity by getting work at *The Capital Times,* the city's evening newspaper, serving intermittently as literary editor and weekly columnist from 1941 to his death. Derleth's uncommonly strong regionalism reminds us of Lovecraft's adhesive relationship with his native Providence, and this is not surprising since it was Lovecraft who urged Derleth to stay in Sauk City, pointing out that "a man belongs where he has roots—where the landscape and milieu have some relation to his thoughts and feelings, by virtue of having formed them" (Alison M. Wilson, *Dictionary of Literary Biography,* Vol. 9, Detroit: Gale Research Company, 1981, p. 203).

In 1924, at the age of fifteen, Derleth sold his first story, "Bat's Belfry," to *Weird Tales,* and spent virtually the rest of his life writing, editing, and publishing books. Because he was such a prolific and versatile writer, the name Derleth means different things to different readers. For some he is the poet whose work, mostly dealing with nature, is showcased in such fine collections as *Hawk on the Wind* (1938), *West of Morning* (1960), and *The Landscape of the Heart* (1970); for others he is the author of the Sac Prairie Saga, a series of regional novels and short stories depicting Midwestern village life from the early 1800s to the present (e.g. *Wind Over Wisconsin,* 1938; *Evening in Spring,* 1941; *The Shield of the Valiant,* 1945; *Walden West,* 1961); and for still others he is the creator of the Judge Peck mystery series and the Solar Pons pastiches (reminiscent of Doyle's Sherlock Holmes tales). Another contingent remembers him for his work with Gothic fantasy; he not only wrote it, but helped promote the works of other writers of the macabre through his Arkham House publications. Derleth, in a self-appraisal appearing in *100 Books by August Derleth,* singles out the short story collection, *Wisconsin Earth* (1948), as "the best cross-section introduction both to Sac Prairie and to [his] work" (p. 120).

In an autobiographical sketch written for *Twentieth Century Authors* (1942), Derleth suggested that he was probably "the most versatile and voluminous writer in quality writing fields." Since he was the author or editor of more than 150 books covering a wide range of subjects and literary types, and since he published thousands of poems, short stories, reviews, and essays in more than 400 magazines and newspapers, Derleth's claim seems justified. Although still very little critical study has been done on the Derleth canon, he seems to have earned an important place in American letters, especially as a Midwestern regionalist. During his lifetime he received a number of distinguished awards, including the Guggenheim Fellowship sponsored by Sinclair Lewis, Helen C. White, and Edgar Lee Masters (1938), the Midland Authors Golden Anniversary Award for Poetry (1965), and the Wisconsin Governor's Award for service to the creative arts (1966).

Most of us have had the rather disappointing experience of being taken on a tour of a magnificent personal library, only to find that the proud owner hasn't read any of the volumes, that the library, in fact, was merely a showpiece. Such was not the case with August Derleth's splendid 12,000 volume collection housed in Place of Hawks. Derleth read his books—a fact nicely demonstrated by the dozens of references to a wide range of fantasy works in "The Fantastic Story." As a matter of fact, it is precisely because Derleth read so widely and practiced the craft of writing so assiduously that his comments in this essay are so valuable. "The Fantastic Story" contains not only a definition of "pure Fantasy" and perceptive assessments of the works of several fantasy authors, but also some helpful suggestions about the writing of fantasy. Perhaps most noteworthy are his comments about the vital importance of an elevated style in fantasy, and his warning that "strangeness of setting and prose style will not make up for an ineffective story insofar as the juvenile reader is concerned." Published in 1946 as part of a full-length text, *Writing Fiction,* "The Fantastic Story" is a pioneering critical study of fantasy literature.

⋅⊶ The Fantastic Story ⊷⋅

August Derleth

Pure fantasy is a kind of dream-world fiction which need not adhere to the orthodox short story plot, and which, very often because it does not adhere to the accepted forms of the short story, is not sustained for even the short novel length. It ranges all the way from the prose of Lord Dunsany to the whimsical tales of many contributors to the late, lamented *Unknown Worlds* magazine, a Street & Smith publication under the same aegis as *Astounding Science-Fiction.*

Dunsany's work is in a class rather largely by itself. It grows out of an original folklore and mythology, and is written in what H. P. Lovecraft has described as

"The Fantastic Story" originally appeared in Writing Fiction, 1946. Copyright © 1946 by The Writer, Inc., Publishers, Boston.

"crystalline singing prose". In his *Supernatural Horror in Literature,* Lovecraft writes of Dunsany that he "draws with tremendous effectiveness on nearly every body of myth and legend within the circle of European culture, producing a composite or eclectic cycle of fantasy in which Eastern color, Hellenic form, Teutonic sombreness and Celtic wistfulness are so superbly blended that each sustains and supplements the rest without sacrifice of perfect congruity and homogeneity." Dunsany's fantasy strives to achieve beauty rather than terror, though there are some effective tales of terror scattered among his collections, *A Dreamer's Tales, The Book of Wonder, Tales of Three Hemispheres, Fifty-One Tales*—the stories of Slith, the thief, of Hlo-Hlo, the spider-idol, and of the Gibbelins, for instance. But work in the manner of Dunsany enjoys a very limited market, speaking from the point-of-view of the contemporary writer. Even H. P. Lovecraft's fantasies, written under the influence of Dunsany, were little published before his death; it was only after his death that the demand for more of his work brought about their acceptance and publication by editors who had previously rejected them. Of Lovecraft's pure fantasies, only *The White Ship* and *The Strange High House in the Mist* were popular among readers of *Weird Tales.*

But Dunsanian fantasy is only a small portion of the field. The fantasy of beauty is, however, as legitimate as the fantasy of terror, and fully as imaginative. For instance, W. H. Hudson's memorably beautiful story of the bird-girl, Rima, *Green Mansions,* is fantasy of a high order. So too is Lafcadio Hearn's wonderfully beautiful short novel, *Chita,* a book which, after it has once been read, cannot be forgotten, but lingers in memory as the perfume of flowers lingers in a room long after they have been taken away. It is Hearn's prose more than anything else which gives *Chita* the aspect of fantasy, and his way of telling the story, for the story of *Chita* is orthodox enough in essence, and it could very well have happened. It is presumably based on a Creole legend of a child found after a hurricane had separated her family, raised by a childless couple, and ultimately finding her father just prior to his death. But it is a story the telling of which seems to set it in that strange borderland between today and tomorrow, yesterday and today, between life and death, belonging fully to neither, a story of undying retrospect, as it were, which violates many canons of good story-telling and yet emerges as one of the greatest of its kind. That it should impress a reader as fantastic is a tribute to a great stylist, for by fantasy we understand generally a story or a theme which, if not absolutely in the realm of the impossible, is at least highly unlikely. W. H. Hudson's Rima is unlikely, but not impossible, but Hearn's *Chita* is not only possible, but it might have been quite likely, not alone as the basis of a legend.

The story of the lost child is very much akin to the profound dislocation of the life pattern typical of those stories in which a tremendous cataclysm, a plague, or the like eliminates from earth almost all life, and the story is concerned with the struggle of the last man or last woman to survive. S. Fowler Wright's *Deluge,* for instance, or M. P. Shiel's *The Purple Cloud.* The writer of successful fantasy is usually a man whose prose style is quite superior to that of the average writer; it should be evident at once that this almost inevitably must be so, because it requires exceeding skill to make fantasy convincing. After all, the writer of a ghost story, or a romantic story, or even of an average pseudo-scientific story can call upon a recognizable background to establish a point of contact with his readers; but the writer of fantasy must very often start from scratch, so to speak, with nothing but similarity of emotions between character and reader.

The symbological setting, such as that in *Perelandra,* by C. S. Lewis, is not superficially apparent, because it cannot be, the author having to face the need of establishing his fantastic setting as setting, without concerning himself with indicating his symbolism. Lewis's is primarily always allegorical on a religious theme, and the allegory, as in *Perelandra,* is very soon apparent. What Lewis does, in effect, is to take a religious thesis and emphasize it most entertainingly in a story which, on the surface, is highly fantastic. Fantasy, then, is not the primary interest of the writer, but only the secondary one, the allegory being all-important. But such stories are no less fantastic, for all that; it is perfectly possible to read C. S. Lewis's novels and enjoy them as fantasy without ever becoming aware of their allegorical significance.

The verisimilitude of a setting in which few aspects strike the note of common human experience is quite difficult to achieve. It is one thing for a novice to describe a landscape, a house, a room, a street, upon reading of which the average reader at once feels at home, drawing upon his own experience to see in his mind's eye just what kind of landscape, house, room, or street the author intends him to see; but it is quite another to make real for such an average reader a world totally dissimilar from anything he has ever seen or imagined. It may be argued that the average man has never seen the far corners of the earth, but that is really not an argument at all, for he has heard of them, he may even have read of them. A man who has never been to Singapore has heard about it, even if only by name in a story by Sax Rohmer, for instance, and it therefore has a certain meaning to him, he believes in Singapore as a place, and, though he may have an entirely erroneous picture of it in his mind's eye, he has already accepted the fundamental fact that Singapore does exist. The writer who employs an utterly alien setting must utilize every skill he has to make his reader believe in his setting; a man who lives in a country of trees and hills will naturally find it a little difficult to "see" in his mind's eye a country of flat, sandy stretches, without trees or bushes, and with every evidence of strange flora and fauna. Yet that is a comparatively trivial parallel when set up alongside some of the settings employed by contemporary fantasists.

M. P. Shiel's *The Purple Cloud* is perhaps of the very best of all novels of fantasy; certainly it is one which is not easily thrust from memory, and Shiel's development of the "last man" theme is very convincingly done. Shiel, of course, is one of the greatest living stylists writing in English. *The Purple Cloud* is the story of a curse which comes out of the arctic to destroy mankind, leaving but one survivor, whose sensations and experiences as he roams through the corpse-littered and treasure-strewn places of the world he had known, and now knows as its unchallenged master, are skillfully done and artistically conceived. Shiel's concession to popular taste, however, mitigates to some extent the excellent impression of the first half of the book; for his survivor inevitably finds that he is not alone, but that a woman has also survived, and they can begin all over again. Despite this concession, however, Shiel's Adam Jeffson is a memorable character—but not because he is Adam Jeffson so much as because he is Shiel's character, for Shiel is a writer who has tremendous potency and magic in his prose. His Adam Jeffson, memorable as he is, is not to be compared with his sinister Dr. Krasinski, and the doctor himself is nobody compared to Richard Hogarth of *The Lord of the Sea,* that wildly improbable but magnificently entertaining epitome of all the adventure stories ever written by man.

It is interesting to examine what Shiel has to say for his work, particularly since his style is manifest even in his communications. "Since the object of Art is to enlarge (or at least to sharpen, or at the very least to refresh) your consciousness of the truth of things, the question is, which of the two is the truer, realism or romance? Well, there can be no question that romance is true, if it be truly realistic, but the truth is that it is not truly realistic, if it be not romantic, since truth is romantic. With the mood of wistfulness in your eyes you look at the moon one night where, as musing she walks amid the stars, and wish that you were there where she muses; wait: before you go to bed you will be where she muses, if our globe be moving that way, and soon you may be soaring not at all far from where Venus at this hour leads the crowd of the starry orchestra with her crown and psaltery," he has written. And examine this succinct description: "She was a woman of twenty-five, large and buxom, though neat-waisted, her face beautifully fresh and wholesome, and he of middle-size, with a lazy ease of carriage, small eyes set far apart, a blue-velvet jacket, duck trousers very dirty, held up by a belt, a red shirt, an old cloth hat, a careless carle, greatly famed."

This matter of style is important to the writer of fantasy. Shiel has a sense of swiftness which is far and away beyond the fastest action of a modern hardboiled detective story; what is more, he has the ability to convey movement of the most electrifying sort in a story in which there is no actual physical movement at all! He does it all with words, nothing more, words and their arrangement and a keen sense of word-meanings and values. If you read Shiel, let us say, *The Lord of the Sea* or *The Purple Cloud* or that breathless novel of mystery and detection, *How the Old Woman Got Home,* you are aware, no matter how critical your approach may be, of having an experience, you are pulled, drawn, almost flown along on a gloriously romantic and fantastic journey, you become conscious of a richness you never knew the English language had before, and you think of such trite words as "gorgeous" and "thrilling" and nothing really adequate to convey to your acquaintances or even to yourself just precisely what the effect of all this wild magic of words and sentences and wonderful people and deeds is, or just how it is gained.

The fact is that Shiel at one and the same time over-writes and under-writes; by that I mean to say that he says no more than is absolutely necessary in the barest sense to tell his readers of matters of speech, action, and movement generally—(he can take you across the city of London as if you were in an aeroplane with an unhampered view on all sides in the space of half a paragraph)—and he permits himself to expand when the matter is one of sensuous imagery, of color, for instance, of scene, emotional experience, and all things pertaining to the senses. In this lies his effect, but ad-

mittedly mine is a barren summary, an explanation not
entirely satisfactory, because Shiel is still more than
this. Arthur Machen, too, is a stylist in more sombre
colors, and Dunsany—in more consciously beautiful
language based on Biblical phraseology.

Style is important to the writer because it means a
great deal to the reader even if the reader is not aware
of it as style at all. A style of one's own is developed
only with time and writing experience, and sometimes
not at all. It is too easy to imitate a style or styles, or
to content one's self with simple prose and dialogue and
emphasize story above everything else. But even simplicity has its mannerisms, and the use of words and
phrases and sentences is very important in achieving
an effect. That this should be true in fantasy more than
in any other kind of writing ought to be obvious; it is
because, as I have written earlier, the fantastic setting
needs more than the prosaic in language to be made
convincing. It is all very well to catalog, which is to
say, to write in such a manner that your description
becomes only a catalog of contents, as for instance:

> The rather barren room contained only two chairs,
> a table, a picture hung askew, and a broken ped-
> estal, on which stood a bowl of colored water or
> glass, through which the sun shone.

Certainly it is all there, pat, and precise. Try it this
way:

> The only light in the room came through the half-
> opened window where the sunlight straggled in
> and shot through a bowl of green-colored water
> or glass, and from there was diffused about the
> room in a soft, emerald radiance which fell im-
> partially upon two chairs and a table, and rather
> more reluctantly, it seemed, on an indistinct pic-
> ture hung crookedly on the wall away from the
> door and window both. At any moment, it seemed,
> the broken pedestal upon which the bowl stood,

might fall, but it did not, it sustained the bowl, and the bowl sustained the sunlight, and the diffused, strange green light in turn sustained and gave life to an otherwise barren room.

The room has not had a stick of furniture added, clearly; but something more has got into it just the same. The cataloging of appurtenances has its place; but its place is not very often in the fantastic story.

But style does not consist in the use of unusual or florid words; it does not consist in thickly-strewn adjectives; it does not grow out of turgidity; style is something substantially constructed, not studied, something that flows easily and comes only from long practise. It is important to learn to write just enough and no more; many an apple has been spoiled by being cooked too much or too little, so to speak. A writer almost never consciously sets out to develop a style; this comes, given time and the will to write—and the writing. It is not only possible but advisable for the young writer who is interested in this matter of style to study a textbook or two on the subject, and to examine the evolution of a stylist's prose manner from his first to his later books.

The field of the fantastic story actually knows no boundaries except the mundane. Fantasy may be the vehicle of a delightful farce or satire. In the past decade at least two writers have been very successful with novels about miracles—Bruce Marshall with *Father Malachy's Miracle,* and Edwin Greenwood's *Miracle in the Drawing Room.* The former is more widely known, because it has been both dramatized and filmed. Its theme is quite simple—a sincere, simple-hearted priest manages to have a miracle performed, but the miracle poses a knotty problem since it a) inconveniences a number of people; b) is unorthodox; c) ought not to have been done at all without the proper authority; and the upshot of the whole matter is that the priest effects another miracle to undo the first. Now this is fantasy of a high order; true, it is primarily a satire, but its entire action depends upon the unfortunate priest's miracle, brought about solely as a point of faith.

This kind of fantasy has a satisfactory audience. So too has a book like Maude Meagher's *Fantastic Traveler*, which is all about David Martin, who took refuge in his imagination from the workaday world and had dreams more wonderful than any ever had by an opium-eater, and, to a lesser extent, because it is a relatively crude performance beside *Fantastic Traveler*, has Thomas Calvert McClary's *Rebirth*, which is based upon the assumption that at a certain hour one day all people forgot everything they knew, and had to begin over with intelligence and ability to think, without memory, customs, habits, etc., a novel idea and one not done too often in any form. E. M. Forster's famous *The Celestial Omnibus*, driven by Sir Thomas Browne and Dante, which carried a lad who loved beauty and a man who prated about it from here to yonder, among the immortals, is likewise fantasy of a high order.

The variations are virtually unlimited. Such popular novels as Oscar Wilde's *The Picture of Dorian Gray* and David Garnett's *Lady Into Fox* stand side by side with such less-known novels as Olaf Stapledon's *Sirius* and Arthur MacArthur's *After the Afternoon*. The symbolical theme of a portrait's representing an aging human soul while the body of its possessor stays young and untouched by time and dissipation. *(The Picture of Dorian Gray)*, the delightful whimsy of a lady's becoming a fox *(Lady Into Fox)*, the amusing parable of an educated and sensitive dog *(Sirius)*, and the Grecian tale of a faun, lover of Aphrodite, who had the power to enter any human body of his choice *(After the Afternoon)* are all alike fantastic, and legitimate stories of fantasy.

One of the most widely-loved books of all time is allegorical fantasy—Lewis Carroll's *Alice in Wonderland;* and one of the most pungent and philosophical of books, broadly mocking a great many beliefs of famous people, is likewise fantasy—Charles Erskine Scott Wood's *Heavenly Discourse.* Any lover of fantasy who has not yet read G. K. Chesterton's *The Man Who Was*

Thursday has a treat in store for him. An increasing taste for sheer whimsy has followed *Lady Into Fox,* and come to its fullest flower in tales of a man who could fly (*The Flying Yorkshireman* and *Sam Small Flies Again,* by Eric Knight), a letter-carrier who slowly turned into a tree (*Mr. Sycamore,* by Robert Ayre), and a man-fish (*The Man-Fish of North Creek,* by Tronby Fenstad). The man-fish story, of course, belongs to the province of folk-lore, as do a great many other tales in the early years of American letters, from Washington Irving's *Rip Van Winkle* to the anonymously invented adventures of Paul Bunyan, Mike Fink, John Henry, Pecos Bill, and a handful of other American folk heroes, all essentially regional Americana. No one has succeeded so well with the fantastic recounting of American folk-lore, to which he has added delightful whimsy and color and inventive genius peculiarly his own, as the late Stephen Vincent Benét, whose *The Devil and Daniel Webster* particularly has already become an accepted part of the best in American legend. Some of the best whimsical fantasy by contemporary writers has been gathered into two notable anthologies, which the would-be writer should not miss—*Two Bottles of Relish,* edited by Whit Burnett (1943), and *Pause to Wonder,* edited by Marjorie Fischer and Rolfe Humphries (1944).

Fantasy and comedy often go hand in hand. That series of collaborations called the "Chester-Bellocs" contains at least one hilariously funny satire which it would be instructive for both readers and writers of the fantastic story to read; it is *The Haunted House.* The Sam Small tales are primarily funny, and so are such tales as that of the languishing lady upon whom a camel came to call (*The Camel,* by Lord Berners, in *Two Bottles of Relish),* and the recent fantasy by Eric Linklater, *The Wind on the Moon,* the story of Dinah and Dorinda and their career of misconduct when the wind is on the moon.

It should be observed also that the realm of fantasy is particularly appropriate for juvenile fiction, if the writer is inclined to try his hand for one of the most critical segments of the American reading public. A great deal of juvenile fiction is fantastic in character, and much of this fantasy is extremely popular. One has only to think of the *Pooh* books by A. A. Milne and of the *Mary Poppins* books by Pamela Travers. Writing fantasy for the juvenile audience has one advantage over that for the adult reader—the juvenile reader or listener is not likely to balk at accepting any setting, no matter how strange—but strangeness of setting and prose style will not make up for an ineffective story insofar as the juvenile reader is concerned.

Once the novice at writing has determined to enter the field of fantasy, and has familiarized himself with outstanding works in the field, he will find his greatest difficulty in avoiding outright imitation. He can hardly avoid influence; the imaginative concepts of writers in the genre are usually potent enough and powerfully enough presented to take hold of the imagination very markedly, and it requires a special effort to shake one's self free of their dominance, particularly if one is at work with the same tools. Even influence ought to be avoided as much as possible, though it may be very difficult at first. The writer who writes a great deal may not even be aware of influences at work in his efforts. It was not until I had put together my first collection of weird tales (*Someone in the Dark,* 1941) and had grouped the stories that I saw clearly that the three groups had been moulded by the work of three past masters—Montague Rhodes James, Mary E. Wilkins-Freeman, and H. P. Lovecraft—though I had done the last-named group of stories in deliberate imitation of Lovecraft's manner in combination with my own lesser additions at Lovecraft's behest, repeatedly made before his death; and, having seen it, I was bound to acknowledge this influence in my introduction to that volume.

Avoiding influences and dominations yet remains secondary to avoiding the mundane; the writer of fantasy who is not possessed of a strong and vivid imagination had better raise his standards in another field.

A vivid and colorful imagination is vitally necessary to the writer of fantasy, an imagination which the prosaic desiderata of every-day life cannot affect in any telling way. Secondarily, a keen sensibility for the shadings of the meaning and color of words and phrases, and an assured skill in putting them together, coupled with a good story sense, are necessary—unless he is determined to write in the field of pure fantasy and eschew the possibility of much remuneration from his efforts. Of all the avenues open to the writer of imaginative fiction, the fantastic story offers the widest basic variety, as distinct from the tale of ghosts, of pseudo-science, and various other types within the boundaries of the imagination.

CLIVE STAPLES LEWIS

(1898–1963)

The following accounts of Lewis's last days and death speak eloquently of the love and esteem in which he was held. "Next morning he was up late, but in time to see his last guest off. As he passed the window, Green turned to wave goodbye to Lewis who was sitting at his desk just inside. There was something in that last look both of affection and farewell that told Green he knew it was 'goodbye' indeed—and he groped his way down Kiln Lane blinded with tears." Roger Lancelyn Green, Lewis's "last guest" is describing, in the third person, his leave-taking from his close friend and former teacher (Roger Lancelyn Green and Walter Hooper, *C. S. Lewis: A Biography,* New York and London: Harcourt, Brace, Jovanovich, 1974, p. 307). A source even closer to Lewis than Green is Lewis's older brother, Warren. By 1963, as the elder Lewis notes in his "Memoir," "the wheel had come full circle," and he and his brother found themselves alone and relying on one another as they had in childhood. Thus it was Warren who found C. S. Lewis unconscious and with only a few minutes to live on November 22, 1963. He recalls the moment. "Even in that terrible moment, the thought flashed across my mind that whatever fate had in store for me, nothing worse than this could ever happen to me in the future"

(*Letters of C. S. Lewis,* ed. W. H. Lewis, New York: Harcourt, Brace, and World, Inc., 1966, p. 25). These two particularly moving testimonials show how deeply Lewis affected those who knew him personally. Many others who now know him through his writings continue to be deeply affected by the thought and masterful style of C. S. Lewis.

We are fortunate that a sizable number of people close to C. S. Lewis have shared their reminiscences of him, and that scholars and critics have analyzed his life and works. Lewis has made his own contribution in his detailed and engaging autobiography, *Surprised by Joy* (1955), which recounts his early years up to his return to Christianity in 1931. In addition to this and to the other works already noted, there is the recent book by Chad Walsh, *The Literary Legacy of C. S. Lewis* (New York and London: Harcourt, Brace, Jovanovich, 1979), that contains a brilliantly succinct but inquiring precis of Lewis's life, private and public.

The following chronology and impressions derive primarily from the aforementioned sources. Clive Staples Lewis was born in Belfast on November 29, 1898. He and his brother Warren, three-and-a-half years his senior, became close lifelong friends. Both of them speak fondly of their early years, particularly those spent in the "new house," Little Lea, to which the family moved in 1905. Little Lea was a rambling Victorian house, honeycombed with passages, the sort that stimulated a child's sense of adventure and imagination. Here, in the attic playroom, "Jackie," as Lewis named himself, wrote stories and illustrated them. These happy years ended in 1908, when the children's mother died and both boys, C. S. for the first time, went away to school. His mother's death triggered Lewis's cynicism about religion, a cynicism that deepened with his very unhappy public school experience. His father finally permitted him to leave school in 1914, to be tutored by W. T. Kirkpatrick, a noted and strictly logical rationalist. Lewis spent several happy years with Kirkpatrick before going up to University College, Oxford.

in 1917. Before his first term ended, Lewis began his officer training. In September he went to the front; he was home again by April, 1918, recovering from a wound. The war seems to have had little effect of any sort on Lewis, and in 1919 he was back at his studies, in which he distinguished himself for the next several years. After some initial frustrations in getting a job—he would go nowhere but Oxford—Lewis became a Fellow at Magdalen in 1925, where he remained as tutor and lecturer until 1954. In 1931 Lewis returned to the practice of the Anglo-Catholic religion, a decision that colored the rest of his life, public and private. He accepted a prestigious position in Medieval Literature at Magdalen College, Cambridge, in 1954, a position he held until his death in 1963.

Lewis's adult life seems to have been quite happy, but not without its burdens. He was for a considerable time poor, largely because for about twenty years he generously provided a home for the mother and sister of a fellow officer, Paddy Moore, who died in the war. Even after he started collecting royalties in the 1940s he remained financially strapped because he put two-thirds of his royalties into a trust fund for charity. The death of Mrs. Moore in 1951, his Cambridge appointment, and increasing royalties made his later years financially comfortable. One of the great joys of his life was his association with the "Inklings," the group of Oxford intellectuals that met a few times a week during the war years and for some time afterward. Fellow Inklings included his brother Warren, Charles Williams, and J. R. R. Tolkien. Warren remembers Lewis's comment, stemming from a particularly happy Inklings meeting, that "no sound delights me more than male laughter" ("Memoirs," p. 14). Despite this chauvinism, another very deep relationship in Lewis's life was his marriage to Joy Davidman in 1956. When they married, Joy Davidman was already suffering from the cancer that ended her life in 1960. The intervening years, according to Warren, provided a short but intense period of great fulfillment for Lewis.

Lewis's public life was an unusually full one. He was a popular lecturer and a sought-after but demanding tutor. Nor did he confine his lecturing to the lecture hall. During the Second World War he visited numerous Royal Air Force bases, lecturing on religion. He also gave a series of religious lectures on the BBC in the 1940s. And all this time he was writing assiduously on numerous subjects and in various literary genres. He wrote works of literary scholarship, works in defense of his Christian beliefs, and works of fiction. He made a considerable impact in all three areas, but he is, and rightfully so, best known for his literary fantasies, in particular for his Outer Space Trilogy and the seven Chronicles of Narnia. The trilogy consists of *Out of the Silent Planet* (1938), *Perelandra* (1943), and *That Hideous Strength* (1945). The Chronicles appeared in rapid succession in the early and mid-fifties: *The Lion, the Witch and the Wardrobe* (1950), *Prince Caspian* (1951), *The Voyage of the "Dawn Treader"* (1952), *The Silver Chair* (1953), *The Horse and His Boy* (1954), *The Magician's Nephew* (1955), and *The Last Battle* (1956). On the basis of these ten books, Lewis ranks with Tolkien as one of the most important fantasists of the twentieth century.

In the few pages of his essay "Sometimes Fairy Stories May Say Best What's to Be Said," Lewis reflects on his reasons for choosing the fairy tale as a "Form," or "the Fantastical or Mythical" as "a Mode" in his fiction. The essay relates particularly to his *Chronicles of Narnia,* which he considers fairy tales. To a lesser degree it also sheds light on his myth-based Outer Space novels (Lewis gave *That Hideous Strength* the subtitle, *A Modern Fairy-Tale for Grown-Ups*). In this sprightly, personal essay, the author discusses the relationship between fairy tales and children. More importantly, he differentiates between genuine children's literature, which can be enjoyed by everyone, and what most adults patronizingly refer to as children's literature, which is most often enjoyed by no one. "Sometimes," one of Lewis's shorter essays, is probably his most succinct statement about a subject that preoccupied him especially in his later years: the fairy tale form of his fiction and the relationship of that form to his audience.

⋅❈ Sometimes Fairy Stories May Say ❈⋅ Best What's to Be Said

C. S. Lewis

In the sixteenth century when everyone was saying that poets (by which they meant all imaginative writers) ought 'to please and instruct', Tasso made a valuable distinction. He said that the poet, as poet, was concerned solely with pleasing. But then every poet was also a man and a citizen; in that capacity he ought to, and would wish to, make his work edifying as well as pleasing.

Now I do not want to stick very close to the renaissance ideas of 'pleasing' and 'instructing'. Before I could accept either term it might need so much redefining that what was left of it at the end would not be worth retaining. All I want to use is the distinction between the author as author and the author as man, citizen, or Christian. What this comes to for me is that there are usually two reasons for writing an imaginative work, which may be called Author's reason and the Man's. If only one of these is present, then, so far as I am concerned, the book will not be written. If the first is lacking, it can't; if the second is lacking, it shouldn't.

In the Author's mind there bubbles up every now and then the material for a story. For me it invariably begins with mental pictures. This ferment leads to nothing unless it is accompanied with the longing for

115

a Form: verse or prose, short story, novel, play or what not. When these two things click you have the Author's impulse complete. It is now a thing inside him pawing to get out. He longs to see that bubbling stuff pouring into that Form as the housewife longs to see the new jam pouring into the clean jam jar. This nags him all day long and gets in the way of his work and his sleep and his meals. It's like being in love.

While the Author is in this state, the Man will of course have to criticize the proposed book from quite a different point of view. He will ask how the gratification of this impulse will fit in with all the other things he wants, and ought to do or be. Perhaps the whole thing is too frivolous and trivial (from the Man's point of view, not the Author's) to justify the time and pains it would involve. Perhaps it would be unedifying when it was done. Or else perhaps (at this point the Author cheers up) it looks like being 'good', not in a merely literary sense, but 'good' all around.

This may sound rather complicated but it is really very like what happens about other things. You are attracted to a girl; but is she the sort of girl you'd be wise, or right, to marry? You would like to have lobster for lunch; but does it agree with you and is it wicked to spend that amount of money on a meal? The Author's impulse is a desire (it is very like an itch), and of course, like every other desire, needs to be criticized by the whole Man.

Let me now apply this to my own fairy tales. Some people seem to think that I began by asking myself how I could say something about Christianity to children; then fixed on the fairy tale as an instrument; then collected information about child-psychology and decided what age group I'd write for; then drew up a list of basic Christian truths and hammered out 'allegories' to embody them. This is all pure moonshine. I couldn't write in that way at all. Everything began with images; a faun carrying an umbrella, a queen on a sledge, a magnificent lion. At first there wasn't even anything Christian about them; that element pushed itself in of its own accord. It was part of the bubbling.

Then came the Form. As these images sorted themselves into events (i.e., became a story) they seemed to
demand no love interest and no close psychology. But
the Form which excludes these things is the fairy tale.
And the moment I thought of that I fell in love with
the Form itself: its brevity, its severe restraints on description, its flexible traditionalism, its inflexible hos-
tility to all analysis, digression, reflections and 'gas'. I
was now enamoured of it. Its very limitations of vocabulary became an attraction; as the hardness of the stone
pleases the sculptor or the difficulty of the sonnet delights the sonneteer.

On that side (as Author) I wrote fairy tales because
the Fairy Tale seemed the ideal Form for the stuff I
had to say.

Then of course the Man in me began to have his
turn. I thought I saw how stories of this kind could steal
past a certain inhibition which had paralysed much of
my own religion in childhood. Why did one find it so
hard to feel as one was told one ought to feel about God
or about the sufferings of Christ? I thought the chief
reason was that one was told one ought to. An obligation to feel can freeze feelings. And reverence itself did
harm. The whole subject was associated with lowered
voices; almost as if it were something medical. But supposing that by casting all these things into an imaginary world, stripping them of their stained-glass and
Sunday school associations, one could make them for
the first time appear in their real potency? Could one
not thus steal past those watchful dragons? I thought
one could.

That was the Man's motive. But of course he could
have done nothing if the Author had not been on the
boil first.

You will notice that I have throughout spoken of
Fairy Tales, not 'children's stories'. Professor J. R. R.
Tolkien in *The Lord of the Rings*[1] has shown that the

---

[1]Lewis almost certainly meant to refer to Professor Tolkien's essay 'On
Fairy-Stories,' to the section captioned 'Children' (pp. 33–46, but especially
p. 42, in *The Tolkien Reader,* New York: Ballantine Books 1966).

connection between fairy tales and children is not nearly so close as publishers and educationalists think. Many children don't like them and many adults do. The truth is, as he says, that they are now associated with children because they are out of fashion with adults; have in fact retired to the nursery as old furniture used to retire there, not because the children had begun to like it but because their elders had ceased to like it.

I was therefore writing 'for children' only in the sense that I excluded what I thought they would not like or understand; not in the sense of writing what I intended to be below adult attention. I may of course have been deceived, but the principle at least saves one from being patronizing. I never wrote down to anyone; and whether the opinion condemns or acquits my own work, it certainly is my opinion that a book worth reading only in childhood is not worth reading even then. The inhibitions which I hoped my stories would overcome in a child's mind may exist in a grown-up's mind too, and may perhaps be overcome by the same means.

The Fantastic or Mythical is a Mode available at all ages for some readers; for others, at none. At all ages, if it is well used by the author and meets the right reader, it has the same power: to generalize while remaining concrete, to present in palpable form not concepts or even experiences but whole classes of experience, and to throw off irrelevancies. But at its best it can do more; it can give us experiences we have never had and thus, instead of 'commenting on life', can add to it. I am speaking, of course, about the thing itself, not my own attempts at it.

'Juveniles', indeed! Am I to patronize sleep because children sleep sound? Or honey because children like it?

FÉLIX MARTÍ-IBÁÑEZ

(1912–1972)

In "The Ship in the Bottle," one of his many brilliant informal essays, Félix Martí-Ibáñez movingly describes the "most tragic day" of his life. That day was in January 1939, at the end of the Spanish Civil War, when he was forced to leave his beloved home in Barcelona, Spain. Martí-Ibáñez recalls walking into the magnificent, ten-thousand volume library he had shared with his father, wavering a long time, and finally choosing one book to take with him as a keepsake, and for inspiration. After tucking the book inside his belted jacket, he sadly walked out the door. "The book," continues Martí-Ibáñez, "was Romain Rolland's *The Universal Gospel,* and to this day it remains, now bound in fine red morocco, among my most precious possessions" (in *The Ship in the Bottle and Other Essays,* New York: Clarkson N. Potter, 1967, pp. 6–7). The anecdote is both poignant and revealing. Félix Martí-Ibáñez had many loves, but none greater than that for the written word. Happily, this grand love affair has manifested itself in some of the finest essays, short stories, travel books, and novels of the century.

Félix Martí-Ibáñez—psychiatrist, author, editor, publisher, medical historian, and world traveler—was born in Cartagena, Spain, in 1912. His father, Professor

F. Martí Alpera, was a renowned European pedagogue who wrote nearly 500 essays and books. His admiring son, Félix, in his "Interview with Myself," remembers him not only as "gentle and brilliant, kind and dynamic," but as an inspirational figure who "encouraged [him] to nurture [his] dreams and to prepare for their possible reality" (The Mirror of Souls, New York: Clarkson N. Potter, 1972, p. 287). Young Félix nurtured many dreams, but one stood above all the rest: his desire to become a doctor. Not content to merely nurture that dream, Martí-Ibáñez enrolled in the medical school of the University of Madrid, pursuing his studies with vigor and enthusiasm. After receiving his Doctorate of Medicine degree, he moved to Barcelona, where he began practicing psychiatry. The practice of medicine, however, satisfied only one of Martí-Ibáñez's twin longings. Equally strong was his desire to write. Despite the demands of his practice, he managed during his years in Barcelona to write two novels (Yo, rebelde and Aventura), and several books of medical history, as well as to edit a number of medical and literary journals. In addition, he traveled throughout Spain, lecturing on a wide variety of subjects. His remarkable talents and accomplishments did not go unnoticed by government officials. In 1937 he was appointed General Director of Public Health and Social Services of Catalonia, and shortly after he was given the position of Under-Secretary of Public Health and Social Service for Spain.

Political events have a way of dramatically changing the course of one's life, however, and the Spanish Civil War profoundly influenced the life of Félix Martí-Ibáñez. For years he had been a loyal supporter of the Republican government, even suffering serious injuries and terrible hardships for it on the Ebro front in May 1937. Had the Republican forces triumphed, Martí-Ibáñez's future in Spain would have been bright indeed; but this was not meant to be. When Franco's forces emerged the victors, Martí-Ibáñez was forced to flee the country, seeking refuge in the United States.

Spain's loss was America's gain. Martí-Ibáñez moved

to New York City, acquired American citizenship, and then proceeded to take up where he had left off during his productive Barcelona days. In the early 1950s he began the publication of several medical journals; in 1956 he was appointed professor and chairman of the Department of the History of Medicine, New York Medical College; and one year later, highlighting his illustrious career as physician-author, he created and launched the medical newsletter, *MD,* serving as its editor-in-chief and publisher. A year earlier, in 1956, the National Academy of Sciences in Cuba presented him with the Order of Carlos J. Finlay in recognition of his outstanding educational work in medicine. During this decade Martí-Ibáñez also presented over 1,000 papers and lectures at conferences held throughout the world; an inveterate traveler, he took pride in the fact that he had gone around the world at least four times. Active and productive till the end of his life, he died of a heart attack on May 24, 1972, in Manhattan.

Martí-Ibáñez was a remarkably prolific writer, especially of nonfiction. Some of his best essays may be found in the two collections that Martí-Ibáñez liked best: *The Crystal Arrow: Essays on Literature, Travel, Art, Love, and the History of Medicine* (1964), and *The Ship in the Bottle and Other Essays.* Also noteworthy is *The Mirror of Souls and Other Essays,* a collection containing some of his most popular editorial essays appearing in *MD* between 1966 and 1971, and *Ariel: Essays on the Arts and the History and Philosophy of Medicine* (1962), the fine collection containing the essay chosen for inclusion in this volume.

While he acquired a reputation for his works related to medicine, he noted in one of his autobiographical essays that his volume of short stories, *All the Wonders We Seek: Thirteen Tales of Surprise and Prodigy* (1963), was among his favorites. The stories, all written in English (he wrote some novels, short stories, and essays in Spanish), have Latin American settings and draw heavily upon the myths, legends, and folklore of this exotic part of the world. Composed between 1954 and

1963, this delightful collection of memorable fantasy stories will compare favorably with the best of the past century-and-a-half.

In "Interview with Myself," mentioned above, Martí-Ibáñez asks himself the question "What do you consider good writing?" and then answers it by seconding W. Somerset Maugham's belief that "a work, regardless of subject matter or length, should be written with lucidity, simplicity and euphony." "Tell Me a Story" offers convincing evidence that Martí-Ibáñez painstakingly followed his own advice. Although very brief, "Tell Me a Story" is a substantive, thought-provoking essay that charmingly describes the value of fairy tales to children. Written in 1959 as an editorial essay for *MD*, "Story" prefigures, in miniature, some of the primary theories Bruno Bettelheim discusses in his important work, *The Uses of Enchantment: The Meaning and Importance of Fairy Tales* (1976). In the best of all possible worlds, "Tell Me a Story" would preface all collections of fairy tales.

⋅⋅✵ Tell Me a Story ✵⋅⋅

Félix Martí-Ibáñez

Tell me a story.... Around the Christmas fireside, in the glow of crackling logs, children are pleading to be told a story. The father, perhaps a physician, may regale the children with morsels of life culled from his daily toil. But the child craves fairy tales. And when he does not get them, he then uses the magic wand of his fantasy to transmute the world around him into a glittering fairyland in which his own home becomes a luminous crystal-walled palace.

I believe in telling children fairy tales. In the past the child was considered "a little man" who had to be fed a steady diet of facts. Today we know that a child is only a child, and even when he becomes a man there still dwells in him a child, who now and then tinkles inside him as the little pebble tinkles inside a jingle bell.

All the expressions of a child are variations on the theme of his search for his own individuality, for an answer to his questions, "Who am I?" and "How can I distinguish myself from my world?" His thoughts resemble the magic thought of primitive people in the sense that he invents his own causality relations and accepts his fantasies as reality. He differentiates himself from his world not through his thinking but through his feelings and his games. Playing for him is a rehearsal of his role in real life. To the adult, play is recreation; to the child, it is hard work and serious business.

The child should be fed not only technical instruction at school but also a fantasy feast at home. The impulses that dominate childhood are biologically even more important than his culture. In the child, to *wish,* which is to dream, is more important than to *want,* which involves action. Actually, the first nourishes the second. But the child confuses them both. To him, the things he desires, however unreal, are more important than real things. If the adult mind makes history, that is, reality, the child's mind makes legends, or the desirable. Myths and legends therefore are the best psychic hormones for the child.

Fairy tales appeal to the child because their fabric is similar to that of his thought. Primitive myths and legends help us to understand the infancy of mankind, just as fairy tales show us the infancy of man.

Myths once governed the creation of European culture. Later, the gods were exiled to earth, wherefrom they still rule our daily life through the image of their mythological deeds. Only artists have remained as custodians of the gods. The rest of us, in our hurried life, do not dream enough, and daydreams are important, for they are both the truest form of dreams and the modern counterpart of myths.

Like primitive man, the child identifies himself with the outer reality in the belief that to manifest his wishes is sufficient to make them come true. In his own world, as in fairy tales, the child allots magic powers to objects surrounding him. To the child the world is a jungle bristling with dangers, as the primeval forest was to primitive man. From his awareness of his disproportion and weakness in face of the gigantic outer world were born such classic tales as *Gulliver's Travels* and *Through the Looking-Glass*.

Wolves, goblins, evil genii are fairy tale symbols of the forces in the adult world that threaten to devour the child's ego. In a tale for a child lost in the fearsome darkness of the forest—which matches that of his own bedroom—the only refuge against such forces is the magic square of gold cast upon the dark forest by the illuminated window of fairy tales. In real life, though, the child may stop dreading the nocturnal darkness once he realizes—as in the story of Madeleine Gekire—that he can with his own imagination "switch on the night," "turn on" the moon and the stars, the crickets and the frogs, and all the other wonderful lights and sounds that are part of the night.

Let us, then, keep telling children tales of wonder. And let us never forget that the most wonderful tale of all was that of a Child born on that first Christmas when Mary "brought forth her firstborn son, and wrapped him in swaddling clothes, and laid him in a manger; because there was no room for them in the inn." This tale is particularly beautiful to us as it was told almost 2000 years ago, in stained-glass words in the Gospels, by a good and kind Greek colleague, St. Luke, the beloved physician.

PETER S. BEAGLE

(1939–   )

·

The medieval alchemist had to be content with the
dream of transmuting lesser metals to precious gold;
Peter Beagle, modern literary alchemist, has made that
dream a reality in the form of his splendid works of
fantasy. This gift of transmutation is evident in all of
Beagle's works: he transforms his interest in, and deep
affection for, animals, for example, into the unforgettable portrait of the slightly neurotic, but sage and philosophical, talking raven in *A Fine and Private Place;*
his love of the ocean breakers becomes, in *The Last
Unicorn,* the liberated unicorns tumbling onto the beach,
"their bodies aching with the streaked marble hollows
of the waves"; and his whimsical thought while carrying out the garbage one day, about what it would be
like to live with a werewolf he later transmogrifies into
"Lila the Werewolf," one of the most original and engaging Gothic fantasies of our time. Yes, the alchemist's dream has become reality in the twentieth
century—thanks to Peter Beagle.

Beagle, one of the younger American writers of fantasy, was born of a middle-class Jewish family in the
Bronx. His ties with both family and city became very
strong, and thus he had great difficulty deciding, upon
graduating from high school, to leave New York so that

he could gain a different perspective. But break away he did, pursuing his education at the University of Pittsburgh. After receiving his B.A. from that institution in 1959, Beagle spent a year (1960/61) at Stanford working under a creative writing fellowship. He then lived and traveled in Europe, spending most of his two years there in Paris. After his sojourn on the Continent he returned to the United States, settling in Santa Cruz, California.

Since his return, he has produced a number of essays, reviews, short stories, filmscripts, and novels. When he is not pursuing his craft, he indulges in one or another of his favorite pastimes: cultivating relationships with animals, even though they often bring on asthma attacks; composing songs, singing, and playing the guitar (he regularly performs in a small restaurant in Santa Cruz, singing the songs of the great French "chansonniers"); and walking along the beach. Although fame and popularity came early for Beagle, he remains congenial and unpretentious (he recently began a presentation at a major academic convention by sincerely wondering aloud, "Why should anyone want to listen to me?"). Beagle now resides in Watsonville, California.

Peter Beagle began his first novel, *A Fine and Private Place* (1960), when he was a nineteen-year-old student at the University of Pittsburgh; it was published when he was just twenty-one. The New York City cemetary setting of this Gothic fantasy hardly prepares the reader for the elegance of his next full-length novel, *The Last Unicorn* (1968), a high fantasy set entirely in a secondary world. It is this work that has firmly established Beagle as one of the most respected writers of fantasy on the contemporary American scene. In between these two novels, Beagle wrote "Come Lady Death," a fantasy short story that was nominated for the prestigious O'Henry Award in 1963. His most recent fantasy work is "Lila the Werewolf" (1974), which returns to the style and New York City setting of his first book. In addition to his fiction, Beagle has written two fascinating works of nonfiction: *I See by My Outfit*

(1965), a delightful account of a transcontinental motor scooter trip that Beagle took in his early twenties; and *The California Feeling* (1969), a colorful commentary on the west coast life-style.

Since the mid 1970s, Beagle has spent most of his time writing for movies and television. His most important movie script was his collaboration with Chris Conkling on Ralph Bakshi's cinema adaption of Tolkien's *Lord of the Rings*. More recently he has been working on film scripts for both "Lila the Werewolf" and *The Last Unicorn*. In "The Self-Made Werewolf," his lively and informative introduction to *The Fantasy Worlds of Peter Beagle* (1979), Beagle confides that he has been "working on a third novel for what seems half [his] life," and that "at present, there are four or five other novels lined up inside [him], shuffling their feet, waiting their turn." Beagle enthusiasts everywhere are hoping that one of these literary prisoners soon breaks free and shuffles its way into the bookstalls.

Beagle's essays are as spellbinding as his fiction, and the review essay of Tolkien's *Lord of the Rings* trilogy (later incorporated in part into his introduction to *The Tolkien Reader*) is of interest not only to Tolkien enthusiasts, but to fantasy readers in general. Through an analysis of his own deep admiration for *The Hobbit* and *Lord of the Rings,* Beagle helps explain why millions read, and reread, these Tolkien masterworks. Although Beagle mentions several attractive features of Tolkien's epic fantasy, he sees one as holding the key to its huge success: Tolkien "believes in his world [i.e., Middle Earth], and in all those who inhabit it." Furthermore, says Beagle, readers, particularly young readers, can quickly "sense the difference between the real and the phony"; thus, sensing the genuineness of Tolkien's secondary world they explore it with trust and enthusiasm. During the past twenty-five years the great popularity of Tolkien's works has generated hundreds of critical articles and books, but none has served as a better appreciation of Tolkien and his works than Beagle's brief essay. Most importantly, perhaps, Beagle succeeds in identifying some of the most significant characteristics of all great and enduring literature.

·•✠ Tolkien's Magic Ring ✠•·

Peter S. Beagle

Three Rings for the Elven-kings under the sky,
  Seven for the Dwarf-lords in their halls of stone,
Nine for Mortal Men, doomed to die,
  One for the Dark Lord on his dark throne
In the Land of Mordor where the Shadows lie.
  One Ring to rule them all, One Ring to find them,
  One Ring to bring them all and in the darkness
    bind them
In the Land of Mordor where the Shadows lie.

Far to the north there are the Iron Hills, the Gray Mountains and the Ice Bay of Forochel; beyond that lies only the great Northern Waste. Farthest to the south is the Haradwaith, land of a dark and fierce people; on the west is the Sea, and far over the Sea are the immortal lands of Westernesse, out of which the Eldar peoples came, and to which they will all return in time. To the east is Mordor, and that was always an evil and desolate country. These are the boundaries of Middle-earth, and this is the world that J. R. R. Tolkien has explored and chronicled in *The Lord of the Rings*. I do not say *created,* for it was always there.

The Lord of the Rings and its prologue, *The Hobbit,* belong, in my experience, to a small group of books and poems and songs that I have truly shared with other people. The strangest strangers turn out to know it, and we talk about Gandalf and mad Gollum and the bridge of Khazad-dûm while the party or the classroom or the train rattles along unheard. Old friends rediscover it, as I do—to browse through any book of the *Ring* trilogy to get hooked once more into the whole legend—and we talk of it at once as though we had just read it for the first time, and as though we were remembering something that had happened to us together long ago. Something of ourselves has gone into reading it, and so it belongs to us.

The country of the book, Middle-earth, is a land much like our own, as mythical, but no more so. Its sunlight is remembered from the long summers of childhood, and its nightmares are equally those of children: overwhelming visions of great, cold shapes that block out the sunlight forever. But the forces that form the lives of the dwellers of Middle-earth are the same that make our lives—history, chance and desire. It is a world bubbling with possibility, subject to natural law, and never more than a skin away from the howling primal chaos that waits outside every world; it is no Oz, no Great Good Place, but a world inhabited by people and things, smells and seasons, like our own.

The Hobbit is our introduction both to Middle-earth and to the tale of the One Ring. Hobbits are a small, burrow-dwelling people, a little shorter than Dwarves: furry-footed, sociable growers and gardeners, fond of fireworks, songs and tobacco, inclined toward stoutness and the drawing up of genealogies. In this book, the hobbit Bilbo Baggins accompanies thirteen Dwarves and a wizard named Gandalf to aid in the recovery of a treasure stolen by a dragon centuries before. During the adventure Bilbo finds a magic ring and brings it home as a souvenir. Its gift, as far as he can tell, is to make the wearer invisible, which is useful if you are trying to avoid aunts and dragons, and Bilbo uses it for both purposes a time or two. But he makes little other use of it in the sixty years he keeps it; he carries it in his pocket on a fine chain.

The Lord of the Rings begins with Gandalf's discovery that Bilbo's ring is in truth the One Ring of the rhyme. It was made by the Dark Lord—Sauron of Mordor, ageless and utterly evil—and the lesser rings distributed among Elves, Dwarves and Men are meant in time to lure the three peoples under the domination of the One Ring, the master of all. But Sauron has lost the ring, and his search for it is growing steadily more fierce and frantic: possessing the Ring, he would be finally invincible, but without it all his power may yet be unmade. The Ring must be destroyed—not only to keep it from Sauron's grasp, but because of all the rings, the One Ring's nature is to turn good into evil—and it is Bilbo's nephew, Frodo Baggins, who undertakes to journey with it to the volcano where it was forged, even though the mountain lies in Mordor, under the eye of the Dark Lord.

The Lord of the Rings is a tale of Frodo's journey through a long nightmare of greed and terrible energy, of his education in both fear and true beauty, and of his final loss of the world he seeks to save. In a sense, his growing knowledge has eaten up the joy and the innocent strength that made him, of all the wise and magic people he encounters, the only one fit to bear the Ring. As he tells Sam Gamgee, the only friend who followed him all the long way to the fire, "It must often be so...when things are in danger; someone has to give them up, lose them, so that others may keep them." There are others in Middle-earth who would have willingly paid that price, but certainly none to whom it would have meant as much.

That is the plot; but the true delight of the book comes from the richness of the epic, of which *The Lord of the Rings* is only a few stanzas. The structure of Tolkien's world is as dizzyingly complex and as natural as a snowflake or a spiderweb: the kingdoms of Men in Middle-earth alone have endured for three ages, and each of their histories, as Tolkien sets them forth in the fascinating Appendix, contains enough material for a ballad as long as *The Lord of the Rings*. And there are other, older peoples—notably the immortal Elves—

whose memories go back to the Elder Days, long before good or evil moved in Middle-earth; there are the Dwarves and the Ents—the shepherds of the trees, "old as mountains"—and there is Tom Bombadil, who belongs to no race, no mission and no age.

Tolkien tells us something of each of these peoples— their songs, their languages, their legends, their customs and their relations with one another—but he is wise enough not to tell all that he knows of them and of their world. One can do that with literary creations, but not with anything living. And Middle-earth lives, not only in *The Lord of the Rings* but around it and back and forth from it. I have read the complete work five or six times (not counting browsing, for which this essay is, in part, an excuse), and each time my pleasure in the texture of it deepens. It will bear the mind's handling, and it is a book that acquires an individual patina in each mind that takes it up, like a much-caressed pocket stone or piece of wood. At times, always knowing that I didn't write it, I feel that I did.

The Hobbit is a good introduction to the dwellers in Middle-earth, the more so as several of its main characters appear again in *The Lord of the Rings*. In addition to hobbits, Dwarves, Elves and Men, there is Gandalf the wizard: a wanderer, known by many names to many peoples, capable of appearing as a bent, frail old man, handy with fireworks, vain, fussy and somehow comical, or as a shining figure of terrifying power, fit to contest the will of Sauron himself. And there is Beorn, the skin-changer, who can take on the shape of a bear at will; a surly, rumbling man, but a good friend. Beorn is not seen after *The Hobbit,* but in a literary sense he is the forerunner of the more deeply realized Tom Bombadil. Both are wary creatures, misliking the great concerns of other peoples. Both are their own masters, under no enchantment but their own; but old Bombadil is song incarnate, and his power is greater than Beorn's. He would be the last to be conquered if Sauron held the Ring.

But of all the characters in both books, surely the

most memorable—and by his own miserable fate, the
most important—is the creature called Sméagol, or
Gollum, from the continuous gulping sound he makes
in his throat. Gollum in ancestry is very close to the
hobbits, and it is he who discovers the Ring in a river
where it has been lost for thousands of years. Rather,
he murders to get it, for no reason that he can say except
that it is more beautiful than anything that has ever
come into his life. His name for it, always, is "the Precious." He flees up the river with it until the river flows
under the mountains, and there he hides in darkness
until Bilbo, lost in the mountains, stumbles on him and
on the unguarded Ring, which he pockets. The Ring
takes care of itself, as Gandalf realizes: it gravitates to
power; it goes where it has to go. But Gollum cannot
live without his Precious, and it is not long before he
leaves the mountains to search for it. In his wanderings,
he eventually picks up the trail of Frodo and Sam, and
is captured by them and made to lead them into Mordor,
where he has once been Sauron's prisoner. From then
on he is either along with them or in sight of them
almost continually until the end of their journey—and
of his own equally terrible odyssey.

At the time Frodo takes him, Gollum is, of course,
quite mad. The dark, silent centuries of living with the
Ring's hunger, and the torments of Sauron after that,
have burned his mind away to a single, glowing cinder
of meaningless desire. He is two creatures now, two
voices that hiss and chatter in him night and day: Gollum and Sméagol—one no person at all, no *I*, but the
Ring's thing; the other somehow still alive, still retaining a few shreds of its own will after all this long time,
and even able to feel a stunted, grotesque yearning
toward Frodo, whom he must betray. He cannot abide
light—even the face of the moon is a physical anguish
to him—and he is afraid of almost everything in the
world, most of all Sauron. Moreover, Gollum is dangerous; he has long been a cannibal, and his ruined
body keeps a rubbery, unnatural strength. Bilbo and
Sam and many others have chances to kill him, but

each time the idea of his suffering, vaguely as they may conceive it (and it takes someone who has borne the Ring, even for a little while, to understand Gollum's agony), prevents them; and so he lives to play out his part in the story of the Ring. In the end he haunts the imagination perhaps more than any other character in *The Lord of the Rings,* which is fitting, for he was already a ghost when the story began.

Sauron himself is never seen, except for one terrifying moment when a hobbit's mind makes contact with his in a *palantír,* a seeing-stone.

But Sauron's servants are as visible as their single-minded energy can make them: Orcs and trolls, bred up by him in mockery of Elves and Ents, as incapable of any creation as their lord, taking no delight but in ugliness; barrow-wights, cold spirits dwelling in the ruined burial mounds of kings; all manner of Men, from barbarians of the woods to the cruel Haradrim, who ride "oliphants," to kings and princes who have fallen into Sauron's various traps of means and ends. Of these latter, the most ill-fated, the most lost and ghastly, are the Nazgûl, the Ringwraiths, each of whom was once a man, a king who came under the power of the Nine Rings that were made for mortal men. Astride great birds or riding black horses they cast freezing shadows as they hunt to and fro over Middle-earth on their master's errands, forever calling to one another in thin voices full of evil and a kind of pitiless sorrow. They are creatures out of a child's dream of clouds across the moon, searching for him, called by the beating of his heart; but they are also men destroyed, and Frodo, seeing them with the Ring on his finger, comprehends the nature of their damnation. Their doom is very nearly his.

For the Ring devours. It is a kind of burning glass through which all the selfishness in the world can be brought to focus, and to wear it is to be naked both to the Eye (for Sauron let a great deal of his original strength go into the making of the Ring, and it calls to him) and to one's own deepest desires for power over others. Like everything else that belongs to the Dark

Lord, the Ring cannot truly create: it can give power, but only according to the wearer's true strength and stature; and its possessor does not die, "but he does not grow or obtain more life," as Gandalf says, "he merely continues." It has stretched Bilbo's life dangerously thin, and Gollum's past his mind's endurance; and the long burden of it has wounded Frodo beyond healing. He speaks for the wretched Gollum and even for the Nazgûl when he says to Sam:

"No taste of food, no feel of water, no sound of wind, no memory of tree or grass or flower, no image of moon or star are left to me. I am naked in the dark, Sam, and there is no veil between me and the wheel of fire. I begin to see it even with my waking eyes, and all else fades."

The book is full of singing. Ballads and poetry and rhymes of lore belong to the daily lives of the peoples of Middle-earth, and epic poetry is their history and their journalism. Each of the different races and tribes, excepting the dwellers in Mordor, has its own traditions of song, and Tolkien renders them all—from the Elvish modes and patterns of rhyming to the proud chanting of Dwarves and the music-hall turns that the hobbits love—with the skill and naturalness of a writer whose own prose is itself taut with poetry. The best of the verses begin to sing themselves as you read them; as do the names of people and places, for that matter—one could almost sing the maps that Tolkien includes with each volume. And the music is never imposed from outside; it springs from the center of this world, as it does from the world of the *Iliad* and the *Nibelungenlied*. Tolkien's people would sing, and they would sing like this.

The books have sold quietly but steadily in the United States since Houghton Mifflin introduced them, but within the last few years the sales have begun to gather momentum. Ballantine Books has published a paperbound version approved by Tolkien, which includes a foreword and some new material.

The real surge of interest in Tolkien's writing has

been among high school and college students. Students make strange and varied works their own, and if there is any significance to their adoption of *The Lord of the Rings*—beyond the fact that it's a good book—the hell with it; one or another of our explainers of the young will take note of it pretty soon. But there is one possible reason for Tolkien's popularity that I would like to put forward, because it concerns the real strength of *The Lord of the Rings*. Young people in general sense the difference between the real and the phony. They don't know it—when they begin to know that difference, and to try to articulate it, then they are adults and subject to all the pains and fallibilities of that state. They can be misled by fools or madmen, but they sense the preacher who doesn't feel a word of his sermon, the mountebank who is putting them on, the society that does not believe in itself. They rarely take a phony of any sort to their hearts.

Tolkien believes in his world, and in all those who inhabit it. This is, of course, no guarantee of greatness—if Tolkien weren't a fine writer, it could not make him one—but it is something without which there is no greatness, in art or in anything else, and I find very little of it in the fiction that purports to tell me about this world we all live in. This failure of belief on the authors' part is, I think, what turns so many books that mean to deal with the real things that really happen to the real souls and bodies of real people in the real world into the cramped little stages where varyingly fashionable marionettes jiggle and sing. But I believe that Tolkien has wandered in Middle-earth, which exists nowhere but in himself, and I understand the sadness of the Elves, and I have seen Mordor.

And this is the source of the book's unity, this deep sureness of Tolkien's that makes his world more than the sum of all its parts, more than an ingenious contrivance, more than an easy parable of power. Beyond the skill and invention of the man, beyond his knowledge of philology, mythology and poetry, *The Lord of the Rings* is made with love and pride and a little madness. There never has been much fiction of any sort made in this manner, but on some midnights it does seem to me that my time is cheating itself of even this little. So I have read the tale of the Ring and some other books many times, and I envy my children, who have not yet read any of them, and I envy you if you have not, and wish you joy.

LLOYD ALEXANDER

(1924–   )

The calendar read December 30 (1978) but the weather suggested a sunny mid-April day, and our visit to Lloyd Alexander turned out to be Christmas and Springtime combined. We had spent several uncomfortable early morning hours, starting out with a New York subway and ending up with a commuter train to finally get to Drexel Hill, outside of Philadelphia, where Alexander, a Philadelphia native, and his wife Janine, live. All of the discomforts vanished when he generously met us between the station and his home, saying, "You never know when it will snow around here."— Alexander is, on the surface, a congenital pessimist. We were imposing on him to gather information for a biographical essay for a book since completed (*Alexander, Walton, Morris: A Primary and Secondary Bibliography*, G. K. Hall, 1981). We gained much more than biographical information; we were treated to warm hospitality and friendship by both Lloyd and Janine (whose cooking is a memorable delight), who made the occasion a joyful one for us. And we discovered one of the reasons that Lloyd Alexander is such a successful writer: he has an affection for the art of writing that embraces not only the creative skills, but also his subjects and his audience.

137

Lloyd Alexander's love for his art dates back at least to a decision he made at age fifteen to become a professional writer, a decision that has exercised great influence over his subsequent activities. He took several different jobs after high school and spent a semester in college, but not finding what he was looking for, he enlisted in the army in 1943. Alexander laughs now at his romantic ideas about the army, which quickly disappeared. But, while getting shot at failed to inspire him, he had a number of experiences which have subsequently enriched his writing. One was that he met and married Janine Denni in Paris in 1946. Another was the considerable time he spent as a member of army intelligence, in Wales where the rugged beauty of the countryside entered his imagination.

Equipped with these experiences, he returned to Philadelphia, where he got a job and pursued his writing at night. Seven years and three unpublished novels (including the war book) later, he decided to write directly about his personal nonwartime experiences, and saw his first book published in 1955 (*And Let the Credit Go*). For several years, he wrote with moderate success in a witty, autobiographical vein, both fiction and nonfiction. *Janine is French* (1959) is the outstanding example of the latter. More complete success came with his decision to write a children's book, *Time Cat*, published in 1963.

Through writing *Time Cat*, Lloyd Alexander discovered that the medium best suited for him to say what he wanted to say is the kind of book that appeals to children, and to adults who are mature enough to enjoy good children's literature. He discovered something else when researching for a chapter on Druids; this was *The Mabinogion*, the chief source of Welsh myth and legend. These two finds provided the medium and the material for what may remain Alexander's most significant work, the five books that comprise the Prydain cycle: *The Book of Three* (1963); *The Black Cauldron* (1965); *The Castle of Llyr* (1966); *Taran Wanderer* (1967); *The High King* (1968). Chief among the many awards these books received was the Newbery Medal in 1968. Responding to the extraordinary number of requests, Alexander did an encore in the form of a number of short stories related to the cycle. These appeared in 1973 as *The Foundling and Other Tales of Prydain*.

Lloyd Alexander had by 1973 achieved his goal of becoming a successful professional writer, and he continues to perform as one. Notable among his several more recent all-ages fantasies is *The Marvelous Misadventures of Sebastian,* which won for him the National Book Award in 1970. He was a finalist for the same award in 1978 for *The First Two Lives of Lukas-Kasha.* Alexander's most recent venture is away from fantasy, though not completely. He has written two books of a projected trilogy which uses the same device Le Guin employs in her Orsinian works, a setting which does not exist but which very closely resembles a real one. In Alexander's case the setting is clearly Western Europe of the Eighteenth Century. The subject is war—interestingly, the same general subject as the first of his unsuccessful early works. This time the author succeeds. *Westmark* (1981) received in 1982 the American Book Award for young adult literature. And *Kestrel* (1982) is perhaps Alexander's finest single novel.

As one might expect of a writer who has devoted himself so single-mindedly to developing his craft, Alexander has reflected upon his profession and has shared his reflections in more than forty essays and reviews. Many of these have appeared in *The Horn Book* and, more recently, in *Cricket,* a very literate children's magazine that Alexander helped to begin in 1973. The essay that follows appeared in *The Horn Book* in 1968, at a time when many young people were questioning society's values. Alexander discusses fantasy as an attractive vehicle of inner values, the chief of which is a capacity for belief in values. Such belief is the foundation of hopeful dreaming, a much more productive activity than wishful thinking. The author is himself, then, encouraged—indeed optimistic—because of the considerable increase in fantasy literature.

Wishful Thinking—or Hopeful Dreaming?

Lloyd Alexander

Anyone close to children—librarians, teachers, maybe even parents—knows they do not hesitate to come out with straightforward questions. I am beginning to learn this for myself, although the process has been a little backwards: Instead of getting to know children first, then writing books for them, the opposite is happening. It is only recently I have had some happy occasions to meet real live children. And not only in schools and libraries. At home I often discover a few hanging around the kitchen or perched on the sofa, swinging their heels. We talk a while, they tell me what a hard day they have had, I tell them what a hard day I have had— there's really not much difference. But they constantly surprise me. The other afternoon one little girl asked, "What would you rather do: be a millionaire or write books for children?"

She asked this question very seriously, and I thought about it very seriously before answering. First, her perception impressed me. She sensed immediately, possibly from the state of the living room, that indeed I was not a millionaire; and she set up her question with two mutually exclusive choices, showing keen insight into basic literary economics.

I gave her an absolutely honest answer. I said I would rather write books for children.

Of course, I added, if somebody felt inclined to give me a million dollars tax-free, in all politeness I could not refuse.

But my answer was truthful. And I believe any serious, creative person—and this includes teachers and librarians, for I've learned how really creative they are—would have said the same. Because—despite our status-oriented society, our preoccupation with "making it," with staying young forever, buying safe deodorants and unsafe automobiles—I think something new is happening.

Whatever our individual opinions, I think each of us senses that as a people we are in the midst of a moral crisis—certainly the deepest of our generation, perhaps of our history. Few of us are untouched by a kind of national anguish. And it hurts. But if we felt nothing, if nothing moved or troubled us, then I fear we would be truly lost. For isn't anguish part of growing up? Without knowing grief, how can we ever hope to know joy?

In the past, we have always been able to find technical or technological solutions to our problems. They have been external problems, for the most part, yielding to external solutions. And so we are not quite used to problems demanding inner solutions. In an article on fantasy, Dorothy Broderick points out that the English have dealt with fantasy more comfortably than we have and comments that perhaps, since England is so much older a nation, Englishmen have had time to ask Why? instead of only How?

It is true we haven't had long years of leisurely speculation. But, ready or not, the time for us is now. A dozen Whys have been put to us harshly and abruptly. And searching for the Why of things is leading us to see that purely technological answers are not enough.

We have machines to think for us; we have no machines to suffer for us, or to rejoice for us. Technology has not made us magicians, only sorcerer's apprentices. We can push a button and light a dozen cities. We can also push a button and make a dozen cities vanish. There is, unfortunately, no button we can push to relieve us of moral choices or give us the wisdom to understand the morality as well as the choices. We have seen dazzling changes and improvements in the world outside us. I am not sure they alone can help change and improve the world inside us.

We are beginning to learn that intangibles have more specific gravity than we suspected, that ideas can generate as much forward thrust as Atlas missiles. We may win a victory in exploring the infinities of outer space, but it will be a Pyrrhic victory unless we can also explore the infinities of our inner spirit. We have supersensitive thermographs to show us the slightest variations in skin temperature. No devices can teach us the irrelevance of skin color. We can transplant a heart from one person to another in a brilliant feat of surgical virtuosity. Now we are ready to try it the hard way: transplanting understanding, compassion, and love from one person to another.

Even as an ardent pessimist, I believe we are starting to think in these terms. Tentatively, gropingly, making a huge number of mistakes. But starting, nevertheless. I think more and more people realize that the status we gain through humanity is more valuable than the status we buy or gain at the expense of others. We know we cannot get ourselves a soul with Raleigh coupons.

I should add that I am not speaking against science or the scientific attitude. The old controversy between the sciences and the humanities is a tempest in an academic teapot. It is a false controversy. One doesn't preclude the other; there is really no essential conflict between the motives and goals of the sciences and those of the humanities.

But I do think we are seeing a shift in emphasis in favor of the humanistic attitude, bringing it into a more active role in our understanding of human nature. Lewis Mumford, for example, in *The Myth of the Machine* stresses that man is a being of restless imagination, an Elephant's Child of insatiable curiosity, a creator not only of tools but of language. Man's inner drives, dreams, incoherent yearnings, his inventiveness more than his inventions, are what made, and still make, Homo sapiens human.

To me, one of the clearest reflections of this changing attitude is a growing appreciation of fantasy in children's literature. The climate for fantasy today is vastly different from what it was twenty, even ten years ago, when the tendency was to judge fantasy as a kind of lollipop after the wholesome spinach of reality—a tasty dessert, but not very good for the teeth.

Now I think we see fantasy as an essential part of a balanced diet, not only for children but for adults, too. The risks of keeping fantasy off the literary menu are every bit as serious as forgetting to brush with Gleem or missing the minimum daily requirements of thiamine, niacin, and riboflavin. The consequences are spiritual malnutrition, tired blood that even Geritol cannot cure.

Most significant are the numbers of professionals who take fantasy seriously as an important facet of children's literature. I say "facet" because, like the facets of a diamond, all aspects of children's literature, and all literature, are indissoluble parts of the same thing. There is, I believe, a unity of all art. If man and nature are one, together in the same life-process, then I think there must be only one basic art-process. The results are different; the impulse is the same.

All art, by definition of the word, is fantasy in the broadest sense. The most uncompromisingly (should I say sordidly?) naturalistic novel is still a manipulation of reality. Fantasy, too, is a manipulation, a reshaping of reality. There is no essential conflict or contradiction between literary realism and literary fantasy, any more than between science and humanism. Technical details aside, most of the things you can say about fantasy also apply to realism. I suppose you might define realism as fantasy pretending to be true; and fantasy as reality pretending to be a dream.

Of course, for practical reasons—and librarians and teachers understand these better than anyone—we are obliged to categorize and separate. Like it or not, we become specialists. The best we can do is make sure we are not nearsighted specialists. We can always keep in the back of our minds the idea that whatever our specialty, it is still an integral part of the whole. Literature for children is not a quiet backwater, but a current of the mainstream.

In addition to being part of the mainstream, children's literature is considerably more functional than a good portion of adult literature. If I were cynical, I might say: Children's books are written to be read; adult books are written to be talked about at cocktail parties.

There may be more truth than cynicism in that statement. My impression is that many adult books are written only to shock the reader (a short-term goal, since shock turns quickly into boredom) or as calisthenics for the author's ego.

On the other hand, children's literature seems an area where books function as they were meant to; where they amaze, delight, and move our emotions. We can respect and admire any number of current adult books, but I find it hard to love them.

And when children love their books, they love them very well indeed. There is a personal relationship between a child and a favorite book that we never quite duplicate after we grow up.

Books of fantasy are certainly not least in a child's affections—and in the affections of many children; more, perhaps, than we suppose.

A number of educators judge that fantasy appeals strongly to the more imaginative, sensitive child and estimate the deepest appreciators of fantasy to be a relatively small minority. This is true, in a way. But, I think, only in a way. We could as well say the deepest appreciators of Bach, Mozart, or Beethoven are a small minority. The number of connoisseurs of anything— food, wine, or fantasy—is small. But the number of enjoyers is large. Fantasy delights more kinds of personalities than we might suspect. Would you believe *Winnie-the-Pooh* a best seller in Russia? And in the

United States, of course, the tremendous popularity of *The Lord of the Rings* is most significant.

Can we say: Scratch a hard-shelled realist and find a lover of fairy tales? Maybe. Because fantasy does offer unique experiences and special values to many readers. And, for the matter of that, to writers.

Writing fantasy has given me more personal joy than anything I have done before. Whatever the merits of the end result, I have never been so caught up in a work, nor loved working so much as I have in these past few years. I daresay most writers of fantasy feel the same way. I am not altogether sure why this should be so. Whatever a writer's reasons, they do not particularly matter so far as the reader is concerned. In the writer-reader relationship, the reader is more important (a truism, though a discouraging number of writers for adults tend to ignore it).

For readers, then, some of the special values of fantasy: First, on the very surface of it, the sheer delight of "let's pretend" and the eager suspension of disbelief; excitement, wonder, astonishment. There is an exuberance in good fantasy quite unlike the most exalted moments of realistic literature. Both forms have similar goals; but realism walks where fantasy dances.

Still, this is only surface. If imagination sinks to mere cleverness, and inventiveness to gimmickry, fantasy drops like a cold soufflé. Below the surface, fantasy must draw on its own deeper resources.

For example, fantasy's ability to work on our emotions with the same vividness as a dream. The fantasy adventure seems always on a larger scale, the deeds bolder, the people brighter. Reading a fantasy, we are never disinterested bystanders. To get the most from it, we have to, in the best sense of the phrase, "lose our cool."

This may be one clue to the growing interest in fantasy. We may be a little weary of being cool. In fantasy, we have more plausible scope for strong feelings, the noble gesture, the eternal passion. (In fantasy, when the hero tells the heroine he will swim oceans for her, he might literally mean it—and do it.) We can fear for the lovers, despise the villain with that delightful hatred with which we honor only the most despicable villains. In short, in all good artistic conscience, we can laugh harder, weep longer—and be a little corny. Bearing in mind the high nutritive value of corn.

These feelings, I suspect, are what children respond to. It may even explain a little why children relish books we judge mediocre or trashy. It is not that children enjoy a silly story more than a good one. But they must find, amid the junk, bits of whatever dream their appetites crave. I think adults do the same.

Another value of fantasy—I'm thinking now of a book by Jean Shepherd, *In God We Trust, All Others Pay Cash,* where he takes a penetrating but very loving look back at his own childhood. He claims he believed in the Easter Bunny until he was twenty; and, talking about his own absolute faith in the Santa Claus of his boyhood, he says: "Later generations, products of less romantic upbringing, cynical non-believers in Santa Claus from birth, can never know the nature of the true dream."

There is a psychological and sociological truth in what he says. In dealing with delinquency—I do not mean the delinquency that poverty breeds, but the kind of cold-hearted emptiness and apathy of "well-to-do," solid middle-class delinquents—one of the heartbreaking problems is interesting these young people in something. In anything. They value nothing because they have never had the experience of valuing anything. They have developed no *capacity* for believing anything to be really worthwhile.

I emphasize the word *capacity* because, in a sense, the capacity to value, to believe, is separate from the values or beliefs themselves. Our values and beliefs can change. The capacity remains.

Whether the object of value is Santa Claus or Sunday school, the Prophet Elijah or Arthur, the Once and Future King, does not make too much difference. Having once believed wholeheartedly in something, we seldom lose the ability to believe. It is like learning to ride a bicycle. Once we know how, we never forget. We may become disillusioned or disappointed with what we believed in. But we can discover better, more satisfying values. Disillusion, however painful, is never so long lasting nor so destructive, to ourselves and to others, as disinterest.

But this capacity for values comes at a fairly early age. The child who does not develop it before adolescence may have trouble developing it at all. Young children yearn for values; the younger they are, the clearer they want those values to be. They crave true heroes, not antiheroes (they can find out about them later); they have a taste for justice, mercy, and courage, which may be naïve and unrealistic to adults. But they will have time to puzzle over the complexities and ambiguities of these virtues in the real world. Indeed, without the simplicities first, they may be ill-prepared to deal with the complexities.

Fantasy can deal with virtues and faults in their simplest terms, in pure primary colors. Again, as Dorothy Broderick says: "The world of fantasy insists that good is always good and cannot be made evil by circumstances; conversely, no amount of pragmatic rationalization can turn evil into good."

Fantasy, by its power to move us so deeply, to dramatize, even melodramatize, morality, can be one of the most effective means of establishing a capacity for adult values.

Having once glimpsed its nature, having once been caught up in a great dream, we can always dream again—and hope the dream will come true.

Perhaps, finally, the ability to hope is more important than the ability to believe. In his book *Images of Hope,* William F. Lynch writes: "Hope comes very close to being the very heart and center of a human being."

But there's a difference between hopeful dreaming and wishful thinking.

Wishful thinking, at no matter what age we do it, is basically passive, withdrawn, and isolated. It implies no effort beyond the wish itself. The wishful thinker says, "If only..." and retreats farther and farther from the real world. He gives himself no chance whatever to have his wish granted.

Hopeful dreaming is an active process. The hopeful dreamer is willing to take his tumbles with the world, not insisting on the immediate gratification typical of infantile demands, but with the patience that is one sign of growing up. The hopeful dreamer says, "If not now, maybe someday...."

Hope is one of the most precious human values fantasy can offer us—and offer us in abundance. Whatever the hardships of the journey, the days of despair, fantasy implicitly promises to lead us through them. Hope is an essential thread in the fabric of all fantasies, an Ariadne's thread to guide us out of the labyrinth, the last treasure in Pandora's box. If we say, "While there's life, there's hope," we can also say, "While there's hope, there's life."

Human beings have always needed hope, and surely now more than ever. This need for hope may be the prime element in the new interest in fantasy.

If so, if we have come to value hopeful dreaming instead of wishful thinking, I read it as a sign of our own maturity. Our ability to accept fantasy joyously and wholeheartedly is one step, a giant step into real adulthood. We, as adults, might have relearned something children already know.

Our growing acceptance of fantasy isn't happening in a vacuum. It is part of the artistic development and upgrading we can see throughout the entire field of children's literature.

The editors of *School Library Journal* suggest that "some distant commentator will look back" and accurately view today's librarians as "living in a Golden Age for serving a young reading audience."

I believe they are right. But I do not think we are in the midst of this Golden Age. More likely we are just beginning. If we can look forward to a Golden Age in children's literature (not wishfully thinking, but hopefully dreaming) we can by the same token look forward to a Golden Age in fantasy.

We have a treasure trove of great fantasies from the past. Now it is our turn to enlarge it with still greater ones for the future. I believe we are ready to do it.

At least—I hope so.

ANDRE NORTON

(1912–   )

Andre Norton is one of the first women and one of the most prolific writers in the fields of contemporary science fiction and fantasy literature. Her first novel appeared in 1934 when she was just twenty-one—at which time she legally changed her name from Mary Alice to Andre. Since then, according to Roger Schlobin's count, in his indispensable *Andre Norton: a Primary and Secondary Bibliography* (Boston: G. K. Hall, 1980, p. xv), Norton has added eighty-six novels and twenty-eight short stories to her list. This list includes historical novels, mysteries, and adventure stories in addition to science fiction and fantasy. While most of the works have a broad, all-ages appeal, a lesser number aim more specifically at young adults.

Though critical attention has been slow in coming, popular attention has been strong and steady. Schlobin points out that her works typically have a long print life, with a number of them exceeding a million sales in paperback; she has been translated into nine different languages; she has been nominated twice for the Hugo award, for *Witch World* (1963) and for *Wizard's World* (1967); and in 1977 she received the Gandalf Award for her "lifetime achievement in fantasy" (Schlobin, xv). She has also received a number of lesser known, somewhat specialized, but nonetheless significant awards, such as the plaque from the Dutch government in 1946 for *The Sword is Drawn,* a historical novel about the Dutch underground in the Second World War. In light of such a rich publishing record, it is indeed somewhat puzzling that Norton does not receive more critical attention. Two reasons that could account for the slightness of such attention are Norton's quiet personality and her ill health, both of which keep her out of the limelight. Until 1967 she had spent most of her life in her native Cleveland, Ohio. She entered college in what is now Case Western Reserve University but had to leave in 1931 after one year, because of the Depression. She continued taking evening classes in writing for some time but never took a degree. From 1932 through 1950 she worked as an assistant librarian in the Cleveland system, with one short excursion to Washington, D.C. (1940–41). In 1950 she retired from the library because of ill health; she worked at the Gnome Press until 1958, after which she devoted herself full-time to writing. Her health finally dictated a move from Cleveland, and in 1967 she moved to Florida where she now continues her prolific writing career. She does not give talks or make public appearances at conventions.

Shyness and ill health may account for her remaining relatively unknown among critics, but it also may be that Norton is simply more devoted to entertaining her fans than she is concerned about her press notices. During her years as a children's librarian she developed original stories for the Special Story Hours. The short novel eventually published as *Steel Magic* (1964; also as *Grey Magic*) is an excellent example of one such work. Like many of Norton's novels, *Steel Magic,* an all-ages fantasy, whisks the readers along with its adventure-filled, engrossing narrative. One can envision the ring of enchanted listeners, as the librarian-become-storyteller casts her spell. Indeed, the Norton style is that of the storyteller; this is where she excels. And Roger Schlobin is probably correct when he suggests that her narrative skills account, ironically, for her critical neglect: "she is a superb storyteller and her command of the narrative form is at times so effective that even the most critical reader becomes too enthralled to reflect and analyze" (p. xiv). After reading (or better yet, hearing) *Steel Magic,* for example, critical readers would agree that the conflicts are slight and that there are some inconsistencies in the work. They would conclude, however, by saying, "but it's a fascinating tale," and that is no small achievement, at least in the view of some. As C. S. Lewis has noted, "Perhaps the pleasure of Story comes as low in the scale as modern criticism puts it. I do not think so myself, but on that point we may agree to differ" ("On Stories" in *Of Other Worlds,* New York: Harcourt, Brace & World, Inc., 1966, p. 3).

While it is difficult to single out individual works from Norton's extensive corpus, it is easy to single out a group as her best work: The Witch World Series. Beginning in 1963 with *Witch World* and continuing, at present, through 1979 with "Sand Sister" (see Schlobin's convenient list, p. 14), Norton has written fourteen short stories and eight novels related to Witch World, a secondary world where magic thrives in a medieval atmosphere. Some of the works belong to a central core; *Warlock of the Witch World* (1967) is one of the best of the core works. Most of the short stories and a few of the novels have more or less distant links to the core works. Among the best of these are *Year of the Unicorn* (1965) and *The Crystal Gryphon* (1972). Sandra Miesel's introduction, in Volume I of the seven-volume Gregg Press edition of the Witch World Series, explains the relationships among the twenty-plus works.

Norton wrote the essay "On Writing Fantasy" to answer the question "Where do you get your ideas?" She cites a number of sources, including historical novels, histories, and encyclopedic reference works in a variety of fields. Historical research is Norton's beginning point. The essay is revealing in other ways. It shows the care she takes in her selection and use of detail. It also provides an invaluable example of how history and the imagination work together to produce what Tolkien has termed a sub-creation. And finally, the essay nicely exhibits the universality of Norton's own tastes in fiction reading.

·✦· On Writing Fantasy ·✦·

Andre Norton

One of the first and most common questions put to any writer is: "Where do you get your ideas?" That is sometimes difficult to answer in particulars, but in general, the one source one must rely on is reading. In fact, the writer must read widely in many fields. For my own books (unless I am dealing with some specific period of history when research becomes highly concentrated) I read anthropology, folklore, history, travel, natural history, archeology, legends, studies in magic, and similar material, taking notes throughout.

But the first requirement for writing heroic or sword and sorcery fantasy must be a deep interest in and a love for history itself. Not the history of dates, of sweeps and empires—but the kind of history which deals with daily life, the beliefs, and aspirations of people long since dust. (And it is amazing to find such telling parallels between a more ancient world and ours, as in the letter from the young Roman officer, quoted by Jack Lindsay in *The Romans Were Here,* who was writing home for money in much the same terms as might be used by a modern G.I.) While there are many things we can readily accept in these delvings into other times, there are others we must use imagination to translate.

There we can find aids in novels—the novels of those inspired writers who seem, by some touch of magic, to have actually visited a world of the past. There are flashes of brilliance in such novels, illuminating strange landscapes and ideas. To bring to life the firelit interior of a Pictish broch (about whose inhabitants even the most industrious of modern archeologists can tell us little) is, for example, a feat of real magic.

Read such books as Price's *Made in the Middle Ages*—then turn from her accounts of the great medieval fairs to the colorful description of the Thieves' Market in Van Arnan's *The Players of Hell*.

Renault's *The King Must Die:* here in Crete, and something within the reader is satisfied that this must be close to reality. Joan Grant's Egypt of *The Eyes of Horus* and *The Lord of the Horizon*, Mundy's *Tros of Samothrace* and the *Purple Pirate*—Rome at the height of its arrogant power but as seen by a non-Roman—the wharves of Alexandria in the torchlight of night, the great sea battles, a clash of arms loud enough to stir any reader.

Turn from those to the muted despair and dogged determination against odds in Rosemary Sutcliff's Britain after the withdrawal of the last legion—the beginning of the Dark Ages—as described in *The Lantern Bearers* and *Swords in the Sunset*. This lives, moves, involves the reader in emotion.

Davis's *Winter Serpent* presents the Viking coastal raids, makes very clear what it meant to live under the shadow of the "Winged Hats." And, a little later, the glories and the grim cruelties of the Middle Ages are a flaming tapestry of color in such novels as Barringer's *Gerfalcon* and its sequel, *Joris of the Rock;* Adam's *Desert Leopard* and Graham's *Vows of the Peacock* are also excellent.

There are "historical" novels, but their history is all sensuous color, heroic action raised to the point where the reader is thoroughly ensorcelled and involved.

So history is the base, and from there to imagination, rooted in fact, sun-warmed by inspired fiction, can flower into new patterns. And those can certainly be ingenious and exciting.

The very atmosphere of some portion of the past can

be carried into fantasy in a telling fashion. Take Meade's *Sword of Morningstar,* which gathers in the telling validity from the author's interest and research into the history of the Robber Barons of Germany and the Black Forest region. Beam Piper's *Lord Kavin of Otherwhen* envisions a world in which the sweep of the migrating Aryan peoples—the People of the Axe—turned east instead of west, flowing through Asia, China, to eventually colonize this continent from the west instead of the east, with an entirely different effect on history.

Though historical novels can furnish impetus for story growth, the basic need is still history. General history can be mined at will, but there are various byways which are very rich in background material.

Herrmann's *Conquest of Man,* a fat volume to open new vistas as it discusses the far range of those Bronze Age traders who set out in their small ships hugging unknown coastlines in the Atlantic, or the North Seas, or went on foot with their trains of laden donkeys into new lands. Thus he presents a wealth of new knowledge barely touched upon by the usual history book.

Four Thousand Years Ago by Bibby—a world spread of history at a single date. What were the Chinese doing when Pharaohs held the throne of Egypt? And what then was going on in Peru, Central America?

Lewis Spense's careful studies of near forgotten legend and lore in his native British Isles, *Magic Arts in Celtic Britain* and the like, are very rich in nuggets to be used.

Rees gives us *Celtic Heritage,* Uden the beautifully illustrated *Dictionary of Chivalry,* Oakeshott's *Archeology of Weapons*—page after page of information on swords, shields, any other armament your hero needs.

Desire a new godling to squat in some shadowed temple? Try *Everyman's Dictionary of Non-Classical Mythology* and be straightway amazed at all the diverse gods the men of this world bowed head to down the ages.

For the layout of a castle, plus the numeration of a proper staff to man it, try Byfield's delightful *The Glass*

Harmonica (which also goes into careful detail on such matters as trolls, ogres, and the training of sorcerers); it is indispensable. And Thompson's *The Folktale,* a careful listing of the basic plot of every known tale and its many variations, is a book to keep to hand.

The professional writer does have to build up his or her own library, though the rich shelves of the public libraries await. Unfortunately, many of the volumes one wishes the most for reference are also the most expensive. But there is an answer—the remainder houses which send out at monthly or six-week periods catalogues of their stock. For one half, one third of the original price one can pick up such volumes when dealing with Marboro or Publishers Central Bureau. And, in recent years, the paperback house of Dover has been reissuing long out of print works in folklore, history and natural history.

So, one has the material, one has the plot—now comes the presentation. One must make come alive for the reader what one has created in one's mind.

Rider Haggard, who was the master of the romantic action adventure at its birth, stated firmly that those who write such books must themselves live in their creations, share every hope and care of their people. And this is the truth; you cannot write fantasy unless you love it, unless you yourself can believe in what you are telling. (Unfortunately, as every writer learns, that which goes on paper, in spite of all one's struggles, is never the bright and shining vision which appeared in one's mind and led one to get to work. At times a scene, a page—if one is exceedingly lucky, a chapter—may draw close to the dream, but one is always left unsatisfied with the whole.)

The approach may be direct in the use of ancient saga or legendary material without much alteration. And this can result in excellence if done by a skillful craftsman who has steeped him or herself in the subject. In this category are such outstanding books as Walton's *Island of the Mighty,* those books by Thomas Swann based on classic myths, Garner's two stories based on

ancient legends of Britain: *Weirdstone of Brisinggamen*
and *Moon of Gomrath*. While Poul Anderson drew first
on Scandinavian sources for *The Broken Sword,* and
then on the Charlemagne cycle for *Three Hearts and
Three Lions,* Emil Petaja works from a classic lesser
known to the general American public when he draws
from the Finnish Kalevala for a series of adventures.
And Sprague de Camp has given us *The Incomplete
Inchanter* with its roots in Spencer's *Faerie Queen: The
Land of Unreason*—Oberon's kingdom plus the legend
of Barbarossa; and *The Wall of Serpents,* another presentation from the Kalevala. Nicholas Gray has turned
directly to fairy tales, writing the haunting and memorable *Seventh Swan* and the amusing *Stone Cage*. The
former "what happened after" in the fairy tale of the
Seven Swans wherein the hero, the seventh brother of
that story, is forced to adjust to living with a swan's
wing in place of his arm. While in the latter, he gives
a new and sprightly version of Rapunzel.

From that background of general legend comes the
work of masters who are so well read in such lore that
they create their own gods and sagas, heroes and mysteries. Tolkien's Middle Earth is now so deeply embed-
ded in our realm that his name need only be mentioned
to provide a mountain-tall standard against which other
works will be measured perhaps for generations to come.

Lord Dunsan is another of the masters. Eddison's
Worm Oroborous is perhaps a little mannered in style
for modern taste, but his descriptions are, like Merritt's,
so overflowing in color and vivid beauty they flash across
one's mind in sweeps of hues and forms one readily
remembers.

To sample some of these earlier writers one can at
present easily turn to the series of books under the
editorship of Lin Carter—issued by Ballantine—where
for the first time in many years some of the older, and
to this generation perhaps even unknown, writers are
introduced again. Such books as *Dragons, Elves and
Heroes, The Young Magicians, Golden Cities, Far* provide small tastes. But this series also reprints in full

length the works of William Morris, Dunsany, Cabell and kindred writers.

Those modern writers who create their own worlds stand well when measured to these pioneers, with some pruning of the dated flourishes of another day.

Hannes Bok, who was an artist with paint and brush, as well as with pen, produced *The Sorcerer's Ship*. Using the classic saga approach of the quest we have such treats as Van Arnan's *Players of Hell* and its sequel *Wizard of Storms*. David Mason gives us two excellent examples of the careful building of an entire world detailed to the full in *Kavin's World* and *The Sorcerer's Skull*. Ursula Le Guin has *Wizard of Earthsea,* an offering which not only presents a strange island-sea planet, but makes clear the training of a would-be sorcerer, and the need for self-control in handling great forces. Jack Vance explores a far future in which our almost exhausted world turns to magic in its last days in his *Dying Earth*. And Katherine Kurtz with *Deryni Rising* pictures a dramatic meeting of alien forces in a strange setting loosely based on Welsh myths.

The common pattern of most sword and sorcery tales which incline to action-adventure is a super-man hero, generally a wandering mercenary (which is an excellent device for moving your hero about). Of this company Robert Howard's Conan is perhaps the best known—unless one may list Burroughs's John Carter thus. Howard's plots may have been stereotyped, but his descriptions of sinister ruins and sharp clash of action move the stories into leadership in the field. We now have John Jakes's Brak, a Viking type wanderer whose adventures tend to get better with each book. There is also Lin Carter's Thonger of Lemuria. And the unbeatable Grey Mouser and Ffahrd whom Fritz Leiber moves about an ancient world seeming to have some parts in common with our own middle east, but highly alien in others.

From the super-man we come to Moorcock's flawed heroes who tend to have massive faults as well as abilities, swinging sometimes to evil. The Elric of the demon-souled sword, and he of the four Runestaff stories are ambivalent.

There are moments of humor in the adventures of the Grey Mouser and his companion in arms, the great northerner Ffahrd. But Sprague de Camp, almost alone of the writers of fantasy, can handle the humorous element as a continued and integrated part of the adventure itself. His teller of tales who is also a doughty fighting man, the hero of *The Goblin Tower,* is something quite different from the humorless Conan or the stormy men of Moorcock. Only the much put-upon magician of Bellairs's *Face in the Frost* can compare with him.

Brunner's *Traveller in Black* is still another type. A troubler of the status quo, he does not fight, merely uses his own form of magic to adjust the scales of alien gods in many lands. Wandering by the demands of some strange pattern he does not understand, on a timeless mission decreed by something beyond the human, he seems to drift, and yet his adventures have all the power of straight action.

These are the heroes, but what of the heroines? In the Conan tales there are generally beautiful slave girls, one pirate queen, one woman mercenary. Conan lusts, not loves, in the romantic sense, and moves on without remembering face or person. This is the pattern followed by the majority of the wandering heroes. Witches exist, so do queens (always in need of having their lost thrones regained or shored up by the hero), and a few come alive. As do de Camp's women, the thief-heroine of *Wizard of Storm,* the young girl in the Garner books, the Sorceress of *The Island of the Mighty.* But still they remain props of the hero.

Only C. L. Moore, almost a generation ago, produced a heroine who was as self-sufficient, as deadly with a sword, as dominant a character as any of the swordsmen she faced. In the series of stories recently published as *Jirel of Joiry* we meet the heroine in her own right, and not to be down-cried before any armed company.

When it came to write *Year of the Unicorn,* it was

my wish to spin a story distantly based on the old tale of Beauty and the Beast. I had already experimented with some heroines who interested me, the Witch Jaelithe and Loyse of Verlane. But to write a full book from the feminine point of view was a departure. I found it fascinating to write, but the reception was oddly mixed. In the years now since it was first published I have had many letters from women readers who accepted Gillan with open arms, and I have had masculine readers who hotly resented her.

But I was encouraged enough to present a second heroine, the Sorceress Kaththea. And since then I have written several more shorter stories, both laid in Witch World and elsewhere, spun about a heroine instead of a hero. Perhaps now will come a shift in an old pattern; it will be most interesting to watch and see.

At any rate, there is no more imagination stretching form of writing, nor reading, than the world of fantasy. The heroes, heroines, colors, action, linger in one's mind long after the book is laid aside. And how wonderful it would be if world gates did exist and one could walk into Middle Earth, Kavin's World, the Land of Unreason, Atlantis, and all the other never-nevers! We have the windows to such worlds and must be content with those.

JANE LANGTON

(1922–   )

In the essay that follows, Jane Langton opines that
what gives a book quality is not so much "the good
idea...systematically worked out" as it is "the interests
and obsessions" of the writer herself. Her own case presents a good example, for it is her obsession with Concord, Massachusetts, and its rich historical and literary
background—the American Revolution; Thoreau,
Emerson, and Alcott—that invests her best writings
with their exceptional quality. In her comments to
Something about the Author, she notes that she is "lucky
in living in a town next to Concord. We go there very
often for shopping, and walking or driving one is wad-
ing through air which to me seems thick with meaning." One of her favorite pastimes is painting her house
which, she points out with a charming smugness, "is
on the shore of what used to be known as Flint's Pond.
Henry Thoreau first wanted to build his house here,
but Mr. Flint wouldn't let him, and he had to make do
with Walden, a mile or two away."

Jane Langton was born in Boston, not far away from
her beloved Concord, on December 30, 1922. She attended Wellesley (1940–42) and the University of
Michigan (B.S., 1944 and M.A., 1945). She earned a
second M.A. from Radcliffe in 1948. From 1955 to 1956

she worked for WGBH television in Boston, doing art work and visual materials for an educational program in the natural sciences called Discovery. She evidently enjoyed the art work but missed school, so Langton took classes for a year at the Boston Museum School for Art. She married William Langton in 1943, and they have three sons. Langton clearly has impressive academic credentials—she is also a Phi Beta Kappa—but does not seem overly impressed by it all; she lists as one of her pleasures, "the confusion of domestic life."

The confusion of domestic life is, in fact, a motif common to most of her writing for young people, including her delightful series of realistic fantasies involving the rich past of Concord: *The Diamond in the Window* (1962), *The Swing in the Summerhouse* (1967), *The Astonishing Stereoscope* (1971), and the most recent *The Fledgling* (1980). On the basis of these works, Francis Molson accurately describes Langton as a writer of "'Nesbitian' Fantasy—but with an American flavor," referring to Nesbit's "distinctive blend of realism and fantasy" (*Twentieth Century Children's Writers,* p. 730). In all four works Langton ingeniously merges present-day Concord with the Concord of the past. Her work is also reminiscent in its blend of realism and fantasy of one of her favorite works, T. H. White's *Mistress Masham's Repose,* a book which she describes as producing "a succession of small effervescent, bursting sensations in the mental taste buds" (*The Horn Book Magazine,* October 1981, p. 565). Her own Concord books are similar treats for children and adults of good taste.

Langton is a polished essayist, as "The Weak Place in the Cloth" demonstrates. She borrows the magical curtain from Nesbit and uses it as an extended metaphor to categorize eight types of fantasy, depending on how one gets through the curtain that divides the real from the unreal. The curtain is a selectively permeable barrier between lands, times, and states of being. In the second part of the essay, Langton gives us a clue to her own success when she speaks of how "realism sharpens fantasy" and of the importance, in this regard, of character development. It is also in this second part that the author comments on what gives fantasy its significance. Langton effectively organizes her discussion according to the three questions that a writer—or reader—of fantasy should ask: "What if? Then what? So what?"

··❖· The Weak Place in the Cloth: ·❖··

A Study of Fantasy for Children

Jane Langton

Part I

Analyzing books of fantasy for children is like explaining a joke after everyone has laughed. Who cares how *Stuart Little* (Harper) differs from *Mary Poppins* (Harcourt)? If you've read them, that's all that matters. But, as a writer of fantasy for children, I want to find out exactly what I've been trying to do so long by intuition and imitation. So I've been sorting and categorizing a lot of old and new favorites to see if I can make some sort of sense out of them. The result is a modest set of conclusions concerning the three primary questions which each fantasy asks and answers *What if? Then what? So what?*

WHAT IF ?

What if rugs could fly? What if pigs could talk? Every writer of fantasy poses a *what-if* question that is the theme of his book. He can ask it in many ways, and all of these ways are different approaches to the dividing line between truth (the real world) and fantasy (the unreal world). For E. Nesbit, the dividing line was a piece of cloth.

> There is a curtain, thin as gossamer, clear as glass, strong as iron, that hangs forever between the world of magic and the world that seems to us to be real. And when once people have found one of the little weak spots in that curtain which are marked by magic rings, and amulets, and the like, almost anything can happen.

There are at least eight different uses which have been made of this cloth by writers of fantasy. In the first, the fabric remains whole. It is merely stretched a little out of shape. The entire story happens on the real-world side of the curtain. These books are tall tales. Who's to say they couldn't happen? What if, for example, someone imitated the Pied Piper and invented a contraption to trap mice with music?

> Through the streets of Centerburg rolled Mr. Michael Murphy.... The mice came running from every direction!... They all went running up the ramps and runways and disappeared in Michael Murphy's musical mouse trap.

A musical mousetrap? Unlikely, but not impossible, not beyond the stretch of the fabric we're talking about. The cloth may be getting a little thin in spots, but it's still whole.

In a second kind of book, the cloth is punctured. The characters leak through the hole into another world. Somewhere near the beginning of all of these books there are episodes like these.

> In another moment Alice was through the glass, and had jumped lightly down into the Looking-glass room.

"This must be a simply enormous wardrobe!" thought Lucy, going still further in and pushing the soft folds of the coats aside to make room.... A moment later she found that she was standing in the middle of a wood...with snow under her feet.

Sometimes the weak point in the cloth is not a place but a thing, a device, a charm of some sort. For the children in one of my books, it is the Astonishing Stereoscope.

There was a great clanging sound. The lenses in front of his eyes rushed outward on all sides, the papery specks and cracks on the surface of the picture disappeared, and Eddy suddenly found himself *inside the stereoscope.*

Edward Eager's children find an extraordinary book on the bottom shelf of the fairy-tale section in the library, which turns on some Seven-Day Magic.

Barnaby nodded excitedly: "It all adds up. Think of it sitting there all those years, with the magic from all those other books dripping down onto it!...And we came and wanted a magic story; so that's what it turned into."

Eleanor Estes invented one of the cleverest devices for tearing a hole in the fabric. The two little girls in her *Witch Family* (Harcourt) draw pictures with crayons, and it is the pictures themselves which create and control what happens on the other side of the cloth. In some of the most celebrated books of fantasy for children, the knife that rips the cloth is not a place nor a thing but a magic person. Peter Pan is one; Mary Poppins is another.

Jane and Michael edged toward Mary Poppins.... "How did you come?" Jane asked. "It looked just as if the wind blew you here.!" "It did," said Mary Poppins.

It is interesting to see how carefully all the writers who tear holes in the fabric of reality patch it up again at the end of the book. The magic volume goes back to the library; the stereoscope is put back under Eddy's bed; the children tumble out of the wardrobe. Mary Poppins flies away; so does Peter Pan. But the reader is often left with the pleasant suspicion that the stitching on the patch isn't very good and that the hole will fray through again.

In a third kind of fantasy, the cloth dividing *here* from *there* is invisible and totally permeable. The two worlds live side by side. No device is needed to turn peculiar events on and off or to escape into the unreal world. It is there all the time, hidden from view. Its inhabitants live uneasily just out of sight of ordinary human beings. In T. H. White's *Mistress Masham's Repose* (Putnam) his young heroine, Maria, stumbles upon a hidden colony of the descendants of Lemuel Gulliver's Lilliputians.

> She saw: first, a square opening, about eight inches wide, in the lowest step...next, she saw a seven-inch door in the base of each pillar...finally, she saw that there was a walnut shell, or half one, outside the nearest door.... There was a baby in it.

Mary Norton's pocket-sized people, the Borrowers, go to great lengths not to be seen by the human beings from whom they borrow.

> "Stillness...that's the thing," Pod whispered to Arrietty the first time he saw Miss Menzies crouching down behind her thistle. "They don't expect to see you, and if you're still, they somehow don't. And never look at 'em direct—always look at 'em sideways like. Understand?"

Of necessity, perhaps, the inhabitants of all of these secret side-by-side worlds seem to be small in scale.

The fourth kind of *what-if* fantasy has its origin in myth, folk tales, and fairy tales. It is the opposite of the first kind. Again the fabric is whole and unbroken, but this time we are on the other side of it. We do not have to find a way through to some fantastic place where anything might happen, because we are there already. We know from the beginning of the story that we are in Once-Upon-a-Time. This realm is no Centerburg nor Cherry-Tree Lane nor domestic establishment under the kitchen floor, but it is a kingdom we all know and recognize and feel at home in. If we were to place it vaguely in space and time, we would attach it to northern Europe and sometime between the fall of Rome and the invention of the internal-combustion engine, and populate it exclusively with wizards, witches, jesters, goose-girls, youngest sons, aristocrats of royal blood, absolute monarchs, and a scattering of peasantry.

"That may be as may be," said the Swan Maiden. "For listen! I serve the witch with three eyes. She lives on the glass hill that lies beyond the seven high mountains, the seven deep valleys, and the seven wide rivers; are you man enough to go that far?" "Oh, yes," said the prince, "I am man enough for that and more too."

The next morning she asked the princess how she had slept. "Slept!" cried the princess. "I didn't sleep a wink!"

Perhaps it is presumptuous to say anything against a form which has survived so long and which still has so many distinguished exemplars, but in my opinion it is difficult in the age of television to say anything fresh in this format. Ten thousand TV cartoons have cranked the life out of it, often cleverly.

> THWUP! The beautiful princess
> turned into a toad.
> "YUK!" said the handsome prince.

"But, dearie," said the toad, "I'm still a
     princes deep down inside."
"Princess, schmincess," said the
     prince.

The fifth kind of fantasy asks the question, "What
if beasts could talk?" In this sort of book, loquacious
animals from the other side of the dividing membrane
punch their way through into the real world and take
over. There is no magic; there are no spells. Everything
is perfectly normal with the single exception that animals behave like human beings. Kenneth Grahame's
Mole and Rat, for example, behave exactly like a pair
of polite Edwardian gentlemen living on comfortable
incomes of a few hundred pounds a year. And listen to
this white mouse, conducting a meeting of the Mouse
Prisoner's Aid Society, in Margery Sharp's *Miss Bianca*
(Little).

"And now," said Miss Bianca, consulting her notes,
"we come to the main item on the Agenda.... Can
everyone hear me at the back?"

In Hugh Lofting's stories about Dr. Dolittle, Polynesia
the parrot is a kind of Rosetta Stone.

Being a parrot, Polynesia could talk in two languages—people's language and animal language.
She was able to explain to the Doctor the mean-
ings of the nose-twitching, ear-scratching and tail-
wagging signals that make up the language of
animals.

This, of course, is the reverse of animals talking like
human beings, since it is Dr. Dolittle who talks like
animals, but the sober domesticity of Hugh Lofting's
beasts is altogether human. All of these books, too, have
ancient beginnings.

But unfortunately, the Hare overslept himself;
therefore when he awoke, though he ran his best,

he found the Tortoise was already at the goal. He had learned that "Slow and steady wins the race."

In the sixth kind of fantasy, there are overlays in time. In some of these stories the present moment dissolves and becomes the past; in others someone from an earlier period in history bursts through the fabric dividing *now* from *then* and emerges among us, to be astonished by washing machines and Chevrolets. In *A Traveler in Time* (Viking) Alison Uttley uses the device of an Elizabethan house as the permanent background for shifting sets of occupants. A child opens doors to find ancestors in ancient rooms, and then returns to the present. But no one merges past and present more seamlessly and masterfully than William Mayne. In some of his settings, the past is embodied in relics and monuments which litter the landscape, it incarnates itself in optical effects of light, it spills out of the cracks in the sky, it moves restively under the soil, it maintains a kind of urgent pressure on the present day. Witness the emergence into the *here* and *now* of Nellie Jack John, Mayne's eighteenth-century drummer boy, in *Earthfasts* (Dutton).

The ground stirred. The stirring did not extend beyond the swelling in the turf. But there was movement, a lot of movement. It was as if someone were getting out of bed. And with the movement came clear drumming.... There was light, increasing light, pure and mild and bleak.

David tried to say that it was the last of the day shining on moving water, but the words would not form themselves, because his jaw was trembling....

It was not light on moving water.... The light was from a little flame. The little flame came out from the hillside, and balanced in the air, and the wind bent the flame over but did not blow it out....

There was a shadow before their eyes, against the hill.... In the dusk the little flame was brighter than they had imagined. It was not standing in the air by itself. It was being held there by a person, and that person was drumming on a side drum, and looking round, and smiling....

"I wasn't so long," said the drummer. "But I niver found nowt."

In a seventh kind of fantasy (ghost stories), the dividing piece of cloth is a shroud, a veil between life and death. The dead pluck at the curtain, draw it aside with their wasted hands, and enter among the living. Behold Sir Edmund Orme.

He stood there without speaking—young, pale, handsome, clean-shaven, decorous, with extraordinary light blue eyes and something old-fashioned, like a portrait of years ago, in his head, his manner of wearing his hair.... He looked again strangely hard at me, harder than anyone in the world had ever looked before; and I remember feeling rather cold and wishing he would say something. No silence had ever seemed to me so soundless.

Henry James has tempted me away from the subject of children's books, but, of course, there are masters of the same tradition writing for young people. Leon Garfield is one.

The phantom stood in the merciless sunshine: a little boy of seven, dressed in an old-fashioned sailor's suit. Its hair was fair and curling; its face was of an unearthly pallor. The clerk gave a harsh scream and clutched onto the area railings. He glared down in rage and terror at the ghost of his childhood.

In this catalogue of an uncataloguable subject there is an eighth and final item, science fiction: a vast body of literature irreducible to a single example. One can only suggest that in such works of the fantastic imagination the curtain hangs between a finite present and a kind of infinite future, a time in which the possibilities of knowledge will be infinitely extended or in which nature itself will be discovered to be infinitely varied.

Part II

Then What?

"When once you have thought of big men and little men," said Samuel Johnson of *Gulliver's Travels,* "it is very easy to do all the rest." He was wrong. It took a Jonathan Swift to decide that the best way to capture a sleeping giant was to attach to the ground every hair of his head. "Big men and little men," was Swift's *what-if.* The Lilliputians' technique for capturing Gulliver was part of his *then-what.* While it is true that the *what-if* question establishes the axiomatic ground-of-all-being for each book and that in itself it must be fresh and interesting, the consequences of this *what-if*—Well, what happens then?—must be worked out successfully. Samuel Johnson to the contrary, it isn't easy. But the more diligently, searchingly, carefully, and cleverly the author figures out what happens, the more convincing and absorbing his book will be.

To ask the question, "Then what?" is to ask what corollaries follow from the original axiomatic "What if?"

AXIOM *(what-if):* What if a New York City mouse went to visit a friend in the country?

COROLLARY *(then-what)*: Like the hero of George Selden's *Tucker's Countryside* (Farrar), he might get hay fever; and, lacking citified things like Kleenex, he would have to blow his nose on a fern.

AXIOM: What if a little girl discovered a secret colony of Lilliputians?

COROLLARY: She might fly one of them in her toy airplane, with disastrous results. (In *Mistress Masham's Repose*, T. H. White thinks up some of the most brilliant *then-whats* of all.)

AXIOM: What if a girl woke up one morning and discovered she had turned into her mother?

COROLLARY: She might stay home from school, watch television, and fire the cleaning lady, as did Annabel in Mary Rodgers' *Freaky Friday* (Harper).

It is important to see that once the fabulous axiom has been stated, the writer must cleave to logic. He must rack his brain to answer the question, "Given such-and-such a situation, what would really happen?" It is the *really* that is to be stressed. *Realism sharpens fantasy*. Take a magic boy, take a Neverland, take some flying children, take a fairy, take all of these fabulous things—what is it that makes this mishmash work? Homely touches that have the feel of truth: The fairy is jealous of Wendy; when Peter Pan loses his shadow, it is sewn back on with a needle and thread.

Of course, the most important key to the *then-what* question is the realness of the characterization. Sharply-drawn characters—whether children, miniature people, elves, or animals—make the cleanest rip in the cloth of reality. Commonsensical Alice, for example, is the handle by which we are able to grasp at Wonderland. Her down-to-earthness throws the Mad Hatter into wild relief. Without her solidity the nonsense would be tenuous and meaningless. And it is the human qualities of Milne's animals that make his Hundred-Acre Wood an enchanted place: Pooh's kindness and humility, his gluttony and courage.

And meet in person young Maria, who stumbles upon the Lilliputians. She nearly rears up off the page in passages like this one.

She was one of those tough and friendly people who do things first and think about them afterward.... Her happiest times were when the Vicar was in London and Miss Brown was in bed with a headache. Then she would be mad with pleasure, a sort of wild but earnest puppy rushing about with the slipper of her imagination, tearing the heart out of it.

Thus when the Lilliputians turn up, we believe in them instantly, because we believe so wholeheartedly in Maria.

Any experienced plotter of books for children knows another dread necessity, another *then-what* question to which he must provide an answer right off-the-bat. The child reading the book must be made to care what happens next, to read on, to be caught on a hook of suspense. The writer must set his stakes high, as soon as possible. In *Rabbit Hill* (Viking) Robert Lawson gets you worrying about his young rabbit hero, Little Georgie, by having him recite for his father a list of the dogs on the route of a journey he must make.

"House on Long Hill: Collie, noisy, no wind—Norfield Church corner: Police Dog, stupid, no nose—On the High Ridge, red farmhouse: Bulldog and Setter, both fat, don't bother—Farmhouse with the big barns: Old Hound, very dangerous."

You can bet Little Georgie is going to encounter that old hound, and so you read on eagerly. Here's another, a terrifying conversation between a tactless sheep and E. B. White's young spring pig in *Charlotte's Web* (Harper).

"Well, I don't like to spread bad news," said the sheep, "but they're fattening you up because they're going to kill you...." "They're going to *what?*" screamed Wilbur.

175

So What?

Two young friends of mine read a thousand books between them one summer when they were about twelve. They will forget most of them, but they will remember some. What is it that makes a book unforgettable? What does it all add up to, the *what-ifs* and the *then-whats?* After all the invention and the action and the pretty devices, *so-what?* What makes for quality?

I can think of two things that set some books of fantasy apart. The first thing, surely, is a strongly realized personal vision. It is the writer himself and his interests and obsessions that count, not simply his vague fondness for children or for the good idea he has systematically worked out. William Pène du Bois is a writer with an obsession. Here he talks about Auguste Piccard's attempts to go a mile up into the sky and a mile down into the sea.

> There was something in this ambition of his which excited me...turned me on.... Thus in my books the most often found prop is the ladder. Peggy Moffit falls down coal holes. Peter Graves goes up, straight up—all of my nuts go up and down. Otto digs dinosaurs. The three policemen go to sea in fish suits. Angels fly to work pulled by kites. The star performer in my latest book, *Bear Circus,* shoots straight up through a hole in a circus tent.

The obsession comes first, and the books come after. The result is a succession of books with a special quality all their own. When you open one of them and turn the pages, you are traveling in a place invented by William Pène du Bois, one that belongs to him and to nobody else. Other writers have discovered and mapped their own personal geographies, and they are places as real to us now as Iowa or Tibet or the Bronx: Laurent de Brunhoff's Celesteville, where Babar is king; the Cherry-Tree Lane of P. L. Travers and Mary Poppins; Maurice

Sendak's land where the Wild Things are; C. S. Lewis's Narnia; the foolish villages of Isaac Bashevis Singer; Milne's Hundred-Acre Wood; Antoine de Saint Exupéry's Asteroid B-612, inhabited by the Little Prince; Edward Lear's Torrible Zone and the hills of the Chankly Bore; Tolkien's Middle Earth; Tove Jansson's Moominland; Hugh Lofting's Puddleby-on-the-Marsh; Margery Sharp's Black Castle and Diamond Palace; the various hilarious provinces of Dr. Seuss. This gazetteer could go on and on. Each of these places is somehow whole and perfect and entire—*real-ized* and altogether there. With the borders of these imaginary territories placed end-to-end, a child's mental dominion can stretch all the way to Homer's Ithaca or Shakespeare's forest of Oberon. A world like this is rich freight to carry around inside any child's head.

The other quality that sets apart some books of children's fantasy is, of course, a second level of meaning—significance, symbolism, allegory; a stab at a moral, a message, a lesson. The meaning may be as bald as the last sentence in one of Aesop's fables ("slow and steady wins the race") or as unpretentious and delicate as the distillation from the modest adventures of Milne's animals (what it means to be a friend). Meaning is not easy. Sometimes the attempt at it is too vaguely vast, too preachy-teachy, too thin and scant. But when it works, the book gains a value that may outlast the short time-span during which a young reader is available to us. It may last him all his life.

James Thurber's *Wonderful O* (Simon) is an example. It is an artful allegory that explains what freedom is. And the famous chapter in *The Wind in the Willows* (Scribner) about the piper at the gates of dawn interjects into the story about Rat, Mole, and Toad an experience of God.

[A]nd, then, in that utter clearness of the imminent dawn, while Nature, flushed with fullness of incredible colour, seemed to hold her breath for the event, he looked in the very eyes of the Friend and Helper; saw the backward sweep of the curved horns, gleaming in the growing daylight....Then, the two animals, crouching to the earth, bowed their heads.

Hugh Lofting's Dr. Dolittle embodies a Schweitzer-like reverence for life. Dr. Seuss's elephant Horton discovers that a person's a person no matter how small. And Seymour Leichman's book, *The Boy Who Could Sing Pictures* (Doubleday), praises art, poetry, and storytelling.

It was like no song they had heard before. His voice was high, sweet and clear. He sang about the farmer and he sang about the land and he sang about the doves and he sang about the river and the rainbow....He knew he would sing forever against the sadness. The miracle did not happen all at once. It happened first when he sang about the doves. And they appeared. And the people saw them. Then the rainbow. And the people saw it. They could see in the air above them, everything that he sang.

Ben saw it too, and more. He looked into their faces, into their eyes and the sadness was gone. They had seen a beautiful thing. Ben left the stage.

No one cheered. You do not cheer a miracle.

You do not itemize and analyze a miracle either, which is what I have been trying to do. And it has leaked through my fingers, spilling numbered headings and subheadings. Now I want to pick it up and rearrange it differently, because there is one thing that hasn't been said. Perhaps it is the only thing that can truthfully be said of all of these books, and it is the secret of their deathless charm.

They are all dreams. They are waking dreams. They make up to us for the sense of loss we feel when we wake up and find our dreams shrinking out of memory. A literary fantasy gives us a dream back to keep. Here is one of Lewis Carroll's, straight from the edge of the bed.

> "He thought he saw a Banker's Clerk
>   Descending from the bus:
> He looked again, and found it was
>   A Hippopotamus."

Most children's fantasies are not as midnight-pure as that, but surely the reason why we are so inexhaustibly delighted by mice that talk and spells that work and the Dong with the Luminous Nose is that we spend a third of our lives asleep, with bankers' clerks dissolving into hippopotamuses. Nonsense pleases. We want the laws and verities to be different from the ones by which we are trapped during the day. Like Dr. Seuss's foolish king we want something new to come out of the sky, not just this everlasting sunshine, rain, and snow, even if the new thing turns out to be sticky green Oobleck, and a disaster. And when the writer of a literary fantasy adds real children to this surreal landscape, when he inserts a flesh-and-blood Alice into his Wonderland, we are given in one package both ends of our daily experience. It is a mixture of waking and dreaming, and that has a pungency that satisfies. It feeds a hunger we didn't know we had.

URSULA K. LE GUIN

(1929–   )

"I still have my first completed [fantasy] short story, written at age nine.... At ten or eleven I wrote my first science fiction story" ("A Citizen of Mondath," *The Language of the Night,* ed. Susan Wood, New York: G. P. Putnam's Sons, 1979, p. 26). So states Ursula K. Le Guin in reflecting on her writing career and the influences on it. The detail with which Le Guin is able to trace the evolution of her writing underlines her almost lifelong and very serious commitment to the art. Her commitment has resulted in a high quality and an unusual diversity and has won for her widespread recognition. She has become an important contemporary American author and is, very possibly, the outstanding practitioner of science fiction and fantasy among contemporary writers.

The outline of Le Guin's career to date is not an unusual one for the talented daughter of talented, scholarly parents. She was born on October 21, 1929, in Berkeley, California, to Alfred and Theodora Kroeber, both well known anthropologists. Ursula also seemed headed for a scholarly, academic career. She went to Radcliffe where she studied French and Italian, graduating as a Phi Beta Kappa in 1951. She took her M.A. at Columbia in 1952 and headed for Paris as a

Fulbright Fellow. There she met Charles Le Guin, a French history scholar; they married in December of 1953. Although she did subsequently teach French in college for a couple of years, she did not continue working for a Ph.D. after her marriage. Rather she concentrated on making a home for her husband and herself and their three children. They live in Portland, Oregon, where her husband teaches at Portland State. "A Look at Le Guin" in Barbara Bucknall's *Ursula K. Le Guin* (New York: Frederick Ungar Publishing Company, 1981, pp. 1–14), provides a good biographical sketch, a nice supplement to the autobiographical "A Citizen of Mondath."

Marriage and a family probably helped to divert Le Guin's career from teaching back to writing. She thus returned to the career that she had begun at the age of nine, a career that had its roots in her early reading of myths, legends, and fairy tales and her listening to her father's rendering of Indian folk tales. She had also discovered a book in her father's library by the classic fantasy writer Lord Dunsany, creator of the land of Mondath in which Le Guin took up imaginative residence. The extent of her more mature, early writing is implied in her statement that by 1960 or 1961 she "had written five novels in the last ten years" (*Language of the Night,* p. 28). Alfred Knopf had turned one of these down in 1951. That novel, like most of her work before 1960, was set in the fictitious land of Orsinia, a country roughly resembling a Central European one. These works defied categorization as either fantasy or realistic fiction, which explains why they were not published. Needing an established genre, she chose science fiction some time after 1960, a few years before she began her remarkable list of successes.

Her first longer work of science fiction to be published, *Rocannon's World,* appeared in 1966. Just three years later, Le Guin won the two prestigious science fiction awards, The Hugo and The Nebula, for *The Left Hand of Darkness.* Even more successful, *The Dispossessed* won the Nebula and Jupiter (given by teachers of science fiction) awards in 1974 and the Hugo in 1975. Relatively few writers have, like Le Guin, won acclaim in both science fiction and fantasy. In the same year that she won her first Nebula (1969) Le Guin won the prestigious Boston Globe-Hornbook award for *A Wizard of Earthsea*, a fantasy for young adults. The second book of this now famous trilogy, *The Tombs of Atuan*, was a 1972 Newbery Honor Book. The third book, *The Farthest Shore*, won the National Book Award for children's literature in 1973. Further evidence of Le Guin's versatility is her volume of poetry, *Wild Angels* (1975); her collection of short stories, *The Wind's Twelve Quarters* (1975); and the 1979 collection of her essays, noted above. She finally got an Orsinian novel *(Malafrena)* published in 1979; her most recent novel is a fantasy entitled *The Beginning Place* (*Threshold* is the English title) which *School Library Journal* picked as one of the best young adult books of 1980.

We are fortunate that Le Guin shares her experiences and talents through articles and teaching in classes and workshops (more examples of her versatility). "Dreams Must Explain Themselves" is a personal essay recounting her "discovery" of Earthsea, the imaginary world of her fantasy trilogy. Le Guin has become conscious that hers is an intuitive approach to writing. She discovers her characters and settings and their names as she writes, instead of sketching them out ahead of time. She also reiterates one of her pet peeves, that adults make an unfortunate mistake when they discount children's literature as beneath them. In the Earthsea Trilogy, Le Guin deals with the subjects of the coming of age, sex, and death, none of which is beneath adult consideration. "From Elfland to Poughkeepsie," Le Guin's statement about style in fantasy literature, is based on a talk she gave at one of the workshops or courses in writing over which she presides almost every year. She follows the first rule of good teaching and gives multiple examples to illustrate both good and bad style. Perhaps more importantly, she defines her style and its particular importance in a work of fantasy. Any aspiring fantasy writer will enjoy and profit from this lesson.

Readers will relish the same spontaneity and felicitous expression in Le Guin's two essays that they find in her fiction. It is interesting, however, that while her fiction is for the most part very serious in tone, her essays reveal humorous twists that surprise and delight. We are fortunate that we have her essays to give us this insight into her personality.

·❧ Dreams Must Explain Themselves ❧·

Ursula K. Le Guin

Andy Porter called from New York earlier this year to try and tell me what he hoped I'd write for *Algol*. The conversation was pleasant, though disarranged by a bad connection, several explosive intrusions by a person at this end who wanted some cookies and attention, and a slight degree of misunderstanding. Andy kept saying things like, "Tell the readers about yourself," and I kept saying things like, "How? Why?"

Some people can talk on the telephone. They must really believe in the thing. For me the telephone is for making appointments with the doctor with and canceling appointments with the dentist with. It is not a medium of human communication. I can't stand there in the hall with the child and the cat both circling around my legs frisking and purring and demanding cookies and catfood, and explain to a disembodied voice in my ear that the Jungian spectrum of introvert/extravert can usefully be applied not only to human beings, but also to authors. That is, that there are some authors who want and need to tell about themselves, you know,

like Norman Mailer, and there are others who want
and need privacy. Privacy! What an elitist, Victorian
concept. These days it sounds almost as quaint as mod-
esty. But I can't say all that on the telephone, it just
won't come out. Nor can I say (although I made a feeble
effort to, about the time the connection failed entirely,
probably because the cat, in despair, had settled for
chewing on the telephone cord) that the problem of communication is a complex one, and that some of us in-
troverts have solved it in a curious, not wholly satisfactory, but interesting way: we communicate (with all
but a very few persons) in writing. As if we were deaf
and dumb. And not just in writing, but indirectly in
writing. We write stories about imaginary people in
imaginary situations. Then we publish them (because
they are, in their strange way, acts of communication—
addressed to others). And then people read them and
call up and say But who are you? tell us about yourself!
And we say, But I have. It's all there, in the book. All
that matters—But you made all that up!—Out of what?

Where Andy and I temporarily misunderstood each
other was at this point: Wanting me to write about the
Earthsea trilogy, the background of it, he said (excuse
me, Andy, for misquoting) something like, "People would
be interested in knowing things like how you planned
the Earthsea world, and how you developed the languages, and how you keep lists of places and characters
and so on." To which I returned some kind of garble-
garble, of which I recall only one sentence, "But I didn't
plan anything, I found it."

Andy (not unnaturally): "Where?"

Me: "In my subconscious."

Now as I think about it, perhaps this is worth talking
about a little. Andy and I surprised each other because
we had different, unexamined notions of how writing
is done; and they were so different that their collision
produced a slight shock. Both of them are completely
valid; they're just different methodologies. As mine is
the one not talked about in writers' manuals, however,
perhaps it needs some explanation.

All my life I have written, and all my life I have

(without conscious decision) avoided reading how-to-write things. The Shorter Oxford Dictionary and Follett's and Fowler's manuals of usage are my entire arsenal of tools. However, in reading and teaching and talking with other writers one does arrive at a certain consciousness of technique. The most different technique from my own, the one that starts from the point farthest removed, is just this one of the preliminary plans and lists and descriptions. The technique of keeping a notebook and describing all the characters in it before the story is begun: how much William weighs and where he went to school and how his hair is cut and what his dominant traits are.

I do have notebooks, in which I worry at plot ideas as if they were old bones, growling and snarling and frequently burying them and digging them up again. Also, during the writing of a piece, I often make notes concerning a character, particularly if it's a novel. My memory is very poor, and if there's something I just noticed about the character, but this is not the right point to put it into the book, then I make a note for future reference. Something like:

W. d not appr H's ing.—Repr!!

Then I lose the note.

But I don't write out descriptions beforehand, and would indeed feel ridiculous, even ashamed, to do so. If the character isn't so clear to me that I know all *that* about him, what am I doing writing about him? What right have I to describe what William did when Helen bit his knee, if I don't even know what he looks like, and his past, and his psyche, inside and out, as well as I know myself? Because after all he is myself. Part of myself.

If William is a character worthy of being written about, then he exists. He exists, inside my head to be sure, but in his own right, with his own vitality. All I have to do is look at him. I don't plan him, compose him of bits and pieces, inventory him. I find him.

There he is, and Helen is biting his knee, and he says with a little cough, "I really don't think this is relevant, Helen." What else, being William, could he say?

This attitude toward action, creation, is evidently a basic one, the same root from which the interest in the *I Ching* and Taoist philosophy evident in most of my books arises. The Taoist world is orderly, not chaotic, but its order is not one imposed by man or by a personal or humane deity. The true laws—ethical and aesthetic, as surely as scientific—are not imposed from above by any authority, but exist in things and are to be found—discovered.

To return circuitously to Earthsea: this anti-ideological, pragmatic technique applies to places, as well as people. I did not deliberately invent Earthsea. I did not think "Hey wow—islands are archetypes and archipelagoes are superarchetypes and let's build us an archipelago!" I am not an engineer, but an explorer. I discovered Earthsea.

Plans are likely to be made, if well made, inclusively; discoveries are made bit by bit. Planning negates time. Discovery is a temporal process. It may take years and years. People are still exploring Antarctica.

The history of the discovery of Earthsea is something like this:

In 1964 I wrote a story called "The Word of Unbinding" about a wizard. Cele Goldsmith Lalli bought it for *Fantastic*. (Cele Lalli gave me and a lot of other people their start in SF; she was one of the most sensitive and audacious editors the field has ever had.) I don't recall now whether the fact is made much of in the story, but it was perfectly clear in my mind that it took place on an island, one among many islands. I did not give much attention to the setting, as it was (as William would say) not relevant; and developed only such rules of magic as were germane to the very small point the very minor story made.

Soon after, I wrote a story, "The Rule of Names," in which both the islands and the rules of magic were considerably more developed (Cele published it too). This story was lighthearted (the other one was glum), and I had fun playing around a bit with the scenery, and with the old island ladies drinking rush-wash tea, and so on. It was set on an island called Sattins, which I knew to be one of an outlying group east of the main archipelago. The main character, a dragon known first as Mr. Underhill and then, when his nature is revealed, by his true name Yevaud, came from a westerly isle called Pendor.

I did not much bother with all the islands that I knew lay between Sattins and Pendor, and north and south of them. They weren't involved. I had the distinct feeling, however, that the island of "Word of Unbinding" lay up north of Pendor. I am not now sure which island it actually is, that one I first landed on. Later voyages of discovery have so complicated the map that the first landfall, like that of the Norsemen in the New World, is hard to pin down for certain. Sattins, however, is on the map, high in the East Reach between Yore and Vemish.

Along in 1965 or 1966 I wrote a longish story about a prince who travels down through the archipelago from its central island, Havnor, in search of the Ultimate. He goes southwest out into the open sea, beyond all islands, and finds there a people who live on rafts all their lives long. He ties his boat to a raft and settles down with them, content with this as the Ultimate, until he realizes that out past the farthest journey of the drifting raft-colony there are sea-people, living in the sea itself. He joins them. I think the implication was that (not being a merman) he'll wear out eventually, and sink, and find the ultimate Ultimate. This story wasn't submitted for publication as it never worked itself out at all well; but I felt strongly that the basic image—the raft-colony—was a lulu, and would find itself its home somewhere eventually. It did, in the last of the Earthsea books, *The Farthest Shore*.

I explored Earthsea no further until 1967, when the publisher of Parnassus Press, Herman Schein, asked me if I'd like to try writing a book for him. He wanted something for older kids; till then Parnassus had been mainly a young-juvenile publisher, putting out the handsomest and best-made picture books in America. He gave me complete freedom as to subject and approach. Nobody until then had ever asked me to write anything; I had just done so, relentlessly. To be asked to do it was a great boon. The exhilaration carried me over my apprehensions about writing "for young people," something I had never seriously tried. For some weeks or months I let my imagination go groping around in search of what was wanted, in the dark. It stumbled over the Islands, and the magic employed there. Serious consideration of magic, and of writing for kids, combined to make me wonder about wizards. Wizards are usually elderly or ageless Gandalfs, quite rightly and archetypically. But what were they before they had white beards? How did they learn what is obviously an erudite and dangerous art? Are there colleges for young wizards? And so on.

The story of the book is essentially a voyage, a pattern in the form of a long spiral. I began to see the places where the young wizard would go. Eventually I drew a map. Now that I knew where everything was, now was the time for cartography. Of course a great deal of it only appeared above water, as it were, in drawing the map.

Three small islands are named for my children, their baby-names; one gets a little jovial and irresponsible, given the freedom to create a world out of nothing at all. (Power corrupts.) None of the other names "means" anything that I know of, though their sound is more or less meaningful to me.

People often ask how I think of names in fantasies, and again I have to answer that I find them, that I hear them. This is an important subject in this context. From that first story on, *naming* has been the essence of the art-magic as practiced in Earthsea. For me, as for the wizards, to know the name of an island or a character is to know the island or the person. Usually the name comes of itself, but sometimes one must be very careful: as I was with the protagonist, whose true name is Ged.

I worked (in collaboration with a wizard named Ogion) for a long time trying to "listen for" his name, and making certain it really was his name. This all sounds very mystical and indeed there are aspects of it I do not understand, but it is a pragmatic business too, since if the name had been wrong the character would have been wrong—misbegotten, misunderstood.

A man who read the ms. for Parnassus thought "Ged" was meant to suggest "God." That shook me badly. I considered changing the name in case there were other such ingenious minds waiting to pounce. But I couldn't do so. The fellow's name was Ged and no two ways about it.

It isn't pronounced Jed, by the way. That sounds like a mountain moonshiner to me. I thought the analogy with "get" would make it clear, but a lot of people have asked. One place I do exert deliberate control in name-inventing is in the area of pronounce-ability. I try to spell them so they don't look too formidable (unless, like Kurremkarmerruk, they're meant to look formidable), and they can be pronounced either with the English or the Italian vowels. I don't care which.

Much the same holds for the bits of invented languages in the text of the trilogy.

There are words, like rushwash tea, for which I can offer no explanation. They simply drink rushwash tea there; that's what it's called, like lapsang soochong or Lipton's here. Rushwash is a Hardic word, of course. If you press me, I will explain that it comes from the rushwash bush, which grows both wild and cultivated everywhere south of Enlad, and bears a small round leaf which when dried and steeped yields a pleasant brownish tea. I did not know this before I wrote the foregoing sentence. Or did I know it, and simply never thought about it? What's in a name? A lot, that's what.

There are more formal examples of foreign languages in the trilogy; in *The Farthest Shore* there are several whole sentences in the Language of the Making, as dragons will not speak anything else. These arrived, spelling (formidable) and all, and I wrote them down without question. No use trying to make a lexicon of Hardic or of the True Speech; there's not enough in the books. It's not like Tolkien, who in one sense wrote *The Lord of the Rings* to give his invented languages somebody to speak them. That is lovely, that is the Creator Spirit working absolutely unhindered—making the word flesh. But Tolkien is a linguist, as well as a great creator.

(In other books I have taken the invented languages further. I knew enough Karhidish, when I was writing *The Left Hand of Darkness*, to write a couple of short poems in it. I couldn't do so now. I made no methodical lexicon or grammar, only a word list for my own reference.)

I said that to know the true name is to know the thing, for me, and for the wizards. This implies a good deal about the "meaning" of the trilogy, and about me. The trilogy is, in one aspect, about the artist. The artist as magician. The Trickster. Prospero. That is the only truly allegorical aspect it has of which I am conscious. If there are other allegories in it please don't tell me: I hate allegories. A is "really" B, and a hawk is "really" a handsaw—bah. Humbug. Any creation, primary or secondary, with any vitality to it, can "really" be a dozen mutually exclusive things at once, before breakfast.

Wizardry is artistry. The trilogy is then, in this sense, about art, the creative experience, the creative process. There is always this circularity in fantasy. The snake devours its tail. Dreams must explain themselves.

It was interesting, trying to write for children (i.e., people over twelve years old). It was hard. What I wanted to send Andy Porter was a long passionate article about the status of "children's books." He wanted something more personal. But believe me, I take the matter personally. Andre Norton had a note on it in a recent SFWA *Forum*, which raised my consciousness several levels with a jolt.

Though I'd like to strike a blow here for the women's movement, I don't really know where to aim it. I know

of no circumstance where, *as a writer,* I have been treated
unfairly or suspiciously or patronizingly on account of
my sex; except one little misunderstanding with *Play-boy,* whereby I consented to become U. K. Le Guin
(Ulysses Kingfisher?), and that was much too funny to
get mad about. But as an SF writer I resent being low
paid in comparison to dreck-writers: and if SF writers
think they're low paid, they should look at writers for
children. I am not complaining personally. Atheneum,
who now publish my children's books, have treated me
well, and with great personal civility; the same goes
for Gollancz in England; and both firms have given me
splendid (woman) editors. What is wrong is the whole
scale—all the publishers' budgets for their children's
books. There is seldom big quick money in kiddylit, but
a successful kids' book has an unusually long life. It
sells to schools, to libraries, and to gift-giving adults,
and it goes on selling, and making money, for years
and years and years. This is not reflected in the ad-vances or the royalties. It is a very badly paid field, in
general.

But the economic discrimination is only an element,
as usual, of the real problem: a reflection of a prejudice.
The real trouble isn't the money, it's the adult chau-vinist piggery.

"You're a juvenile writer, aren't you?"

Yeth, Mummy.

"I love your books—the real ones, I mean, I haven't
read the ones for children, of course!"

Of courthe not, Daddy.

"It must be relaxing to write *simple* things for a
change."

Sure it's simple, writing for kids. Just as simple as
bringing them up.

All you do is take all the sex out, and use little short
words, and little dumb ideas, and don't be too scary,
and be sure there's a happy ending. Right? Nothing to
it. Write down. Right on.

If you do all that, you might even write *Jonathan
Livingston Seagull* and make twenty billion dollars and
have every adult in America reading your book!

But you won't have every kid in America reading your book. They will look at it, and they will see straight through it, with their clear, cold, beady little eyes, and they will put it down, and they will go away. Kids will devour vast amounts of garbage (and it is good for them) but they are not like adults: they have not yet learned to eat plastic.

The British seem not to believe publishers' categorizations of "juvenile," "teen-age," "young adult," etc. so devoutly as we do. It's interesting that, for instance, Andre Norton is often reviewed with complete respect by English papers, including the *Times Literary Supplement*. No pats, no sniggers, no put-downs. They seem to be aware that fantasy is the great age-equalizer; if it's good when you're twelve it's quite likely to be just as good, or better, when you're thirty-six.

Most of my letters about the Earthsea books from American readers are from people between sixteen and twenty-five. The English who write me tend to be, as well as I can guess, over thirty, and more predominantly male. (Several of them are Anglican clergymen. As a congenital non-Christian I find this a little startling; but the letters are terrific.) One might interpret this age difference to mean that the English are more childish than the Americans, but I see it the other way. The English readers are grownup enough not to be defensive about being grownup.

The most childish thing about *A Wizard of Earthsea*, I expect, is its subject: coming of age.

Coming of age is a process that took me many years; I finished it, so far as I ever will, at about age thirty-one; and so I feel rather deeply about it. So do most adolescents. It's their main occupation, in fact.

The subject of *The Tombs of Atuan* is, if I had to put it in one word, sex. There's a lot of symbolism in the book, most of which I did not, of course, analyze consciously while writing; the symbols can all be read as sexual. More exactly, you could call it a feminine coming of age. Birth, rebirth, destruction, freedom are the themes.

The Farthest Shore is about death. That's why it is

a less well built, less sound and complete book than the others. They were about things I had already lived through and survived. *The Farthest Shore* is about the thing you do not live through and survive. It seemed an absolutely suitable subject to me for young readers, since in a way one can say that the hour when a child realizes, not that death exists—children are intensely aware of death—but that he/she, personally, is mortal, will die, is the hour when childhood ends, and the new life begins. Coming of age again, but in a larger context.

In any case I had little choice about the subject. Ged, who was always very strong-minded, always saying things that surprised me and doing things he wasn't supposed to do, took over completely in this book. He was determined to show me how his life must end, and why. I tried to keep up with him, but he was always ahead. I rewrote the book more times than I want to remember, trying to keep him under some kind of control. I thought it was all done when it was printed here, but the English edition differs in three long passages from the earlier American one: my editor at Gollancz said, "Ged is talking too much," and she was quite right, and I shut him up three times, much to the improvement of the whole. If you insist upon discovering instead of planning, this kind of trouble is inevitable. It is a most uneconomical way to write. The book is still the most imperfect of the three, but it is the one I like best. It is the end of the trilogy, but it is the dream I have not stopped dreaming.

·❖· From Elfland to Poughkeepsie ·❖·

Ursula K. Le Guin

Elfland is what Lord Dunsany called the place. It is also known as Middle Earth, and Prydain, and the Forest of Broceliande, and Once Upon a Time; and by many other names.

Let us consider Elfland as a great national park, a vast and beautiful place where a person goes by himself, on foot, to get in touch with reality in a special, private, profound fashion. But what happens when it is considered merely as a place to "get away to"?

Well, you know what has happened at Yosemite. Everybody comes, not with an ax and a box of matches, but in a trailer with a motorbike on the back and a motorboat on top and a butane stove, five aluminum folding chairs, and a transistor radio on the inside. They arrive totally encapsulated in a secondhand reality. And then they move on to Yellowstone, and it's just the same there, all trailers and transistors. They go from park to park, but they never really go anywhere; except when one of them who thinks that even the wildlife isn't real gets chewed up by a genuine, firsthand bear.

The same sort of thing seems to be happening to Elfland, lately. A great many people want to go there, without knowing what it is they're really looking for, driven by a vague hunger for something real. With the intention or under the pretense of obliging them, certain writers of fantasy are building six-lane highways and trailer parks with drive-in movies, so that the tourists can feel at home just as if they were back in Poughkeepsie.

But the point about Elfland is that you are not at home there. It's not Poughkeepsie. It's different.

What is fantasy? On one level, of course, it is a game: a pure pretense with no ulterior motive whatever. It is one child saying to another child, "Let's be dragons," and then they're dragons for an hour or two. It is escapism of the most admirable kind—the game played for the game's sake.

On another level, it is still a game, but a game played for very high stakes. Seen thus, as art, not spontaneous play, its affinity is not with daydream, but with dream. It is a different approach to reality, an alternative technique for apprehending and coping with existence. It is not antirational, but pararational; not realistic, but surrealistic, superrealistic, a heightening of reality. In Freud's terminology, it employs primary, not secondary process thinking. It employs archetypes, which, as Jung warned us, are dangerous things. Dragons are more dangerous, and a good deal commoner, than bears. Fantasy is nearer to poetry, to mysticism, and to insanity than naturalistic fiction is. It is a real wilderness, and those who go there should not feel too safe. And their guides, the writers of fantasy, should take their responsibilities seriously.

After all these metaphors and generalities, let us get down to some examples; let us read a little fantasy.

This is much easier to do than it used to be, thanks very largely to one man, Lin Carter of Ballantine Books, whose Adult Fantasy Series of new publications and reprints of old ones has saved us all from a lifetime of pawing through the shelves of used bookstores somewhere behind several dusty cartons between "Occult" and "Children's" in hopes of finding, perhaps, the battered and half-mythical odd volume of Dunsany. In gratitude to Mr. Carter for the many splendid books, both new and old, in his series, I will read anything his firm sends me; and last year when they sent me a new one, I settled down with a pleasant sense of confidence to read it. Here is a little excerpt from what I read. The persons talking are a duke of the blood royal of a mythical Keltic kingdom, and a warrior-magician—great Lords of Elfland, both of them.

> "Whether or not they succeed in the end will depend largely on Kelson's personal ability to manipulate the voting."
> "Can he?" Morgan asked, as the two clattered down a half-flight of stairs and into the garden.
> "I don't know, Alaric," Nigel replied. "He's good—damned good—but I just don't know. Besides, you saw the key council lords. With Ralson dead and Bran Coris practically making open accusations—well, it doesn't look good."
> "I could have told you that at Cardosa."[1]

At this point, I was interrupted (perhaps by a person from Porlock, I don't remember), and the next time I sat down I happened to pick up a different kind of novel, a real Now novel, naturalistic, politically conscious, relevant, set in Washington, D.C. Here is a sample of a conversation from it, between a senator and a lobbyist for pollution control.

> "Whether or not they succeed in the end will depend largely on Kelson's personal ability to manipulate the voting."
> "Can he?" Morgan asked, as the two clattered down a half-flight of stairs and into the White House garden.
> "I don't know, Alaric," Nigel replied. "He's good—damned good—but I just don't know. Besides, you saw the key committee chairmen. With

[1] Katherine Kurtz. *Deryni Rising*, New York: Ballantine Books, August 1970, p. 41.

Ralson dead and Brian Corliss practically making open accusations—well, it doesn't look good."

"I could have told you that at Poughkeepsie."

Now, I submit that something has gone wrong. The book from which I first quoted is not fantasy, for all its equipment of heroes and wizards. If it was fantasy, I couldn't have pulled that dirty trick on it by changing four words. You can't clip Pegasus' wings that easily— not if he has wings.

Before I go further I want to apologize to the author of the passage for making a horrible example of her. There are infinitely worse examples I could have used; I chose this one because in this book something good has gone wrong—something real has been falsified. There would be no use at all in talking about what is generally passed off as "heroic fantasy," all the endless Barbarians with names like Barp and Klod, and the Tarnsmen and the Klansmen and all the rest of them— there would be nothing whatever to say. (Not in terms of art, that is; in terms of ethics, racism, sexism, and politics there would be a great deal to say, but fortunately it has all been said, indirectly and therefore with all the greater power, by Norman Spinrad in his tremendous satire *The Iron Dream*.)

What is it, then, that I believe has gone wrong in the book and the passage quoted from it? I think it is the *style*. Presently I'll try to explain why I think so. It will be convenient, however, to have other examples at hand. The first passage was dialogue, and style in a novel is often particularly visible in dialogue; so here are some bits of conversations from other parts of Elfland. The books from which they were taken were all written in this century, and all the speakers are wizards, warriors, or Lords of Elfland, as in the first selection. The books were chosen carefully, of course, but the passages were picked at random; I just looked for a page where two or three suitably noble types were chatting.

Now spake Spitfire saying, "Read forth to us, I pray thee, the book of Gro; for my soul is afire to set forth on this faring."

"'Tis writ somewhat crabbedly," said Brandoch Daha, "and most damnably long. I spent last night a-searching on't, and 'tis most apparent no other way lieth to these mountains save by the Moruna, and across the Moruna is (if Gro say true) but one way…"

"If he say true?" said Spitfire. "He is a turncoat and a renegado. Wherefore not therefore a liar?"[2]

"Detestable to me, truly, is loathsome hunger; abominable an insufficiency of food upon a journey. Mournful, I declare to you, is such a fate as this, to one of my lineage and nurture!"

"Well, well," said Dienw'r Anffodion, with the bitter hunger awaking in him again, "common with me is knowledge of famine. Take you the whole of the food, if you will."

"Yes," said Goreu. "That will be better."[3]

"Who can tell?" said Aragorn. "But we will put it to the test one day."

"May the day not be too long delayed," said Boromir. "For though I do not ask for aid, we need it. It would comfort us to know that others fought also with all the means that they have."

"Then be comforted," said Elrond.[4]

Now all those speakers speak English differently; but they all have the genuine Elfland accent. You could not pull the trick on them that I pulled on Morgan and

[2] E. R. Eddison. *The Worm Ouroboros*, New York: Ballantine Books, April 1967, p. 137.

[3] Kenneth Morris. *Book of the Three Dragons*, Junior Literary Guild, Copyright 1930, New York: Longmans, Green and Company, p. 8.

[4] J. R. R. Tolkien. *The Fellowship of the Ring*, New York: Ballantine Books, October 1965, p. 351.

Nigel—not unless you changed half the words in every sentence. You could not posssibly mistake them for anyone on Capitol Hill.

In the first selection they are a little crazy, and in the second one they are not only crazy but Welsh—and yet they speak with power; with a wild dignity. All of them are heroic, eloquent, passionate. It may be the passion that is most important. Nothing is really going on, in those first two passages: in one case they're reading a book, in the other they're dividing a cold leg of rabbit. But with what importance they invest these trivial acts, what emotion, what vitality!

In the third passage, the speakers are quieter, and use a less extraordinary English; or rather an English extraordinary for its simple timelessness. Such language is rare on Capitol Hill, but it has occurred there. It has sobriety, wit, and force. It is the language of men of character.

Speech expresses character. It does so whether the speaker or the author knows it or not. (Presidential speech writers know it very well.) When I hear a man say, "I could have told you that at Cardosa," or at Poughkeepsie, or wherever, I think I know something about that man. He is the kind who says, "I told you so."

Nobody who says, "I told you so" has ever been, or will ever be, a hero.

The Lords of Elfland are true lords, the only true lords, the kind that do not exist on this earth: their lordship is the outward sign or symbol of real inward greatness. And greatness of soul shows when a man speaks. At least, it does in books. In life we expect lapses. In naturalistic fiction, too, we expect lapses, and laugh at an "over-heroic" hero. But in fantasy, which, instead of imitating the perceived confusion and complexity of existence, tries to hint at an order and clarity underlying existence—in fantasy, we need not compromise. Every word spoken is meaningful, though the meaning may be subtle. For example, in the second passage, the fellow called Goreu is moaning and complaining and shamelessly conning poor Dienw'r out of the only thing he has to eat. And yet you feel that anybody who can talk like that isn't a mean-spirited man. He would never say, "I told you so." In fact, he's not a man at all, he is Gwydion son of Don in disguise, and he has a good reason for his tricks, a magnanimous reason. On the other hand, in the third quotation, the very slight whine in Boromir's tone is significant also. Boromir is a noble-hearted person, but there is a tragic flaw in his character and the flaw is envy.

I picked for comparison three master stylists: E. R. Eddison, Kenneth Morris, and J. R. R. Tolkien; which may seem unfair to any other authors mentioned. But I do not think it is unfair. In art, the best is the standard. When you hear a new violinist, you do not compare him to the kid next door; you compare him to Stern and Heifetz. If he falls short, you will not blame him for it, but you will know what he falls short of. And if he is a real violinist, he knows it too, In art, "good enough" is not good enough.

Another reason for picking those three is that they exemplify styles which are likely to be imitated by beginning writers of fantasy. There is a great deal of quite open influencing and imitating going on among the writers of fantasy. I incline to think that this is a very healthy situation. It is one in which most vigorous arts find themselves. Take for example music in the eighteenth century, when Handel and Haydn and Mozart and the rest of them were borrowing tunes and tricks and techniques from one another, and building up the great edifice of music like a lot of masons at work on one cathedral: well, we may yet have a great edifice of fantasy. But you can't imitate what somebody does until you've learned how he does it.

The most imitated, and the most inimitable, writer of fantasy is probably Lord Dunsany. I did not include a passage of conversation from Dunsany, because I could not find a suitable one. Genuine give-and-take conversations are quite rare in his intensely mannered, intensely poetic narratives, and when they occur they

tend to be very brief, as they do in the Bible. The King
James Bible is indubitably one of the profoundest for-
mative influences on Dunsany's prose; another, I suspect, is Irish daily speech. Those two influences alone,
not to mention his own gifts of a delicate ear for speech
rhythms and a brilliantly exact imagination, remove
him from the reach of any would-be imitator or emu-
lator who is not an Irish peer brought up from the cradle
on the grand sonorities of Genesis and Ecclesiastes.
Dunsany mined a narrow vein, but it was all pure ore,
and all his own. I have never seen any imitation Dunsany that consisted of anything beyond a lot of elaborate
made-up names, some vague descriptions of gorgeous
cities and unmentionable dooms, and a great many sentences beginning with "And."

Dunsany is indeed the First Terrible Fate that Await-
eth Unwary Beginners in Fantasy. But if they avoid
him, there are others—many others. One of these is
archaicizing, the archaic manner, which Dunsany and
other master fantasists use so effortlessly. It is a trap
into which almost all very young fantasy writers walk;
I know; I did myself. They know instinctively that what
is wanted in fantasy is a *distancing from the ordinary*.
They see it done beautifully in old books, such as Mal-
ory's *Morte d'Arthur,* and in new books the style of
which is grounded on the old books, and they think,
"Aha! I will do it too." But alas, it is one of those things,
like bicycling and computer programming, that you have
got to know how to do before you do it.

"Aha!" says our novice. "You have to use verbs with
thee and thou." So he does. But he doesn't know how.
There are very few Americans now alive who know how
to use a verb in the second person singular. The general
assumption is that you add *-est* and you're there. I remember Debbie Reynolds telling Eddie Fisher—do you
remember Debbie Reynolds and Eddie Fisher?—
"Whithersoever thou goest there also I goest." Fake
feeling: fake grammar.

Then our novice tries to use the subjunctive. All the
was's turn into were's, and leap out at the reader snarl-

ing. And the Quakers have got him all fouled up about which really is the nominative form of Thou. Is it Thee, or isn't it? And then there's the She-To-Whom Trap. "I shall give it to she to whom my love is given!"—"Him whom this sword smites shall surely die!"—Give it to she? Him shall die? It sounds like Tonto talking to the Lone Ranger. This is distancing with a vengeance. But we aren't through yet, no, we haven't had the fancy words. Eldritch. Tenebrous. Smaragds and chalcedony. Mayhap. It can't be maybe, it can't be perhaps; it has to be mayhap, unless it's perchance. And then comes the final test, the infallible touchstone of the seventh-rate: Ichor. You know ichor. It oozes out of several tentacles, and beslimes tessellated pavements, and bespatters bejeweled courtiers, and bores the bejesus out of everybody.

The archaic manner is indeed a perfect distancer, but you have to do it perfectly. It's a high wire: one slip spoils all. The man who did it perfectly was, of course, Eddison. He really did write Elizabethan prose in the nineteen-thirties. His style is totally artificial, but it is never faked. If you love language for its own sake he is irresistible. Many, with reason, find him somewhat crabbed and most damnably long; but he is the real thing, and just to reaffirm that strange, remote reality, I am placing a longer quotation from him here. This is from *The Worm Ouroboros*. A dead king is being carried, in secrecy, at night, down to the beach.

> The lords of Witchland took their weapons and the men-at-arms bare the goods, and the King went in the midst on his bier of spear-shafts. So went they picking their way in the moonless night round the palace and down the winding path that led to the bed of the combe, and so by the stream westward toward the sea. Here they deemed it safe to light a torch to show them the way. Desolate and bleak showed the sides of the combe in the wind-blown flare; and the flare was thrown back from the jewels of the royal crown of Witch-

land, and from the armoured buskins on the King's
feet showing stark with toes pointing upward from
below his bear-skin mantle, and from the armour
and the weapons of them that bare him and walked
beside him, and from the black cold surface of the
little river hurrying for ever over its bed of boul-
ders to the sea. The path was rugged and stony,
and they fared slowly, lest they should stumble
and drop the King.[5]

That prose, in spite of or because of its archaisms,
is good prose: exact, clear, powerful. Visually it is precise and vivid; musically—that is, in the sound of the
words, the movement of the syntax, and the rhythm of
the sentences—it is subtle and very strong. Nothing in
it is faked or blurred; it is all seen, heard, felt. That
style was his true style, his own voice; that was how
Eddison, an artist, spoke.

The second of our three "conversation pieces" is from
Book of the Three Dragons, by Kenneth Morris. This
book one must still seek on the dusty shelves behind
the cartons, probably in the section marked "Children's"—at least that's where I found it—for Mr. Carter
has not yet reprinted more than a fragment of it, and
if it ever had a day of fame it was before our time. I
use it here partly in hopes of arousing interest in the
book, for I think many people would enjoy it. It is a
singularly fine example of the recreation of a work magnificent in its own right (the *Mabinogion*)—a literary
event rather rare except in fantasy, where its frequency
is perhaps proof, if one were needed, of the ever-renewed
vitality of myth. But Morris is also useful to my purpose
because he has a strong sense of humor; and humor in
fantasy is both a lure and a pitfall to imitators. Dunsany is often ironic, but he does not mix simple humor
with the heroic tone. Eddison sometimes did, but I think
Morris and James Branch Cabell were the masters of
the comic-heroic. One does not smile wryly, reading

[5] E. R. Eddison, pp. 56–57.

them; one laughs. They achieve their comedy essentially by their style—by an eloquence, a fertility and felicity and ferocity of invention that is simply overwhelming. They are outrageous, and they know exactly what they're doing.

Fritz Leiber and Roger Zelazny have both written in the comic-heroic vein, but their technique is different: they alternate the two styles. When humor is intended the characters talk colloquial American English, or even slang, and at earnest moments they revert to old formal usages. Readers indifferent to language do not mind this, but for others the strain is too great. I am one of these latter. I am jerked back and forth between Elfland and Poughkeepsie; the characters lose coherence in my mind, and I lose confidence in them. It is strange, because both Leiber and Zelazny are skillful and highly imaginative writers, and it is perfectly clear that Leiber, profoundly acquainted with Shakespeare and practiced in a very broad range of techniques, could maintain any tone with eloquence and grace. Sometimes I wonder if these two writers underestimate their own talents, if they lack confidence in themselves. Or it may be that, since fantasy is seldom taken seriously at this particular era in this country, they are afraid to take it seriously. They don't want to be caught believing in their own creations, getting all worked up about imaginary things; and so their humor becomes self-mocking, self-destructive. Their gods and heroes keep turning aside to look out of the books at you and whisper, "See, we're really just plain folks."

Now Cabell never does that. He mocks everything: not only his own fantasy, but our reality. He doesn't believe in his dreamworld, but he doesn't believe in us, either. His tone is perfectly consistent: elegant, arrogant, ironic. Sometimes I enjoy it and sometimes it makes me want to scream, but it is admirable. Cabell knew what he wanted to do and he did it, and the marketplace be damned.

Evangeline Walton, whose books, like Kenneth Morris's, are reworkings of the *Mabinogion,* has achieved her own beautifully idiosyncratic blend of humor and heroism; there is no doubt that the Keltic mythos lends itself to such a purpose. And while we are on the subject of humor, Jack Vance must be mentioned, though his humor is so quiet you can miss it if you blink. Indeed the whole tone of his writing is so modest that sometimes I wonder whether, like Leiber and Zelazny, he fails to realize how very good a writer he is. If so, it is probably a result of the patronizing attitude American culture affects toward works of pure imagination. Vance, however, never compromises with the patronizing and ignorant. He never lets his creation down in order to make a joke, and he never shows a tin ear for tone. The conversation of his characters is aloof and restrained, very like his own narrative prose: an unusual kind of English, but clear, graceful, and precisely suited to Vance's extraordinary imagination. It is an achieved style. And it contains no archaisms at all.

After all, archaisms are not essential. You don't have to know how to use the subjunctive in order to be a wizard. You don't have to talk like Henry the Fifth to be a hero.

Caution, however, is needed. Great caution. Consider: Did Henry the Fifth of England really talk like Shakespeare's Henry? Did the real Achilles use hexameters? Would the real Beowulf please stand up and alliterate? We are not discussing history, but heroic fantasy. We are discussing a modern descendant of the epic.

Most epics are in straightforward language, whether prose or verse. They retain the directness of their oral forebears. Homer's metaphors may be extended, but they are neither static nor ornate. The *Song of Roland* has four thousand lines, containing one simile and no metaphors. The *Mabinogion* and the Norse sagas are as plainspoken as they could well be. Clarity and simplicity are permanent virtues in a narrative. Nothing highfalutin is needed. A plain language is the noblest of all.

It is also the most difficult.

Tolkien writes a plain, clear English. Its outstanding

virtue is its flexibility, its variety. It ranges easily from the commonplace to the stately, and can slide into metrical poetry, as in the Tom Bombadil episode, without the careless reader's even noticing. Tolkien's vocabulary is not striking; he has no ichor; everything is direct, concrete, and simple.

Now the kind of writing I am attacking, the Poughkeepsie style of fantasy, is also written in a plain and apparently direct prose. Does that makes it equal to Tolkien's? Alas, no. It is a fake plainness. It is not really simple, but flat. It is not really clear, but inexact. Its directness is specious. Its sensory cues—extremely important in imaginative writing—are vague and generalized; the rocks, the wind, the trees are not there, are not felt; the scenery is cardboard, or plastic. The tone as a whole is profoundly inappropriate to the subject.

To what then is it appropriate? To journalism. It is journalistic prose. In journalism, the suppression of the author's personality and sensibility is deliberate. The goal is an impression of objectivity. The whole thing is meant to be written fast, and read faster. This technique is right, for a newspaper. It is wrong for a novel, and dead wrong for a fantasy. A language intended to express the immediate and the trivial is applied to the remote and the elemental. The result, of course, is a mess.

Why do we seem to be achieving just that result so often, these days? Well, undoubtedly avarice is one of the reasons. Fantasy is selling well, so let's all grind out a fantasy. The Old Baloney Factory. And sheer ineptness enters in. But in many cases neither greed not lack of skill seems to be involved, and in such cases I suspect a failure to take the job seriously: a refusal to admit what you're in for when you set off with only an ax and a box of matches into Elfland.

A fantasy is a journey. It is a journey into the subconscious mind, just as psychoanalysis is. Like psychoanalysis, it can be dangerous; and *it will change you*.

The general assumption is that, if there are dragons

or hippogriffs in a book, or if it takes place in a vaguely Keltic or Near Eastern medieval setting, or if magic is done in it, then it's a fantasy. This is a mistake.

A writer may deploy acres of sagebrush and rimrock without achieving a real Western, if he doesn't know the West. He may use spaceships and strains of mutant bacteria all he pleases, and never be anywhere near real science fiction. He may even write a five-hundred-page novel about Sigmund Freud which has absolutely nothing to do with Sigmund Freud; it has been done; it was done just a couple of years ago. And in the same way, a writer may use all the trappings of fantasy without ever actually imagining anything.

My argument is that this failure, this fakery, is visible instantly in the style.

Many readers, many critics, and most editors speak of style as if it were an ingredient of a book, like the sugar in a cake, or something added onto the book, like the frosting on the cake. The style, of course, *is* the book. If you remove the cake, all you have left is a recipe. If you remove the style, all you have left is a synopsis of the plot.

This is partly true of history; largely true of fiction; and absolutely true of fantasy.

In saying that the style is the book, I speak from the reader's point of view. From the writer's point of view, the style is the writer. Style isn't just how you use English when you write. It isn't a mannerism or an affectation (though it may be mannered or affected). It isn't something you can do without, though that is what people assume when they announce that they intend to write something "like it is." You can't do without it. There is no "is," without it. Style is how you as a writer see and speak. It is how you see: your vision, your understanding of the world, your voice.

This is not to say that style cannot be learned and perfected, or that it cannot be borrowed and imitated. We learn to see and speak, as children, primarily by imitation. The artist is merely the one who goes on learning after he grows up. If he is a good learner, he will finally learn the hardest thing: how to see his own world, how to speak in his own words.

Still, why is style of such fundamental significance in fantasy? Just because a writer gets the tone of a conversation a bit wrong, or describes things vaguely, or uses an anachronistic vocabulary or shoddy syntax, or begins going a bit heavy on the ichor before dinner— does that disqualify his book as a fantasy? Just because his style is weak and inappropriate—is that so important?

I think it is, because in fantasy there is nothing but the writer's vision of the world. There is no borrowed reality of history, or current events, or just plain folks at home in Peyton Place. There is no comfortable matrix of the commonplace to substitute for the imagination, to provide ready-made emotional response, and to disguise flaws and failures of creation. There is only a construct built in a void, with every joint and seam and nail exposed. To create what Tolkien calls "a secondary universe" is to make a new world. A world where no voice has ever spoken before; where the act of speech is the act of creation. The only voice that speaks there is the creator's voice. And every word counts.

This is an awful responsibility to undertake, when all the poor writer wants to do is play dragons, to entertain himself and others for a while. Nobody should be blamed for falling short of it. But all the same, if one undertakes a responsibility one should be aware of it. Elfland is not Poughkeepsie; the voice of the transistor is not heard in that land.

And lastly I believe that the reader has a responsibility; if he loves the stuff he reads, he has a duty toward it. That duty is to refuse to be fooled; to refuse to permit commercial exploitation of the holy ground of Myth; to reject shoddy work, and to save his praise for the real thing. Because when fantasy is the real thing, nothing, after all, is realer.

MOLLIE HUNTER

(1922–   )

Although many twentieth-century fantasists have gone to the cornucopia of Celtic myth, legend, and folklore for ideas and inspiration, few have used their source as effectively, carefully, and lovingly as Mollie Hunter. Indeed, Hunter uses not only the raw materials of Celtic folklore, but also the techniques of the Celtic storyteller. This superb blend of Celtic form and content has given Hunter's children's fantasies their charm, vibrancy, and authenticity, and has established her reputation as one of the finest literary craftsmen in the fantasy field.

It is relatively easy to find reviews and a few critical essays on Mollie Hunter's fiction, but impossible to find detailed biographical information. The standard reference tools and children's literature texts supply no more than an acorn-cup of facts: Maureen McIlwraith, née McVeigh (Mollie Hunter is her pseudonym), was born on June 30, 1922, in Longniddry, East Lothian, Scotland; she attended Preston Lodge School in East Lothian and then, on December 23, 1940, at the age of eighteen, married Thomas McIlwraith, a marriage which produced two sons, Quentin Wright and Brian George; her present home is "The Shieling," Milton, near Drumnadrochit, Invernesshire, in the Scottish Highlands.

Perhaps this is all that Mollie Hunter wants us to know about her life. In *Contemporary Authors,* she confides that she is a congenital nonjoiner, adding that she particularly enjoys "places without people" (Volumes 29–32, p. 402). Furthermore, in an essay, "The Last Lord of Redhouse Castle," she points out that she lives "in isolation from other writers, and always [has] done" (in *The Thorny Paradise: Writers on Writing for Children,* Edward Blishen, ed. Harmondsworth, Middlesex, England: Kestrel Books, 1977, p. 129). However, in the same essay she also speaks of her "ebullience," her "gift of the gab," and her "instinct to perform" (p. 128). The picture that begins to form is one of an articulate, dynamic woman who, although enjoying the company of others (especially children), prefers to lead a private life, a life dedicated to her family and craft. More appealing to her than the public limelight is the "gentle, ever-changing" light that bathes the rugged hills around her Scottish Highlands home ("Redhouse Castle," p. 134). From her beloved native land comes the inspiration for her works of fiction and thus, quite understandably, she prefers a lifestyle that keeps her close to her roots.

When Mollie Hunter was twelve years old, Mr. Miller, the president of the local literary society, told her the spine-tingling tale of the Black Douglas of Redhouse Castle, an infamous Scottish nobleman who was hanged for murdering his brother. So captivated was Hunter by the grisly story that she promised herself she would "study history properly and find out lots of things" ("Redhouse Castle," p. 128). She has kept her promise. Hunter's extensive study of Scottish history (especially the fifteenth and sixteenth centuries) and Celtic folklore, her two great loves, has not only made her an expert in these fields, but has provided her with the raw materials for her novels.

Most of Hunter's novels can be divided into two categories: fantasies based upon Celtic folklore, and historical novels. Her career as fantasist, and as a writer of children's books, began in 1963 with the publication of *Patrick Kentigern* (published in America as *The Smartest Man in Ireland,* 1965), a novel that was written at the "insistence" of her two young sons. This charming work was followed in rapid succession by several other fantasy novels for young children, including *The Kelpie's Pearls* (1964), *Thomas and the Warlock* (1967), *The Ferlie* (1968), *The Bodach* (1970; published in the same year in America as *The Walking Stones: A Story of Suspense*) and *The Haunted Mountain,* a Notable Children's Book of 1972. Her self-termed "'prentice effort" as a writer of juvenile historicals was *Hi Johnny* (1963). After this fascinating study of King James the Fifth came *The Spanish Letters* (1964), *A Pistol in Greenyards* (1965), *The Ghosts of Glencoe* (1966), *The Lothian Run* (1970), *The Thirteenth Member* (1971), and *The Stronghold* (1974), for which she received the Library Association Carnegie Medal in 1975. She also won the 1973 Child Study Association Annual Award for *A Sound of Chariots* (1974), a poignant autobiographical novel. Besides her fiction, Hunter has written two plays and has also contributed articles to *The Scotsman* and *The Glasgow Herald.* In addition to the awards already mentioned, she has received the Scottish Arts Council Literary Award (1972).

Although the version of "One World" appearing here was taken from the pages of *The Horn Book Magazine,* the essay was first presented as a library lecture on April 29, 1975. We can easily imagine the pleasure and enthusiasm with which it must have been received, for it exhibits all the traits of a superlative lecture: sound organization, coherence, concreteness, lucidity, and personal charm. Perhaps most impressive, however, is its solid foundation of carefully researched material. Hunter approaches her subject not only as writer, but also as anthropologist, archaeologist, and cultural historian, generously sprinkling her perceptive examination of the folklore roots of fantasy literature with colorful and highly detailed illustrative examples, many of which are based upon her own personal experience with the topography, inhabitants, and legends of the

Orkney and Shetland Islands. From start to finish she treats her material with such confidence, authority, and familiarity that we cannot do other than nod our heads in agreement with her central thesis: fantasy is basically a "succession of folk memories filtered through the storyteller's imagination." Whether using the expository or fictional form, Mollie Hunter convincingly demonstrates her love for, and knowledge of, Celtic folklore.

·•❧ One World ❧•·

Mollie Hunter

PART I

"There's a ghost in Baker's Wood," said my sister. And we said—half wanting to believe her and half afraid to—

"Go on, there isn't! You're making that up."

"No, I'm not. It's the ghost of a baker that hanged himself. Why d'you think it's *called* Baker's Wood?"

None of us could think of an answer to that. Besides, although she was only twelve years old, my sister was still the oldest child there—which made the rest of us pretty small fry. And, of course, there was that bit in us that wanted to believe her. We fled past the darkness of Baker's Wood and fetched up half a mile away, still frightened, yet giggling with delight in ourselves. We'd tricked that old ghost, we had!

Everyone has some recollection of a similar childhood incident. Tucked away at the back of the mind perhaps, but still there, is some memory of the imagined

terror that has such fascination for children; and many
people must also have recall of one further experience
common in childhood—the feeling that around any corner one might catch a sudden glimpse of something
strange and wonderful. I remember vividly how I longed
for this something with an oddly poignant yearning;
and as a writer now, I find that the form of children's
literature which best exemplifies both the fascinated
terror and the yearning is what—for lack of a more
exact name—we refer to as fantasy.

The title is inexact, of course, because this is such a
wide-ranging genre, covering everything from "Snow
White and the Seven Dwarfs" to the adventures of as-
tronauts in future time. But the basis of all such tales
is the same. Their ingredients have a common source
in recurring elements of the tales from folklore with
which we in the Western world are familiar. Moreover,
all successful essays into fantasy have one result in
common, and my purpose now is to examine the background of this result and from this to assess its significance in children's literature.

A brief look at the technicalities of writing fantasy
is a first necessary step in this, so many writers having
tried the form and failed for lack of realizing one simple
truth. Fantasy is not simply absurdity piled upon absurdity until some climactic point is reached. However
skillful the writer may be in handling such a situation,
the initial credibility gap will still be too wide for the
main outline of the story to be acceptable; and even if
the reader perseveres in trying to bridge this gap, interest will fall away simply because the story contains
no natural and easy means of identification with its
characters.

True fantasy, on the other hand, is always firmly
rooted in fact or in some instantly recognizable circumstance acceptable to the reader—even if that circumstance is itself fantastic. One may say, for instance,
"There was a boy once made himself a whistle," or "The
starship Endeavour took off for an unknown universe."
The first is the factual type of opening which provides
instant reader identification with a character. The sec-

ond opening postulates a circumstance which in itself is fantasy in the sense of its being technically impossible; yet it is still so recognizably a projection from known facts that the reader can instantly associate with these and thus once again identify.

In the case of the first type of opening, the writer's skill must be directed towards pursuing this reader-identification to the point where character and reader are mutually engaged in some experience involving creatures of fantasy. In the case of the second, the reader's initial acceptance of a fantastic circumstance is furthered by peopling it with real—i.e. human—characters, and then similarly achieving mutual involvement of characters and reader.

The "fantastic fact" story basis can of course be placed far back in time as well as far forward as, for instance, "There was once a dwarf lived all alone in a dark forest"—an opening which postulates a circumstance so old in story terms that the reader's mind slides back in time as automatically as it jumps forward for a fantasy of the future. *Racial memory* or *ancestral memory* are the terms variously used to explain this easy reaching back to ancient thought patterns, and the phenomenon is one which is at least partly responsible for ready acceptance of all the folklore elements in fantasy. Paradoxically, also, one has only to glance at the most apparently modern of fantasies—the starship odyssey—to see immediately how some of these elements occur.

The Captain of this starship is always an identifiably human person, but always also he is its ultimate authority figure and thus the folklore equivalent of "the king of that country." Who, then, is the creature who stands at his elbow advising him—the being who hails from a planet other than earth and is gifted with paranormal powers? One of his interplanetary crew, of course, but also the folklore equivalent of the court magician.

The starship is threatened by the inhabitants of another planet—a race possessing an inexplicably advanced technology. In folklore terms, the king finds he has to counter magic. Lieutenant Magician, however, is able to explain that all the power of this technology is controlled by a device worn by the alien ruler—in folklore terms, the ring or amulet which is commonly pictured as conferring magic power. To capture the device therefore becomes the Captain's aim. But alas, possession of this is guarded by the impenetrable casket in which this ruling figure sleeps—paralleled again in the thicket around the Sleeping Beauty and in the glass case around Snow White; or else it is hidden in some complex of underground caves—a parallel with innumerable folk tales of dwarfs guarding treasure deep in the mine under a magic mountain. And so the story proceeds, taking a little bit here from this tradition of folklore, a little bit there from that, and proving in the process that Ecclesiastes was right in saying, "There is nothing new under the sun"—not even the adventures of a starship!

Further support than this is needed, however, for the claim that all fantasy is rooted in folklore, and the support comes first of all from defining the word *folklore* itself. The key to this definition is *lore*, which is derived from an Old English root interpreted as meaning either the act of teaching or that which is learned. Thus folklore is what people have learned and passed on through the ages—in effect, the traditions, beliefs, customs, sayings, stories, superstitions, and prejudices preserved by word of mouth among the common people and, even where no oral chain of communication existed, within their racial or ancestral memory.

A very long stretch of time is implied in this definition; in the case of the stories which embody most other aspects of folklore, a much longer period than illustrators of the first recorded versions would have us suppose. Indeed, to find the origins of such tales, we must go as far back as the first imaginative uses of speech, for folk tales are not a spontaneous act of invention. Far from this, they are the result of diverse experience over a long period in a wide variety of settings, with imagination only very gradually shaping the accreted knowledge of this experience into story form. With justice, in fact, they might well be called a people's record of events dating from prehistoric times, as perhaps one example could serve to demonstrate.

In the Orkney Islands, to the north of Britain, there is a structure known as Maes Howe. A *howe* in Orkney dialect is a hill, and Maes Howe from the exterior does present the appearance of a rounded, grass-covered hill. Its interior, however, shows it to be a megalithic monument of unique grandeur, a stone tumulus constructed with superb precision to be the burial hall of priests or kings. For more than thirty centuries Maes Howe has dominated the Orkney plain on which it stands, and—in the words of the late Eric Linklater—it shows that the men who built it had "a working knowledge of mathematics, a priest-king to whom they listened, and immortal longings."

Thirty centuries ago, on a tiny windswept island in the wild waters of the North Sea? Who could have visualized the existence of such a people or of such an achievement in building? And when the grass grew over the outer walls of Maes Howe, who could have believed the story of the great hall it concealed?

No one did, in fact; no one except the humble fishermen and farmers of that same island. It was they, century after century after century, who preserved the tale of Maes Howe as an artificial structure instead of the natural hill it seemed to be, and such was the strength of this legend that other men eventually heeded it. A party of twelfth-century Viking warriors broke through the roof of this strange tomb to plunder the treasure of its buried priest-kings. They left a record of their exploit in runes carved on the interior of its stone walls; and in their turn, they too were absorbed into the folk tale of Maes Howe. But still it remained only a folk tale, despised as a source of accurate information about the past until late in the nineteenth century when the resurgence of interest in folklore caused heart-searching among at least some of the learned people who had previously been so contemptuous. Maes Howe was among the phenomena investigated during this period, and the truth so long preserved in the folk tale was finally proved.

The mind conditioned to accept rapidly-changing patterns of culture finds it difficult, of course, to appreciate just how slowly all such tales have accreted—difficult also to grasp how very gradually imagination has transmuted the long experience they span and how folk memory alone has transmitted them. In yet another group of these northerly islands, however, there is most striking evidence of the circumstances that made all this process possible—physical evidence in the shape of a small area of settlement continuously occupied for more than three thousand years from the Stone Age onwards.

Jarlshof is the name of this settlement. It lies on one of the Shetland Islands, and the site it occupies is a complex of building-remains which show houses of the Bronze Age constructed among and around and on top of the earlier Stone Age dwellings. A wheelhouse and a broch of the Iron Age are planted squarely among the Bronze Age ruins. The ninth-century farmhouses of Norse settlers stand cheek by jowl with those buildings of prehistory. Later buildings by thirteenth-century Norsemen have been supplanted by a medieval farmstead, and towering over all these remains are the high, broken walls of a sixteenth-century mansion.

A great variety of artifacts and other physical evidence of occupation has been uncovered in these ruins, and much of it goes to show that the different cultures involved were not only contiguous but widely overlapping—stone tools continuing to be used well into the era of bronze, and bronze weapons until late after the working of iron was well-established, with household utensils, food, and methods of cultivation all showing similar degrees of overlapping. Jarlshof, in brief, is an excellent demonstration of the fact that social development in past time was not the stratified process into which it has been simplified by modes of thought prevailing in the nineteenth and early twentieth centuries, and where there has been an intermingling of physical cultures, there must inevitably also have been inter-mingling of all those component parts which make up the definition of folklore.

This is where we see the chain of communication through the centuries—the long, unbroken line of folk memory stretching in the case of Maes Howe from Megalithic times to the present day and channeled en-route by those Norse raiders seeking plunder in the tomb of legendary priest-kings. This is where we begin to see the reality behind the fantastic façade of the tale and to sense how the tale itself has grown from the interweaving of events and situations known to one age, only dimly remembered by ages following, and em-bellished by the imagination of later ages. This, finally, is where we should begin to appreciate that no such thing as pure fantasy exists. There is only a succession of folk memories filtered through the storyteller's imag-ination, and since all mankind shares in these memo-ries, they are the common store on which the modern storyteller must draw in his attempts to create fantasy.

Closely related to this is my other stated contention on the technicalities of writing fantasy. A solid base of fact or apparent fact is required for the reader to be able to identify, and as an example of how this operates in folklore terms, I instance a type of tale which very clearly demonstrates how fantasy springs from the folk-tale mixture of the known, the remembered, and the imagined. There may be variation of detail in this type of story—which I always think of as the Princess leg-end—but the broad lines of it are always the same.

A kingdom is troubled by some great danger. The King tries every method to combat it and fails. In de-spair, he offers the hand of his daughter and half his kingdom to the champion who will rid the kingdom of its danger. All the knights of the court take up the challenge. All fail. All the brave men of the country also take the test and fail. Finally, a challenger appears from outside the charmed circle of the brave and knightly—a poor boy from some unregarded corner of the kingdom or from outside it altogether. He applies resourcefulness where blind courage has failed, wins the hand of the Princess and half the kingdom. And when the old King dies, poor boy and Princess reign in his stead over the whole kingdom and live happily ever after.

This, on the surface, is pure fantasy; but its charm is no more than a façade for certain stern facts of sociopolitical life in prehistoric Europe. For *kingdom* in this setting, one must read *tribal unit;* and for *King, the husband of the tribe's matriarch,* for the situation embodied in the tale clearly points to a time when such tribal units managed to preserve identity and territorial rights through the system of matrilinear succession.

The idea behind this rule of succession was that a man cannot count on having sons who will rule wisely, but he *can* choose a son-in-law who will serve this purpose. Thus, succession to the ruling rights devolved through the eldest daughter of a line, with a husband carefully tested for more than his obvious qualities; and, to avoid consanguinity or internecine plotting, from as far beyond the court circle as possible.

Rule over half the kingdom was the further sensible device adopted to induct this young man into a share of the chieftainship at the moment the physical authority of the matriarch's husband was reckoned to be passing its peak—the matriarch and her aging husband gaining thereby from the authority of the young man's physical strength, the young couple by the advice of the older pair. And on the death of the older man, the young man achieved the full position he had won by marriage.

"They lived happily ever after" is the seal the storyteller finally sets on what started out as fact, and through a long, slow working of memory and imagination eventually took on the air of fantasy. Yet still it is a story which continues to *seem* grounded in fact, for this is the true art of the storyteller—to make his tale appear to relate to the lives of his hearers. The poor boy of the tale is no faceless character but an anti-hero with whom we can laugh and sympathize. The champions who fail are part of the established privilege he topples. The Princess, perhaps, is the spoiled brat we would all like to see suitably tamed. All the initial elements in the tale have some comparable dimension in real life, and thus we start out with so firm a grip on seeming fact that we never notice the point where this takes off into fantasy and carries us, soaring, with it.

This is a process that applies even to the furthest realm of fantasy—the supernatural. Yet once again, there is often writing which strives so hard for effect that it fails altogether to place the supernatural truly in context in fantasy and fails, accordingly, to reach the take-off point that carries the imagination of the reader soaring effortlessly into that furthest realm. And so once again also, we need an objective look at folklore—this time to define the significance of the role played in it by the supernatural.

PART II

A contradiction in terms becomes immediately evident in any attempt to define the role of the supernatural in folklore, some aspects of this appearing clearly to be founded in fact. The initial step in this must therefore be to divide all these aspects into two broad categories, the first one taking in creatures and objects which were themselves natural but which were thought to have supernatural powers.

The barrel of meal which gave an endless supply, for instance, is an obvious example of wish-fulfillment. And just as obviously, the frequent tales of the stranger hero who appears riding a horse which runs faster than the March wind point to a time when the horse was a previously-unknown and therefore impressive phenomenon to certain primitive peoples. Thus far one can go with the aid of deductive reasoning, but research can take us even further in examining this category of the supernatural, and here I would particularly instance the seal legends common in the north of Scotland and the islands of Orkney and Shetland. It is within this area that the great breeding grounds of the gray Atlantic seal are located, and these legends all concern the seal's supernatural power to shed its skin and take human form. In this way, it was said, seals could come ashore to marry and even interbreed with humans— as happened on one occasion when a young Shetland fisherman was walking late on a moonlit night by a lonely beach.

Suddenly the young man heard music—girls' voices singing on a strangely high and sweet note. The next moment he saw the girls. They were dancing, and singing as they danced. Their hair flowed free. Their bodies were white and supple in the white moonlight. Enchanted, the young man hid behind a rock to watch them, and close to his hand discovered a pile of seal-skins. Instantly then, he understood the meaning of the scene and determined to have one of those beautiful girls for his own. Snatching up a skin, he made off with it, and all the other seal-women immediately ran to recover their skins and plunge back into the sea.

The girl whose skin he had stolen was helpless to do this. Without the skin she could not assume her seal form again, and so she followed him, begging and pleading to have it returned. But the young man was adamant. Marriage to this particular beauty was what he planned, and seeing no help for it, the girl agreed to become his wife. The couple had two children—two boys who could not understand why their mother searched everywhere in the house whenever their father was away at sea and wept as she searched.

"What are you looking for, Mammy?" they kept asking. And always she answered them:

"Nothing you would understand. Nothing you would understand."

The younger of the two boys was not satisfied by this. Still he persisted with his questions, and driven beyond endurance by this at last, the mother told him:

"It's just an old sealskin your Daddy's hidden somewhere. That's what I need to find."

The boy had the sharp eyes of childhood, and long ago he had discovered where his father had hidden the stolen skin.

"Is that all?" said he and led his mother to the hiding-place.

The mother seized the skin, recognized it for her own, and hurried back to the sea with it to take her seal form again, although—the story most touchingly ends— "she grat sore to leave the bairns." That is, "she wept bitterly to leave the children."

There is an odd little ring of truth in this last, moving detail. Indeed, for all the fantasy of the concept behind it, the whole story is an interestingly circumstantial one, and research has indicated a primitive source in contacts that once existed between the natives of Shetland and other islanders they referred to as *Finns*. They came from an island group lying off the Norwegian port of Bergen, these Finns, and were known to use tiny canoes of sealskin, which they handled most skillfully. This gave them the power to exact a sort of tribute from the fishermen of Shetland, and the legends of Shetland portray these Finns as magicians with the sealskin boats as their true skins. Robbed of these skins, therefore, their magic was rendered harmless. Lacking them, they could not escape back to the sea; and so there seems little doubt that this kind of story also rests very solidly on factual circumstance ignorantly perceived and imaginatively interpreted.

To turn now to the second category of the supernatural in folklore is to consider all those creatures whose form and substance are only apparent, in the sense that they are simply manifestations of a world which itself has no physical existence. Chief among these, it is generally thought, are the fairies of folklore, but fairies are not so easily categorized. Some theorists see strong affinities between our familiar fairy lore and a much wider-ranging body of tales rooted in the religious influences of prehistoric times. Anthropologists, on the other hand, instance this familiar material as an example of folk memory preserving a strong tradition of the small-statured tribes which once inhabited Northern and Western Europe.

My own feeling is that fairy lore owes something to each of these sources—a theory I have dealt with at suitable length in another lecture; but for the time being at least, it can be said that fairies do not conclusively come within this second category. The beings which do properly belong to it, however, are both as varied and as truly insubstantial as the fears which bred them—the wraiths and fetches of Celtic legend, for instance, the hound of death, and all other apparitions of foreboding. One could further instance such concepts as earth godlings like the *gruagach* of the Scottish Highlands, which had to be given its libation of milk every day in case it would take the strength of the cows in the dairy, the mischievous Puck of English legend (which name in turn derives from the Slavic *bog* through the Scots Gaelic *boucca*—all of these, again, meaning an earth spirit), the closely-linked *pooka* of Irish legend (which was a mischievous spirit in animal form), the kelpie or water-horse of Scottish legend, together with goblins, demons, and every other kind of unearthly form. Yet all of these are still no more than personalized manifestations of some fear or longing, a projection of the imagination on a situation or setting which inspired emotion of some kind.

How these beings first entered into folklore is something that would require a book in itself to examine, but perhaps the best illustration of how they have persisted is in the Irish Puck Fair at Killorglin in County Kerry—the "Pook" Fair, as it is pronounced there; for here we can see the relationship to the pooka in the pook (i.e. the puck, or wild mountain goat) which is captured for the occasion and reigns for three days as King of the Puck Fair. All sorts of stories are told to explain the origin of this festival, which takes the form of a three-day orgy of drinking, dancing in the streets, and a horse-sale that brings tinkers and farmers from all over Ireland flocking to Killorglin. But the people of that place themselves admit that no one really knows why or when it all began, and only the atavism of the ritual proceedings involved points to the truth.

The Puck is brought into the village with great ceremony, riding on a cart filled with flowering heather. Following this come other carts, carrying young girls dressed in white and handing out bunches of heather to the waiting crowds. At the center of the village is a platform, built sixty feet high for this occasion. The procession halts at its foot, one of the girls crowns the Puck with a golden crown, and a band plays while the other girls dance in his honor. The Puck is then hoisted onto the platform itself and tethered there with food and water to last him for the three days he will reign over the Fair. And there he stays, high above all the horse-dealing and the dancing, the gypsies telling fortunes, the stalls selling hot *crubeens,* long eyes winking amber under his golden crown—an elemental creature at the heart of an elemental celebration.

Is he the *pooka* in visible, living form? One could reasonably guess that the intent originally was to show him so, but all one could truly say of him and his ilk is that man was very near the taproot of his existence when such creatures were first visualized. His senses were all keener than they were ever to be again, his body was tuned to the pulse of life all around him, his mind sensitive to every emanation of thought and feeling. Man was a fearful creature, with the imagination to invent danger even where none existed—a thinking creature who had to find some way to explain to himself all those curious sensations of mind and body. And so he was an animist, imputing a spirit of life to everything in his world—sun, grass, wind, water, tree, stone.

Man's imagination gave shapes and names to these hidden presences, forms without substance which were yet as real to him as anything which could be seen or touched; and thus, by personalizing his fears, he was able to define them. He invented a magic to counter the power he sensed in their unseen world; and thus he succeeded in controlling his fear of it, making this manageable even to the point where he could enjoy frightening himself with tales of the supernatural. And—perhaps—hold a Puck Fair!

A background of inherited thinking like this was inevitably a potent factor, too, in tales springing from events and situations in folk memory—especially since all these are rooted in times when magic continued to be commonly practiced and was universally believed to be effective. The subjective viewpoint which accepted magic as an agency of any event or situation, the appetite for the marvelous which is no more than the old childhood longing to glimpse the strange and wonderful around every corner—these were the other ingredients of the thinking which automatically seized on the supernatural as an explanation of the otherwise inexplicable in folk memory: the horse that could run as far as the wind, the meal barrel that never became empty, the seal which turned into a beautiful young woman. Time and the storytelling imagination did the rest, gradually achieving the apparent fantasy of the folk tale from this wholly natural and therefore perfect and inevitable blend of fact and fancy.

Compare now the workings of this sort of mind with that of the modern child reading a fantasy drawn from these same sources. The very early years of this child will also have been a totally animistic period, when spatial concepts were so incompletely grasped that objects could inexplicably leap out to hurt him, when favorite toys had names and therefore personalities which had fantasies of adventure woven around them, and when unseen, uncomprehended forces like a strong wind felt like the hand of some giant creature lifting him up. By his scale of measurement also, everything beyond his immediate surroundings belongs to a giant world, which is therefore full of menace for him. His physical senses are at their most acute, his emotions at their most perceptive. His delights are all in things which seem to have some magical significance—notice the face of a small child listening for the first time to the tick of a watch. His fears are the fears of the unknown, the inexplicable—watch the face of a small child seeing a storm for the first time.

In the first few years of life, in effect, the modern child undergoes a compressed form of all the physical, mental, and emotional experiences through which his primitive forebears developed; and when he reaches reading age, he has not entirely left this fantasy world behind him. Total memory of it will be dim, but the delights will stand out all the sharper for that. Language will have given him a point of reference for his fears, so that he will be able to control his memory of them—even to the point where they, too, take on the edge of delight which comes from knowing there is some ultimate safety from them. Becoming bolder with this knowledge, he will actually invent new terrors—as we did with the ghost in Baker's Wood—just for the sake of enjoying that dangerous edge of delight; and the further he grows from them in terms of years, the more he will be able to manipulate the balance of those fears and pleasures that engage his deepest nature.

Yet still there are forces within this growing child that urge him inexorably on towards the adult world of rational concepts, so that for some years of his growth, he is a divided personality. From the age of about eight, say, to around twelve years, one half of him longs to remain in his now-manageable fantasy world; the other half is eager to be accepted into the real world of adults, and the story which appears naturally to merge these two worlds in one can be his imaginative release.

This is the significance that fantasy has in children's literature, and this is the result that all successful essays into fantasy have in common. They integrate the real and the imagined world so closely into one wholly believable one that the child reader is no longer conscious of any division in his own personality. For the time the story lasts, at least, there is no "pull devil, pull baker" between his inherited subjective feelings which accept magic and the supernatural and the growth of his objective viewpoint which urges him to put aside those feelings.

The transition from one mode of thinking to the other will come eventually, of course; but in the child's good time when, by his own volition, he is wholly ready to accept it. Moreover, if the writer of fantasy has served him well enough, there will always be some talisman—a sight, a scent, a sound, a touch—which can take him back to this world where imagination and experience were so closely integrated—this perfect, one world of fantasy. The return will be brief, of course, and the occasions of return will grow fewer over the years, but this is a natural progression and most people would not wish it otherwise. The world of reality, after all, has no room for wistful backward-looking; and even if it had, there are no more than a few people who actively retain the desire for something known in childhood or have the capacity to evoke it at will. These few, moreover, soon become strangers to their fellows, for they are the incomprehensible ones—the dreamers who take the sky for their skull, the ribs of mountains for their bones, who sense always with the faculties of the primitive, and see always with the wondering eye of the child.

They are the ones who never pass a secret place in the woods without a stare of curiosity for the mystery implied in all its mounds and hollows, who still turn corners with a lift of expectation at the heart. And to be a writer of fantasy, one must be among those few—those fortunate few; for, to produce a work that answers all the demands of fantasy, is suddenly to turn the corner which does at last show something strange and wonderful waiting to be seen, and—most gloriously—to know that long-ago sense of yearning at last fulfilled.

KATHERINE KURTZ

(1944–   )

Katherine Kurtz had never written a novel, but in 1968 with the proper blend of timidity and confidence— and a dash of naïveté, as she readily acknowledges— she submitted and had accepted her proposal for the trilogy now known as The Chronicles of the Deryni. By 1980, the date of the interview essay that follows, this trilogy was into its seventh printing and had deservedly become a fantasy classic. And this trilogy was only the beginning.

Katherine Kurtz was born on October 18, 1944, in Coral Gables, Florida. In an earlier age, her entrance would have been viewed as something portentous, since it occurred in the midst of a hurricane. She became an avid reader, even before she entered elementary school, very likely because her mother began reading fairy tales to her when she was still an infant. Upon graduating from high school, Kurtz received a four-year science scholarship to the University of Miami at Coral Gables. She continued to excel and upon graduating with a B.S. in chemistry in 1966, she was admitted into medical school at the same university. After completing one year in this program, however, she decided upon a change. Kurtz quit medical school in the spring and enrolled the following fall as a graduate student in history, again at Miami, transferring to U.C.L.A. in the winter of 1968/69. For the next few years, in addition to attending classes, she wrote her first novel, (*Dernyi Rising*, 1970) and worked full-time as an administrative assistant with the Los Angeles Police Department. She completed her M.A. requirements and received her degree in 1971. For the next ten years, while working as an instructional technologist for the police department, she wrote five novels, the last two of which were in the vicinity of five hundred printed pages. In August of 1980 Kurtz made the "difficult decision" to "break with the world of salaries and shift to writing full-time," a decision she found "both exciting and scary."

Kurtz has commented on her reasons for following the path she has. She decided to leave medical school because it left her less and less time to pursue her love of reading and her more recent desire to write fiction. Both of these pursuits had been nurtured, Kurtz recalls gratefully, by her professors in the numerous humanities courses that she fortunately elected. In particular it was an honors humanities program in her freshman year that stimulated her love for the art, architecture, and ideals of the middle ages and the renaissance, a love that is so evident in her Deryni books. She notes that "nowadays, I read straight history and philosophy and religion for pleasure, as much as I read fiction— probably more."

Some of her comments help us to understand how Kurtz has been able to accomplish so much in a relatively short period. She views her very formal training in academic writing as of great assistance to her and recommends "a strong background of grammar, spelling, and punctuation." Her scientific training has instilled a sensitivity to detail and also has helped her work out the genetics of the very impressive Deryni family trees found in appendixes to several of the novels. During her work in history, Kurtz learned medieval Latin and acquired the skills in the research that is the foundation for her fiction. Although she much prefers her more recent regimen of full-time research and writing—she has been to England twice in the past two years gathering material—she was able, while working full-time, to write forty or fifty pages of manuscript on a good weekend, and she could edit this work during her lunch hours.

Kurtz's chief accomplishments are, of course, the books themselves. Her major works are the two Deryni trilogies, set quite specifically in a Celtic-English atmosphere of the early middle ages. The first trilogy, The Chronicles of the Deryni, consists of *Deryni Rising* (1970), *Deryni Checkmate* (1972), and *High Deryni* (1973). The Chronicles of Camber, named after the central character, comprise the second trilogy: *Camber of Culdi* (1976), *Saint Camber* (1978), and *Camber the Heretic* (1981). In the interview essay that follows, Kurtz explains her reservations about the short story form. She has recently modified these reservations, evidently because her novels have provided a larger tapestry that allows for, in fact suggests, spin-off stories or decorations that don't fit directly into the main subject. She has already produced three or four such decorations, one of the most recent of which is an elegantly woven story entitled "Bethane" (in *Hecate's Cauldron,* New York: Daw Books, 1982). She is now planning a collection of her Deryni short stories.

Kurtz keeps her readers informed about her forthcoming publications and works in progress through a "Progress Report" that she writes for *The Deryni Archives,* a journal put together by Kurtz and her Los Angeles fans. Her most recently completed work, due to appear early in 1983, is a World War II thriller entitled *The Lammas Option.* At present the tireless Kurtz is working on the first volume of the next Deryni trilogy, which picks up two years after the conclusion of *High Deryni,* and is also doing preliminary research for a biography of Dion Fortune, a fiction writer, psychologist-occultist, and member of The Golden Dawn, a mystical order which flourished just after the turn of the century, and whose members also included such a luminary as William Butler Yeats. In the October the

1981 *Deryni Archives* (Volume 7), Kurtz expresses the hope that she will write "a Deryni and a non-Deryni book per year from now on" (p. 3).

Fortunately for both Kurtz and her fans, she does unwind. She is a member of the Society for Creative Anachronism, an organization, as Kurtz defines it, dedicated to re-creating "the positive aspects of the Middle Ages as they existed in Western Europe." In the S.C.A. she is known as Countess Bevin Fraser. The Countess enjoys making and wearing medieval costumes and participating in various activities ranging from calligraphy and needlework to jousting ("at rings") on horseback. Kurtz is also owned by four cats.

The interview essay that follows is a considerably shortened version of one that appeared in two successive issues of *Fantasy Newsletter* (May and June, 1980). It was so successful that we decided to keep the question-answer format, rather than to put it into a typical essay. Most of the portions omitted in the current version are biographical; we have distilled this information and included much of it in the foregoing headnote. We are much in the debt of Dr. Jeffrey Elliot who arranged the interview, and developed the excellent questions. Katherine Kurtz has been a model of medieval "courtesie" in helping us to update the information. The reason we use the term "interview essay" is because several of Kurtz's responses are, in effect, short essays (she wrote out the answers and sent them to Elliot) dealing with a variety of subjects ranging from her own works to the more general concern of how one creates a secondary world. Of particular interest is her distinction between other kinds of fantasy and her own "historical fantasy." Another area of particular importance is her discussion of style, which Kurtz views somewhat differently than does Le Guin. In the series of responses that follows, Katherine Kurtz treats us to glimpses of the Deryni realm and to insights into the more inclusive world of fantasy.

·•❧ Interview Essay ❧•·

Katherine Kurtz (and Jeffrey M. Elliot)

Elliot: When asked which author most influenced your approach to writing fantasy, you cited Frank Herbert and his classic novel, *Dune.* What did Herbert teach you about the genre? Did he influence your attitude toward writing? What about the actual process itself?

Kurtz: I think what impressed me most about *Dune,* at the time, was the deft handling of characterization. I studied the way Herbert made his characters interact, how he wove together dialogue and action so that it flowed. There were very few slow spots in *Dune,* even when the characters were only talking. He had a very visual style in that book, and that was the way I wanted to write. I actually took apart a few of his scenes and analyzed them for this unique blend of talk and action which was successful for him in that particular book, so that I could figure out how he did it. I don't think I've ever done that with any other book, at least in writing, though there will be scenes here and there that I'll stop to re-read, to appreciate the artistry which makes a particular scene outstandingly successful. But Herbert was only a jumping-off point, so far as learning that particular lesson. Far more useful, in terms of sheer craftsmanship, was writing *Star Trek* scripts back in

1968—and I heartily recommend this kind of exercise to any writer who's still trying to perfect his or her dialogue and pacing sense. The idea is to take a television series that you particularly like—*Star Trek* was ideal, since it had very strongly realized characters and a good, solid universe to work with—and to write a sample script for it. Format is not particularly important for the exercise—though, if you pick a show that's going to be on the air for a while, there's always the chance (granted, slim) that you might be able to sell the script. What is important is that: First, you have to fit your story into a somewhat artificial but disciplined structure of a teaser and four approximately equal length acts, each ending on a cliffhanger or other note that will make the reader want to come back after the commercials (the same principle applies to chapter endings); and Second, you already know how the characters talk, how they phrase things, so you can worry about writing believable dialogue which will carry your plot, instead of having to worry about whether the character will hold together. (It can be extremely difficult to keep all the points in mind at once, when you're just starting out; hence, you concentrate on just a few things at first.) From there, it's much easier to ease into writing one's own material, with original characters and universes.

Elliot: Unlike most fantasy writers, you achieved professional status almost overnight, going from an unpublished writer to a writer with a contract for three books. Can you relate the events which led to the sale of the Deryni trilogy?

Kurtz: I guess I was too naïve to realize that people don't sell three-book contracts their first time out. I had written a short story, "Lords of Sorandor," while I was still in college, and when I came to California, I started toying with the idea of expanding it into a novel. When I went to Baycon, the World Science Fiction Convention in Oakland in 1968—my first science fiction convention, ever—I met a man named Stephen Whitfield, who had written the very successful *The Making of Star Trek,* for Ballantine Books. We got to talking, and I told him about my idea, and he said, "Hey, Ballantine is just beginning to look for original fantasy for their new Adult Fantasy series. Your idea sounds like it would be perfect. But don't write one book; write a trilogy." "You've got to be kidding," I said. "I haven't even written one, and you want me to write three?" "No problem," he replied. "What you do is, you write the first few chapters of the first book, with a page per chapter outline of the rest, and then you write a paragraph or so about each of the other two books. I'll tell Betty Ballantine to expect it." Well, after several gulps, and many questions, all delivered in a very small, timid voice, I decided that maybe I could do it, after all. I didn't have enough experience to realize that the odds were almost astronomical against such a thing succeeding. So I wrote my outline and my sample chapters and I sent them off—and two weeks later, got back that magical letter from Ballantine saying, "Hey, we really love your idea, and how does a contract for three books sound, with thus-and-so terms?" Talk about being blown away. Anyway, I accepted—and then settled down and began to work in earnest on *Deryni Rising.* It was well received, especially for a first novel, and I continued working on *Deryni Checkmate* and *High Deryni.* By the time those were finished, I had begun to establish a small but loyal following among fantasy and science fiction readers. And when I started the Camber Trilogy, things really started to take off. As of July, I'm more than halfway through with the third and final Camber book, *Camber the Heretic,* and the del Reys and I have mapped out at least the next six books in the Deryni universe. We've also talked about a mainstream novel which has the potential to be a best-seller, and I'm working on closing a contract for a film version of *Deryni Rising,* hopefully before the end of this year.

Elliot: As you assess your present situation, has this instant rise to professional status proved to be a totally positive thing—that is, would you be a better writer today had you been required to serve an apprenticeship? Where was your training-ground to fail?

Kurtz: I think my experience has been a positive thing. There are still times, though, when I sort of stand back and look at how far I've come and think, "Wow, is this really me?" Though I've had to work full-time at another job while I've been getting myself established as an author, I still am in the unusual position of actually making a living doing what I love to do—and unfortunately, not too many people are able to do that. Hopefully, by the end of this year, I'll really be doing what I love to do—writing my own things full-time. As for a training-ground to fail, I think I've had that; I've just not had it as public as many writers do, since I don't do short stories, as a rule. (There's one, "Swords Against Marluk," in *Flashing Swords! #4,* but that's really part of a novel that I'll be getting around to in the next year or two.) I think that authors who go the short story route get much more accustomed to the chanciness of writing. A novelist does his or her work in much larger chunks, so there's more time to work out glitches and more chance that a good editor will catch you before you go to press and make you fix the awful things that might get through in a short story. I'm not knocking short stories; I just don't care for them. I don't like to read them, and I don't particularly like to write them—and the same reason holds for both dislikes. Perhaps it's a lack of discipline, but I can't seem to confine myself to that short a format. My ideas are just too big, and I feel constricted by having to squash them down. I don't like to read them, either, because just when a story starts getting good, it's over. So I avoid short stories, for the most part. (And having said that, I have to tell you that I will probably be doing one next year sometime, since an incident has come up in the current novel, *Camber the Heretic,* which doesn't fit there, but wants to be told. So I will probably write it.) I have had my failures, by the way, both in science fiction. One was a short story that I wrote as a favor to a friend, and then he didn't like it for the anthology he was putting together. The other was a science fiction novel that I did for a publisher which shall remain anonymous, to the publisher's formula, and which, when finished, didn't match the formula which the publisher *then* said was what we'd agreed on. And, of course, because the book had been written to a formula, it wasn't fit for anything else in that form, so I've done nothing further with it. Someday, I'll go back and do it the way I should have done it the first time; but for now, it's just stuck in a drawer. There's a good story there, though.

Elliot: You've described your particular brand of writing as "historical fantasy." What does this term imply? How does it differ from what is commonly thought of as "fantasy" or "sword-and-sorcery?"

Kurtz: I would describe "historical fantasy" as fiction which is set in a universe which closely corresponds to our own history, so far as sociological and religious background is concerned. In the Deryni books, I've tried to be very careful to give a real historical flavor to what I've written, drawing very heavily on my background as a cultural historian and trying to instruct as well as entertain. Very much of what I talk about, in terms of horses, falconry, sailing ships, food, armour, costume, etc. is drawn from our own historical background. The saints I mention, for example, are all pre-tenth century or else they're made up. When I ordained Camber in *Saint Camber,* I took the ordination from pre-tenth century ecclesiastical practices. And when I do stray from a technological level, such as giving Morgan's ship *Rhaffalia* a jib, which really wasn't developed until several hundred years later in our own world, I try to give a plausible explanation for the difference. In a way, my world is an alternate or parallel of our own, with the divergence probably having occurred about the fifth or sixth century. Regular fantasy does not pretend to parallel our own history, except in the broadest sense. It

239

tends to be more fairy-tale medieval, for the most part, though it may draw heavily on mythological background of various cultures. And sword-and-sorcery goes even more eclectic, tending toward more action and less characterization, in general, with magic that may be almost entirely of the hocus-pocus variety and inhabited by creatures which never walked the world we know, except, perhaps, in nightmares. I think that characterization and internalization are important to the kind of fiction I like to read, and I think my writing shows this. Regular fantasy and sword-and-sorcery tend not to stress these points as much as I would like. I suppose that's one reason I started writing my own. Many writers get their start writing out of sheer preservation, because they can't find enough to read, of the type they want.

Elliot: How extensively do you draw on history in your fantasy, both for plot ideas and story details? What does history enable you to do, as a writer, that intuition doesn't?

Kurtz: As an historian, I'm convinced that we can and should learn from our history, both the mistakes and the successes. But if a person hasn't studied history except as the series of dates and battles and royal reigns, such as we discussed earlier, then he may not be aware of the valuable lessons to be learned from history. So I am constantly on the lookout for points of history that have relevance today, and for those connections of philosophy which are universally valid, regardless of the outward trappings. Handled skillfully, these can be both entertaining and enlightening experiences for the reader, not to mention the writer who puts them all together. I learn things from every book I write. The research and the bringing together of all the elements are half the fun of creating. As for intuition, that is often the catalyst which takes two or three only-possibly related elements and from them synthesizes a new way of looking at something. Sometimes the characters themselves take the elements and forge something wasn't expecting. Something magical happens when your characters start showing up at your story conferences with yourself. The first time Camber looked over my shoulder, I nearly fell out of my chair. Javan, Conhil's middle son, did that just the other night.

Elliot: One would imagine, upon reading your work, that you read and write Latin quite fluently. Is this the case? The Deryni fantasies make superb use of Latin terminology, but not to an excess. How do you know when to stop, when you're approaching overkill? What functions does the Latin serve in your fiction?

Kurtz: I fake Latin very well. Most of the Latin used in the books is taken directly from the Latin Missal or other liturgical sources. I do read Latin reasonably well for the purposes of translating old records, but the rest comes from faking it, as I said. I also have several priest friends who bail me out, from time to time. They like the books, by the way. The purpose of using the Latin in the first place is partially to give the flavor of the times—after all, the medieval Church was a great, overshadowing influence on all walks of life, in the real middle ages. I guess I just have a good sense of balance, as to how much is enough but not too much. In the case of any strange word, I try to use it in a context so that the reader has at least an idea what it means. Then, if he looks it up, too, that's even better. But at least I've planted another word in his unconscious, and hopefully he's going to be the richer for it. All human endeavor can enrich others of the race. Even negative human acts can instruct and give us a better appreciation for the positive human values.

Elliot: The Deryni fantasies draw heavily on your background in medieval history, patterning the imaginary kingdom of Gwynedd after ninth century Wales. Why did you choose this specific time period? What about this period, from an historical viewpoint, makes it productive for such a series?

Kurtz: Wales provides only a part of the background for the Deryni series. When I wrote the first book, I had never been to Great Britain, and I had this intellectual fascination with Wales that was based solely on what I had read and intuited about that fantastic country. When, between the completion of *Deryni Rising* and *Deryni Checkmate,* I actually went to Wales, that fascination was confirmed; but I also went to Scotland for the first time, and the Yorkshire area—and those really turned me on. If there's such a thing as reincarnation, and I tend to think there is, then I've been in Scotland before. Crossing the border was almost a physical sensation; it was like I'd gone home. Consequently, a lot more of Scottish and English flavor came into the later books, not just the Welsh influence. Lately, since I've been to Ireland and read more on the folklore and traditions of all these areas, my view of the Eleven Kingdoms has become even more eclectic. I think it makes for a much richer tapestry. As for time settings, I'm covering a two hundred year span just now, from around 916 to the early 1100s; and that's a period that's far enough removed in our own history that there's a great deal we don't know about it. That leaves me a lot of latitude in my speculations.

Elliot: What are some of the explicit and implicit assumptions which underlie the Deryni universe? Are they readily apparent in your fiction? How apparent do you try to make them?

Kurtz: I would say that the most explicit assumption is that magic works, though this has several aspects. We can define "magic" as any occurrence which seems to operate by means which we can't explain, especially if there seems to be no causal connection supported by scientific evidence. It's also been defined as science not yet understood, as it might be viewed by superstitious, non-scientific people. Much of what the Deryni do, that's considered magical by their contemporaries, is what we are beginning to call science today: telepathy, telekineses, teleportation, healing. They use hypnosis, too, though they have the added advantage of forcing a receptive state, which we do not, in this universe. Much of their so-called magical activity seems to take place within the trappings of what we might call "ceremonial magic," but there are also things which are mystical, bordering on the religious. And then, there are things which even they can't explain; they simply work "spells," and things happen. Of course, modern psychologists would point out, and rightly, that the purpose of ritual is to achieve a certain mental set, to get one into the right "head-space" to be able to turn the mind loose to realize special potentials which are not normally accessible at the conscious level. And this is true. But understanding how a phenomenon works doesn't make it any less valid. Whether the "spells" which the Deryni use are simply mnemonic devices to trigger certain mental sets, short-hand procedures for previously used rituals, is not important. What is important is that these are ways which work, for them, for gaining access to these higher human potentials. The fact that the Deryni discovered that these potentials can be awakened in some humans simply illustrates my belief that we all have some of these potentials, to some extent, and that if one works at it, one can always become better than one was. In this, the Deryni are embarked upon the classic quest for the Philosopher's Stone, the aim of the ancient alchemists. It wasn't really to make gold out of lead; it was to refine the human spirit and make it more valuable than it started out, to burn away the dross and reveal the perfected man. Now, the Deryni are far from perfect, but they do understand the need for this constant quest for perfection, knowing that they can never *reach* it, but knowing, also, that if no one tries, no one will ever rise any higher than he is. They do the best they can, with what they have been given. And a man's reach must exceed his grasp, else what's a heaven for?

Elliot: Can you discuss the process of inventing an imaginary world, one that is both interesting and believable? How do you go about the actual task of constructing such a world?

Kurtz: Constructing an imaginary world is both easier and more difficult than the uninitiated might think. A lot depends on how large a story you have to tell, how far-ranging you're going to be in your story-telling—a lot of things. For a world that's going to show up in more than one book, one almost has to have a map. I have one, and I try to be very scrupulous about putting new places on it, as I use them in the stories. This is the only way to avoid geographic inconsistencies. I also keep genealogies, since so many of my characters are related in some way; I keep lists of members of difference groups, with ages and any distinctive features such as the color associated with their magic, if they're Deryni; drawings of ground plans of buildings where my characters spend a lot of time, especially if I plan for them to go back there again; coats of arms; places mentioned but not yet placed on the map; who's associated with what lands. I'd be lost if I didn't keep my lists. I also do time-lines of events, as I've found out that's the only way for me to keep my interwoven plots and subplots from getting hopelessly tangled. The key to the whole thing is consistency; and this is the key. I don't care what kind of world one is writing about.

Elliot: Do you do extensive research in the course of writing a novel? Is all your research of a library nature? Do you ever do any personal experiments in order to understand a problem you're writing about?

Kurtz: I do some library research. I haunted the Loyola Library, the week I was working on the scene in *Camber of Culdi* where Cinhil's first son is baptized. I didn't have a Latin translation of the ceremony at home, and I nearly went crazy finding one. I did a lot of that kind of research on excommunication and ordination, too. My references to horses are largely gleaned from actual experience, when it comes to talking about their behavior. As for experimentation, in a way, I've done some of that. I recall that when I was writing that scene in *Deryni Checkmate,* where Morgan has been drugged with merasha and has fallen down the chute under St. Torin's shrine, and he's coming to—I got down on the floor and tried out that passage, to see what he really would have seen. Often, when I'm sitting at my typewriter, I'm making the facial expressions and gestures of my characters, as I write about them. Of course, all the background on hypnosis is authentic, too. My training as a hypnotist goes back many years, and my interest even farther. Hypnosis is not quite as versatile a tool for us as it is for the Deryni, but it's useful, nonetheless.

Elliot: The Deryni universe is clearly distinguished by your mastery of historical costuming. Have you read extensively in this area? Have you made many medieval costumes? Have you ever worn such costumes? Has your practical experience in this area enriched your fiction?

Kurtz: It wasn't until I came to California and discovered the Society for Creative Anachronism (SCA) that I really discovered the joys of historical costuming. I learned to sew when I was around seven or eight, and long ago reached the point where I'm not afraid to tackle much of anything, so far as a sewing project is concerned. Sewing medieval clothing is a little different, though, since you don't work with patterns, in the usual sense. That took a little getting used to; and I've had my share of disasters, and done my share of ripping out. But making and wearing medievals, as we call them in the SCA, is still one of my favorite ways to unwind. And, of course, making and wearing these clothes teaches you a lot about what one could and could not do while wearing them, and the reasons for some of the design features. These range from use intended for the garment, type of fabric available, *width* of fabric available—for, you have to remember that in the very early medieval times, the size of the loom was limited, so when you had to hand-weave every piece of fabric, you were going to want to make optimum use of that piece, and you weren't going to want to cut it anymore than necessary. Remember that the lady of the manor was responsible for clothing the entire household. She might have ladies to help her with the spinning and weaving and sewing, but this was pretty much a year-round occupation, just keeping clothing on everybody's back. When you have to go through that, you use and re-use every scrap of fabric, and cut down adult clothing for the children, and so on. We re-cycle clothes today, too.

Elliot: There are at least three, if not more, major themes in your fantasy: First, there is nothing wrong with being different; different does not necessarily imply bad; Second, power in itself is neither good nor evil; it is how one uses it; and Third, it is not good to misuse the gifts one's been given; instead, one has an obligation to use them as wisely as possible. Could you explain each of these themes in the context of your fiction?

Kurtz: I think you've stated the themes very well. The first theme gets down to the basic notion of prejudice, I suppose. We encounter all kinds of prejudice today—racial, religious, ethnic, social class. The point is, prejudice is so unfair. It isn't right to judge an individual on the basis of a group to which he belongs, especially if it's something over which he has no control. I suppose we could say that there are some areas of prejudice over which a person *does* have control, like religion or social class, since, at least in theory, a person could change his religion or make a million dollars and bring himself up to a better social class. But things like skin color, or Deryniness—these can't very well be changed. Furthermore, it isn't right to expect that people should have to change. None of these things I've mentioned hurt anybody else, in themselves. Certainly, things can be misused—but the qualities, in themselves, are neutral.

As for the second theme, the amoral nature of power, it's the use of power which takes on moral coloring. Atomic energy is an obvious modern example: the bomb vs. nuclear medicine. Or, to shade the judgment a little, a reactor which goes critical—power intended for good but gone astray—versus a well-run nuclear generator which benignly produces energy to power a whole state. Getting into the more human resources, we might use the example of a brilliant scientist doing research in bacteriology. He can look for a cure for cancer, or he can develop items for bacteriological warfare. The same genius, but turned to different ends. Among the Deryni, the contrasts are even more obvious, some of them using their enormous power to protect, some to destroy; some to heal, some to subvert the weak. Wencit of Torinth, for example, without his drive to regain what he felt was his, by whatever means possible, might have turned out quite differently. There was enormous power and potential there; yet he ended up as just so much cooling corpse—and it had to be that way.

Finally, the theme of using one's gifts wisely. I think this is a definite area which carries over into our lives. Everyone has various potentials, but they have to be realized. First, one has to recognize that they've got these potentials; and then, one has to develop them. Cinhil is probably the best example in the books. He fights like hell to avoid doing and being what he was born to do and be. The problem with Cinhil is that he was born to do and be several things, and the society in which he lives can't handle him doing both. He's led a peaceful and fulfilling religious life for most of his years when we first encounter him. He's a good priest and contemplative. He could have spent the rest of his life behind the cloister walls, and been perfectly content. He probably would have made a positive contribution to the life of his religious community, too. But he's also a prince of the royal blood, the only one left. And there comes the time when the need for him in this other, secular role, is greater than the need for him to stay in his monastery. You'll recall that poignant conversation he has with Archbishop Anscom, the night he's to be married to Megan, in which the Archbishop points the new duties that call. And Cinhil knows that Anscom is right, at least in his head. But he never manages to convince his heart, and that plagues him for the rest of his life, though he does attain a measure of personal fulfillment, once he resumes his priestly offices in private—especially once he confides in Alister-Camber and has someone with whom to share this aspect of his life.

Elliot: You've written extensively on the genetic code of Deryni inheritance. What is the basis of the code? How does it operate? What surprises does it hold?

Kurtz: The notes on genetic aspects of Deryni inheritance were a first crack at figuring out how the powers are transmitted. In the beginning, I postulated the Haldane potential being carried on the Y chromosome, which would endow all males of the line with the capability to have Deryni-like abilities put on them. This is consistent with what I'd developed in the beginning, concerning the Haldanes. Genetically speaking, there's no reason that all Haldane males couldn't assume Deryni powers; but because they've been told that only the king can hold the power at any one time, they think that the others can't. We'll see, in a later book about Kelson, that this is not true. Conall will learn this lesson very tragically. This particular potential is only male-linked, so we won't see any women receiving a magical potential in this manner. As for actual Deryni inheritance, I had originally envisioned it as being a single factor transmitted on the X chromosome, but I've realized, since I wrote that original speculation on genetics, that there have to be multiple factors involved. We know, for example, that the Healing factor is a separate one, that not all Deryni can heal. In fact, only a small percentage of Deryni can heal. The Healing factor also seems to be preferential for males, though we'll see a few female Healers. Rhys and Evaine's fourth child, a daughter named Jerusha, will be a born Healer. But there are definitely multiple factors at work here, because even Rhys and Evaine's children aren't all Healers. Two of the four are—a boy and a girl. One of these days, I'm going to sit down and rework the genetic theory covering this. I suspect that the factors involved are more like the ones that determine eye color, for example. You can get different degrees of involvement. And, of course, inherited Deryniness is definitely a potential. Born Deryni still have to be trained to realize their abilities. Otherwise, you get people like old Bethane, who learn just enough to be dangerous. We'll see a little of Gabrielite training of Deryni, some of them Healers, in *Camber the Heretic*. It's a shame the Gabrielites had to be wiped out, because they were really impressive people. We could use some of them around today.

Elliot: In the course of writing the Deryni fantasies, you've wrestled with the problem of logic and consistency. Is this a major worry in a series as vast and as complicated as yours?

Kurtz: A lot depends upon how large your concept is for the universe you're developing. Authors who set out to write one book, with no thoughts of continuing in that universe, tend to write themselves into corners and out of the possibility of sequels. If they later decide to do a sequel, they may have a rough time of it. *Dune Messiah* is a good example of this. Frank Herbert wrote a monumental masterpiece in *Dune,* but he wasn't thinking in terms of a sequel. By the time he went on to do *Dune Messiah,* he had a lot of corners to write himself out of, and the book suffers as a result. But he planned ahead for *Children of Dune,* and that book, while not as good as *Dune,* was infinitely better than *Dune Messiah.* Then there are authors who drive their readers crazy by not worrying whether every little detail is consistent from book to book, so long as each book is consistent within itself. Marion Zimmer Bradley, who is one of my very favorite people, does this a bit in her Darkover books, and it's certainly understandable, considering the vast time span over which she's written the books. Some of the inconsistencies she merely shrugs off. There's one, however, that I love, where she explains away a differing account by saying that this particular character was under a great deal of stress at the time a specific incident occurred, and he may not have remembered exactly how it happened, that his memory may have been mercifully blurred. It takes a rare and special talent to pull off that kind of escape from inconsistency, and Marion is an expert.

Elliot: In the course of reading the Deryni series, one cannot help but be impressed by the meticulous attention to detail (e.g., costuming). Is this talent an outgrowth of your training as an historian? Do you consider this a trademark of your writing? Is there the possible danger of loading the reader down with too much detail?

Kurtz: I don't think my attention to detail is so much a product of my historical background as it is just a part of me. I'm a very visual person. I have a vivid imagination, especially for scenes and colors and sounds. Some people have commented that the opening of *Deryni Rising* reads as though written for the screen—which is interesting, since I'm in the process of selling that book to a major producer for a feature film. I didn't necessarily have that in mind when I wrote it, though. That's just the way I saw it. If anything, it's the result of the scientific observation I was taught before I ever entertained the idea of being either an historian or a writer. Certainly, it's possible to go into too much detail. But it's not so much how *much* you tell, as *how* you tell it, that makes the difference. A good description, if it's properly balanced with action and dialogue, can be a great asset to creating the proper atmosphere in a story. If it's overdone, it can drag the whole thing down. Oddly enough, I've been criticized both for too much and not enough description. I suspect that the too-much advocates are the ones who are not strong visualizers themselves—and there's nothing wrong with that—and they really *do* get bogged down with too much detail that they just can't see in their minds' eyes. Early on in the books, about the time I was starting the Camber books, Lester del Rey called me on omitting some of that detail, though. As I recall, I'd talked about setting Wards Major several times, in the course of several books, and tried a short-hand description of what happens in that process. Lester came back and said, "Katherine, you have to remember that some of your readers are picking up any given book for the first time, and they may not have read the expanded version of what is old-hat to you, by now. Besides, they love your magic. They want it in all its details. So don't shortchange them." He's right, of course. The trick is to retell those things that have become familiar to me, in ways that are fresh and won't bore me or my faithful readers, yet will still give that first-time excitement to the reader who is encountering it for the first time.

Elliot: Can you discuss the genesis of the Deryni series? How did the idea come about? How did it develop?

Kurtz: The original idea for the series—or, I should say, the idea which later led to the Deryni concept—came from a dream I had back in about 1965. That was just the ghost of the story later told in *Deryni Rising.* Jehana was the one who had to assume the dead king's power, and Kelson was an infant in arms. There was also the possibility of a romantic interest between Morgan and Jehana. I wrote that in a short story called "Lords of Sorandor," which I've since published in the *Deryni Archives,* a magazine put out by some fans under my supervision. It was that story which I described to Stephen Whitfield, in an expanded version. And reading that story today, it's interesting to see what parts got translated almost intact in the final novel, and what things changed radically. I can't tell you where the Deryni themselves came from. They weren't in "Lords of Sorandor," at least by name. I wish I could remember how I discovered them, but it's been too long, and I've been too intimately involved with them for too long, to be able to recapture that discovery process. It really is more of a discovery process than a creative one, by the way. My readers have remarked, but not before I'd realized it myself, that at times, it's as though I'm recounting real history, not just telling a story I've made up. It's enough to make one wonder if it isn't possible, perhaps, to tap into another dimension. Maybe there really *are* Deryni, somewhere, somewhen. When one of those characters takes a storyline and runs, it certainly seems like there's something at work besides mere imagination.

Elliot: Many avid readers of fantasy, particularly those who enjoy the Deryni series, can cite several very strong lead characters in your work. What makes characters, such as Morgan, or Duncan, or Cinhil, so memorable?

Kurtz: I suppose the major difference between my characters and a lot of other fantasy characters is that mine are full of very human foibles and faults, even the heroes. By the time you've gotten to know a Morgan or a Duncan, you know a lot about what makes them tick. They're complex. And the heroes aren't all white, and the villains aren't all black. I'd say that the ones my readers identify most closely with are Morgan, of course, Duncan, Derry (which was something of a surprise to me, since he started out as a very minor character), Rhys, Evaine, and Camber. I feel closest to Camber, myself, with Duncan probably a close second. Camber is sort of a Deryni Thomas More, in many respects, with a lot of extra added attractions. He's an extremely ethical man who has to deal with situation ethics a great deal of the time, and it bothers him, even though he really believes he's doing the right things for the right reasons. Cinhil is another character that I feel I know very well, though I don't like a lot of the things about him. He goes a long way, from the time we first see him living in his monastery until he dies in *Camber the Heretic*. So does Camber, for that matter. Camber is very real for me. I'd know him if I ran into him on the street. (I should. He's peered over my shoulder at the typewriter often enough!) I'm very fond of Rhys, too, though I don't understand what makes him tick, as well as I do Camber. And Evaine is like me in many respects, especially her passion for learning about things and solving puzzles.

Elliot: Speaking of your characters, one wonders how you went about selecting their names. Did you select names that were prominent in this period: Did you invent many of the names? How did they originate?

Kurtz: I collect names. Whenever I go to a foreign country, I look for books on "What to Name Your Baby." I have them from England, Wales, Scotland, Cornwall, and Ireland, to name but a few. I like the Celtic flavor, and I like formal-sounding names. I hate nicknames, for the most part, especially the diminutives— Bobby, Johnny, Billy, Tommy. Yuch! The fastest way I know of, to get my fur bristled the wrong way, is to call me Kathy. So many people think they're indicating friendliness by calling a person by a nickname, even when they've been introduced by a given name. When I introduce myself as Katherine Kurtz, it's because I think of myself as Katherine, and I want to be called that. If I wanted to be called Kathy, I'd introduce myself that way. That's one of my few pet peeves. I always call someone by the name they want to be called. Names are very important. I would never name a child of mine a name that could be corrupted by unthinking clods— at least not a name that could have a diminutive ending put on it. My little nephew's name is Graham, for example. No way you're going to put a "*y*" ending on that and have it sound like a cutesy name. And I have a half-sister named Brenda. Again, no way to shorten that badly. As for my characters' names, I use historical names and made-up ones. I'll often use a less common spelling, like Brion. Occasionally, a character will address another by a shortened form, such as Alister addressing Jebediah as Jeb in a casual situation—but not a diminutive!

Elliot: Most science fiction and fantasy writers steer clear of religion as a major theme in their work. Yet, the Deryni fantasies are heavily steeped in religion, drawing extensively on custom, myth, ceremony, etc. Why do many writers in the field avoid this subject? Why do you place such important emphasis on religion? Do you have a particular view of religion or approach to religion that you attempt to incorporate into your writing?

Kurtz: It isn't particularly surprising to me that science fiction writers tend to steer clear of religion in their stories. I think the modern trend is to feel that somehow religion, especially in the realm of faith, is increasingly unimportant in the light of scientific sophistication. People brought up in a technological age, especially those with a strong scientific education, tend to distrust anything they can't see or measure. They view religion as the opiate of the masses, a psychological crutch which the progressed man doesn't need anymore. They think that organized religion, with its myths and customs and ceremonies, is out of date in these modern times. And if it's out of date now, it will surely be out of date in the future. Hence, when you encounter religion as a salient point in most science fiction, it's in the context of either a decadent civilization or a primitive planet where the progressed Earthmen are going to release the natives from theocratic bondage. Perhaps this is a harsh judgment, and there are exceptions to this generalization, but this is my impression. Even when most science fiction writers do try to deal with religion in a meaningful way, they come up short because they try to invent an alien religion without realizing what religion really means, and they aren't able to get into the emotional range of what religion is all about. The result is that the religions *do* come out as shallow and un-sophisticated, thereby proving the writers' theories that religion is an unimportant appendage of human psychology, and not worthy of the sophisticated and educated modern man. Fortunately, some science fiction writers do eventually reach the point of some of their really advanced scientist brothers and sisters, who have discovered that, in the long run, they *have* to acknowledge some universal Creative Force. Beyond a certain point, the most sophisticated scientists seem to come to the almost unanimous conclusion that there has to be Something to account for the majesty and order of the universe. This is basically a return to the foundation of religion, albeit in a more nebulous, less formal manner. Unfortunately, when most people reach this undeniable acknowledgement of that Great Something, when they've experienced the Great Awe, they become inarticulate about it. Theologians will write about it, but scientists generally don't. That's a shame, because I think they could give us some beautiful insights, from their unique point of view.

I *am* surprised, though, that more fantasy writers don't deal with religion, since they tend to have a liberal (as opposed to a hard science) education, and should have been exposed to human history in greater depth than one would expect of a scientist. Given a historical orientation, it's almost impossible not to realize that the Church in the Middle Ages, especially, was the single, overpowering influence that touched the life of every man, woman and child, even more than kings and warriors. Since most fantasy writers draw heavily on a medieval or quasi-medieval background, it's amazing that so many of them ignore this important point. Again, perhaps it's because they're uncomfortable talking about something which is really so close to the human center, whether you're talking about Judeo-Christian religion or the gentler aspects of the Old Religions. Modern man doesn't often have time to seek a mystical experience; and I think this is reflected in what is being written today, not just in fantasy and science fiction, but in all kinds of literature. Drug culture used this quest for the mystical as an excuse for their activities, but drugs have a tendency to become the end rather than the means. Some people are discovering that a mind-high is much better than a drug-high, and with no nasty side-effects, but achieving this state only with your own head takes a lot more discipline and control than just popping a pill or lighting up a joint or shooting up something. I don't take drugs; I don't even like to take an aspirin unless it's really necessary. But I've had some experiences that were absolutely mind-boggling. The mystical experience is something that still gives me shivers of sheer awe. I suppose I've drawn a little on that in the Camber books, especially. Remember, I told you that there was a lot of me in Camber. I've used this religious approach in the Deryni books both because of the historical framework and because I guess I want to try to share a little of the magic of what religious experience can be. And if you put that kind of thing in a fantasy novel, people who ordinarily would be a little skittish about acknowledging this part of them, in their modern, scientific educations, are often able to taste it just a little. And some of them go on and explore further on their own. Religion can be the opiate of the masses, as some folks charge; but if you take it a few steps beyond dogma and get to the archetypical foundations, the mystery of existence, you can find something that is valid and has meaning, at different levels for different people. The outward form isn't that important. Personally, I'm most comfortable in a Judeo-Christian framework similar to what I describe in the books; but I can also be comfortable in any of a number of other frameworks. People may call their gods by different names, and acknowledge Him or Her different ways; but it all goes back to the Source, in the end. There are many valid paths to the Godhead.

Elliot: Has the Deryni series bridged the gap between the fantasy audience and the mainstream audience? Are there tangible signs that mainstream readers are

buying and enjoying the books? Do you aspire to branch
out into other fields? If so, which ones?

Kurtz: I think it has, to a certain extent. I've had reports
that people who never read fantasy before have picked
up my books and gotten hooked on them, and then
started branching out to other fantasy and science fiction. People who like straight historical fiction also like
the books. They've also been great for getting junior
high and high school kids to start reading—kids who've
never read a whole book before in their lives. I've had
some amazing reports from teachers who use the books
as catalysts for getting kids to read. I do plan to do
other things besides the Deryni, though. I mentioned
the book on the medieval sheriff. I also have a couple
of mainstream-type projects that I'm going to do one of
these days.

Elliot: Some critics have argued that the early Deryni
books are not as deftly written as the later ones. Would
you agree? If so, why?

Kurtz: Of course, the earlier Deryni books are not written as deftly as the later ones. I wrote *Deryni Rising*
in 1969; I was ten years younger and less experienced
then. Also, *Deryni Rising* was a much simpler book, in
terms of plot and characters, than any of the later ones.
People don't usually realize, until I point it out to them,
that *Deryni Rising* is very unusual in that it all takes
place in little more than twenty-four hours, other than
the opening chapter. There's just so much you can do
in twenty-four hours, especially if it's a first novel and
you're still finding your literary balance. If I were writing *Deryni Rising* today, there are some things I'd add;
and when the film version eventually comes out, folks
will see some things added. It doesn't change the basic
story; but the script is much more the way the story
would have gone, if I'd written it today. It's a bit expanded, shows a little more of the relationships between
Morgan and Brion and Kelson. We actually see Morgan

257

before he goes off to Cardosa, and a little of his relationship with Kelson. It's going to be great fun. As for progress, I would certainly hope that the later books are the better ones. If they aren't, it means that I haven't been learning my lessons as an author. I'm told, for example, that *Saint Camber* is the best one to date, and I have to agree. I like that book very much. I still re-read passages from time to time and think to myself, "Wow, that's neat. Did I really write that?" And the neatest part of all is that I did! If I didn't enjoy writing so much, I wouldn't do it. It's nice that other people like to read what I've written, but if it didn't please me, too, I certainly wouldn't spend all those hours behind the typewriter.

Elliot: In what sense could it be said that you've grown as a writer? Can you see clear signs of improvement in your work? What do you do better today than when you began writing? What areas still require further effort?

Kurtz: Language seems to be the thing that's criticized most by reviewers. They seem to think that fantasy has to be full of thee's and thou's and lots of archaic language. That can be good, if it's done well, but it can make a book limp along very badly if it isn't just right. From as objective a point as I can manage in answering that charge, I would have to say that I'm not J. R. R. Tolkien or C. S. Lewis, and I don't think it's valid to criticize the Deryni books because my language is not theirs. I try to keep blatant modernisms out of the language, but I *am* writing for modern readers, and communication is sometimes more important than formal style. There are those who can handle this epic language beautifully, and I admire them for it; but I don't think that the stories I have to tell would benefit from being couched in that form. I could cite Mary Stewart's Merlin books as beautiful examples of language handling. And there's a novel called *The White Hart,* by Nancy Springer, that will be coming out from Pocket Books shortly, that's marvelous. But I don't think either of those ladies could tell the Deryni series as well as I can. Different kinds of tales call for different ways of telling. Still, I am aware of the fact that my language usage bothers some folks, and I'm trying to broaden the epic sweep of what I'm doing.

Elliot: Asked about the chief differences between male and female fantasy writers, you stated that the best epic fantasy today is being written by women. What accounts for this fact? Which writers come most readily to mind? Is there a major difference in the kind of fantasy being written by women as opposed to men?

Kurtz: I can't explain why the best fantasy is currently being written by women. It's simply been my observation that this is true, at least for the kind of fantasy I like to read. One can start with Anne McCaffrey and Andre Norton, go on with Patricia McKillip and Tanith Lee and C. J. Cherryh and Marion Zimmer Bradley, and wind up with a new writer, like Nancy Springer. Some of these women also write science fiction, or mix science fiction and fantasy, but their common point is that they all write *good* fantasy. I should also mention Mary Stewart and Evangeline Walton, of course; and I've undoubtedly left out some important ones. I think, perhaps, that women tend to be more intuitive, as opposed to being hard-science oriented—more concerned with people rather than things and events; and perhaps it's this which gives us a slight edge in writing the kind of fantasy I enjoy. Notice that I qualify good fantasy as the kind that I enjoy, which is entirely subjective. But that's what counts in reading tastes, in the long run. Sometimes one can tell why one likes a particular work; sometimes one can't—but one can almost always say whether one likes or doesn't like it. It's greatly a matter of personal taste. Not that I don't like and admire some of my male colleagues, like Poul Anderson—far from it. But some of the things most hyped in the past have been things I've enjoyed the least—and they have tended to be written by men. I can't explain the correlation.

Elliot: Finally, what plans do you have for the Deryni series in the future? Will it continue to expand indefinitely? Do you see an end-point in sight? Will you be disappointed when that end comes?

Kurtz: I have at least another six-to-eight books to do in the Deryni series, though I expect to do some other things along the way, too. And if more ideas come along for more Deryni books, I'll do them, too, as long as I continue to enjoy writing them. In addition to the three-book sequences on Morgan's childhood and origins, and what happens to Morgan and Duncan and Kelson two-to-three years after the first trilogy, I'd like to do a book just about Deryni magic, excerpting all the ceremonies and procedures and going more into the theory and such. I think that could be a very interesting project, and one which I know that a large number of my readers are interested in. There are all kinds of possibilities. I don't see any definite end in sight—partly because that would mean a cessation of the creative processes. When you create a whole world, if you've created it in multiple dimensions, you can't help but have it continue to generate more stories. There's always the question cropping up, of, "What happened then?" Or, "What happened before that?" Or, "What about So-and-So?" The concepts and characters will vary, and the way I look at them, as I grow in my awareness and in my skill at transmitting that awareness to my readers; but the possibilities are extensive. I see other, non-Deryni projects on the horizon, and perhaps they will eventually take precedence over the Deryni; but if they do, it will only be because I have grown into other areas of concern, and have other tales to tell, and other lessons to teach, and other wonders to discover.

MICHAEL MOORCOCK

(1939–   )

Michael Moorcock is a good example for a lesson on the perils of making hasty generalizations about people. He combines interests and pursuits that are not often found in one individual. In a largely autobiographical essay, *"New Worlds: A Personal History,"* he notes that he "had a relish for contemporary forms of fiction as well as a passion for the classics" (in *Foundation,* no. 15, 1979, p. 8). Thus he enjoys Charles Dickens and Leo Tolstoy as well as Ronald Firbank and Fritz Leiber. His broad taste in literature holds true also for music, embracing Mozart and the Beatles alike.

Another unusual combination is Moorcock's personal flamboyance and his professional conservatism. Charles Platt, a long-time associate, remembers the way Moorcock would appear at a monthly social gathering of British science fiction fans: "Moorcock looked somewhat out of place—tall, rotund, long-haired, bearded, dressed dashingly in a pale caramel suit, lavender shirt, paisley tie, and wide-brimmed felt hat" (*Dream Makers: The Uncommon People Who Write Science Fiction,* New York: A Berkley Book, 1980, p. 207). Such a portrait does not usually fit an editor who attacked, as Moorcock did, the "undisciplined and directionless romanticism in popular art," and the "contemporary enthusiasm for comic strips and technology and bizarre sexual imagery which had come with the Swinging Sixties" (*"New Worlds,"* p. 14). In attacking the fads and other excesses of the sixties Moorcock recognized and evidently enjoyed the fact that he was attacking what some people erroneously associated with him and his magazine. As an editor Moorcock was likewise looking for authors that were technically innovative—Borges, Peake, Calvino—but who were also both talented and disciplined. "We needed," he says, "more rigorous criticism" (*"New Worlds,"* p. 8).

A final instance of yoking apparently disparate pursuits is Moorcock's iconoclasm and his idealism. One need not venture far before encountering one of Moorcock's acerbic attacks against contemporary "establishment" writers: "I found most English fiction of the fifties and sixties worn-out, cliché-ridden, laborious, seemingly the tail end of a literary movement which had begun in the twenties and petered out by the forties" (*"New Worlds,"* p. 8). Moorcock, however, recognizes that such outrageous and usually unsupported statements arise from his own tendency to overreact. He frankly notes that many of his early articles were "often fiercely opinionated and probably over-stated" (*"New Worlds,"* p. 9). But what primarily motivated Moorcock was, he insists, not the wish to "shock anyone." Rather what he and his contributors shared that set them apart as *New Worlds* (the term "new wave" also applies) writers was the use of a "romantic idiom-using symbolism, imagery, and irony" to write "courageous stories" in order "to grapple with very large issues" (*Dream Makers,* p. 210). He reflects, with a measure of disillusionment, that "naïvely, we had honestly expected that these readers would be more open to new kinds of writing" (*"New Worlds,"* p. 11). In short, Moorcock and his new wave colleagues idealistically strove to revitalize literature and to confront serious social issues.

The numerous references to *New Worlds* in the preceding assessment underscore the central importance of this magazine in Moorcock's career. He edited this popular science-fiction magazine from 1964 to 1967; from 1967 until 1971, when it ceased to be published regularly, he was both editor and publisher, and he has brought out several special issues since then. Although he was only twenty-five when he became editor, he had already held three previous editorial posts, starting in 1956 when he was only seventeen, with *Tarzan Adventures,* a magazine for juveniles.

Another of the Moorcock paradoxes is that while he has been involved as an editor primarily with science fiction, he has done most of his writing in heroic fantasy. He launched his fantasy-writing career with the first of a series of linked short-stories, "Sojan the Swordsman," which appeared in 1957 in his own *Tarzan Adventures.* Since this first story, Moorcock has written close to sixty novels and ten collections of short stories, an unusual number of which stubbornly refuse to go out of print.

In 1967, Moorcock won a Nebula for the best novella, "Behold the Man," expanded and published as a novel two years later. In 1972 he won the British Fantasy Award for *The Knight of the Sword. The Condition of Muzak* won the 1977 *Guardian* Fiction Prize. It is the last of the four-volume Jerry Cornelius series, which is Moorcock's most unusual work, a blend of science fiction and contemporary satire. Moorcock has written several sword-and-sorcery series, the most important of which centers around the figure of Elric. Probably the best approach to the series is through its DAW Books revision, beginning with *Elric of Melniboné* (1976). Before leaving Moorcock's writings, it should be noted that readers will encounter different titles for a number of Moorcock's works. This situation exists because of different British and American titles or because Moorcock is constantly reworking his earlier works and chooses to assign a new title when they are reissued.

The essay that follows, "Wit and Humor in Fantasy," will doubtless give rise to a good deal of controversy—like author, like essay. In the first place, a passage or two may seem obscure, but, as the editor who first published the essay pointed out, "this essay forms part of a longer work (a study of epic fantasy entitled *Heroic Dreams*) and...references which may seem fleeting or obscure here are not so in the context of the whole book." Beyond this point, some may judge Moorcock's definition of comedy to be too narrow. Others may understandably bridle at an occasional abrasive, iconoclastic, and unsupported remark. On the other hand the essay demonstrates Moorcock's idealism—while he most admires irony, he refuses to justify works that he sees as "dismissive ironies." And the essay shows its author's passion for definition and critical standards. Most importantly, Moorcock is one of a very few writers to call our attention to the pervasiveness of humor in fantasy and to the unique historical partnership between humor and fantasy. A final note: Rayner Unwin, the son of Tolkien's editor, like Moorcock, failed to catch the humor in *The Lord of the Rings*. Tolkien responded:

I return Rayner's remarks with thanks to you both. I am sorry he felt overpowered, and I particularly miss any reference to the comedy, with which I imagined the first 'book' was well supplied. It may have misfired. I cannot bear funny books or plays myself, I mean those that set out to be all comic; but it seems to me that in real life, as here, it is precisely against the darkness of the world that comedy arises, and is best when that is not hidden.

The Letters of J. R. R. Tolkien,
Boston: Houghton Mifflin Company, 1981, p. 120.

Tolkien and Moorcock agree—at least in theory.

·✷· Wit and Humour in Fantasy ·✷·

Michael Moorcock

Father, I remember marking the flowers in the frame of carved oak, and casting my eye on the pistols which hang beneath, being the fire-arms with which, in the eventful year of 1746, my uncle meant to have espoused the cause of Prince Charles Edward; for, indeed, so little did he esteem personal safety, in comparison of steady high-church principle, that he waited but the news of the Adventurer's reaching London to hasten to join his standard.

> Scott, Introduction *Peverile of the Peak,* 1820

Scott's wit redeemed his work and makes it possible for us to enjoy it today in spite of its long windedness, its unlikely plots, its unfashionable sentiment. His humorous characters relieve the sober heart-searchings of his main characters. Scott, inheriting the style of the great 18th century novelists, could hardly fail to supply that wit, though he spread it as thinly as he spread the rest of his talents.

Fantastic fiction is happily very rich in comedy, from Thomas Love Peacock to Mervyn Peake. Comedy demands paradox—the juxtaposition of disparate images and elements—just as fantasy does. The square peg was never more delightful than when trying to fit itself into the round hole of a de Camp and Pratt fantasy. Comedy—like fantasy—is often at its best when making the greatest possible exaggerations—whereas tragedy usually becomes bathetic when it exaggerates. Obviously there is a vast difference between, say, Lewis Carroll and Richard Garnett but the thing that all writers of comedy have in common is a fascination with grotesque and unlikely juxtapositions of images, characters and events. The core of most humour, from Hal Roach to Nabokov. Somehow, too, the attraction to wholehearted mythological subject matter is often coupled to a comic talent as in the work of Mark Twain and James Branch Cabell. With *A Connecticut Yankee in King Arthur's Court,* Twain produced one of the greatest classics of its kind, which has influenced more than one generation of fantasy writers. What gives Twain's romance a power which its imitators have in the main lacked is the undercurrent of pathos and tragedy running through the whole story. It is a substantial and enduring book because, although it is funny, it does not deny the facts and implications of its subject matter. The death of England's chivalry before The Boss's electric fences and gatlings is all the more poignant for the comedy which precedes the scene.

Jokes are not Comedy and stories which contain jokes are not comic stories. The art of ironic comedy is the highest art of all in fiction and drama but it is by no means the most popular art. James Branch Cabell's success with *Jurgen* (1919) was based on the public's mistaken idea that the book was filthy. It introduced enough people to Cabell's work, however, to give him a reasonably large audience through his life-time. His work today is rarely reprinted, as Peacock's is rarely reprinted, partly because it is an acquired taste (like Meredith's novels) and no publisher is prepared to publish enough of his work to let anyone acquire that taste. A vicious circle. Here is an example of Cabell:

Thus it was that, upon the back of the elderly and quite tame dragon, Miramon returned to his earlier pursuits and to the practice of what he—in his striking way of putting things—described as art for art's sake. The episode of Manuel had been, in the lower field of merely utilitarian art, amusing enough. That stupid, tall, quiet posturer, when he set out to redeem Poictesme, had needed just the mere bit of elementary magic which Miramon had performed for him, to establish Manuel among the great ones of the earth. Miramon had, in consequence, sent a few obsolete gods to drive the Northmen out of Poictesme, while Manuel waited upon the sands north of Manneville and diverted his leisure by contemplatively spitting into the sea. Thereafter Manuel had held the land to the admiration of everybody but more particularly of Miramon,—who did not at all agree with Anavalt of Fomor in his estimation of Dom Manuel's mental gifts.

—The Silver Stallion (1926)

It seems always to have been true that the more grandiose, the more portentous, the less concise, the less truthful, the more humourless a writer is, the more successful he is; at least in immediate terms.

I think my own dislike of J. R. R. Tolkien lies primarily in the fact that in all those hundreds of pages, full of high ideals, sinister evil and noble deeds, there is scarcely a hint of irony anywhere. Its tone is one of relentless nursery room sobriety. "Once upon a time," began nanny gravely, for the telling of stories was a series [*sic*] matter, "there were a lot of furry little people who lived happily in the most beautiful, gentlest countryside you could possibly imagine, and then one day they learned that Wicked Outsiders were threatening this peace..."

There are, of course, some whimsical jokes in Tolkien, some 'universal ironies', but these only serve to exaggerate the paucity of genuine imaginative invention. The jokes are not there to point to the truth, but to reject it. The collapse down the centuries of the great myths into nursery tales is mirrored in recent fiction.

We have gone from hobbits, to seagulls, to rabbits and a whole host of other assorted talking vermin in a few short years and reached the ridiculous stage where there is often more substance to the children's books of writers like Garner, Garfield, Aiken and Cooper than there is in those fantasies apparently produced for adults! That such nostalgic pre-pubescent yearnings should exist in England is bad enough, but that they should have spread throughout the world is positively terrifying. To find them flourishing in the land of Twain, Mencken and Damon Runyon is deeply distressing. But one should not be naive. America has her own brand of such stuff and much of it is to be found in modern science fiction.

There is a specific method employed by the bad writer to avoid the implications of his subject matter, to reduce the tensions, to minimise the importance of themes which he might in pretending to write a serious book, inadvertently touch upon. This is the joke which specifically indicates to the reader that the story is not really 'true'. I'm reminded of my favourite line from Robert Heinlein's *Farnham's Freehold* where the daughter of the family, undergoing painful and primitive childbirth, pauses in her efforts to speak to her father. "Sorry about the sound-effects, daddy," she remarks.

The laboured irony, as it were, of the pulp hero or heroine, this deadly levity in the face of genuine experience, which serves not to point up the dramatic effect of the narrative, but to reduce it—and to make the experience described comfortingly 'unreal'—is the trick of the truly escapist author who pretends to be writing about fundamental truths and is in fact telling fundamental lies. An author of this kind cannot bear to confront reality for a second and will find any means of ignoring facts. Such wounded souls would be joking about the weather in Florida while they burned in Hell...

The great gaudy war-horses of heroic fantasy may look very fine in their silks, their cloth-of-gold, their silver, their iron, their richly decorated leather; they may roll their eyes and flare their nostrils and their huge hooves may dance proudly, but they are inclined to shy at the first whistle of shot, to whinny in terror at the sight of blood, and return to the safety of their high-fenced field to make somewhat nervous jokes about the real issues not being decided in the mud and filth of the battle—but on some higher, cosmic plane.

What genuine humour can do, as in the work of Tolkien's contemporary, Mervyn Peake, is to emphasise the implications of its subject matter, to humanise its heroes, clarify its issues and intensify its narrative. Humour is intrinsic to the *Gormenghast* trilogy (1945–59). Sonorous though much of the writing is, it is constantly saved from bathos by its wit, its shifts into dark comedy; melodramatic though many of the scenes can be, they are off-set by visual ironies, by comic juxtaposition, by sardonic descriptions, as with the Bright Carvers and their annual offerings. The injustices existing in Peake's world are injustices familiar to us all—cynicism, unfeeling self-involvement on the part of the powerful; confusion and fear on the part of the weak; unthinking brutality and inequalities, frustration and misery—yet these things are never harped upon; more often than not they are laughed at—while the author bides his time.

There are genuine comic grotesques in Peake—the Prunesquallors, the Teachers, Swelter, Barquentine, the sisters Cora and Clarice—the Earl and the Countess of Groan themselves. Even the central character of the first two novels, the infamous Steerpike, is made to behave somewhat ridiculously on occasions—and, when he takes his revenge on innocence—on those at whom we have laughed in earlier chapters—their plight is all the harder to endure: the pathos and misery of their situation is amplified and we see their fate in an altogether changed light. This is what the genuine comic writer can do, time after time. He can make us laugh only to pause with shock at the recognition of what we are actually laughing at: misery, despair, loneliness, humiliation, the fact of death.

Here is a short passage from the under-rated third

volume, *Titus Alone* (1959) where Titus has been arrested and is being tried for vagrancy:

> The Magistrate leaned forward on his elbows and
> rested his long, bony chin upon the knuckles of
> his interlocked fingers.
>
> 'This is the fourth time that I have had you
> before me at the bar, and as far as I can judge,
> the whole thing has been a waste of time to the
> Court and nothing but a nuisance to myself. Your
> answers, when they have been forthcoming, have
> been either idiotic, nebulous, or fantastic. This
> cannot be allowed to go on. Your youth is no ex-
> cuse. Do you like stamps?'
>
> 'Stamps, your Worship?'
>
> 'Do you collect them?'
>
> 'No.'
>
> 'A pity. I have a rare collection rotting daily.
> Now listen to me. You have already spent a week
> in prison—but it is not your vagrancy that trou-
> bles me. That is straightforward, though culpable.
> It is that you are rootless and obtuse. It seems
> you have some knowledge hidden from us. Your
> ways are curious, your terms are meaningless. I
> will ask you once again. What is this Gormen-
> ghast? What does it mean?'
>
> Titus turned his face to the Bench. If ever there
> was a man to be trusted, his Worship was that
> man.
>
> Ancient, wrinkled, like a tortoise, but with eyes
> as candid as grey glass.
>
> But Titus made no answer, only brushing his
> forehead with the sleeve of his coat.
>
> 'Have you heard his Worship's question?' said
> a voice at his side. It was Mr Drugg.
>
> 'I do not know,' said Titus, 'what is meant by
> such a question. You might just as well ask me
> what is this hand of mine? What does it mean?'
> And he raised it in the air with the fingers spread
> out like a starfish. 'Or what is this leg?' And he

stood on one foot in the box and shook the other as though it were loose. 'Forgive me, your Worship, I cannot understand.'

'It is a *place,* your Worship,' said the Clerk of the Court. 'The prisoner has insisted that it is a *place.*'

'Yes, yes,' said the Magistrate. 'But where is it? Is it north, south, east, or west, young man? Help *me* to help *you.* I take it you do not want to spend the rest of your life sleeping on the roofs of foreign towns. What is it boy? What is the matter with you?'

A ray of light slid through a high window of the Courtroom and hit the back of Mr Drugg's short neck as though it were revealing something of mystical significance. Mr Drugg drew back his head and the light moved forward and settled on his ear. Titus watched it as he spoke.

'I would tell you, if I could, sir,' he said. 'I only know that I have lost my way. It is not that I want to return to my home—I do not; it is that even if I wished to do so I could not. It is not that I have travelled very far; it is that I have lost my bearings, sir.'

'Did you run away, young man?'

'I rode away,' said Titus.

'From...Gormenghast?'

'Yes, your Worship.'

'Leaving your mother...?'

'Yes.'

'And your father...?'

'No, not my father...'

'Ah...is he dead, my boy?'

'Yes, your Worship. He was eaten by owls.'

The Magistrate raised an eyebrow and began to write upon a piece of paper.

Of all modern fantasists Mervyn Peake was probably the most successful at combining the comic with the epic to produce a trilogy which can be read and re-read for its insights into our own lives, showing our hopes and fears in a light which is often outrageously funny. The trilogy ranks with Meredith's *The Amazing Marriage* (1896) for the skill with which epic, comic, tragic and moral elements are blended together. It stands above all other works of its type; the *Gormenghast* trilogy is the apotheosis of that romantic form which had its crude beginnings with *The Castle of Otranto,* in which the vast, rambling, semi-ruined castle is a symbol of the mind itself.

"The optimist proclaims that we live in the best of all possible worlds," says Cabell, "and the pessimist fears that this is so."

The optimist and the pessimist constantly war within the writer of fiction as he gives shape to his chosen subject matter. But it should be the subject matter, not the author's wishes, which ultimately speaks for itself. If the author forces the material one way or another to achieve a happy or an unhappy ending and thus denies the implications of what he has written he is betraying both the reader and himself.

While I admire the work of James Branch Cabell I find his ironies too relentless. He cheats in order to show everything as an example of mere human folly. In contrast to Twain, he uses his talents almost always to avoid pain, though he uses them very cleverly. Nothing is important, says Cabell, therefore nothing hurts. One becomes weary, after a while, of dismissive aphorisms. Like Vonnegut, he seems primarily concerned with showing how ridiculous all human activity can be; how pointless is human sorrow; how silly is human ambition; how pathetic is human concern and sentiment. It is anxiety-quelling of a sort which pretends to realism. It tells us that nothing is really worth suffering for to the extent that people are prepared to suffer; and that we debase ourselves by means of our self-deceits, our ridiculous vanities. But in the end this view is as untrue to our experience of life as that of the ponderous writer who insists that all issues are Large Issues, and that all Quests are in the end Fulfilled, if He Who Makes The Journey is Noble and Virtuous and given to inappropriate sentimentality. Cabell's kind of fiction may well act as a fine antidote to Tolkien's, but neither is very satisfying to the demanding reader in the long run. The impulse to write dismissive ironies often emerges in reaction to an overdose of portentous and meretricious sobriety; but one, though pleasanter to read and considerably more palatable to digest, is finally no more enduring than the other.

Melodrama and irony work very well together; the best fantasies contain both elements, which maintain tonal equilibrium—but a work of fantasy must, like all good fiction, be something more than aesthetically pleasing—though we should be grateful for the little that is merely that. It should have at its source some fundamental concern for human beings, some ambition to show, by means of image, metaphor, elements of allegory, what human life is actually about. As with listening to the music of Mozart, of Ives or Schoenberg, we wish to be entertained, to escape the immediate pressures of the world—but we also wish, when we read, to be informed, to try to understand how we may deal with these problems and how we may respond positively, without cynicism, to the injustices and frustrations which constantly hamper the needs of the spirit.

The messianic fervour amongst the more outlandish supporters of Heinlein or Tolkien shows, well enough, that the reader expects more than simple entertainment from his fantastic fictions. I doubt if there are many imaginative writers who have not had at least one letter—possibly hundreds—from readers who believe that a work of fiction has changed their lives, helped them through a difficult time, caused them to re-assess themselves and their society, and so on. To be a victim of one's own messianism is terrible—to become the victim of someone else's is even worse. By introducing an element of comedy into his work a writer can maintain perspective for himself and his readers. Wit is the best enemy of perverted or fanatical romanticism.

Comedy and fantasy are close companions. If fantasy is real life exaggerated, more colourful and, perhaps, simpler—if the extremes of life are represented by giants and fairies, dragons and heroes—then the vicissitudes of life are represented in comedy by a pratfall or a custard pie, an embarrassing misunderstanding, and the losing of one's trousers at a formal function. To off-set the grandiose, the pompous elements in fantasy, the writer like Fritz Leiber will introduce comedy to 'humanise' the characters and make the reader much more concerned in their fate than they might otherwise be. The degree of irony one employs can often determine the degree of sentiment one uses and if one does want to touch on matters about which one feels deeply, then it is often better to use a comic context. One feels no less seriously about something, but one is able to face the implications with a steadier eye. Even in heroic fantasy garb it is possible to canter towards the guns and not shy away from the first or even the second cannonade.

Horace Walpole said that life was a comedy to those that think, a tragedy to those that feel. Since it is fair to guess that the majority of us both think and feel it is fair to expect fiction which appeals to both our thoughts and our emotions. When fantasy attempts to understand the real world tragic subject matter and comic style can often be the best combination. Byron says in *Don Juan:* "And if I laugh at any mortal thing/ 'Tis that I May not weep."

But a writer must entertain before he has any right to try instruction (even if his only attempt is to instruct the reader's sensibility). A writer has a natural reticence to shout at the same volume the same slogans as those people, quite as miserable and angry as himself, whose protests at such barbarism as modern war takes a more direct and political form. An artist cannot be much of a politician, unless it is during his time off.

If one *is* primarily concerned with telling a moral tale in the exaggerated form called 'fantasy' then comedy can have a humanising influence on what might otherwise be merely a portentous or over-distanced epic narrative. It also enables an author to cope with an idea on more than one level. If he is working a form where the ironic tone seems largely unsuitable he can supply a balance by having a character whose function can be to offer an ironic commentary on the protestations and ambitions of the hero. Thus in Leiber Fafhrd is fundamentally gloomy, while the Mouser is fundamentally optimistic. No matter how serious the drama, humour may help humanise the character and, on a simple level, the use of humour is the secret of the success of most of the popular film-thrillers, from *The Maltese Falcon* to *Jaws, The Wind and the Lion,* to *The Man Who Would Be King*. One thing that can be said for *Star Wars* (dreadful though the script is) is that it may well have banished the tone of Awful Seriousness which seemed to overtake even fairly good directors when faced with the prospect of doing quite an ordinary or minor science fiction subject.

To try to distinguish between different forms of humour here would be as silly as trying to define different kinds of fantasy and science fiction. It ranges from the wit of Meredith to the comedy of Dickens.

From Homer onwards the world's epics and fables have given us comic characters, including, of course, the original Conan, the buffoon, companion of Finn and the Red Branch heroes, yet there are surprisingly few such characters in the vast numbers of recent heroic fantasies claiming the mythological romance as their particular heritage. The comic strips offer a wider selection of humour, particularly in the *Star Reach* group of comics and the *Howard the Duck* series.

That comedy and fantasy may combine to delightful effect (as in *A Midsummer Night's Dream*) was shown by *Unknown* where writers like de Camp and Pratt, Anthony Boucher, Fritz Leiber, Henry Kuttner and many others came into their own. It is probably not a coincidence that the best writers have almost all shown themselves capable of producing marvellous comic stories. A strong sense of comedy or irony in a genre writer ensures that his chosen genre, at least in his hands, never becomes stale and over-formalised. Chandler and Hammett introduced sophisticated humour into the thriller without for a moment destroying the dramatic power of their work and gave the detective story a lease of life it retains to this day, as well as improving the overall level of aspiration of writers.

It seems to me that if fantasy fiction is to avoid the stultification that has befallen commercial science fiction it would do well to recall its strong bonds with comedy.

"To love Comedy," says Meredith, in his great essay *On The Idea of Comedy and the Uses of the Comic Spirit,* "you must know the real world, and know them, though you may still hope for good." To keep a form vital you must draw your inspiration not from other books in that form but from life itself, from experience, from knowledge of men and women, and, where fantasy fiction is concerned, from an enthusiasm for the epic, the myth, the noble metaphor which speaks to us on a hundred levels. And to make such things speak to their fellows in as many voices as possible, writers must employ comedy to remind their readers that no matter how intense the images, how grand the themes, how awe-inspiring the terrors, one is still writing about reality.

SUSAN COOPER

(1935–   )

In her acceptance speech for the Newbery Medal in 1976, Susan Cooper pointed out an element of irony. The American Library Association, celebrating its centennial in the year of the bicentennial of the United States, awarded its highest honor "to a Limey" ("Newbery Award Acceptance," *The Horn Book*, August 1976, p. 361). Cooper is perhaps better described as Anglo-American. She has lived near Boston with her American husband since 1963. Her previous record is, however, all British, and there is no question that it is this influence that dominates all her writings.

She was born on May 23, 1935, in Burnham, Buckinghamshire, England. She refers to her generation as children of World War II and has vivid memories as a six-year-old of air raid sirens and bombs and walking to school the next day collecting bits of shrapnel ("Newbery Award Acceptance," p. 365). These memories played an important part in her writing later on. Cooper attended Somerville College, Oxford, for English studies (1953–56) and earned her M.A. there in 1956. She became a successful reporter and feature writer for the *London Times* for several years, eventually writing Sunday features and becoming a deputy news director. In 1963, she married an American, Nicholas J. Grant, and moved to the United States. She has one son, one daughter, and three stepchildren. Although she resides in the United States she travels each year to England. She and her husband have also built a house on an island called Great Camanoe in the British Virgin Islands. They spend summers and winter vacations there, and it is there that she does much of her writing. Cooper remains very attached to her native England. "I'd never really mastered my homesickness, and I suppose I never shall" ("Newbery Award Acceptance," p. 364).

And it is, as already noted, her native England which has chiefly inspired her writings, particularly her famous series of five novels, *The Dark is Rising*. She traces the source of the novels, in her Newbery acceptance speech, to her "endless reading about Britain, prehistory, Britain, myth, folk tale, Britain..." (p. 364). The first in the series, *Over Sea, Under Stone,* appeared in 1965 and was an American Library Association Notable Book that year. The idea for a series did not occur to Cooper until a number of years later. *The Dark is Rising* appeared in 1973 and won the Boston Globe-Hornbook Award, was a Newbery runner-up, and also an American Library Association Notable. *Greenwich* appeared in 1974, followed by *The Grey King* in 1975, for which Cooper received the Newbery Medal in 1976. The final book of the series is *Silver on the Tree* (1977). She attributes her preoccupation with "the ancient problem of the duality of human nature" in *The Dark is Rising* to her childhood experiences of this good-evil phenomenon in World War II ("Newbery Award Acceptance," p. 365). Cooper is, with ample justification, compared to Tolkien and C. S. Lewis in her use of myth and legend in these books. Like Alan Garner she relies heavily on Celtic materials, though unlike Garner she employs the Arthurian legend to a considerable extent.

In addition to the series, Cooper has written an adult science fiction novel, *Mandrake* (1964), a documentary called *Behind the Golden Curtain: A View of the U.S.A.* (1965), and a charming illustrated fantasy for children, *Jethro and the Jumbie*. In this last mentioned work, she uses the setting and dialect of her Virgin Islands winter home.

In a fairly recent *Horn Book* essay, "Nahum Tarune's Book" (October 1980), Cooper attempts to identify the ingredient that makes good fantasy so special. She uses a book that has been a favorite of hers for thirty years, Walter de la Mare's anthology of poetry *Come Hither*, as an example of a book that has "the mysterious quality... evanescent as a rainbow" (p. 498) to which readers respond so deeply. She identifies the quality by the depth of the reader's response: "that magical shiver of response," "stab of joy," "lovely shock." In the essay included here, she goes a step further and notes, as would Jung, that writing a fantasy involves discovering elements from her unconscious and that the reader shares in this process of discovery. In short, the writer— and reader—of fantasy are discovering archetypes. Cooper, then, discovers much of her material as she goes, much the way Ursula K. Le Guin does (compare "Dreams Must Explain Themselves"). As corollary to the Jungian subject, Cooper offers an intriguing view of the different levels on which fantasy appeals to a reader at different ages and how it becomes a means of self-discovery. She also compares fantasy and mainstream writing on the basis of how they stimulate this self-discovery. And she couches these potentially heavy and academic subjects in a pleasing poetic style.

·✦· Escaping into Ourselves ✦·

Susan Cooper

The legs turn toward the library, the hands reach for a novel. Why? "Well, I read for pleasure, of course." Of course: but what's the root of the pleasure, the reason why anyone, child or adult, reads fiction?

The reason, simply, is entertainment. The novel entertains by offering refreshment, solace, excitement, relaxation, perhaps even inspiration: an escape from reality. And the escape, in turn, brings encouragement, leaving the reader fortified to cope with his own reality when he returns to it. So I hear the slam of the door sometimes as my twelve-year-old Kate, feeling the weight of the world upon her slender shoulders, retreats into her room; and I know that she will shortly be curled up in there with a book—and will, afterward, feel better.

In "realistic" fiction, the escape and the encouragement come from a sense of parallel: from finding a true and recognizable portrait of real life. In those pages we encounter familiar problems, but they're *someone else's* problems; involved but secure, relaxing into the story, we watch while the other fellow copes. If the ending is happy, we are reassured; even in a difficult world, all may be well at last. If the ending is tragic, the ancient cathartic effect of pity and fear takes over and we are reassured just the same, by the courage or steadfastness or simple humanity of the hero/heroine. We small people enjoy reading—need to read—about big people; at one end of that scale is the newspaper gossip column, at the other the New Testament.

Comic novels, thrillers, biographies, romances all have the same kind of appeal. So does science fiction, which does unearthly things to space and time but is still realistic fiction at heart. In all such books the reader knows, beneath the suspense of the story, what to expect; the "straight" novelist will not tamper with the limits of human behavior, nor the science fiction writer cheat by changing the laws of thermodynamics. Their greatest charm is that they play an exciting game according to rules.

There is just one kind of fiction which differs from all these. Why does anyone read, or write, fantasy?

Fantasy goes one stage beyond realism; requiring complete intellectual surrender, it asks more of the reader, and at its best may offer more. Perhaps this is why it is also less popular, at any rate among adults, who set such store by their ability to think. Among small children, who have not yet begun to think much about the stories they hear, fantasy reigns supreme. No realistic story has yet attained the universal affection they give to fairy-tale, except possibly, in the United States, *Goodnight Moon*—which is not a story at all, but a deceptively simple ritual. Very young children, their conscious minds not yet developed, are all feeling and instinct. Closer to the unconscious than they will ever be again, they respond naturally to the archetypes and the deep echoes of fairy story, ritual, and myth.

But after that, learning begins, as it must; the child is launched on his long quest for understanding. As he discovers the world around him, and the books which show him that world, his tastes in reading veer naturally toward realism. Some children not only reach that point but stay there; shunning fantasy as "babyish," they grow up to become those adults who seldom read novels at all, and find their escape and encouragement from those other contemporary escapist phenomena, which range, as Ursula Le Guin once wryly observed, from television soap operas to "that masterpiece of total unreality, the daily Stock Market Report." But others, born with a different chemistry, go on seeking out fantasy all their lives, instinctively aware that so far from being babyish, it is probably the most complex form of fiction they will ever find.

And what do we, and they, find, when we read fantasy? The escape and encouragement are there, for sure—but in a different form. This time, when we depart from our own reality into the reality of the book, it's not a matter of stepping across the street, or into the next county, or even the next planet. This time, we're going out of time, out of space, into the unconscious, that dreamlike world which has in it all the images and emotions accumulated since the human race began. We aren't escaping out, we're escaping in, without any idea of what we may encounter. Fantasy is the metaphor through which we discover ourselves.

So it is for the writer, too. Every book is a voyage of discovery. Perhaps I speak only for myself, perhaps it's different for other writers; but for me, the making of a fantasy is quite unlike the relatively ordered procedure of writing any other kind of book. I've never actually *thought:* "I am writing fantasy"; one simply sits down to write whatever book is knocking to be let out. But in hindsight, I can see the peculiar difference in approach. When working on a book which turns out to be a fantasy novel, I exist in a state of continual astonishment. The work begins with a deep breath and a blindly trusting step into the unknown; I know where I'm going, and who's going with me, but I have no real idea of what I shall find on the way, or whom I'll meet. Each time, I am striking out into a strange land, listening for the music that will tell me which way to go. And I am always overcome by wonder, and a kind of unfocused gratitude, when I arrive; and I always think of Eliot:

We shall not cease from exploration
And the end of all our exploring

Will be to arrive where we started
And know the place for the first time....

One of our best "realistic" novelists (how I hate these labels—but there's no way round them) said to me once, cheerfully rude, "Oh, you fantasy people have it so easy, you don't know you're born. If there's a problem in your plot—bingo, you bring in a bit of magic, and the problem's gone."

No, no, no, fantasy doesn't work that way; anyone cherishing such theories is bound for trouble. If he or she tries to sail our perilous sea in such a ship, he is likely to end up with a book which may be beautifully written, hugely entertaining, full of bits of magic—but which somehow isn't fantasy. True fantasy is John Masefield's *The Box of Delights,* or Alan Garner's *The Owl Service:* books which cast a spell so subtle and overwhelming that it has overpowered the reader's imagination, carried him outside all rules, before he has noticed what is happening. To some degree I doubt whether Masefield or Garner or the rest knew what was happening either; they simply heard the music, and employed all their very considerable talent to write it down. You can't write fantasy on purpose. It won't come when called. Like poetry, it is a kind of happy accident which overtakes certain writers before they are born.

In case I seem to be portraying those of us who write fantasy as The Chosen, I might add that all other specific gifts within the large realm of fiction are just as slippery, just as arbitrary. Very few writers can sow their seed successfully in more than one or two fields. Once, when I was young and very poor, I decided to chase an instant income by writing short stories for women's magazines. This wasn't my favorite occupation, but I knew I could write, and—believing that therefore I could write absolutely anything—I did my best. The stories were uniformly terrible and not one of them was published. Wiser and less arrogant—and still poor—I went back to the kind of writing I was born to do: that is, to the limited range of ideas that my imagination would offer unbidden. And those writers with a different kind of imagination, hearing a different music, went on writing very good short stories.

An entry in one of my working notebooks reads: "We are all at the mercy of the quality of the imagination we inherit. The book can never be better than that."

A writer's notebooks are perhaps the best illustration (better in some ways than the books themselves) of the way his mind works. Some consist of detailed blueprints for books or plays, set out with mathematical precision; some are filled with discursive examinations of character, building up backgrounds which may never appear in the story but which show the writer getting to know the people he has made. My own notes are mostly cryptic and random, full of images, scattered with quotations and ideas which often seem totally irrelevant to the book in hand—though they weren't at the time. Rereading them, I have always again the *feel* of what it is like to write fantasy, though whether any of this can be communicated by the notes themselves I do not know.

This book is mountains and lakes and valleys, birds and trees, with the sea in the distance glimmering, waiting. The last book is the lost cantref off the estuary, the drowned land where the bells sound. The long sands, the open sea and sky; the dunes.

If you wear agrimony, you may see witches. And if you look into their eyes, you see no reflection of yourself. The scarlet pimpernel is a charm against them.

Names of fields in Hitcham: Great and Lower Cogmarthon; Upper and Lower Brissels; Homer Corner; Hogg Hill.

The sword comes from the drowned land.

The opening of doors. Wakening of things sleeping. Revealing of old things forgotten.

Don't forget: "The mountains are singing, and the Lady comes."

Bird Rock. The birds remember. It is the door.

The "brenin bren y Ganllwyd," the great king oak near Dolgellau, felled in the early 18th century. Bole contained 609 cubic feet, and above this towered four great branches, each long enough for a mill shaft.

Sandpipers run, and scoot off into the air, in pairs and tens and little flocks. One leads Will somewhere.

Triad from the 13th century Exeter *Chronica de Wallia:* "These are the kingdoms which the sea destroyed.... The second kingdom was that of Henig son of Glannog; it was between Cardigan and Bardsey, and as far as St. David's. That land was very good, fertile and level, and it was called Maes Maichgen; it lay from the mouth (of the Ystwyth?) to Llyn, *and up to Aberdovey....*"

The Doors come back, perhaps in Book Five.

In Welsh, "glas" can mean green as well as blue, silver, greyish-white and slate-colored. The Welsh word for "grass" is "glas-wellt" (lit. green straw).

"Three freights of Prydwen went we into it,
But seven came back from Caer Siddi."
The seventh is Arthur, and we never see him. No one does, but Merriman.

A sailor tattooed with a star between thumb and forefinger.

Bran/Herne/Arthur. Perhaps to the very last minute I shan't be sure whether he stays or goes.

Corona Borealis, the Crown of the North Wind, just dipping over the northern horizon at midsummer.

The sea level was changing in the fifth century, causing floods; same time as the Saxons were harrying the Romano-British. Irish invading too. In the peace of Arthur, the English had Sussex, Kent, Norfolk but not Bucks, Middlesex, Oxford. Twenty-one years between Badon, and Arthur dying at "Camlann." When does the Tree grow? Well—now, I suppose. Or outside Time.

At the last battle, Will glimpses all the lost faces: Owain, Gwion, the king. Even a girl throwing him a red rose. You never did use that red rose....

In the "Poetics" Aristotle said, "A likely impossibility is always preferable to an unconvincing possibility." I think those of us who write fantasy are dedicated to making impossible things seem likely, making dreams seem real. We are somewhere between the Impressionists and abstract painters. Our writing is haunted by those parts of our experience which we do not understand, or even consciously remember. And if you, child or adult, are drawn to our work, your response comes from that same shadowy land. Like us, you are escaping into yourselves.

I have been attempting definitions, but I am never really comfortable when writing about "fantasy." The label is so limiting. It seems to me that every work of art is a fantasy, every book or play, painting or piece of music, everything that is made, by craft and talent, out of somebody's imagination. We have all dreamed, and recorded our dreams as best we could. How can we define what we are doing? How can a fish describe what it's like to swim?

So having asked those questions, I sat in my study brooding hopelessly over a proper dispassionate description of the nature of fantasy, when I heard slow careful footsteps on the stairs. My daughter Kate came in, carrying a dish of water in one hand and some curious funnel-like instrument in the other. I said, "I'm stuck."

Kate smiled vaguely but ignored this, just as she had ignored the prohibition against Disturbing Mother at Work. She said, "Watch," and she dipped the funnel into the dish and blew through it, and out of the funnel grew the most magnificent bubble I have ever seen, iridescent, gleaming.

"Look at it from here," said Kate, intent. "Just look at the light!" And in the sunlight, all the colors in the world were swimming over that glimmering sphere— swirling, glowing, achingly beautiful. Like a dancing rainbow the bubble hung there for a long moment; then it was gone.

I thought: *That's* fantasy.

I said: "I wish they didn't have to vanish so soon."

"But you can always blow another," Kate said.

NEW AVON ⦿DISCUS TITLES

LADY SACKVILLE: A BIOGRAPHY   63701-4/$3.95
Susan Mary Alsop

Clever, devastatingly beautiful and the toast of late-Victorian society, Victoria Sackville was a high-living aristocrat who became embroiled in some of the greatest scandals of her generation. "Vivid...with an effervescence reminiscent of Lady Sackville herself."   *Time*

NEW GUINEA TAPEWORMS
AND JEWISH GRANDMOTHERS   64006-6/$3.95
Robert S. Desowitz

Dr. Robert S. Desowitz, Professor of Tropical Medicine at the University of Hawaii, explains the intricate relationships betwen humans, parasites and microbes, and why health programs aimed at chemical—and not environmental—controls have failed. "Compelling...illuminating, and delightfully written."   *The New York Times*

STUFF OF SLEEP AND DREAMS:
Experiments in Literary Psychology   63719-7/$4.95
Leon Edel

The Pulitzer Prize-winning biographer of Henry James explores the relationships between authors' psyches and their art, offering provocative insights into the unconscious of many famous writers, including Joyce, Cather, Woolf and Eliot. "Thought-filled, ingenious... dazzling."   *Washington Post Book World*

AVON ⦿ DISCUS PAPERBACKS

NEW FROM ◢◣ AVON BARD

DISTINGUISHED MODERN FICTION

SENT FOR YOU YESTERDAY
John Edgar Wideman   82644-5/$3.50
In SENT FOR YOU YESTERDAY, John Edgar Wideman,
"one of America's premier writers of fiction" (*The New York
Times*), tells the passion of ordinary lives, the contradic-
tions, perils, pain and love which are the blood and bone of
everybody's America. "Perhaps the most gifted black novelist in his generation." *The Nation*

Also from Avon Bard: **DAMBALLAH** (78519-6/$2.95) and
                     HIDING PLACE (78501-3/$2.95)

THE LEOPARD'S TOOTH
William Kotzwinkle   62869-4/$2.95
A supernatural tale of a turn-of-the-century archaeological
expedition to Africa and the members' breathtaking adventures with the forces of good and evil, by "one of today's
most inventive writers." (Playboy).

DREAM CHILDREN
Gail Godwin   62406-0/$3.50
Gail Godwin, the bestselling author of A MOTHER AND
TWO DAUGHTERS (61598-3/$3.95), presents piercing,
moving, beautifully wrought fiction about women possessed of imagination, fantasy, vision and obsession who
live within the labyrinths of their minds. "Godwin is a writer
of enormous intelligence, wit and compassion...DREAM
CHILDREN is a fine place to start catching up with an extraordinary writer." *Saturday Review*